THE CRASH
OF HENNINGTON

THE CRASH
OF HENNINGTON

Patrick Ness

Harper*Flamingo*Canada

The Crash of Hennington
Copyright © 2003 by Patrick Ness.
All rights reserved. No part of this book may be used or reproduced
in any manner whatsoever without prior written permission except in
the case of brief quotations embodied in reviews. For information
address: HarperCollins Publishers Ltd., 2 Bloor Street East,
20th Floor, Toronto, Ontario, Canada M4W 1A8

www.harpercanada.com

HarperCollins books may be purchased for educational, business,
or sales promotional use. For information please write:
Special Markets Department, HarperCollins Canada,
2 Bloor Street East, 20th Floor, Toronto, Ontario, Canada M4W 1A8

First edition

National Library of Canada Cataloguing in Publication

Ness, Patrick, 1971–
The crash of Hennington / Patrick Ness.

ISBN 0-00-200529-8

I. Title.

PS3614.E52C7 2003   813'.6   C2002-904708-0

HC 9 8 7 6 5 4 3 2 1

Printed and bound in the United States
Set in Stempel Garamond

For Marc Nowell

And in memory of my remarkable great aunt,
Ingeborg Utheim
1915–1999

'Souls have complexions, too: what will suit one will not suit another.'

GEORGE ELIOT, *Middlemarch*

Prologue. In.

She smelled dawn even before the sun looked over the horizon. A low mist clung to the sleeping bodies surrounding her at intervals across the lea. Breath clouded up from her great nose in increasing puffs as wakefulness filled her body. She raised her head and glanced around the sloping green of the meadow.

The first one awake. Usual and expected. The way it should be and was.

She turned her head to the sunrise coursing down from the hilltop. A low flood of light illuminated the mist and cast the dozing members of the herd as gray, rocky islands in a sea of white. She breathed in as the morning reached her lips and, leaning back to gather the proper force of weight, hoisted herself to her feet.

Time to move into the daybreak.

Part I.

Welcome to Hennington.

1. The Solari.

The front lobby of the Solari was made entirely of marble, even the sunlight. Any hotel guest – say, this one here, with the inappropriate clothes and the reminiscing smile – standing at the entrance to the second most opulent and expensive hotel in Hennington could see in detail the shiny yet persistently flat white-flecked black marble that made up the sprawling floor, though he would be hard pressed to find a seam, the expense apparently having been poured into the material's quality rather than its beauty. Given that the outside of the Solari was as shiny and edged as a precisely folded piece of foil, it might be surprising to this particular visitor, though perhaps not, that the interior, with its deep black expanses peppered with spots and streaks of white, could be so ominous and still. A blanket of the universe wrapped up as a present, perhaps.

Stepping inside the lobby's marble rhombus, the visitor would see marble planters, marble doorways, a marble waterfall tastefully placed beneath a marble sculpture (of a marble-worker), a marble bellhop stand (currently vacant), marble directional signs and an enormous single marble front desk, fully twelve meters long, in the shape of a sperm whale beaching itself seemingly because of unfathomable heartbreak in the deep, deep sea. Looking behind the behemoth, the guest, if he ventured further indoors, which it seems he has, would lay his eyes on the first organic thing he would have seen so far in the lobby of the Solari, representational whales notwithstanding: a person in the form of Eugene Markham, Solari front desk clerk.

It is with surly, unhappy Eugene that this story truly begins.

Eugene sat on his back-paining swivel chair behind the whale, thinking about suicide. Not seriously considering it, just mooning over the act in the manner of many a pale twenty-something with a broken heart. His girlfriend had left him for another man, a non-Rumour no less, but that had happened so often in life it was an insipid topic of insipid pop songs. Speaking of which, Eugene's band, Dirges For Betty, hadn't written any, pop songs that is, or at least any good ones or for that matter even any insipid ones, and Eugene was beginning to believe no one ever slept with the bass player anyway. Then there was the scaly chrysalia which had suddenly broken out all over his genitals and which was shaping up to be the only lasting legacy of his now-former relationship. And, oh, yes, he had just been demoted from catering to front desk. So one might forgive Eugene for being less attentive than usual when the shimmery-haired stranger – the selfsame guest who had sized up the Solari, now having made his way to the front desk – checked in. He (Eugene) was too caught up in wondering whether you slashed your wrists parallel or perpendicular to your palm and whether, since your palm was more or less square, this was even the right question to ask.

—Do you have any rooms available?

Eugene peeled back the skin from a hangnail on his thumb. The strip pulled off all the way back to the first joint. It bled and it hurt like hell, but it was also kind of impressive in its own macabre sort of way. Though he was unaware of it, Eugene cracked a smile.

—Now why would you want to go ahead and do a thing like that?

Eugene teleported back from his languor and at last noticed the man standing before him.

—Can I help you?

—I might very well ask you the same thing, my good fellow.

The man was dressed entirely in black, incredible given that Hennington was in the thick of summer, when Hilke's Winds blew off the Brown Desert, turning the city into a humidity-free place of chapped lips, bloody noses and queer tempers, where the heat rarely dipped below forty during the day despite the best efforts of a calm, cool ocean that seemed as intimidated by the heat as those unfortunate Hennington residents without air conditioning, which, oh yeah, was another of Eugene's problems. The man in black looked like he was either approaching or leaving behind fifty, but he exuded health like a pheromone. His skin was bronzed almost to the tan of Eugene's own Rumour hue, but this man was no Rumour. His nearly black hair was clipped short and neat and contained, Eugene was surprised to find himself thinking, a well-nigh dazzlingly handsome sprinkling of gray. The man's eyes were a green so light it neared pastel, contrasting, even highlighting, his long black coat, black shirt, black pants, black belt and black boots. All in all, a preposterous outfit in this weather. There was another thing. This man had, what was it?, an *aspect* about him, a warm calmness, a smile that invited, a glance that seemed to show patience as well as an invitation. Maybe it was something as simple as charisma. Maybe he was just an exceptionally good-looking man. Whatever it was, the result was this: Eugene liked fucking girls (a lot); nevertheless, he was aware of the erection pressing against the crotch of his uniform, causing the chrysalia to itch all the more.

—Let's start again. I'd like a room.

The spell dissipated. Eugene's confusing hardness faded. Something lingered, though, and Eugene's mind, in its own

7

ham-fisted way, toyed with the something that hovered around this man. If it hadn't been for a single red pimple near the bridge of the man's nose, Eugene might have convinced himself he was seeing a vision. Or even a god, maybe.

—How long will you be staying?

—I'm not sure. Just got off the train and I'm here. A week. A month. I'm not sure. What's your name?

—Eugene.

—Tybalt Noth.

Tybalt Noth offered a hand. Eugene, surprised again, accepted the shake.

—Unusual first name.

—A ridiculous name given by ridiculous, if loving, parents. I go by Jon.

—So an open-ended stay is what you're looking for?

—You have summed up the matter admirably.

Jon né Tybalt smiled.

—I'm visiting an old friend, you see. I don't know when I'll be leaving.

—An open-ended reservation ought to be fine. We're not that crowded.

—Because it's so damned hot.

The man betrayed not one drop of sweat, despite having recently arrived from the oven outside. Eugene took his identification and credit card and entered them into the computer.

—You might want to change clothes, sir. The heat doesn't look to let up anytime soon.

—Call me Jon, please, and I know about the weather. I'm from here. I can remember many a pressure-cooker summer.

—Really?

Why was it so surprising that this man was a Hennington native? Yet it was, most definitely.

—I just haven't been back in a long time. These are my traveling clothes. Trust me, Mr Eugene, I brought appropriate attire.

He took the card key Eugene offered him.

—Room 402.

—Thank you, Eugene.

—And my name's Eugene if you need anything else.

Jon blinked.

—Thank you again. I'll remember that. I hope you find whatever it is you're looking for, Eugene.

He grabbed his bag, hitherto out of Eugene's sight below the rolling back of the sperm whale. Eugene started making sounds about getting a bellhop, but Jon waved them off.

—I like to carry my own bag.

He smiled again, warmly and, it struck Eugene, incongruously for being dressed like a fallen angel. He turned and walked to the elevators. He seemed shorter than at first sight, but he moved with a sense of balance so sure and smooth that he seemed to glide. At the elevators, he turned.

—Is The Crash still hovering about town?

—Of course. They never change.

—Ah, that'll be something to see again.

The elevator arrived. Jon disappeared into it. Eugene looked back at his computer screen. Jon Tybalt Noth's return address was in the Fifty Shores, which meant that he had traveled three and a half thousand miles across the widest expanse of the Brown, by *train*, dressed in black. Eugene entered a note reminding the evening staff to check if Jon needed any other cooling amenities. He thought for a minute, erased the note, and decided to ask Jon himself at the end of his own shift.

Poor Eugene. He never knew what hit him.

2. A Confluence of Nudity.

Many years before she became *the* Cora Larsson, legendary Mayor of Hennington and remembered in a generation of matronymics, Cora Trygvesdottir went sunbathing in the nude and met the man who would become her husband. The scene: infamous Conchulatta Beach, that prime piece of land hooking its way over the southern entrance to Hennington Harbor, its crescent stretching from calm harbor to violent strait to calm ocean. Cora went alone, a not uncommon occurrence during a final year at college spent fleeing the daily catastrophes of two flatmates. Her natural inclination for serenity left her unable to really enjoy the boom crash of college life. That she excelled at it and later at law and still later at politics seemed to Cora to be the same sort of infuriating fate joke as penguins being such great swimmers: you did what you were good at and tried to ignore the fact that your flippers were really handicapped wings.

And so here was Cora, hatless and tanned, humming to herself, marching down to the beach, having parked her hasty in the last available slot. She carried a law coursebook, but even she knew that it was more or less a pretext. Henningtonians were not an especially beach-worshipping bunch, but neither were they beach-foolish. There were rules. The beach was a place where she could expect quiet and calm, especially if she read from an unattractive book of laws and even more so if she removed her bathing suit, *de rigueur* as the beach edged west. A naked sunbather was a serious sunbather, and Cora could wear her nudity as a shield against bothersome, over-friendly beachwalkers.

Along with her law book, Cora carried her hasty keys, a tube of sunblock with a much too low defense level, a small bottle of water, and a Mansfield U beach towel. She wore only sunglasses, sandals and a bikini, more appropriate attire having been left in the hasty's trunk. For a Wednesday, the beach was crowded, but Cora made good time heading past the unseemly hordes of casual visitors. As she got further west, the families thinned and solitary sunbathers became more common. No one was in the water. It was hammerhead season and even with the iffy safety nets, you only swam if you were suicidal or drunk.

She grew faintly aware that the female-to-male ratio on the beach was beginning to tilt in favor of the men. She was a confident young woman, but still she relaxed a bit as the number of muscled, oiled bodies covered in the tiniest of suits began to grow. She removed her bikini top, bunched it in her hand, and received nary a glance from the men baking in the sun. Still further and the tiny suits shrunk all the way into not being there at all. She began to glance an impressive variety of penises in an ever-more impressive variety of states of excitement. Slowly, the lone sunbathers became pairs of sunbathers who now paused in their activities and watched Cora curiously as she passed. Seeking only solitude, Cora followed etiquette and kept her eyes to the middle distance, pausing just long enough to remove her bikini bottom once the danger of any male who might leer had thoroughly passed. Now on the ocean side, she selected a spot at the edge of some brush that led back to the base of the cliffs. She spread her towel, piled her belongings, and lay down to read.

She was awakened some time later by a voice.

—Good God, you're about to burst into flames.

Cora opened her eyes, and the pain began there.

—Ow.

—No shit, ow, are you going to be able to walk?

Cora forced her eyelids the rest of the way up and saw her   11 future husband, Albert Larsson, for the very first time. He was clothed only in sandals and a concerned expression. Cora turned a little and reached for something to cover herself up, but the excruciating pain from the burn quickly overtook any notions of modesty. She croaked out a question.

—Is it as bad as it feels?

She felt her lips crack as she finished the sentence. She tasted blood.

—I think you're going to live, but we've got to get you inside somewhere.

And so Albert referred to himself and Cora as 'we' in the third sentence he ever spoke to her. Whenever she told this story in the years to come, both less and more often than you might think, Cora left out how suddenly comforted Albert's simple 'we' had made her feel. If, as she believed, every story needed a secret, Cora's was that she had loved Albert from sentence number three.

—Let me help you up. Slowly, now.

With much care and the lightest of touches, Albert got her to her feet. He gathered her few wayward things and delicately placed a hand on an unburnt spot to help her walk.

—You're going to have this two-tone problem for a while. Your backside is as white as virgin pearl.

—A moan will have to suffice for a witty rejoinder.

—I'll pretend to be dazzled.

She still could only barely see him, but her painful squints revealed first his nudity, second that he seemed Cora's age or a bit younger (she was right but only just; when they met, they were twenty-two and twenty-one), and third that the reddish-blond hair on his head matched exactly the reddish-blond hair that led down from his belly button. What made a bigger impression was the kindness she felt in his hands.

They were so gentle on her skin that they seemed to be the

only thing keeping her from spontaneous immolation as they trudged back up the beach.

—How did you get here?

—I drove my hasty.

—Well, you're not driving it home.

—Clearly.

—Do you have anyone who could come get you?

—My flatmates, I guess.

—I recognize that tone. Don't worry. I'll drive you, and let's talk no more of it.

—Ow.

—We're getting there.

Step by painstaking step, Albert supported Cora, and they walked, naked as a bridal bad dream the night before the wedding, past staring groups of volleyball players and disc throwers. Cora's burn was so awesome there weren't even any catcalls. The onlookers knew they were in the presence of something tremendous.

—Pavement.

Cora's step jarred on the stone, sending a canvas of pain up her front.

—Ow.

—My car's just right here.

—So close? You got here early.

—I'm not very proud to say.

Something occurred to Cora.

—Did you come to the beach naked?

—No. I was having sex with a man in the bushes behind you. We dozed, and when I woke up, he was gone and so were my clothes, towel and all various and sundry, save for the sandals I had somehow managed to not take off.

Cora let out a surprised laugh in the form of a grunt.

—I'm laughing less at the story than at your candor.   13

Through another squint, she could see him grin.

—I'm Albert.

—Cora.

—How about I take you to my lonely apartment, cover you with aloe, and put you in a cold bath, Cora?

—I'm in no position to decline.

Albert slipped off his left sandal, lifted up a flap, and pulled out his car key. Cora watched him with burnt eyebrows raised.

—You know, that's a really good idea.

Some time later, after Albert more than made good on his promises, he wrapped her in a sheet, laid her on the couch, and fed her with bits of melon and cool water.

—I want to take you out to dinner to repay your kindness.

—Are you asking me on a date?

—You had sex with a man on the beach today. Are you askable on a date?

—It's a big world. I like lots of things. I'm askable.

—All right then, I'm asking.

They married four months later. Though they occasionally indulged in sharing a boy, theirs was a rock-solid, faithful, and devoted union. Such was their bond, in fact, that by the time Cora was elected Mayor a surprisingly short seventeen years later, local Hennington argot referred to an especially strong contract as an 'Albert and Cora' to demonstrate its solidity.

3. The Crash on the Hill.

She was concerned about the dust.

The air smelled heavily of it, but it should have been too early in the year for there to be dust, although the last rains were well gone. There was ash in the dust as well and a distant smell of burning. She paused before she led the herd up to the top of the hill that marked the northern entrance to the descending fields, a place completely lacking in the malodorous homes of the thin creatures. This was just a grassy area, and she shouldn't have been able to smell dust at all.

(An Arboretum groundskeeper leaned against his rake, watching The Crash from behind a stand of trees. He could see them grazing in the field, Maggerty mooning along after as usual, and he also had a pretty good guess where they were going to head next.

He frowned.)

She looked at the rest of the herd behind her. A lightness of mood permeated the group but left her unaffected. She was the only one who bothered at the dust in the air. The rest of the herdmembers shuffled aimlessly about, pulling at the grass with agile lips, some of the younger calves even playing, gamboling on the lea, if anything so bulky could ever truly be said to gambol. Lush green surrounded them. Families of birds sang to each other in the trees and to those symbiotic brethren who made a meal of the ticks and other annoyances in the herdmembers' hides. A breeze teased its way through the glade where the herd was gathered, and to every herdmember there, save one, all was well.

She sniffed again, reaching with her nose, even squinting her eyes, their weakness more than compensated for by sensitive nostrils and nimble ears that now also turned and grabbed at any evidence that might linger in the air. Nothing. There was the usual amount of thin creatures scattered in the fields, easy to sense with their eerie strangled cries and halved footfalls, oddities not excepted by the thin creature who constantly followed the herd, also present in her catalogue of senses. Nothing out of the ordinary but the dust.

15

She snorted and waved her great horn to get the others' attention. The message communicated itself through the group, and the herd began to file behind her. Yet even as they crossed into the ever more verdant gardens that leapt their way down the hillside, she could still smell the dust, its persistence meaning only one thing.

Hard times were coming.

4. Luther in Limbo.

Luther Pickett, beloved foster son of Archie Banyon and heir apparent to both the Chairmanship of Banyon Enterprises and the Banyon family fortune – though there *was* the matter of the last name – kept an immaculate desk in the middle of an overwhelming office. Taking up fully three quarters of the forty-fifth floor (the leftover fourth given to elevators and Luther's four secretaries), it contained a conference room, a lengthy reception hall, a full bathroom with shower, an exercise room with spa and relaxation tub, a dining room, and a whole separate apartment where Luther could quite comfortably spend the night if he chose, which he never had, not once. Luther's desk sat in the office's main chamber, a room whose vaulted ceiling reached so high it took up a sizable portion of the forty-*sixth* floor, giving Luther a two-story wall made entirely of glass. In late afternoon, the sun poured in, filling the office to the brim with a spectacular view of Hennington out into the Harbor and beyond. Aside from Archie Banyon's own office (the three-story penthouse with the pool, driving range, and ice rink; Archie was an athletic man), Luther's office was the most impressive, most talked about, most envied, and to the extent that smaller budgets would allow, most copied in the city.

So it should surprise no one that Luther Pickett was desperately unhappy. Really, just look at his desk. A notepad, a file, a few papers, neatly stacked. A blotter, a telephone with intercom, a computer to one side. Barely anything else. No personal photos, no mementos from company milestones, no sample Banyon Enterprises products. Even the coffee mug was black and unmarked by logo or design. Most definitely *not* the outward reflection of an unfettered soul.

The minimalism (some would say sterility) reached to the gray carpet and on up the undecorated walls. After three years in this office, the intended inoffensive-yet-very-expensive abstract expressionist paintings were still packed in crates thirty stories below, waiting futilely for the day when Luther would finally allow them to breathe fresh air. And there was the silence, too. No bustle, no music, not even a hum from the air conditioning, just Luther's pen scratching across a paper or the fading click of typing on the keyboard. Yet the atmosphere was not cold but melancholic, a funeral parlor's viewing room rather than a prison cell, Luther the grieving relative and not the angry inmate. Luther at thirty-eight (grapevine verdict: 'looks younger, seems older') appeared at once tense and exhausted. His tanned, handsome face rarely smiled, his broad chest rarely expanded into laughter, his step never betrayed any lightness. His secretaries worried frantically about him.

The intercom lit up.

—Yes, Lois?

—You're going to be late for your 9.30.

Luther glanced at the clock.

—Shit. Call Jules, please, and tell him I'm on my way.

—I already have.

Archie Banyon and Luther Pickett had a thrice-weekly tennis match, played on the grass court Archie had installed on the uppermost floor of his own office. It was meant as a friendly game between friendly rivals, father-son in intent, if not perhaps in genuine feeling; still, it was not the corporate death-saga it might have been. Luther was strapping, tall, muscular. He was bald across the top and kept the rest of his hair cropped extremely short, a *trompe l'oeil* that made his head seem like a single sleek muscle as well. His tightly compacted litheness paired with a set of small silver-rimmed spectacles to make Luther look for all the world like a terrifically strong man trying not to appear so. In spite of this – and spite definitely entered into the equation – Archie Banyon had an impressive game and a more impressive tenacity. Luther usually lost two out of three, even given Archie's extra five decades.

What the matches amounted to were three opportunities a week to speak with Archie. Three times a week to deliver the prepared speech that Luther had written and rewritten, the prepared speech that laid it all in the open at last and forever, the prepared speech that would probably kill Archie Banyon, not merely because of what it meant for Luther, but because of what it meant for Archie's biological son, Thomas, a distasteful little caveat that helped matters not at all.

Luther gathered his tennis clothes and bolted to the elevators. He shot up through eighteen floors of computer banks and safes, film libraries and records, corporate histories and hidden crimes, eighteen floors of valuable information that Archie had placed between himself and Luther because he only felt comfortable if he was on one end and Luther on the other. —To protect it, Archie said, like sentinels. The elevator doors snapped open. Luther spotted Jules, Archie's assistant, arranging Archie's equipment off to the side of the court. Jules flashed Luther a wan, impish smile.

18   —Piss off, Jules.

—Is that any way to greet your umpire?

—Where's Archie?

—*Here!*

Archie called from the far end of the court, behind Luther. Luther turned. One week. One week, and there would be no turning back. He would either give the speech or he wouldn't. In one week, if he hadn't said no, his silence would have answered yes.

5. Maggerty.

Maggerty the Rhinoherd was not the rhinoherd, but the misnomer served a humane purpose. Though the resolute, quiet and massive Crash needed no tending, the presence of Maggerty could only otherwise be explained by madness, an explanation with which the polite citizens of Hennington privately agreed but publicly tended away. The Crash offered no product, neither meat nor milk nor leather; their eating patterns were too erratic and wandering to be a real benefit to agriculture (there were no farms in the city anyway, which was where The Crash wandered more than half the time); and the individual animals were impossible to tame, ignoring Henningtonians with a determination that would have seemed like arrogance had The Crash not also asked so little in return: a few hay bales during drier times and the right to free range. The Rhinoherd did nothing but follow. He was more disciple than caretaker. Hennington sensibilities to the side, it was an occupation for a fanatic or an imbecile. Fortunately, Maggerty was both.

He was born in the farmland to the south of Hennington, the only son of middle class rent-farmers. Odd from the beginning, his destiny was set at six years old when he was 19 kicked between two ribs under his left armpit by a goat he tried to suckle. This – the attempted suckling – was not done out of hunger but out of simple entrancement with the goat and its wheaty, dirty, shitty goat-smell. Crawling past the small, electric dairy works; past the Rumour farm-maidens tending to the hens and the sheep; under the nose of the giant Rumour overseer asleep in his chair, head cocked towards a computer terminal, one hand somnolently gripping the erection that raged in his pants as he (the overseer) dreamed; moving quietly through the gate, held fast so the latch didn't clatter; literally following his nose to the furthest pen, Maggerty came face to face with the bored she-goat, munching her hay, distracted and oblivious.

Trailing his fingers on the wall, Maggerty circled the goat slowly. She took no notice of him after her initial sizing-up, exuding the offhand confidence so peculiar to farm animals who weren't also sheep. She was a greenish brown with white bony legs and sharp – Maggerty was soon to discover – hooves. With caution, or rather, with *reverence* Maggerty placed a hand on the goat's hide. The goat jumped a little, but it seemed to Maggerty to be more out of surprise than abhorrence. When he touched her again, she didn't move.

He began to stroke her, slowly, like a pet. She had birthed a litter less than three weeks before, but her kids had already been taken from her. Her udder, plump to the point of hardness, glistened with a liquid Maggerty assumed to be sweat. He knew, as all farm children knew, that udders issued milk, and he was deliriously overcome with a desire to drink, to sup rich sustenance from the goat, to bring the pulsing, thrumming warmth of another existing aliveness into himself. A contempt was there, too, for the goat's refusal to regard him, to notice his need, but that did not stop his desire for the milk.

He knelt. Heat buzzed in the air. He felt his heartbeat in his temples. A tingling spread over his body along with a sort of ecstasy, if he had known the word at six, but it was like the ecstasy of those screaming streetcorner preachers who haunted Hennington's desolate east side and who would shit right out in the open and leave it stinking in the sun for want of interrupting their sermons. Maggerty leaned in and put his lips to one of the long teats. He had not even properly gotten his mouth around the nipple when the goat kicked him, slicing a deep, precise cut between two ribs just below his left armpit, leaving a wound that never healed. Never.

This was the unacceptable thing. A child ridiculously exploring a goat could be explained, heaven knew such things and worse had happened on southern Hennington farms since time immemorial, but a child with a wound that never stopped bleeding, never scabbed nor scarred, now *this* was a thing to be wary of. The expected ostracism and isolation followed ruthlessly in the farming community, ringing outwards from friends to schoolmates to teachers and onward, until finally Maggerty's own mother regarded him only grudgingly on the rare occasions when she regarded him at all.

As he stumbled down the road after The Crash, Maggerty distractedly put his hand to the wound. Years and years and years had passed. The wound never got worse, but it never got better either. It also never stopped hurting, and it was this, the never-ending pain coupled with the oddity of the never-healing wound, that had driven Maggerty irretrievably into madness sometime in the teenagedom when he had picked up with The Crash, still accompanying them all these many long years later.

He ate grass and roots with them. He drank from the streams and canals and lakes as they did. He rarely approached them – the experience with the goat had taught him not to 21 meddle with an animal that weighed one hundred times as much – but he also never left them, nesting with them through winters and storms, famines and droughts. He began to be called Maggerty the Rhinoherd not long after taking up his patronage. At first, municipal thought considered forcibly separating him from The Crash, but as he apparently did no harm to the animals and as they did not seem to mind or indeed acknowledge his presence, he was left alone.

And so it stood. Maggerty the Rhinoherd. Before the year was out, he would have a second never-healing wound, but only because it would first take his life.

6. The Mayor's Office and its Discontents.

The speakerphone on Cora's desk crackled.

—Mayor?

—What can I do for you, Adam?

—The Arboretum just called.

—Let me guess. The Crash bruised a blade of grass and molested a squirrel.

—More like trampled a rare species of terrestrial phalaenopsis. The botanists are screaming about irreplaceability.

—Adam?

—Yes, Mayor.

—'Terrestrial phalaenopsis'?

—That's what they said.

—They couldn't say 'orchid', like normal folk?

—I guess they figured you'd know.

—On the basis of nothing.

—What should I tell them?

—That they shouldn't have planted terrestrial phalaenopsi where one hundred rhinoceros could tread on them.

—Well, they are *terrestrial* phalaenopsis.

—And it is an equally terrestrial Crash. Surely there are paths The Crash doesn't take. The botanists can plant their orchids there.

—I think all they want is a fence.

—In whose lifetime do they see that happening? The Arboretum's been an open park for ninety years. That's not going to change on my watch just because a bunch of botanists are crying over orchids.

—I like orchids.

—I have another call, Adam. Issue settled.

She released his line and pressed another flashing light.

—Yes?

—Deputy Mayor Latham on the line.

—Put him through. Max? Make me happy.

—Unlikely, I'm afraid.

—You can't make the fundraiser.

—I can't make the fundraiser.

—This is my thought, right this second: 'Why do I even bother?'

—Talon is sick.

—Oh. Well, all right then. What's wrong with her?

—Battery Pox.

—Poor thing. Started the shots?

—We're driving home from the doctor's office right now. She'll be fine. She's just throwing up all over everything.

—And a sitter is out of the question?

—Cora . . .

—All right, all right, all right, I'm civilized. I'll just have to work myself up for a sparring match with Archie Banyon.

—He can't be too upset if I have a sick daughter.   23

—He won't be upset at you. He'll be upset at *me*.

—You can handle Archie Banyon.

—I know I can handle Archie Banyon. Doesn't mean I look forward to it. Where are you now?

—Driving down Eighth. Just about to cross Medford.

—Look out for The Crash. They're around there somewhere.

—The Arboretum called, didn't they?

—I don't want to talk about it.

—Sorry about tonight.

—I don't want to talk about it.

But she did.

—How can you expect to be elected if I do all your campaigning for you?

—You got elected four times. Why fix something that's not broke?

—Don't be cavalier. They're not going to make you Mayor just because I tell them to.

—They might.

—Well, yes, they might, but still, Max—

—I'll make it up to you.

—So you say. Are you even going to *vote*?

—Mercer Tunnel. Breaking up. Gotta go.

—Liar.

She cut him off and pressed a private speed dial.

—We're flying solo tonight.

—Hi, sweetest. Max pulled out again?

—Yep.

—How does he expect to get your job if he never shows up to anything? Politics is nasty and brutish, but you at least have to play at it.

—Talon's got Battery Pox. Apparently, she's vomiting everywhere.

24

—How vivid. All right, whatever, we'll pull in the dough for him once more.

—He says thanks.

—No, he doesn't, but at least he means it.

As was his wont, Albert disconnected without saying good-bye. Cora dialed her secretary.

—Angie, get me Archie Banyon on the phone, please.

—Max canceled again, didn't he?

—Just get Archie on the phone and let me out of my misery.

She clicked off and saw lines lighting up as Angie tracked down Archie Banyon. Cora steeled herself. He would let her off, but he wouldn't do it without making her pay.

7. Father and Daughter.

Max Latham was trying to become Mayor of Hennington, but he wasn't trying very hard. He still wasn't sure if his heart was in it, which he often thought should have been proof enough that his heart *most definitely* was not in it. There was the sticky question of destiny, though. He had worked for Cora nearly thirteen years, since he was fresh out of law school, first as an intern with a brilliant mind for policy – if a little less so for politics – then as an advisor, then as Chief of Parks, until his current position as Deputy Mayor, the youngest person ever to have held such a post. Now, with Cora retiring after twenty adored years in office, everything had crystalized, just at this moment, for him to fulfill an awaiting slot in history, to step forward and seize the waiting gold ring, to set so many records atumble.

If elected, and as there was no present credible competition and as he was riding on Cora's enormous popularity, getting elected seemed almost foregone, he would be Hennington's first Rumour Mayor, quite a coup when Rumours were still, if you believed the census takers, a minority in the city. He would also be the youngest Mayor ever in the Recent Histories, beating the record by the two years he was younger than the previous recordholder, Cora, on *her* first election. Max had yet to even breach forty. More esoterically, Max would also be Hennington's first unmarried Mayor, the mother of his daughter having drowned before plans for their wedding could be finished. All these impressive footnotes that would be for ever attached to his name.

And yet.

He looked in his rearview mirror for a glimpse of Talon, piqued in the back seat.

—How're you feeling, sweetheart?

—My head weighs a hundred pounds.

—We're almost home. Let me know if you need to throw up again.

—Okay.

Talon at ten was the spitting image of her father, high cheekbones, dark wavy hair, skin on the lighter side of the usual Rumour tan. But she had her mother's chin cleft, a mark that could still spark fresh pain in him when he saw it, even all these years later. Max slowed his car to watch The Crash, still so magnificent after uncountable sightings, wander across to a side street. He idled to a stop as the last animals lumbered through the intersection. The Rhinoherd shuffled along with them twenty paces behind.

—Look, honey. The Crash.

—I can't sit up, Daddy.

—Of course, sweetie, I'm sorry. We're almost home.

Was not being sure if you wanted to run for Mayor a good sign that you shouldn't run for Mayor or a good sign that you had enough self-doubt and introspection that you were in fact a perfect candidate for Mayor?

—Daddy?

—Yes, sweetie?

The sounds of coughing. Max turned around and stroked the back of Talon's head while she retched into the bag the doctor had given her.

—Just take your time, honey. It hurts less if you relax.

He felt sweat dampening her hair as he stroked it.

—Take all the time you need, sweetheart. We've got all the time in the world.

8. Mathematica.

Jacqueline Strell sat in her office and bathed in numbers. They flooded her desk in wave after wave, pages of numbers blocked in charts, scraps of numbers scribbled in pencil, computer analyses of numbers bracketed and cross-referenced to other rivers of numbers filed away in the cabinets behind her, numbers on cards, numbers on machine readouts, numbers on computer screens, numbers on the desk itself put there when, in a flurry of activity, Jacki chose not to flip over a page but continued onto the hard wood. Even her fingernails sported numbers, whimsically painted there this morning when she was in a whimsical mood. The time was rapidly approaching when she would need more whimsy. Oh, yes.

Her office nestled in the back half of the Hennington Hills Golf Course and Resort Administration Building. She loved it. Spacious table tops flung out from her desk in wings towards her office door, room enough to keep the flood of numbers churning and churning in their never-ending whirlpool. Cabinets lined the three walls behind her and to her right and left, streams and cauldrons of bubbling, stirring, steaming numbers. She had fourteen different clocks decorating her walls, all set to the same time but all with different number fonts.

This was the reason Jacki was an accountant: she, alone among everyone else she had ever known, understood infinity. This understanding was innate. No epiphany, no trumpet blast of the everlasting had ever filled her brainpan. The eternal had always whiled away its time in her gray matter. She had been intimate with the infinite from the time she could even speak such words. The human mind was not supposed to be able to truly grasp the never-ending, but she could close her eyes and set her mind running off into forever, tripping lightly away on a line with no beginning and no end.

This was the reason Jacki understood infinity: she understood numbers. Infinity, aside from its unfathomable physical existence, could only and would only ever be expressed in numbers. Jacki looked scornfully on the small-minded 'appreciation' of the layman towards an infinite set. 'Really, really big, then even bigger'. They didn't see it. Jacki *saw* it. More, she felt it, smelled it, could almost touch it. Numbers adding and adding and adding and adding exponential upon exponential upon exponential and then all those numbers were still as nothing because infinity remained, brightly spilling itself infinitely forward.

Jacki leaned back in her chair and sighed. She was tall, generously boned, with loopy brown hair that matched the gawky, unconfined sprawl of her body. She rubbed her hand across her high forehead, inside which was an increasingly throbbing ache. Yes indeedy, it was time for whimsy again, most definitely. She opened the top drawer of her desk and pulled out a vial and syringe. With practiced movements, she filled the hypodermic, tapped it for bubbles, raised the hem of her skirt, and injected her thigh with 50ccs of the purest Forum you could get anywhere in Hennington.

Because there were three more things about Jacki:

1) Besides being an accountant with a comprehension of infinity, she was totally, utterly, wholly, paralytically and absolutely addicted to Forum.

2) Because of *this*, Jacki also worked as a prostitute for her boss, Thomas Banyon, biological son of Archie Banyon and general manager of the Hennington Hills Golf Course and Resort, lent out to clients to feed a specific need, thereby pleasing Thomas and causing him to provide her with more Forum, although of course never quite enough. These shifts were in addition to the full day's work she put in as Thomas' Head Accountant. Never let it be said that Thomas Banyon lacked a darkling sense of humor.

3) And all of *this* was true because, at age forty-one, with her youngest child fifteen years old, Jacki still produced, on a daily basis, nearly two pints of breast milk, and there were a surprising number of men who would pay a surprising amount of money for just such a delicacy. Thomas Banyon was not a man to let potential income go unexploited.

Her phone rang. Alone in her office, she mouthed an expletive.

—Hello?

—Jacks.

Jacki frowned, but the Forum was already dribbling its way through her veins and she began to feel her consternation melt away, butter in boiling water.

—Yes, Mr Banyon?

—I have a clip for you tonight. Are you up for it?   29

As if there was a choice involved.

—Of course, Mr Banyon. It would be my pleasure.

—It's Councilman Wiggins. You remember the good Councilman, don't you?

Remember? She had to put salve on her nipples for nearly a week after the good Councilman displayed a tendency for toothiness. This memory too, though, floated away into the shimmering mirage of the drug.

—Certainly, Mr Banyon. What time?

—Say ten?

—All right. Ten it is. Usual place?

—Usual place.

—I'll be there.

—I truly appreciate that, Jacks. I've got some really wonderful merchandise here that I had been hoping to share with you. I want to thank you for giving me the opportunity.

—I'm grateful for your indulgence, Mr Banyon.

—You're a good girl, Jacks.

He clicked off. Jacki closed her eyes. She was deep into butterscotch warmth now and glorious waves of light and color filled her head. The anguish, thank the heavens, was winding its way clockwise down the drain, spiraling blissfully out of her presence.

God bless Forum. Forum's name be praised.

9. Hospitality.

—Mr Noth?

Eugene Markham knocked again. After a lengthy pause, Tybalt 'Jon' Noth opened the door. He was wearing one of the Solari's bathrobes. His hair was wet, and he held a towel in his hands. Still, he smiled when he saw Eugene.

—Eugene! What can I do you for?

—I was just checking to see if everything is to your satisfaction.

—Slow day for you then?

—Yes.

—And you still have yet to manage a proper smile.

Eugene almost smiled at this, but not quite.

—That was pitiful, Eugene. And enough of 'Mr Noth'. I told you to call me Jon.

—All right, then. Jon. Is everything to your satisfaction?

—I've only been here long enough for a shower, but the bathroom fulfills most accepted definitions of nice.

Jon smiled again, more warmly this time. Maybe he was a preacher. Maybe that was it.

—Are you some kind of preacher?

—How is it that I just *know* this surliness is something you're trying to overcome and that there's a perfectly personable individual in there somewhere struggling to get out rather than just plain old dour Eugene?

—You smile a lot, is all I mean.

—Your perception is bizarre, Eugene, but somehow, perhaps accidentally, it may even be correct. Interesting.

Eugene blinked. He wasn't sure if he was being agreed with.

—So ...

—I have been called a preacher in my time, Eugene, but even then, it could have been wrong. As for now, definitely not.

Eugene blinked again.

—'Why don't you come on in and talk for a while, Eugene' is what you're waiting for me to say, yes?

—I don't mean in any male-male sex kind of way, but—   31

—I didn't think you did. Why don't you come on in and talk for a while, Eugene?

Eugene, surprising even himself, smiled, stepped over the threshold, and entered Jon's room.

10. The Crash at the Bridge.

Once, early on in her time as leader, the search for food had forced her to take them across the bridge that flung itself over the bay away from the city, a difficult, frightening and lengthy journey. The whole way along she could only smell salt water and the noxious metallic scent of the boxes that the thin creatures rode in. The wind drowned out all sound as the herd picked its way through the stopped boxes, the thin creatures inside staring out impassively. It was slow going, with much nervous lowing and braying among the members of the herd until, perhaps inevitably, disaster struck. About two thirds of the way across, some of the older animals started to panic, the confinement of the bridge causing a claustrophobia unknown to them even in some of the city's starker alleys.

She attempted to keep some sort of order, firmly shaking her head, stepping forward and back. She snorted and affected a prance to try to hold their attention, but the wind snuffed her out. An old male began to get aggressive in his fear, knocking some of the smaller animals out of his way. An old female stumbled, accidentally pushing over a pregnant mother. The final stroke was the appearance of a flying box carrying some of the thin creatures. (— ... *so avoid the Firth Roundabout if you can at all. And finally, it looks like we've got a serious traffic jam on the Harbour Bridge, caused by The Crash of all things. As you can see from SkyCam5, cars are just at a* standstill. *Looks like rush hour's going to be even longer tonight all over the city. Back to you in the studio . . .*) Hovering to the side of the bridge, the box brought a swirling roar that proved too much for the more nervous animals. They turned and charged, running full gallop back the,way they had come, leaving her and more than half the rest of the herd standing near the far end of the bridge.

The herd must not divide.

She ran to overtake the fleeing animals, to try to get in front of them to lead them again, to get them off the bridge and back into a calmer state. She arrived too late for some. The aggressive old male had given himself a mortal wound charging into the scattered boxes over and over again, his horn cracked, his ears bleeding. The old female who had knocked over the expectant mother had been turned against and was being forced over the side by a cadre of enraged herdmembers blinded by fright. She reached the group only in time to see the old female vanish over the edge with a low, terrified moan.

She quickened her pace, passing charging herdmembers on her right and left, weaving through the thin creature boxes, some of which were trying to move out of her way and only causing more problems. Her mouth foamed at the effort, her ears filled with the roar of her blood, but near the end of the bridge, almost a mile later, she was in front of the herdmembers that were fleeing. Assuming her entire authority in what she did next, she turned, faced the entire herd, and stopped right at the line where the bridge returned to the soil. Astonished, the escaping herdmembers careered to a halt in front of her. There were pile-ups as those charging behind were slower to stop, but eventually she faced the herd in its entirety, save for the two now lost. Even stopped, chaos still rattled the members as they jostled and tussled, some still panicking to get off the bridge.

She paced in front of them purposefully, walking back and 33 forth, back and forth, until all heads were turning following her movements. With a loud snort and without slowing her step, she turned and headed away from the bridge. The animals followed her in shaky unison. In a short amount of time, the bridge was cleared of all animals except for the dying old male, who thankfully had knocked himself into unconsciousness before he died.

It was difficult to lead, but she led them once more.

11. Orthopediae.

Thomas Banyon was born with legs so bowed he was said to have been straddling his mother's womb rather than resting in it, that his mother had wished for a boy and had given birth to the wishbone instead, that his parents had copulated on horseback, in a tunnel, with pliers, et al. Fortunately, his parents had been – his father still was – very, very wealthy: erstwhile Hennington City Council Members, owners of the Hennington Hills Golf Course and half of everything else in Hennington, stables full of horses, maids in the houses, unused yachts. These remarks about his legs were never said to Thomas Banyon's face. This did not mean he was unaware of them.

Before Thomas had been alive a year, his parents had paid for five surgeries to correct his legs. He had three more by the time he was six and had not actually learned to walk until he was seven. He attended rigorous physical therapy on up into adolescence with Joe. Joe, 'Just Joe', the therapist, was a former soldier who had served with Thomas' grandfather in the Gentlemen's War nearly fifty years previous and was purported to be the best physical therapist in Hennington. But Joe, and there's really no getting around this, was an out-and-out sadist. His stated goal from day one was to get Thomas to cry.

Said Joe, in that indecipherable accent of his: —No pain, no advancement.

Years passed, and Thomas' pleas to his parents fell on four deaf ears. The sessions grew longer and longer, with Thomas holding out for as long as he could against the onslaught of drills, weights, endurance tests, water exercise, and on and on. If Thomas had been able to fake crying, if Joe had taken even one small modicum less of obvious pleasure in inflicting the torture, Thomas might have grown up to be an altogether different person. But being of a spiteful, resentful disposition, he had developed the two natural and inevitable results.

Thomas Banyon had grown very strong, and Thomas Banyon had grown very mean.

At sixteen he was asked, because of his family's position, to escort one Rebecca Turkel to Rebecca's coming-out cotillion. Thomas, whose now vaguely straighter legs had the muscular mass of an elephant, could not dance, would not dance, and scorned the very idea of dancing. Rebecca, being a nice girl if a bit unobservant of behaviours human, responded by smiling, saying things like 'Oh, pooh', and 'You old grouch', never imagining for one moment that Thomas might be serious. On the big night Thomas, thinking the matter clarified, squired Rebecca down the winding staircase to the adulation of the white-gloved crowd below. When, at the bottom of the stairs, the crowd parted, the music began and Rebecca turned to Thomas to begin the traditional dance, he was sure he had been duped. Thomas Banyon, already most of the mammoth size he was working to become, loudly yet clearly spouted at Rebecca Turkel a most foul four-letter word that reached the ears of every guest and sister-debutante at the cotillion. To punctuate the oath, Thomas took his boutonniere and crushed every last carnation petal in the palm of his hand. He left Rebecca standing stricken and alone. She moved out of Hennington not three weeks later. 'Medical school' was the given reason, but everyone knew the most Rebecca Turkel had ever expressed about medicine was 'Ouch'.

As punishment, because cotillions – however ridiculous to even Thomas' father Archie – were *not* to be taken lightly, Thomas was made a gardener at the golf course. Delivering an astonishing blow to precedent, Archie Banyon even declined to send Thomas to college. Said his father with a wan smile, —You can pick up the trade on the job. Externally at least, Thomas took the hint from the gardening assignment, but he knew just exactly how much he would pick up about business from tending to a golf course. Ever the surprisingly smart son, though, he kept his opinions to himself. Not coincidentally, this was the time Luther Pickett arrived on the scene. Suddenly, Thomas had a pre-teen younger brother, an orphaned son of some fucking shipping clerk in some obscure fucking Banyon Enterprises satellite investment. Luther was described by Archie to Thomas as having 'promise'. The implication was obvious. Well, so fucking what? Thomas would learn all about fucking 'promise'.

Despite the unstated intentions of his father, Thomas *did* learn quite a bit from the golf course. Important things like where and when to seize what power and for how long and just how to use it once you got it. Gardening turned into supervising turned into course designing at a rapid and bloody rate. Privately, Thomas' father approved of the casualties left in Thomas' wake, admiring the ambition of an otherwise thwarted youth, but Archie Banyon blanched a little at the glee Thomas seemed to feel in it. Publicly, though, the father simply smiled and kept promoting his son. Inside of ten years, brief but still too long for pretty much anyone but Thomas to work at a golf course, Thomas Banyon, bandy-legged, bad-tempered, debutante-insulting son of a billionaire, was CEO of Hennington Hills Golf Club and Resort and loving it. What should have been a dishonorable, low-salaried (for an heir), do-nothing job had somehow morphed into a private fortune and personal pleasure, because nepotism or no, Thomas was *very* good at what he did: mainly terrifying his subordinates and keeping his members happy. Surprisingly, Thomas found the latter as entertaining as the former. He gained a reputation for providing for the illicit tastes of the richer and seamier sides of Hennington, which as usual were often one and the same. Drugs? Thomas could purloin a selection to fill a convenience store. Inside information? Thomas could make and break fortunes simply by frowning instead of smiling. Sex? Now, sex was where Thomas flourished.

Sex, oh, could Thomas acquire all kinds of sex for whatever persuasion was requested. Whilst a mere gardener, Thomas had already seen the perks that a quick hand job received from a grateful married man in a sand trap. You only had to do the actual act a few times before the more delicious avenues of blackmail opened. Thomas didn't need the money, but he discovered quickly how having power over someone turned into other advantages. When those men and women thought they were taking something from the bulky, muscular, smiling, friendly teenager, Thomas knew otherwise.

Nowadays, the locker-room jerkoffs and sauna blowjobs, the limousine pussy-eating and private apartment fuckings (of pussy *and* ass; opportunities were opportunities) were left behind as mere child's play, the youthful desire to put in the personal appearance. Almost all of his employees at Hennington Hills had extra, special duties that Thomas required of them now and again. Peter Wickham, the waiter with the delightfully elegant sexual organ; Jacki Strell, the milk-bearing accountant; Maggie Bonham, the gift shop manager about whose head-giving epic poems should have been written; silver-haired chief chef Hartley Chevalier, who appealed quite dramatically to equally silver-haired women; Paul Beck, assistant mechanic, whose sad eyes and cunnilingual talents left him very little time to actually fix any of Hennington Hills' vehicles; Tracy Jem-Ho, barmaid with a whip. And so on. All of these people owed Thomas something, and none of them would, *should* ever think of leaving. Besides, Thomas thought, he treated them well, paid them well, never asked them too far over the edge, certainly not to any point where they couldn't come back. He *cared* about them, he thought. Any of the entertainment might disagree, but Thomas was sure that was beside the point.

Upon his perch in the golf cart from which he surveyed his grounds and shook the hands and caressed the egos of its utilizers, Thomas Banyon was offering JH Williams Roth VIII an imported cigar of the highest purity and utmost illegality.

—Taste good?

—Exquisite. Like a young girl just having smoked the finest cigar.

—I can arrange for you to make the comparison first hand, if you'd like.

—I was unaware that I had to ask any further than I already have.

JH Williams Roth VIII raised his eyebrows haughtily. Thomas smiled. This prick would get his cigar-smoking girl. He would also get a raging case of the Mud. Maybe Thomas was a gofer and a pimp, but you didn't treat him like one. The mobile phone in the cart rang. He lowered his voice, turning away from the prying ears of the soon-to-be-oozing

38   JH Williams Roth VIII.

—Thomas Banyon.

—It's Luther.

—Hello, brother.

—I was wondering . . .

A long pause. Thomas liked making him wait.

—He'll be there at the usual time, Luther.

—Thank you.

Luther hung up. Thomas smiled to himself. Wasn't providing what people wanted all the power you ever really needed?

12. The Melting Sanctuary.

The scented smoke whorled around Jarvis Kingham's bearded face and on up into the shafts of light fingering through the corrugated skylight. Other than the row of candles marking the entrance to the sanctuary across from Jarvis' pulpit, the skylight was the only source of illumination. It wasn't much. Jarvis' nose was filled by incense, plain old candle smoke, and a spectacularly effusive cloud of sweat emanating from his parishioners. Didn't any of these people use antiperspirant?

Be nice, Jarvis, he thought.

He coughed and tried to stifle a second by clearing his throat. Despite his years of training, despite his strongly felt and sincere devoutness, despite his recognition of its place as the holiest of holy days in the Bondulay religion, Jarvis had never really cared for the Collingham Sacraments. The service was, frankly, the dreariest of the entire Bondulay sacred calendar: a dark room filled with candles on a hot summer day with pew upon pew of worshippers overdressed in their too-hot church finest sweating up a storm. What fun. Jarvis shifted his shoulders a little under his thick, wool robe. Droplets gathered to form rivulets of sweat cascading from his armpits and ample stomach. His eyes stung from the salt, and his fingers left wet prints on the pages of the Sacraments. Water, he thought, even as his lips sounded out the canticle.

—*And, lo, the man who would be penitent before the Almighty shall have his transgressions rescinded without question;*

—*And, lo, the woman who would be penitent before the Almighty shall have her past wrongs erased without recompense.*

Jarvis made a quick pass with his tongue to catch the drops of sweat dangling precariously from his mustache.

—*But the penitence does not end at the expunging of past faults;*

—*The true penitent carries on in a never-ending quest to keep their past lies from being spoken again;*

—*To keep their past wrongs from being committed again;*

—*To keep their past thievings from being stolen again;*

A verb-subject problem that seemed to have arisen in the translation.

—*To keep their past grievances from being redressed;*

—*So say the Sacraments.*

The congregation answered, a little wistfully in the heat, —*And so say we all.*

At least you get to sit down, Jarvis thought, then pushed the thought immediately away. The Collingham would have been slightly more tolerable if it weren't also so long. Jarvis had been speaking for almost an hour and had only gotten through four canticles. There were seven to go. He shifted his feet and noticed that a quite literal puddle of sweat had formed between his sandals. Oh, Heavens above, he thought, enough is enough.

—Good people, I think, perhaps, in deference to today's rather . . .

And here he paused to give both weight to the word and to signal a reluctance to make his request, a reluctance he no more felt than he did current personal comfort.

—... *astonishing* heat, I am wondering, perhaps, if it might not be prudent to move directly to the canticles of blessing.

He was surprised to hear some mumbling among the parishioners.

—And grant ourselves some comfort on this day of atonement.

The murmuring grew into outright conversation, and so quickly, too. Jarvis couldn't quite believe his ears, but he was hearing protests. As achingly somnolent as they were, did they actually want to go through seven more canticles? A lone but distinctive voice rose over the murmurs. Jarvis only just halted a cringe. Theophilus Velingtham stood in the sweltering darkness to speak. Theophilus had been Head Deacon forever, at least since long before Jarvis, and spent most of his time as a one-man performance review committee.

—Father, I, and I believe the rest of the congregation, would find it difficult to countenance your request.

—I beg your pardon?

Even given Theophilus' penchant for self-righteous droning, the man couldn't seriously be suggesting two more hours.

—The Collingham Sacraments are our highest holiday, Pastor. What does a little discomfort mean to the true penitent?

More murmurs, this time of assent.

—How can a little overheating, and I'll grant you, it *is* rather warm in here—

There was some appreciative chuckling. Theophilus wore a smile that Jarvis could see even in the dimness of the sanctuary. He tried hard not to also read malevolence there.

—I was only thinking of the extremity of the discomfort, 41

Deacon Velingtham. Surely, the Collingham was not meant as an exercise in suffering.

—Surely what *better* situation could there be for the transgressor to reflect upon the gracious penitence of the Sacraments than to receive those Sacraments in a session of extreme discomfort?

There were calls of 'hear, hear' and 'amen' from the crowd now.

—It must be forty degrees in here, Deacon, maybe forty-five. I'm thinking of the safety issues—

—I, for one, am willing to risk it for the precious absolution that the Collingham offers.

Now there were outright calls of agreement.

—Continue on!

—The entire Collingham!

—Praise be to the Sacraments!

Theophilus' voice again, splitting the room like a cleaver.

—I think of Sarah the Downhearted in the desert, walking mile after mile to gather the cactus leaves necessary for her—

—Yes, Deacon, we are all familiar with the parable.

—I was merely—

—Do you all really wish to proceed?

If he was going to have to do all eleven canticles then he might as well get on with them without having to listen to Theophilus blabber about a parable taught to children. The veritable shouts of 'yes' from the congregation sealed the matter.

—Well, I must say I am heartened and delighted and much humbled by your reverence for the Sacraments. It strengthens not only my faith in the text, but my faith in you, my good people. Blessed are you, and faithful. You are truly children of the Sacraments.

42   *Zealots*, Jarvis thought, and cautioned himself again on his

lack of charity. He caught a glance of Theophilus sitting down again in the gloom, a look of sour triumph on his face. Jarvis stifled another unkind thought and looked back to his text.

—Then if you'll all turn with me to the beginning of canticle five . . .

13. Maggerty Eats.

The circumstance wasn't noteworthy, but the sensation was.

Maggerty was hungry.

He had, more or less, ceased noticing hunger years before. The constant swirly, inky fog in his brain helped to push the subject away, and he had also managed to achieve a certain self-sufficiency that kept the deepest pangs in abeyance. He knew where to get fruit in the Arboretum, where to get vegetables from the larger local gardens, and where easiest to steal prepared goods from those shopkeepers who turned a blind eye when Maggerty ambled in. No one wished the Rhinoherd any ill and all did their distant best to see that he was provided for. Even in these conditions, if Maggerty got hungry enough, he would just eat grass with The Crash. It tasted unspeakable, but he had also learned the habit of ignoring his tongue.

So, in fact Maggerty was often hungry, but rarely noticed because there was always something in the way of provision, making it more accurate and more disturbing, then, to say now that Maggerty was *aware* that he was hungry. Acutely aware. The fruits on the trees were smaller than usual; the vegetables in the gardens also. The prepared goods were still theftworthy, but Maggerty had caught the eyes of more than one shopkeeper frowning at his repeat business. The grass was also different. There was still plenty of it, of course, there was always plenty of grass, but Maggerty's tastebuds were becoming less successful at ignoring the bitterness, mainly because they had only been taught to ignore the sickly sweetness of the greenest grasses of Hennington.

No, there was no doubt about it. Maggerty was hungry, hungry enough to momentarily clear his fogged brain and require him to take notice. His stomach paced up his torso in gurgly steps. A little while later it paced back down. He followed it with his attention every time, fingering his wound distractedly. Beneath the grime and under the lowered face – but oddly enough *not* underneath a beard; it remained one of the central mysteries of the Rhinoherd that he never grew facial hair, never grew it for there was certainly no way he could be *shaving* it off – Maggerty frowned. It was an effort for so expressionless and calcified a face to show much emotion, but there it was, an honest-to-goodness frown.

Somehow Maggerty knew the leader of the herd was also bothered about the grass. He had been with The Crash long enough to have seen her assume her leadership, albeit reluctantly, and had followed the herd faithfully through her entire tenure as leader. He could tell when she was bothered, even when it seemed the other animals in The Crash couldn't. There was a look to her, a shaking of the head, a leveling of the eyes, there was *something* that Maggerty keyed into through the murk in his brain, something that addressed the unsettled aspect of him, which was a considerable aspect indeed. Maggerty, that wariest of suspects, could follow wariness in others, even rhinoceros, *especially* rhinoceros, with nary a batted matted eyelash.

He plucked a pinkish-green cherry from a wan cherry tree tucked away in the northern corners of the Hennington Arboretum. The branch did not give up the under-ripe fruit willingly, and Maggerty nearly mashed it into nothing before he got it off the limb. When he finally ate it, it was so sour the tears temporarily blinded him. He let out a little gasp. After his vision cleared, he noticed the leader of The Crash regarding him. Not looking, but sniffing in his direction, her spearhead ears rotating this way and that, taking their measure of him. He croaked out some words to her.

—They're green. Not ripe yet.

She looked off into the distance, but somehow Maggerty could tell she was still giving him her attention. She snorted, shaking her head and shuffling her front feet.

—What's going on?

But of course she had no answer. She turned and moved off further among the rest of The Crash, all grazing happily in the green lea. They were in an area where a concentration of aeries hovered at the top of nearly every tree, homes to the massive Hennington Grey Eagle. She directed her attention to the treetops, as if pondering a question. Maggerty looked up as well. The huge nests seemed abandoned, ghost nests waiting to fall. The eagles were nowhere to be seen.

—Where did they go?

And again she had no answer.

14. Peter on the Move.

Peter Wickham unplugged the charger from his motorcycle and maneuvered out of the garage. His waiter's uniform was neatly folded into a back compartment. Underneath his protective jacket and helmet, he was dressed in an expensive pair of black pants and a white, frilled shirt that was ridiculous. Big Boss Thomas Banyon had selected it though and thus discussion of its merits stopped there.

Peter had been brought from over the border the year   45 before by Thomas Banyon, ostensibly as a waiter, but really because one of Thomas' regular young bucks had the gall to go and get himself murdered, under circumstances Thomas preferred not to spell out, leaving him short one Rumour boy to lease for general entertainment. Thomas' experience was such, though, that the word 'general' rarely applied for long, and Peter ended up being not quite so 'general' after all. It turned out that Peter had a member just subtly shaped, curved, and pliant enough to be a perfect fit for those male and female clients whose tastes tended towards the mysterious pleasures of the anus. Thomas being Thomas, Peter had to work as a waiter anyway, so tonight he had pulled a full shift at Hennington Hills Golf Course and Resort's Savannah Restaurant before heading out to what had turned into a regularly scheduled Wednesday-night clip. He pushed the cycle onto the freeway out of town heading for the immaculate but somehow sad home of one Luther Pickett, businessman.

Peter was remarkably unresentful of his clips. He wasn't foolish enough to ever believe that Thomas Banyon would for one second make good on his promises of releasing Peter after the three-year work permit was up when Peter would be able, theoretically anyway, to look for work away from his sponsor. Peter brought in too much money and too many intangibles to the Golf Course and Resort, and he was well aware he would be used until his looks, talents, and penis were no longer so often requested. But that was the future; it would take care of itself. He shared in none of the griping the other employees of Hennington made about old men with bad smells or fat women with pudgy, inept fingers.

There was no doubt Peter had gone through his share of awful clips: the woman who, after sex, had walked into her bathroom and calmly died of a cerebral hemorrhage; the teenage boy who, halfway through the act, had begun to insist that Peter start punching him; the man who had held him at gunpoint demanding that Peter fuck his large, blonde dog, not believing Peter when he told the man that he had requested the wrong employee. Thomas, in an act that could have been mistaken for kindness, had released this last man from the clip list. You never threatened the entertainment. Never. Unless, of course, that *was* your particular brand of entertainment.

Despite all this, as Peter drove towards Luther's home, he was heartened, even a little excited. Though never having been with a man during his whole life across the border, Peter had unexpectedly made the rookie mistake of falling dangerously and recklessly in love with Luther Pickett, the boss' stepbrother. Somehow, through his three or four clips during the week, through all the fakery and fucking he performed, through all the varying degrees of hygiene and taste that he put up with, this regular Wednesday appointment made up for it all.

He rounded a long curve in the freeway and slid down the offramp. He turned up into the hills, humming to himself as he went. Luther's house was at the end of a private road, removed from most neighbors and traffic. A lovely house, Peter thought for the nth time as he parked his bike to the side of the garage. When he walked around to the front door, Luther was already there, waiting for him.

—Peter.

—Hey, Luther.

They kissed.

—Come in. I made chook. Hope you're hungry.

Here was another thing: Luther Pickett seemed to be the only clip in the history of Hennington Hills to make dinner for the entertainment.

—Smells good.

—I hope so. I'm a little worried about the spices.

They stopped at the entrance to the kitchen for a longer embrace and kiss.

—It's good to see you.

—I'm very glad to be here.

And there was the sad look again, the look that had caused Peter to fall.

—What's wrong?

A laugh.

—Oh, you know, the usual.

—Yes, but you never tell me 'the usual'.

—Just a little personal failure today. Nothing to worry about. Here, take off your jacket. Get comfortable.

—Do you like this shirt?

—Sure.

—You don't have to lie.

—Then, no.

—I don't like it either. Banyon insisted I wear it. Said it was all the fashion, as if he would know. Do you have a T-shirt I could borrow?

—Absolutely.

Luther disappeared for a moment and returned with a shirt. He watched while Peter changed. He sighed.

—Are you sure nothing's up?

—I'm sure. Don't worry about it. We're here to have a good time.

'We', thought Peter.

—Why don't we eat then? And after that, I can help you relax.

—I'm all for that plan.

Luther smiled, and there was genuine warmth in it, Peter was sure.

15. An Offer.

—Good veal. Your room service has performed well, Eugene.

—First I've ever had.

—First room service?

—First veal. I'm Rumour. We don't normally go for veal.

—Oh, that's right. It's seafood or nothing, isn't it?

—The Official Entrée of the Rumour Nation.

—And what nation would that be?

—A hypothetical one, so far.

—So far? There are ambitions afoot to make it not hypothetical?

—If you believe my father.

—Do you?

—Do I what?

—Believe your father.

—Before or after he died?

—Either.

—Then no and no.

—Ah, the bitterness of youth. We're ignoring the, what is this?, crumb cake would be my best guess.

—Blueberry-cinnamon bundt.

—How very exact.

—I work here. I've seen the menu.

Jon cut his way into the bundt with a knife. A quivering blueberry goo slumped out of the middle of the slice.

—I think that's as far as I'm willing to go.

—You're not going to eat it?

—Look at it.

—It looks good.

Eugene cut himself an enormous piece. He seemed so

pleased while eating it that Jon could have sworn he heard
him humming. He *was* humming. A tune, even.

—What are you humming?

—What?

—That song. What are you humming?

—I'm not humming.

—Yes, you were. Just now.

—No, I wasn't.

Said with an unusual sternness that Jon took as a dismissal
of the subject. So be it.

—All right then. You weren't.

—It's almost eight. I should be going.

—There's no need for that just yet.

—I thought you had somewhere to go, too.

—Not tonight.

—Why would you spend the first night of your vacation
in a hotel room?

—It's not a vacation. I told you, I'm visiting an old friend.

—Well, still. Why stay here? Why not visit your friend?

—I have found out she's occupied this evening.

—She?

—She. Old passion from my past, I'm afraid.

—And she doesn't know you're coming so that's why she's
occupied.

—How very observant from one who has seemed hereto-
fore so opaque. I mean that as a friend.

—No, I know fuck all about most things. My girlfriend
just dumped me.

—A-ha. So you're currently attuned to the caprice that is
occasionally named 'woman'.

—What?

—Women can sometimes ruin you.

—Goddamn right.

He angrily speared another quivering bite of bundt.

—What do you want to be, Eugene?

Eugene smiled sourly, blueberries in his teeth.

—You mean when I grow up?

—How old are you?

—Twenty.

—Then, yes, definitely, when you grow up.

—I don't know.

—Surely there must be something.

—Nope.

—At all?

—At all. I wanted to be a musician. I'm a bass player.

—If you *are* a bass player, then why the past tense? Sounds like you're already a musician.

—Fuck it, I don't want to talk about it.

—Surely you don't want to work here the rest of your life?

Eugene said nothing, shoving more bundt into his mouth.

—How would you like to come and work for me?

—You just met me.

—I'm an excellent judge of people.

—Not if you're offering *me* a job.

—Self-deprecation is more destructive than you can possibly imagine, Eugene.

—A job doing what?

—Being my assistant.

—I'm flattered, but like I said—

—Look, I don't want to bed you or your single-tracked mind.

He turned his full gaze on Eugene. Apple-green eyes resting in a lined, deeply tanned face. Cropped salt-and-pepper hair pulling back from strong temples. A small nose resting above a generously lipped mouth. A chin that only seemed on the weaker side until you heard the voice pouring from above it. Eugene began to sweat. He felt his skin pulling into goosebumps. He was entranced, trapped.

—I am not an average man, Eugene, and I don't mean that in a boastful way. In fact, it has often worked to my detriment, but I do know a few things. My destiny is here in Hennington. I'm not prepared to share that destiny just yet but know this, I am not mistaken, misled, or delusional. I'm not just offering you a job, Eugene, I'm offering you a chance. A chance to be there.

And then it was gone, vanishing like steam off an athlete. Jon leaned back and smiled with a casualness that seemed to emerge from nowhere. Eugene could only cough for a moment before he spoke.

—Why me?

—Why not you?

—Why would you want me to work for you?

—I'm not sure. Doesn't it seem right, though?

—You just met me.

—So you've said. I told you. I'm a good judge of people.

—I just met *you*.

Jon shrugged.

—You've got blueberry dribbling down your chin, Eugene.

It was a full moment before Eugene took his napkin and wiped the blue conflagration from his face, but by then he was already a former employee of the Solari Hotel.

16. Why Archie Banyon Feels the Way He Does About Women.

—Maybe I can talk her out of it. It's not too late. Ballot's not for another four months. She could get a waiver on registration. Tell the people she's reconsidered because of their support. She'd be re-elected by fucking *acclamation* if it came to that. She's fifty-eight years old. She's got at least two more terms in her. Three, even.

Archie Banyon's limo was caught in traffic, which meant that Jules was going to have to listen to even more of this blather than usual.

—I've known her for ages now. Ages. Since before she was Mayor. She was my lawyer, don't you know, and a right pain in the ass she was then. Right pain in the ass she is now, but a damn fine Mayor. Damn fine. She shouldn't be retiring. Don't trust that Max. Seems like a nice enough kid, but 'kid' is the problem word there. Cora's got more sense than Max does. Hell, Max's little whipper's got more sense than Max does, and she's what, ten?

—Maybe the Mayor wants some time with her family.

—What fucking family? She's got Albert and whatever stud they're currently fucking. That's not family. That's not even a card game.

—Would it be out of place for me to ask you to cut down on the cursing?

—Yes.

—I thought so.

—I don't understand people who get power and then just give it up. Just say, 'Oh, what the fuck, I just don't want it anymore. I'm *retiring*'.

He literally spat the last word, contemptuous saliva hitting the limo's floor.

—Not everyone's like you, Mr Banyon.

—And thank God for that. What a pain in the ass the world would be then.

—Would it be out of place for me to agree with you?

—Out loud, yes.

—I thought so.

—And what for the love of God does she see in Max?

—If you don't mind me saying so, your opposition to Max Latham seems out of proportion to anything he's done.

—I'm not against Max Latham. I'm *for* Cora Larsson.

—And why would that be exactly? Again? Sir?

Archie's history was populated by the ghosts of dead women. He should have known something when his first wife was named Belladonna. Archie and Belladonna married young and desperately in love. Belladonna, whose formidable bearing and pomegranate lipstick eschewed any attempt at a nickname, gave birth to four daughters in rapid succession: Dolores, Soledad, Ariadne, and Proserpina, Belladonna's sense of humor showing an appealingly dark shade. When Thomas was born, Archie intervened. Belladonna had wanted to call him Actaeon.

Archie's mother, who had died when Archie was a teenager but who at the time of his wedding could be dealt with as a sad memory rather than the ominous beginning to a macabre chain, had been strict and loving with Archie until her death, instilling him with confidence, kindness, and a respect for self, a parenting trick that Archie was constantly sad not to have learned. Archie's mother was the reason he loved women so much and also the reason for the manner in which he loved them. Not in the big-rack-hot-ass sort of way that his friends so perplexingly did. Archie just found them easier to talk to, easier to share a meal with, easier to take advice from. It was clear to everyone that Archie had found a wondrous and powerful match in Belladonna, a brilliant, passionate, dark-eyed lawyer who was the only daughter in a family of eight sons.

Belladonna's misfortune was to thumb her nose at fate one too many times. One day, when Poison and her daughters

Pain, Solitude, Corrupted Innocence and Bad Marriage were sunbathing on the fourth-story roof of Archie's northeast Hennington estate, an earthquake opened up the ground and reduced the building and the five women to rubble. Archie had been inspecting a vineyard on a horse which hadn't even thrown him during the tumult. Thomas turned up later full of unsatisfactory explanations.

Archie's grief, a deep and powerful thing even if he hadn't been by then the richest man in Hennington, was finally only mollified by an endocrinologist called Maureen Whipple, a name Archie thought inoffensive enough not to anger the gods. Copper haired with copper-rimmed eyeglasses, Maureen was an amateur lepidopterist and singularly devoid of risky imagination. But she liked Archie quite a bit, and he liked her quite a bit right back. Eleven days after their fourth wedding anniversary, she was killed when a derailing train hurtled through her windshield.

Archie's third wife, Anna Grabowski, about whom the less said the better, barely made it down the aisle before perishing in a trapeze mishap.

His fourth wife was a devil-may-care whirlwind named May Ramshead. Eight years older than Archie, she was a zoologist with a wild streak. She rappelled off of cliffs, swam with sharks, and had spent time as a rodeo clown. Two and a half years of blissful marriage later, May died peacefully in her sleep when her heart failed.

Archie finally took the hint and settled, at age sixty, for a single life with female friends. That was when he met and hired Cora Larsson. Contrary to the whisperings of those few existing enemies of Cora, Archie wasn't responsible for Cora's success. True, Archie had sent Cora poking into some fishy business dealings of then-Mayor Jacob Johnson, but it was Cora who had followed the now-infamous trail to the mysterious death of Johnson's father and the millions stashed away in accounts under the name of Johnson's mistress, a story so familiar it needs no rehashing here.

It was, however, Archie's suggestion, with a helping hand from Albert, that Cora run for Mayor some twenty years ago. Archie was thirty years Cora's senior, but he was, if the truth be known, in love with her and always had been. Thank goodness she was already married to Albert and also that Archie realized marriage to him meant certain death. He merely had to be her friend. He gave her money and advice when she ran for Mayor and threw the inaugural ball when she won. She was also the reason Banyon Enterprises hadn't cheated the city in over two decades. Archie respected her too much to ever want to face the disappointment of her certain litigation. He loved her, and that was that, more than enough reason to support her.

—What's with this traffic?

—It seems to be clearing up, sir.

—Thank God for that.

—Yes, sir. Thank God, indeed.

17. 'The Tale of Rufus and Rhonda'.

—How's your head, baby?

—I want to cut it off.

—But then you wouldn't have one at all.

—I don't care.

—Medicine's not helping?

—I guess. It makes me tired.

—Try to sleep, then.

—I can't keep my mind clear. It races and races and it's

all just thing after thing after thing.

—That's the fever, darling. It can't be helped.

—I'm so tired.

—Do you want me to tell you a story?

—Don't you think I'm a little old for that?

—Do *you* think you're a little old for that?

—Depends on the story.

—I'll make it age-appropriate, how about that?

—Maybe.

—Okay, let's see. 'There was once a girl named Talon . . .'

—Stop. I don't want to be the heroine.

—Why not?

—I just don't. Please?

Max thought for a minute.

—All right. How about this?

There once was a great king called Rufus the Swarthy. (—What was he king of?) He was king of all the land. (—Which land?) He was king of all the Southern Lands. (—What were they called? —Just flow with me here, Talon.) He had arisen to the throne after his father was killed in a great war with the people to the North that had raged on and on for generations. King Rufus didn't believe in war. (—That's a pacifist, right? —Very good.) He had seen war take the lives of all of his friends and classmates and all the rest of the young men in his land. Now it had taken the life of his father, and King Rufus decided enough was enough. He was going to end the war, once and for all.

The war had gone on for so long, hundreds of years, it turned out no one could remember what the war was being fought over. So the first thing King Rufus did was send his Royal Researchers to work. They worked night and day for months on end, going back further and further into history, 57 searching the research, combing the catacombs, delving into the delvements. (—Is that a word? —Probably.) At last, on a bright, cold morning, they found the reason. Forty-seven generations before, the King of the Southerners had stolen a rhinoceros out of the Northern King's private zoo. (—That's it? —Wars have started for less. —But that's stupid. —Precisely.) King Rufus couldn't believe that so many thousands of lives and hundreds of years had been wasted on something so small, especially since both the cities of the North and the cities of the South had grown over time despite the war and each side had more than their share of zoos chock-full of rhinoceros.

He decided a symbolic gesture was in order. He would give a present to the ruler of the Northerners, who during this time was Queen Rhonda the Stout. King Rufus ordered his kingdom's zoologists to select the top male and female rhino from his stock and prepare them for a journey to the North. Rufus himself would then deliver them to the Queen in person, unaccompanied by any guard. He sent word to Queen Rhonda's court of his plan, and she sent word back that he would be allowed to make the journey unmolested.

For one hundred and twenty-two days, King Rufus walked with the male and female rhinoceros towards the North's capital city, through sun and rain, light and dark, all alone save for the rhinos. The three lived off the land, Rufus hunting game for himself and finding lush spots for the rhinos to graze. At last, late one afternoon, King Rufus reached the castle doors of Queen Rhonda. He entered through a long hallway that led from chamber to chamber, on and on and on through one hundred separate rooms, the male and female rhinos with him at every step, until finally, he reached the throne room of Queen Rhonda. (—And she was beautiful and they fell instantly in love. —Yes and no. They fell in love, but she wasn't beautiful. —Oh, I like that.)

58

'The Stout' turned out to be a kind nickname for the Queen. Exceedingly short and overwhelmingly plump, Rhonda nevertheless exuded a kind of vitality and vigor that struck Rufus' eye immediately. Now, it should be said that looks-wise, Rufus was no great shakes either. (—Good.) His wild mane of red hair was so long that it often tangled itself in his equally long beard. Underneath all the hair and matting was an extremely handsome if overly thick-fingered man, but on the surface he seemed like a golem made of burlap. Plus, he had a cold sore. But it was love at first sight for them both anyway. And for that, the Northern cities and the Southern cities rejoiced. Everyone everywhere was equally sick of the war.

Queen Rhonda immediately accepted the gift of the male and female rhino, and offered her kingdom's hospitality to King Rufus while the details of the armistice were worked out. One day later, the Queen, with Rufus' permission, also ordered her lawyers to draw up a pre-nuptial agreement. They attended feasts together, hosted parties welcoming delegates from Rufus' kingdom, and generally spent a lot of time staring into each other's eyes and sighing.

But all was not well. There was a wizard in Rhonda's court named Ted. (—Ted? —Yes, Ted. —*Ted* the Wizard? —Yes, may I continue?) Ted had never loved Rhonda but had arranged with her father at her birth to be the one to marry her when she reached adulthood. Fortunately for Rhonda, her father had died when she was a child, also fighting the war like King Rufus' father. (—Aw, Dad. —It's just a fairy tale, honey. Don't worry.) By the time Rhonda came of age, she had exercised her queenly powers to have the agreement with the wizard voided, for she had no desire whatsoever to marry a man who was only interested in her power. She regarded him as more annoying than evil, though, so she kept him around and had ceased giving him much thought after the matter was settled.

Ted hadn't forgotten though, and when he learned of the wedding plans of Rufus and Rhonda, he finally realized his chance for revenge. Working with all the black magic at his command, calling on all the evil forces he knew or was at least acquainted with, using every last magic chemical he had in his storehouse, every trick he ever learned, he cooked up an evil curse. Revenge would be his.

The wedding day arrived, sunny but cool. Nearly every resident of both kingdoms had crowded onto a huge field to watch the ceremony. Even the male and female rhino were present, chewing happily away on the grass. Rhonda the Stout stoutly rhondled her way down the aisle to her awaiting groom. Rufus had been cleaned up for the occasion and swept up his bride-to-be for a pre-ceremonial kiss.

This was where Ted popped in.

'STOP!' he cried with a booming voice. 'I, Ted the Splendid, curse this union.'

There were gasps among the guests. Rhonda wasn't impressed.

'What is it now, Ted?' she asked.

'I curse this union thusly,' said Ted. 'Marry if you will, love if you will, rule if you will, but kiss at your peril.'

'Meaning . . . ?' Rhonda said.

'If you kiss the lips of your beloved,' said Ted, 'both of you will transform immediately and forever into rhinoceros, of the type that brought this cursed union together in the first place.'

'You can't do that, Ted,' said Rhonda.

'Oh, but I can, Your Majesty. And have done.'

'Ted, as Your Sovereign,' said Rhonda, 'I command that 60 you lift this curse.'

'Too late, Your Majesty,' said Ted. 'What's done cannot be undone.'

With that, he let out an evil wizardly laugh and disappeared in a plume of foul-smelling green smoke.

Rufus and Rhonda didn't know what to do. They were standing at the altar, waiting to consummate their vows, and bring peace at last to the Southern and Northern cities. Thousands of expectant faces watched silently as Rufus and Rhonda stared into each other's eyes.

'What should we do?' asked Rufus.

'There seems to be only one thing we *can* do,' said Rhonda.

They kissed. (—Oh!) In a flash, where the King and Queen were standing, there were suddenly two rhinoceros, face-to-face, each with a crown hooked over their respective horns. Slowly, they turned to face the crowd, and without a word, for everyone knows rhinos can't speak, they walked back up the aisle, pausing only to be joined by the male and female rhino already present. The two kingdoms watched as the four rhinoceros ambled for the horizon and set to grazing.

The townsfolk stood in silence for a while. Nobody knew what to do. Then someone from the South remembered that Northerners were said to go to the bathroom where they slept, and the Southerner felt the need to mention this to a Northerner nearby. Then someone from the North remembered that Southerners were supposed to have scars on their backsides from having their tails cut off when they were babies, and the Northerner felt compelled to ask a Southerner to show it to him. Then someone from the North spat on someone from the South. Then someone from the South slapped someone from the North.

A new battle began that day, one so intense that King Rufus and Queen Rhonda and the other two rhinos were forgotten.   61

When one hundred years had passed and the new, even-worse war had destroyed both kingdoms so thoroughly that even their histories had been erased, no one among the few remaining survivors could remember where the wandering crash of rhinoceros had come from. The end.

—So but wait. Is that where The Crash comes from?

—No, sweetie, I just made that up. It's as true as any other story, though, I suppose.

—Why did Rufus and Rhonda kiss each other?

—I guess they loved each other so much they would rather have spent their lives as rhinos than not be able to kiss.

—But rhinos can't kiss.

—Says who?

—But didn't they know about the war starting up again?

—Probably.

—But didn't they have a duty to their kingdoms, then?

—Yes, but it's a moral question. Which is more important? Love or peace?

—What's the answer?

—That's the whole point, there is no answer.

—How is that supposed to make me sleep? I'm going to be up all night debating love versus peace. I'm *ten*, Dad. I have no idea.

—Okay, what about this one? 'There was once a chipmunk named Terry who was having trouble getting his library card renewed—'

—Good night, Dad.

—Oh, good, a laugh at least. Are you feeling better?

—A little.

62   —Think you can sleep?

—I think so.

—Okay, baby. Do you want me to stay with you a while until you do?

—Yes.

—My pleasure, honey.

18. Mingle, Mingle.

—Archie! Good to see you.

—That's overly solicitous for you, Cora. Is something wrong?

—Not even a moment for pleasantries, huh?

—Don't tell me. The Boy Prince is a no-show yet again.

—Why weren't you a detective, Archie?

—Because I preferred to be rich. What's his excuse this time?

—His daughter's sick.

—If it's anything less than plague, I'm not buying it.

—It's Pox.

—Did she get the shots?

—Yes.

—Then he could have gotten a sitter.

—Archie—

—I left my kids home on plenty of nights when business called.

Another voice came in from behind.

—It's a different day and age than when we were young, Archie.

—I'm thirty years older than you, Albert. There's no 'we' involved at all, though I suppose you knew of this conspicuous absence as well.

—Family called, apparently, and it's actually thirty-one years. But how are you this fine evening?

—My arches are falling.

—Isn't that the first line of a sonnet?

Cora took Archie by the arm.

—Come. Eat something. You'll be happier.

—Oh, yes, why don't you rub my belly and tell me I'm a good dog while you're at it.

—Has that been the secret all along?

—What's to stop me from just going straight back home?

—Archie, please. Now the situation is this.

—Would you get me a whiskey, Albert?

—Straight up but very, very cold, if I remember correctly.

—Good lad.

—The situation, as I said.

—Yes, get on with it.

—Is that Max isn't here because his little girl is sick. None of these people are really here to see him anyway. They all want to hobnob with me.

—I know that's *my* preference.

—So Max gets sympathy points for brave single fatherhood, as well as for having his priorities straight.

—His priorities straight? What if a tidal wave is heading for the city but Max's daughter has a little cough?

—It's a different time now, Archie.

—The second time I've heard that inside of five minutes.

—Only because it's true.

—Is it?

—Yes. We'll have an *in absentia* fundraiser. It'll be the talk of the town.

—It might be the talk of a very, very dull town, but even only there if it was the first time it had happened.

—The last time was my fault. A head of state had died. I had to send a representative.

—Poppycock. Oh, God bless you, Albert.

—That ought to smooth the evening out a bit.

—So, I'm an alcoholic, now, am I?

—Isn't that really something for you to decide for yourself?

—Why did you marry this man again?

—He has an enormous penis.

—So 'it's not the size that counts' has been a lie all along?

—'Fraid so.

—Bring me another, then, and let's get this thing over with.

—Champagne?

—What *I'm* concerned about is the Bondulay creeping into our schools if he's elected.

—What do you get when you cross a Rumour with an octopus?

—I think he's very handsome.

—Harold, please. This is neither the time nor the place.

—I don't think his race is an issue at all.

—Do you have any Cluvot?

—I've heard he's part of the Rumour Underground.

—Creeping how?

—Oh, please, he hasn't looked at a woman since his fiancée died.

—I don't know but it sure can pick a head of lettuce.

—That doesn't mean he won't ever.

—Any what?

—Oh, you know how they are.

—Oh, *yawn*. Everyone knows that doesn't exist.

—It sure doesn't seem to be.

—Harold!

—'They'?

—I think he's wrapped up in being a father.

—Oh, sure, you act shocked now, but you'll be laughing on the car ride home.

—They call it a cultural experience and then suddenly we're all listening to their music.

—And she's such a sweet little girl, too.

—Secret societies control all centres of government.

—Cluvot. It's from the North.

—I wonder what he looks like naked.

—I most certainly will not.

—What does that have to do with religion?

—He's Rumour, so probably a hairy chest.

—And you'll be telling everyone you know at the office tomorrow.

—Maybe Hennington's a little more enlightened than we thought.

—You're paranoid.

—Not necessarily. I went out with a Rumour guy in college, and he was smooth.

—Are you really this clueless, Harold?

—You sure he wasn't waxed?

—There aren't any wines from the North.

—It's all stepping stones, is what I'm trying to say.

—Nobody was doing it back then.

—What? What did I say?

—Doesn't mean he couldn't have tweezed.

—It's made from pears.

—A whole chestful of hair? I doubt it.

—Stepping stones.

—Precisely. I mean, he's leading in the polls and the city's what? A quarter Rumour?

—Have you even seen him here yet?

—Little baby steps until all of a sudden we're overrun.

66   —To think otherwise is naïve.

—I heard someone say something about his daughter being sick.

—I have no response to that, except of course that the answer is no.

—That'd be just like him to stay home with her.

—Max is a Rumour.

—I'm not even sure Max Latham is a member of the Bondulay Church.

—Have you ever even met him?

—Forget it, then.

—If even that.

—No shit, but he should at least be able to take a joke.

—I prefer to think of it as sanity.

—No, but it just seems like the kind of thing he'd do.

—Of course he is. He's Rumour. They all are.

—I think it's something to be proud of.

—Champagne?

Albert declined another glass with a wave of his hand.

—There are some well-nigh terrifying people here, Archie.

—But terrifying people with money. That's the important thing.

—I'd wager half of them aren't even registered on our side of the hustings.

—Max is going to win. You always put money on the winner, no matter who you might vote for.

—Tragic but true. Makes for a nicely tense party though, don't you think?

—I always feel like I've barely escaped with my life.

—That's because you have.

—Where's Cora?

—Over there. Hijacked by Harold Baxter. A rescue might be in order.

—Let her stay. Punishment for allowing me to be here and Max to not.

—She *is* my wife. A rescue is chivalrous. Come with me.

—No, I . . . Harold, how are you, you old son-of-a-bitch?

—Doing well, Archie. You know, I was just telling Cora here that—

—Cora, my dear, I'm leaving.

—But you just got here.

—Ninety-three minutes ago. Everyone is as cocktailed-up as they're going to be. Besides you've already gotten my money and the milkings of most of the rest of this crowd.

—He even got money out of Miriam Caldwell.

—Good Lord, Archie. Did you have to join her church?

—No, no, she's terrified of me. It was easy. But as I've said, I'm leaving. Walk me to my car.

—Of course. Nice talking to you, Harold. Albert, be a dear and get me another soda water.

—Certainly.

Cora and Archie walked towards the car park.

—Cora, I have concerns.

—I suppose I'm not surprised.

—I'm wondering if we've got a bit of a paper tiger on our hands here.

—Don't worry, Archie. The campaign is months away, and though you admittedly haven't had an opportunity to hear it, Max can be a very persuasive campaigner in his own way.

—He'd better be, is all I'm saying.

—What's on your mind, Archie?

—There were some rumblings in the crowd in there.

—Rumblings about what?

—About Max being Rumour.

—Oh, Archie, you can't be serious.

—I'm quite serious. He'd be the first. I'm not sure they, them, in there, are sure they're ready for it.

—But everyone knew that going in. His poll numbers are high, he's viewed with integrity—

—He's still a Rumour. It could be the old story that people are afraid to say they wouldn't vote for him because they don't want to look prejudiced.

—I suppose I can see your point, Archie, but don't you think we're past that? We've had Rumour Councilmembers, Rumour Department Heads—

—I'm not saying he's not going to win. I'm just saying it might be tougher than you, *we* expect it to be.

—I don't have any illusions that there might be an element out there that might not vote for a Rumour.

—The trouble is that it's a volatile element that could be open to persuasion as well as growth in size.

—Persuasion by whom? He's unopposed.

—Just because there's not a credible opponent now doesn't mean there won't be at some point.

—Who?

—I don't know, Cora. Good grief. I'm speaking hypothetically. Just keep your eyes open is all I'm saying. This could be a bigger challenge than it appears on the surface.

—I wasn't born yesterday. My last race was against Jake Caldwell, remember? All those churchkin of Miriam's with their picket signs, pretty much calling me a wayward wife who should go back to the kitchen. Whoever thought those loonies would get thirty per cent? But at the end of the day, the voters did the right thing, and they're going to do the right thing this time.

—Fair enough, but stay on your guard.

69

—That's very sweet, Archie. I appreciate your help tonight.

—I hardly did it to be sweet.

—But you did it anyway.

—And thank God it's over. Ah, there's the limo.

—Have a good night, Archie.

—Remember what I said, Cora. I'm an old man. Our bodies make up in clairvoyance what they lose in malleability. There are rumblings afoot. Whether they'll bring anything noteworthy to pass is anyone's guess.

Albert came up behind her as Archie sped away.

—Here's the soda water.

—Thank you, my love.

—What did Archie want? A percentage of Talon Latham's future income?

—He thinks Max is going to have problems because he's Rumour.

—Well, no shit. A secret conference just for that?

—I guess he wanted to impress upon me the gravity of the issue.

—A-ha, he was drunk.

—Looked that way. Let's go back inside.

—Must we?

—Duty calls.

19. Duty Calling.

Deep in the distant far side of Hennington Hills Golf Course and Resort, Jacki Strell waited on the bed for Councilman Wiggins to finish his cleanup in the bathroom. The excitable Councilman had spilled all over himself inside of twenty minutes. As usual, he had tried to hold out and Jacki had attempted the methods she knew to slow him down: giving it a finger flick on the head, grabbing a single pubic hair and pulling it out, etc. All to no avail. Given that the entertainment was informally scheduled for an hour, Jacki faced the familiar problem of dead air with Councilman Wiggins. Most of the time, they tried half-heartedly to bring him to a second climax, a climax for Jacki, of course, being the furthest thing from either of their minds. He usually just ended up biting too hard on her nipples while fumbling ineffectively with her round bottom.

Jacki sighed pleasurably. She had so much Forum in her bloodstream that Councilman Wiggins could bite away and she wouldn't even notice until the next day rolled around and salve would be required for her inflamed, maltreated aureoles. Taking Forum was like kicking back in a hot bubble bath you could take along anywhere. The world became one movable, ongoing massage. It was fair to say she couldn't remember what life was like before Forum, back in those non-prostitute, number-filled days with her sons and ex-husband, but one of the side effects of Forum was the peculiar accompanying belief that all of a sudden there *wasn't* a life before Forum, that it was always there, that it would always be there, that no problem was ever too big or too unpleasant that it couldn't be washed away in the enveloping stream of Forum. She barely registered the Councilman coming out of the bathroom looking both sheepish and peeved.

—I thought you said you were going to learn some new things to keep that from happening.

—It's okay—

She blanked on his name.

—Darling. It happens to a lot of men.

—But you said you could slow things down, that it wouldn't be a problem.

71

—I did slow things down, but let's face it, you're a little soldier who wants to shoot as soon as he gets to the firing line.

—Little.

She sighed, but didn't lose the smile from her face.

—I don't mean literally little. I meant it as a term of endearment.

—I'm not little.

He was. He was almost six inches shorter than Jacki, a good two stones slighter, and his genitalia, while proportional, were on the smaller side of what Jacki had seen in her most recent business days.

—No one's saying you are.

—You just did.

—I didn't, but we were having such a fun evening. Come here. Come back to bed. We'll have a nice, relaxing time for the rest of the hour.

Wiggins looked skeptical.

—Maybe we can make you go twice.

—You think so?

—Honey, I'm sure of it.

What were these words? Where did they come from? She didn't even call her children 'honey', had never addressed her husband during the eleven years they were married as 'darling'. And what were these clothes? She was a mathematician, for pity's sake. Mathematicians didn't wear rubber panties or silicon bras with zippers down the front of each breast. Accountants sure as hell didn't wear black hosiery attached to a black metal band that gave a slight electric shock when touched. At least not on a regular basis, they didn't. Who was she? Who was she right now?

Sometimes with Forum came the Lions, and they could kill you if you let them drag you away. Jacki closed her eyes and fought. Forum had a vibration, and while Councilman Wiggins resumed sucking down her nutrient-rich breast milk (also, incidentally, Forum-rich; Councilman Wiggins had quite unknowingly developed his own habit), she concentrated on working her way back into Forum's vibe. She could even see it when she closed her eyes. It was honey-colored and shimmering and just out of her reach.

Breathe, Jacki, breathe.

The Lions were at her heels, trying to drag her back to the present, if she could just, if she could only, if she could—

There it was. Oh, my, yes. There it was.

Everything's all right, honey. Nothing could be finer, darling.

Was she talking aloud?

She exhaled slowly, and her unconscious hand tenderly stroked the Councilman's thinning brown hair.

20. In the Hours Before Morning.

The questions were as old as time itself, but no less rigorous for their familiarity:

Are there reasons for love? And are they all intangible? If not, what if intangibles are the only things I have? Am I justifying all of this for my own wishful thinking? Is that love then, or is it just rationalization? Is this what we *do* when we're in love? Is there nothing real? Or is he just beyond my reach? And what does he think of me? Is he reminded of me during the rest of the week? Does my name enter his mind at work? Do I exist for him when I'm not here?

Peter hadn't slept much. He glanced over Luther's slumbering neck at the clock. It was still a little while before dawn. Staying for the whole night was another rarity in a clip, especially since Luther had already paid and Peter had logged in a completion over the phone hours ago. He put his face to the back of Luther's neck, inhaling a funk that verged on the offensive but steadfastly remained deeply sexual. It was a smell only lovers got. A stranger would have wrinkled his nose at the presumption.

Luther stirred.

—Are you awake?

—Oh, sorry, Luther. I didn't mean to wake you.

—I wasn't sleeping.

—Me neither.

—Why not?

—Just thinking.

—What about?

—Just things. How about you? You've got to get up for work in a couple of hours.

—I know.

—So why are you awake? I don't go on shift until tonight. I can afford to waste sleeping time.

—It's not as if I'm choosing to.

—What's bothering you?

—It's nothing.

—I've heard that before.

—You wouldn't understand.

—Do you have any idea how insulting that is?

—Sorry. I didn't mean it that way. I only meant that *I* don't quite understand it, and that's why I'm awake, because I can't figure it out.

—Maybe I could help you.

—You wouldn't want to get involved in my problems.

—Why wouldn't I?

In the blue darkness, Luther turned to face Peter.

—Why *would* you?

Luther's eyes reflected the moonlight that crept in through the slats in the windowblinds. He held on to Peter's arm and peered deeply into Peter's face, as if the answer were literally written there and he would have to make it out in the dark somehow. Peter could feel the pressure of full attention. Here was, if not *the* moment, then certainly *a* moment, a turning point where wished-for but unexpected advancement just might be possible, where the door opened a crack and a small light flung its way toward the promising. Peter couldn't catch his breath. He could actually feel the sweat coming off of his brow.

But, curses until the end of time, it was too early for him to rise to the occasion.

—I think . . . I mean, you're a great guy.

—Oh. Well. Thanks. That's very sweet.

He kissed Peter on the forehead.

—I think you're great, too, Peter.

—I just mean—

—You don't have to say any more. It's all right. Just me and my boring problems. Let's just try to get some sleep, okay?

Luther turned back around, away from Peter. Peter nuzzled closer to him. Neither of them slept during what remained of the rags of the early morning, Luther lost in his thoughts, Peter berating himself for not saying something, *anything* better. And so neither of them found out what there was to find out, neither of them spoke when the opportunity was there. Which was too bad, because if either of them had had that tiny bit of bravery available right at that moment, so much of what followed could have been avoided.

21. The Crash Before Dawn.

It was still dark, and the sleeping bodies of the herd were scattered across the Arboretum's wide main field like boulders thrown from a volcano. Maggerty slept in a nervous curl at the base of a tree, somnolently shooing away a murder of dream crows that pecked at his bare dream feet. A clear sky huddled overhead, the stars whispering in urgent tones about some universal matter or other. There was no artificial light on the hill of fields, but the moon was bright enough to cast crisp shadows of the many clutches of snoozing rhino hillocks. All was quiet. It was late enough for the olive bats and Hennington flying foxes to have finished their nocturnal feedings and scoot themselves off to inverted slumber. Even the breeze had settled down to rest.

But she was awake. She wasn't upset, she probably couldn't have even been called troubled, but there was definitely a disquiet in her. For hour upon hour now, she had been unable to work it out. She was lying down and had pulled distractedly at the grass within reach of her lips until a bald spot had appeared in a semicircle around her. Even then, she kept at it until she tasted nothing but dirt. Finally, she just sat up, twisting her ears this way and that, listening for the usual sounds of the deepest part of the night, hearing some, not hearing others.

Everything was wrong and nothing was. Her nostrils could smell the hint of dust in the air, yet that in itself wasn't troubling. The eagles weren't in their nests, but maybe they had just started mating season a few weeks early. The grass tasted bitter, but maybe something had just gotten into the groundwater. Maybe her anxiety was misplaced. The rest of the herd didn't seem to notice anything wrong. The birthrate had held steady, and the nine calves that had been born this year were neither more nor less healthy than in previous years. The last animal to die was almost two years ago when an ancient male was unable to pull himself out of a mud bog and the animals had to mill around helplessly while he slowly bleated his way to death by dehydration. There was no disease in the herd, no malnourishment, no hoof or skin malady.

So what was bothering her? The herd might be oblivious but the thin creature that always followed them had sensed something, too. He gave off a horribly forlorn and confused smell in the best of times, but lately it had increased to the point of almost being distracting. He also stuck closer to the herdmembers than he had before, even daring to nap in the middle of the herd while they grazed. It didn't prove anything, but at least she wasn't alone.

The sky began to change color, glowing slightly along one horizon. She hadn't rested all night, but forcing herself, she laid her head down onto the dirt mat to snatch whatever slumber she could before full-fledged daybreak. It was still a long while before she finally slipped off to shallow, fitful sleep.

Part II.

There Are No Ends, Only Changes.

22. Marmalade Leviathan.

Eugene's first job for Tybalt 'Jon' Noth was the procurement of a car (—Something black, Eugene, maybe a convertible, a sun roof at the very least), so when Eugene pulled up in front of the Solari in his brother's seventeen-year-old orange Bisector, the one with the sideboards that kept killing old ladies before they moved the bus benches further away from the road, to say that Jon was non-plussed was quite possibly to understate the matter.

—And just what under the expanse of great blue heaven above is this?

—It's my brother's.

—Is he adopted?

—It's the only car I could find.

—What a curious search that must have been.

—Well, I just thought that, you know.

—Oh, I don't have even the slightest idea where you're going with this, Eugene.

—*Anyone* can get a rental car.

—Of course they can. That's the whole point. Convenience, you see, matched with desire. It's called capitalism.

—I thought, I guess, you wanted something, I don't know, singular.

—Singular?

—Yeah.

Jon blinked.

—Singular.

—My brother's on a fishing boat for the next four months.

—So this . . . mobile clown cutlery is at our disposal.

81

—Look, if you don't like it, I can get you something different. I just thought—

—I know. Singular.

—Fuck it, I'll take it back.

—No, wait.

In truth, there *was* something spectacular about it, if Jon was going to be honest about things. The car was gargantuan with a long sloping roof that ultimately made its way to a third row of seats near the back. The half-dome hood swooped down to meet the twelve-bar radiator with a thud that could have raised mountains. Eugene's brother had gotten the optional fifth door that served as a convenient escape hatch in case of fire or police stop. And then there were those lethal protruding sideboards. Bisector, It Divides the Road, had quickly entered the lingo as Vivisector, It Dices Wide the Old. Uniambic perhaps, but accurate. Eugene's as-yet unnamed brother had kept it spotless and buffed to a point where both the wooden and chrome parts shone with equal glare. Such a monstrosity could never have been called beautiful, but it certainly was *something*. Singular, indeed.

—I've either grossly over-estimated you, Eugene, or grossly under-estimated. Either way, I'm curious as all hell as to how things are going to go.

—So you'll use the car?

—'Car' doesn't quite cover it, does it?

—You're not the easiest person to figure out, you know that?

—You've no idea.

Jon opened the passenger side door. Eugene looked surprised.

—I'm driving?

—Wouldn't you rather drive?

82   —Yeah, but—

—If I'm going to be seen in this Day-Glo meteorite, I think being chauffeured is probably the only route to take. Wouldn't you agree?

—Whatever you say.

—That's what an employer likes to hear.

Eugene shook his head. Jon smiled.

—Good. It'll be easier if you think I'm loony.

—What'll be easier?

—To City Hall, Eugene.

—City Hall?

—I have an appointment with the Mayor.

—The Mayor.

—Yes.

—Don't tell me she's—

—Yes, she's the friend.

Eugene turned the key. A sound like a two-story house being shat out the asshole of a zebra ripped through the dashboard. Jon had to strain to hear what Eugene said next.

—She's married, you know.

—Yes.

They exchanged a long look until Eugene finally shrugged, put the car in gear, and thrust off in a cloud of purple smoke.

23. Comfort for the Uncomfortable.

Jarvis Kingham's lifelong intellectual ambition had always been academic theology and that he ended up a practicing priest instead was maybe not the ironic hair-splitting that some of his more cynical friends presumed. For was not active ministration simply theology in action? While he had moments where he wished he could spend more time with his books and while the vigor of some of his parishioners 83 sometimes scared the daylights out of him – Head Deacon Theophilus Velingtham to name just one – the benefits, both personal and spiritual, more than rewarded the decision he had made to follow this slightly divergent path.

He actually remembered the exact moment. An already bearded seventeen year old, he had entered the Bondulay Divinity School up in the Mallow Hills southeast of Hennington, a place packed with seminary students, sand blown over the hills from the Brown, and really nothing else save for the occasional chuckwalla or poisonous rattleback. This was six years after Currie *vs* Madam Montez' School for the Sensual Arts, so by that point female seminary students were fully integrated into school life. Celibacy rules, even the temporary ones among students not studying for the priesthood, were still in force – no court was ever going to have any say over that issue – but the number of 'immaculate' conceptions at the school among female students was less than the all-male faculty had feared and predicted. As a matter of fact, the salutatorian of Jarvis' graduating class was the one and only Lyric O'Mahoneyham, overthrower-to-be of Archbishop Carl Sequin, and probably on her way to the Bondulay High Papacy had Hennington's future not taken the route it did.

(At that point, though, that was all a good ways off – and still remains a ways off now, though becoming uncomfortably close for more vaguely clairvoyant Henningtonians. If Archie Banyon's body had been more specific about what awaited, he might not have given up smoking after all.)

Jarvis toddled along unremarkably and had just begun his third year when he met the woman who should have been the love of his life. Her name was Diana. Long brown hair cascading in waves around a breathtaking face without a trace of make-up; a serious, challenging brow that let you know you had better have more to your argument than just opinion; a nose slightly too wide over lips slightly too crooked placed on a face just slightly too large. Diana was stunning, not in the euphemism-for-beauty way, but actually stunning, as in it was difficult to find words for small talk when you first met her and equally difficult not to feel like you were trying to squirm out of the truth when she questioned your ideas. Most of the cocksure, popular, handsome boys at the seminary were terrified of her, and there was more than one malicious and erroneous story floated along the grapevine by those who felt threatened, which was more or less everyone.

Jarvis, on the other hand, too engrossed in his studies and too chaste in his temporary celibacy vow to notice any female, wouldn't have registered Diana at all if she hadn't insulted him publicly during a History of the Sacraments seminar. The class had reached the contentious subject of Hildegard Robham's schism from the Bondulay during the Gentlemen's War. In the old story of Pacifism pitted against The Regrettable Use of Force, Jarvis had taken the mildly surprising but by no means unprecedented position of agreeing with Robham's pacifist principles. Diana had turned to face him from her seat in the seminar, nostrils blazing.

—I suppose I can understand your abhorrence to war, but to eliminate all use of force under every circumstance is naïve, suicidally idealistic, and in the most morally repugnant sense shirks adult responsibility. Pacifists allow their consciences to be free while still subsisting on the fruits of war.

Jarvis tried to argue back, but it was too late. He was already in love.

—How can you call the anonymous killing of strangers you've never met morally justified under any humane religion?

—In a theoretical argument about an uncomplicated world, 85

you're completely right. In this world, however, your argument is complete sheep's balls!

—*Miss Avisham!*

—Sorry, Professor, but suppose, whatever-your-name-is, we'd taken a pacifist stance against Pistolet? Where would we be then?

—Don't you believe the moral high ground would have eventually won out?

—Eventually? *Eventually?* You arrogant, self-satisfied, brainless pile of treacle. How many more people would your 'eventually' have allowed Pistolet to kill? How many more millions deserved to be tortured, raped, and murdered because of your grand 'eventually'?

—Surely you concede that if we'd acted earlier on, with diplomatic means—

—I concede nothing! War is a horrible, atrocious, awful, awful thing, but war was *not* the monster, Pistolet was. You're applying an absolute principle to an in-absolute world.

—But we're talking about dogmatic philosophy, not practicum.

—And you're hiding behind your hot air, you coward!

Diana held up the main textbook for the course.

—The world doesn't exist in this. The world exists out there.

Jarvis didn't have time to duck before the book connected with his nose and broke it. Later, remarkably not expelled and courteously walking home the newly bandaged and cotton-packed Jarvis, she had clarified her points.

—I'm sorry about your nose, but you were completely in the wrong.

—That's all wight—

—I just get so mad at scholars who cave themselves in book-learning and then in perfect riskless safety advocate an adherence to the Sacraments regardless of the real-world human suffering it causes. It's immoral. I get sick of the skewing of God's messages to further some intellectual ideal. That's why I threw my book at you.

—It's okay—

—Don't you think the central message of the Sacraments is to care for your neighbor as if he were your brother? And if that message has to be applied imperfectly in an imperfect world, then so be it. It's our moral responsibility to God to do the best we can in the situations He provides to us.

—I'm wif you all de way—

—I don't want to waste my time bothering with all this esoteric nonsense that keeps you completely out of God's big, messy, wonderful world. That's the whole reason I'm entering the priesthood.

—Me, too.

Snap judgment guided by passion that it was, the priesthood turned out to be a surprisingly good fit. Jarvis excelled in his studies, turned out to be a better orator than he expected, and was able to take most of his classes with Diana. He was aware of the perversity of only being able to please the woman he adored by entering lifelong celibacy for her, but dumber things have been done in the name of love. When graduation day arrived, he and Diana hugged platonically. Before he set off on his first assignment less than twenty miles away in urban Hennington, he went with her to the docks in the Harbor, from where she was to set sail for *her* assignment, across the ocean on the entire flip side of the world map. They waved as the ship set to sea, her long hair tangling wildly in the wind, his beard catching flecks of sea foam. As she disappeared over the horizon, Jarvis realized how easy it would be to keep his vow of chastity. The only woman he ever loved was receding thousands of miles away, and Jarvis' desire receded with her. He had heard that sex was overrated anyway – sweaty, sticky, brief, and ultimately depressing. He tucked away his tired, sad, and sore heart, telling himself he could probably get more joy out of gardening.

In this, he was entirely correct, though the measure of his joy was not reflected in the bounty of his garden. He had long since accepted that his fingers were many shades away from green, but that didn't stop him from celebrating small victories: a tomato large and red enough to be edible; a double-digit strawberry harvest; blueberries that didn't make the church children vomit. He had once managed an avocado and parsnip pie for an after-church potluck that the Widow Jesslyn Mitcham had even called 'tart in the best sense of the word'. This morning, he was on his knees, trying to coax a clutch of basil leaves into taking root. The man at the greenery had told him that basil was the best seasoning to use for the summer squash he anticipated (hoped hoped hoped for) in a month or two. Coincidentally, basil had been on sale that day, so Jarvis had purchased a few cuttings to try to grow in his garden.

—You can do it. Here's some water to make the ground lovely and moist, and these little blue pellets will make you grow green and tasty. You're going to love it out here. It's a beautiful place, if you'd only make that little bit of effort.

—Father Kingham?

Jarvis sat upright and stared down at his basil in surprise.

—Am I interrupting?

Jarvis swung around and looked up.

—Mrs Bellingham! Of course you're not interrupting. For a minute there, I thought my basil was talking to me.

—Oh! I say!

—Or would that be 'my basil *were* talking to me'? No matter. What can I do for you this fine, warm, beautiful day?

—Do you have a few moments, Father?

—Always.

He motioned her inside the church to his office and sat her in a chair opposite him across his desk.

—What's on your mind?

She gave a slightly embarrassed little frown.

—It's kind of silly, Father.

—Coming from you, Mrs Bellingham, I highly doubt that.

—That's very kind, Father, but, well . . .

—You can feel free to tell me absolutely anything, sister. Not only do you have my strictest confidence and good faith, you've also got a legal system that says that I never, ever have to tell anyone.

Mrs Bellingham smiled.

—All right, then. How can I begin? I'm not a superstitious woman, Father.

—I've always admired your levelheadedness.

—But lately, I've been having these dreams.

She paused.

—Dreams, Sister?

—Well, one dream in particular, but over and over again.

—Is it an especially bothersome dream?

—Yes, to be frank.

She paused again.

—Why don't you tell me your dream, Mrs Bellingham? And take your time.

—If you insist.

And she told him.

24. Closing the Deal.

—The secret is all in where you place your feet.

—Mm-hmm.

—If you get them square with your shoulders, then step a little bit apart, you can just let your center of gravity carry the swing away from you.

—You don't say.

Thomas Banyon pulled another drag on his cigarillo as he waited for Armand Odom, President and COO of Odomatic Incorporated, purveyors of fine dried and canned meats, to just shut up and take his fucking swing already. They had been at the fifteenth tee for nearly ten minutes while Odom shifted and wiggled and realigned and rebalanced and talked and talked and talked. Thomas was letting the prick win, currently by all of two strokes, and Odom had got it into his head that Thomas should be the beneficiary of his own obviously superior skills and knowledge. Thomas held the smoke in his lungs. The things you went through to get a new customer.

—See, I think your problem might be that you're rushing it, pushing yourself to just hit it as hard as you can without first getting the feel for your tee.

—Interesting.

—I mean, we can talk more about your putting problems when we get to the green, but remember, putting doesn't matter if you can't get there first.

—Makes perfect sense.

Thomas closed his eyes and dragged again on the narcotic-spiced cigarillo. They were made specially for him by a shady agribusinessman from over the border and contained a delightfully mild narcotic formed when one particular species of beetle laid its eggs on the leaves of one particular species of shrub, of which shrub the shady agribusinessman owned every single known specimen. When the beetle eggs hatched, the grubs would, in an action apparently unique in the natural world, attack and eat only the stems of the fern, causing the leaf to fall to the ground whole, beetle-egg husks still attached. The husks decomposed as the leaf dried up, igniting a most unusual chemical reaction that resulted in a dried fern leaf with black speckles. These leaves were then gathered by trained harvesters, mixed with regular cigarillo tobacco, and then hand-rolled in zero-humidity humidors into slender, smoke-able sticks. The whole process cost an obscene fortune, but the results were exquisite: a smoke that elated without cloudiness, relaxed without lethargy, and painted the world pink without painting it red. Thomas received them *gratis*. The shady agribusinessman, whose name was Dylan or Declan or some D name Thomas always forgot and preferred not to know anyway, recognized a good retailer when he saw it, and Thomas was the best retailer of shady agribusiness products in all of Hennington. The wholesale boxes of Maria John, posh, itch, Brown Dog, and katzutakis arrived like clockwork every fortnight, along with a fresh box of TB's Special Blend.

—Now watch where my arms are when I bring the club back. Can you see how I've only got my elbows just slightly crooked? And look where the head of the club is.

Thomas kept his eyes closed.

—I see.

It was worse at the green.

—Your approach wasn't bad, but did you see where I placed mine? I purposely hit it long to take advantage of the slight incline.

Thomas had purposely hit his own ball short to take advantage of a subtle groove he knew rested just below the hole. 91

Now, he would have to shank even that. He blew smoke out of his mouth and reinhaled it through his nose. Odom missed his putt, sending it wide.

—See, I pushed it, just like you do the tee shots. That's what happens when you rush. Goddamnit!

Thomas was going to have to three-putt a one-meter shot to keep this moron in the lead. He wondered whether it was possible to miss the hole that many times without looking drunk or blind. He picked up his ball and pocketed it before Odom could complain.

—I'll give you the hole. Why don't we call it a day and get some drinks inside? On the house, of course.

—But how will you learn?

—I think I've got enough to absorb today.

The clubhouse barmaid, Tracy Jem-Ho, was ready in the clubhouse with cocktails, one with twice the alcohol for Odom, who remarkably was still protesting.

—But a real sportsman would never quit a game in the middle.

—You were ahead. Your victory was inevitable.

—Still, a final score has a certain—

—We water the course every Thursday. We would have been wet by the eighteenth hole.

—You don't water every morning? Pre-dawn watering is generally considered par for the course, if you'll excuse the—

—Every pre-dawn except Thursday, when we water at this time.

—What on earth for?

—Drink up, Mr Odom. It's free.

—Whew. Strong one.

—That's the way we like them here at Hennington Hills. Now. Mr Odom.

92   —Could I get another one of these?

—Of course. Tracy? Have you met Tracy?

—It's a pleasure.

—Interesting you should put it that way, Mr Odom.

—I beg your pardon?

Thomas paused. Was nothing ever easy? But then, easy wasn't fun, was it?

—Surely you've heard one or two stories regarding all that we have to offer here at Hennington Hills.

—Oh, yes, it's a beautiful course, and I hear the others are just as nice. The grounds are quite something.

—But you must have heard, I don't know, a story or two? Regarding the facilities?

Tracy placed another drink in front of Odom. Thomas could tell by the small amount of blue at the bottom that this one was nearly pure alcohol. Good girl.

—I'm not following you.

—About the things we can also provide besides those things that are only, how can one put it, apparent on the surface.

—I'm sure I don't know what you mean.

Oh, for fuck's sake.

—You didn't just come to me for a round of golf and a country club membership, Mr Odom.

—What else would I have come for?

Odom took another long draft from his cocktail schooner, set it down on the countertop, and looked Thomas straight in the eye. He didn't say another word. You'll pay for this, Thomas thought. Literally, in amounts you'll barely be able to afford but will somehow be unable to keep yourself from spending. I will take you down, and I will do it in the worst possible way, by making you beg me for it.

—We offer our members amenities not available at your run-of-the-mill country club. We are also expert providers in   93 the more, shall we say, *sensual* areas of relaxation that the modern businessperson is so often in desperate need of.

—Uh-huh. And what would those be?

Enough.

—It matters very little if you're taping this, Mr Odom. I've investigated your background, and I already have some interesting tidbits that would keep you from using any recording against me. So if you're working undercover to take care of some past ugliness, why not turn it over to me rather than let the soiled hands of law enforcement make you a puppet? And if you're recording this for your own protection at a later date, I can assure you from experience that such protection is both unnecessary and irrelevant.

Odom's face went ashen. Gotcha, fucker, and on a guess, no less. Odom took another drink and remained silent.

—I can't think of any reason why your entry into Hennington Hills should be anything other than a pleasant, worry-free experience for both of us. Come. Give me the tape.

Odom drank again, then slowly reached in his pocket and pulled out a micro-recorder.

—How did you know?

—It's not uncommon. Trying to get me to say the first questionable thing and so forth.

—It was for the second reason, by the way, my own protection. I'm not undercover or anything.

—I know.

—How?

—Is it really important? What's important is that you're here, that we've gotten past these awkward formalities, and that you begin to learn all the wonderful things we can offer you at Hennington Hills.

94   —So what they say is true?

—Where have you been, my good man? I thought I'd at least gotten past the level of mere hearsay.

—And I can join?

—Mr Odom, I wouldn't think of letting you leave *without* joining.

Thomas smiled as Tracy set down an already-completed application form in front of Mr Odom.

—You'll see the membership fees are a bit steep, but we think they're worth it. I'm sure you'll agree.

Odom took the pen lying next to the application and signed it without another word. He set down the pen and took another drink.

—I'm sorry about the tape.

—Already forgotten.

—It's just, you see—

—Say no more, Mr Odom. You were merely protecting yourself. It was admirable.

—So . . . I'm in?

—Irretrievably.

—When can I start?

—You're almost there, Mr Odom. You just need to answer me one simple question.

Thomas took a last long drag and extinguished the end with a slow turn in the ashtray.

—What's the question?

—I want you to think about this clearly, Mr Odom – may I call you Armand? – Armand, because it's the most important part of your application, the most important question we have here at Hennington Hills. The question is.

—Yes?

—What do you like?

25. Maggerty in the City.

The young man in the apron swept the sidewalk in front of the store with a petulant snap of his wrists. He was the son of the owner and would naturally have rather been doing anything else in the world than sweeping the sidewalk in front of the store. It was hours before noon, but the sun was already promising another hot day, perfect for the illegal No Margin Surfing off of Darius Point that the young man, whose name was Jay, loved to sneak away to with his friends. NMS was a sport for those who thought themselves invincible, hence only those under twenty were ever interested. You paddled your board out over currents that could grab you and pull you down three hundred feet, collapsing your lungs before you even had a chance to scream, but that was only if the sharks, which were everywhere, didn't get you first, which they would eventually. Jay had already lost three fingers on his left hand down the gullet of a hammerhead. No big deal. Forty-one stitches didn't take all *that* long to heal. But the currents and the sharks were only the beginning. If you managed to make it around the Point alive, what awaited were waves sixty feet high traveling at forty nautical miles an hour. If you then actually managed to catch one of these monstrosities, you still had to navigate it perfectly to expel yourself out the end of the tube and into open water before the wave slammed you into the solid rock cliffs that comprised the western side of Darius Point. None of this was at all possible without being thoroughly twinged on itch which, if it didn't help your navigation much, at least got you out on the water in the first place. No Margin. Meaning no mistakes.

Jay ran his hand absentmindedly over the flat packet of itch in his back pocket. He looked up at the sun again and frowned. Fuck, man, it wasn't fair. He went back to pushing the broom angrily across the concrete. He was just about finished and ready to go back inside (and maybe, just maybe, say sayonara to the old man and take off for some NMS anyway, maybe if the old man was sleeping, maybe), when Maggerty stumbled down the street, heading right for the store. Jay looked around for The Crash and saw them passing along a cross-street one block up. Maggerty's reason for straying was obvious. Jay's father sold produce in slanted racks out in front of the store, packed full with the morning's delivery of apples, oranges, cantaloupes, strawberries, blackberries, haggleberries, and huge, pink bonnet melons with the vines still attached, as well as a generous helping of yesterday's white corn and a solitary jumbo kiwi sweating juice through its hide of erect hairs.

Maggerty reached the middle of the street and stopped about ten yards away. Somehow, without even looking up, he seemed to notice the young man with the broom standing in front of the piles of fruit. Traffic had been cut off by The Crash up at the main intersection, so there were no cars to honk Maggerty off. He shifted from foot to foot, looking at different patches of ground that hopped into and out of his line of vision.

Here was a moment of expectation. If there had been no one there, Maggerty would simply have taken something and the morning would have continued onward. But there *was* someone there and so this moment was necessary. He had made his peace with it. He knew that he had only to stay where he was before he would either be given food or he would not. Sometimes this latter version of events involved being chased away, but not often. Only wait, and something would eventually happen to kick the day forward again. His breathing slowed. He touched his wound and brought his fingertips briefly to his nose to smell the nature of the suppuration. He tapped his bare, filthy toes on the warm blacktop and scratched between his buttocks. He waited for an outcome.

Jay rubbed his hand across the packet of itch again and stared at the Rhinoherd. He had never seen him this close before. He had only heard the regular town folklore of Maggerty – something about a goat and fairly obvious madness – along with all the usual talk at the high school, where 'Maggerty' was pejorative for any poor kid with a hygiene problem. But at this hour of the morning, when the sun was already squint-worthy and shadows turned you into a mountaintop, there was only himself looking into the street at the Rhinoherd, who seemed to be dancing in a shuffling, fidgety sort of way. A faint, foul smell reached Jay's nostrils, but it was more animal than filth, more sad than disgusting.

He walked slowly over to the fruit without taking his eyes off of Maggerty. He took hold of an orange and palmed it up into the air and down again. He leaned backwards against the wood of the fruit rack and felt the itch pressing from his back pocket. Silently but with the efficient motion of a muscled No Margin Surfer, he tossed the orange underhand towards the Rhinoherd. It hit Maggerty in the shoulder and rolled clumsily to the pavement.

Maggerty roused from his stopped-time stupor. There was fruit at his feet. He reached down to pick it up. A bonnet melon rolled across the concrete into his reach. An apple appeared there, too, and then a soft, wet jumbo kiwi. It was as much as Maggerty could carry, and he scooped them up into his arms. He stumbled away down the street back towards the already disappearing Crash, pressing the fruit into his mouth.

Jay watched the Rhinoherd turning the corner a block

away. He touched the itch in his pocket again without realizing it and reluctantly returned to sweeping.

26. What Do You Want?

—You wanted to see me, Cora?

—Have a seat, Max.

—So it's one of those kinds of talks.

—Actually, come to think of it, maybe you *are* in trouble. You're the one who's going to have to figure that out, I think.

—Why do I feel like I did when my parents wanted to know if I smoked hash in the eighth grade?

—Did you?

—Smoke hash? No. But then again you already know that. 'No skeletons allowed', if I remember my first job interview correctly.

—I was merely being a smart politician, Max. However megalomaniacal it may sound, I do have a legacy, and I don't want to leave it to just anyone. Which brings us conveniently to the point.

—Look, I'm sorry again about the fundraiser, but Talon was sick.

—Yes, I know, that's not the issue. We raised over eighty thousand for you last night. That puts your pot at over 1.2 million. More than enough for airtime, signs, get-out-the-vote projects, the rest of your campaign staff. In short, pretty much enough for the whole race, including your inauguration ball and hair of the dog the morning after. Now, if you would just *start* your campaign any time in the near future, why, that would be lovely, too. Oh, don't sigh at me, Max. I've known you for ten years. Something's going on, and I want to know what it is.

—Nothing's 'going on'.

—Then answer me this simple question. Do you want to be Mayor or don't you? Because if you don't, you'd better tell me right now, as in this morning, or a lot of people are going to be plenty peeved. Fundraising is bad enough, though I am happy to spend my evening touting your real and considerable assets. That's not bull. I think you'll make a great Mayor. But explaining to all those folks whose behinds are wet with my saliva why their money might not be going where they thought it was would be much worse.

—I said, I'm sorry for not being there.

—Not the point. I know you model yourself as a kind of brooding idealist—

—I do not.

—You do. You do, and that's fine. Money to soup kitchens, needle-exchange programs, hunger relief for The Crash, all good stuff, but it's the idealism catch that's been around forever: in order to accomplish anything idealistic, you have to first be in a position of power to do something.

—That's not quite true. Volunteers implement a lot of idealistic ideas.

—Oh, for God's sake, Max, quit being argumentative. It's a simple equation. Idealism without implementation equals moral impotence. I know you find politicking distasteful, so do I, but why come this far just to not get over that final qualm? Is it a case of nerves? Is it a matter of requiring a simple pep talk? Because I can do that if that's all you need. But I'm worried that it might be something more. Well, not worried exactly, but *aware* that something's at work here. So stop being evasive and start talking.

—Cora, there's nothing I could tell you that would ease your mind.

100   —So don't ease my mind. Shake it up a bit. I'll manage.

—All right then. It's this whole question of the inevitability of it all.

—You mean the election being a foregone conclusion?

—Well, yes, in a way, but I also mean for myself. I haven't done anything since I got out of law school except work here and stay on this career fast-track. I'll be forty in three years, and I've never done anything else.

—My suspicion is that that's probably just cold feet, Max. It's natural to question your motivation, especially just as you're about to join the battle to move to the next level.

—I wouldn't believe you've ever gotten cold feet about anything.

—Every time I've run. Hell, I get cold feet when I decide where to go for dinner. 'Do I really want noodles?' Perfectly natural, even more so for someone like you who's introspective to a rather large and annoying degree. You commit five years of your life by becoming Mayor, more if you include the campaign.

—It's not the time commitment that bothers me, although it's odd to think that Talon will be about to graduate from high school before my first term is up. I don't like to think I'd be slighting her. But more to the point it feels as if I've been heading for this and only this from the beginning, that Mayor is what I was destined to be. At least that's what people seem to say when they talk to me, that fate has selected me out because of whatever reasons fate has and everything's lined up to lead me directly to this, as if I've had no choice in the matter.

—But it's hardly as if this has been handed to you, Max. You've worked hard to do what you've done, to get where you are. This hasn't happened *to* you. Surely there must have been some motivation there, if not just right this second, then at some point. And if you had it once, you'll have it again.   101

—That's just it. I look at my life, I look at my daughter, and sometimes I can't remember how I got here.

—So are you saying you don't want to be Mayor or that you don't know?

—I'm saying I don't know.

—Is this serious enough to make you drop out of the campaign?

—I don't know. Maybe.

—Well, I've got to be honest if it kills me, I suppose. It's not too late to quit. You'd lose a little face, and there are people who'd be mighty disappointed, but four months is enough for someone new to step in if they had to. I've no idea who, frankly, but you need to do what you need to do.

—I don't know if I want to quit. I'm not sure.

—Then how about this? Why not take tomorrow off and just have a three-day weekend? Spend a ton of time with Talon, don't think about the campaign, although you've been doing a pretty good job of that on your own already, and just, I suppose, reflect. Search your heart and mind, Max. Being Mayor is something you shouldn't do half-assed. There's a lot of nonsense you have to put up with, and the job is only worth it if it's worth it to you.

—I'm not sure that's going to help.

—It either will or it won't. Do it anyway. Unfortunately, the way things lie, I'm going to have to know one way or another when you come in on Monday. As much a martinet as it might make me, I want to have *some* say over who the next Mayor is, and if you're out, there are a mind-boggling number of things to be done.

—All right. Sorry for the wrench in the plans.

—No, no, my fault. I've been the advisor in this whole thing. I thought you were having doubts, but I thought they'd take care of themselves. I was wrong. Take the weekend.

Hell, go home right now. Let me know what you decide on Monday, okay?

—I can agree to that.

—My grandmother always told me that if you search yourself top to bottom, then there's no such thing as a wrong decision. Whichever way you decide will ultimately be the right way, Max. I trust you.

—I'm assuming your grandmother didn't tell you the part about how we sometimes make wrong decisions so we can be taught unpleasant lessons.

—Of course she didn't. My grandmother was a very smart woman.

27. 'Cleave' Has Two Meanings.

Luther Pickett was born in Tishimongo Fair, that small, incongruously wet burg stuck deep in the crook of the Molyneux Valley, near the disputed Mohair Pass on the mountain border to the Rumour Land. Besides its more common and justified reputation as a literary bedrock – being the birthplace of both Joan Reachpenny *and* Christina Ungulate, as well as the summer home of Midge and Lolly Tottering and the location of the Alms Hotel where Shelbert Shelbert famously ended his life with Fergus Pangborn's triple-barreled rifle – Tishimongo Fair was also the primary production spot of Archie Banyon's Vallée de Molyneux Merlot, a 'deeply spicy wine with a tart sensuality' that made Hennington society matrons blush as they reached for another sip. Lachlan Pickett, Luther's father, was the winery's head of distribution. Having been raised by teetotalers, Lachlan knew effectively nothing about wine, but he was good with a clipboard, had a strong profile with a virile haircut, and exuded a calm confidence that deflected attention away from what was marginal competence at best. He had all the usual blessings of the physically beautiful: an equally beautiful wife, an array of jocular friends, and a golden son with a beatific smile and the usual knack for sports. This last, of course, was Luther.

The memories of Luther's childhood before the tragedy were lit by warm, soggy sunlight. Tishimongo Fair caught both the rain from the mountains on either side and the heat that came north from the Rumour deserts. Long, steamy summers melted into long, steamy winters. The family wasn't especially wealthy – Luther's mother Annika was a stubbornly unsuccessful portrait photographer – but he could never recall wanting for anything. He remembered his home as a casual place with friends dropping by for dinner parties, baby showers, the whole list of middle-class fêtes. Luther was popular at school, did well in his studies to the surprise of his perplexed but proud father, and was a child of whom the dreadful word 'potential' was often applied. In short, he was happy, which just couldn't last.

At twelve, the tragedy, shocking enough in its casualness to hit the newspapers and ultimately enter Tishimongo lore, came along and took Luther's parents. On an unusually chilly autumn night, the Pickett family slept soundly in their beds. Sometime during their slumber, a Caucasus Asp, out of season and no doubt freezing to death, slithered into their house through an open vent near a basement window. The basement, unfortunately, also served as the master bedroom for Lachlan and Annika Pickett. The snake, sensing the room's most potent source of heat, slowly coiled itself under the sheets, between their warm, dozing bodies.

First Annika stirred and was bitten, then Lachlan. Neither of them woke up before their deaths, witnessing only sudden and permanent ends to dreams. Wondering about breakfast, young Luther found them lying there the next morning. He jostled his father's shoulder but was unable to rouse him. When he did the same to his mother and touched her exposed, cold skin, he realized something more was at work than simple oversleeping. His jostling awakened the snake, which now realized that its haven had cooled. The Jungle Dangers training Luther had taken at school probably saved his life. He stayed completely frozen while the red-and-white-speckled asp slunk across the floor to another snug sanctuary at the bottom of the linen closet. Luther dialed Crisis Services on his parents' phone and waited, wide eyed and quiet, on the front walk until the paramedicals arrived.

At the same time, Archie Banyon was in town, making the dreaded annual inspection of his Molyneux vineyards. The dismal weather was not encouraging. His merlot required day after day of steamy sun, to the point where the grapes almost boiled on the vine. Drear could turn the year's harvest sickly sweet if it stuck around too long. He was irritable and opprobrious and growing increasingly furious with the head shipping clerk for having the insolence to be late to a morning meeting where he would be asked to share his portion of the blame for the weather. Archie had, in fact, gone as far as making a great show of firing Lachlan Pickett *in absentia* in an attempt to strike fear into the vineyard's other managers. He was mid-rant when the police showed up.

There is no more potent driver of charity than saving face, a fact which coupled nicely with the realization that Archie had also been in a vineyard when his wife and daughters had perished. He felt some fateful request was being made of him. Perhaps it was a reprimand for firing a dead man. Conversely, maybe the fates were giving him a child as recompense for the loss of his own. Whatever the reason, Archie adopted the blond-haired, serious-browed Luther without hesitation, 105 sweeping him out of Tishimongo Fair and installing him in a hilltop mansion overlooking Hennington.

To Archie's surprise and delight, Luther immediately turned out to be the 'son I feel I've never had', always whispered out of earshot of Thomas, of course. Young Luther Pickett – he never considered giving up his last name, and Archie, in a rare show of modest sensitivity, never pushed it – was courteous, intelligent, hard-working, and showed an interest in Archie's work. All of which could also be said of Thomas Banyon, aside from courteous, but Luther was just so much more *likable*. He wore none of Thomas' surliness, none of that considerable anger that threatened to flash in inappropriate places, and perhaps most importantly, none of that resentment that made Archie seethe. Moreover, Luther owed him. Archie Banyon was a kind and generous man, but he was also rich, a rich that went very deep down. He was more comfortable being owed than owing.

What Archie completely failed to see was that Luther was also in an ongoing, all-consuming state of shock. When Luther found his parents' bodies lying peacefully in their beds, he realized that the world could not, would not, and should not ever be counted on. Luther, perhaps even subconsciously, accepted that whatever Archie gifted him with was bound to be snatched away sooner or later, a feeling that was probably responsible for his extraordinary success in business. He had unwittingly given up having any stake whatsoever in the outcome. Therefore, his work was relaxed and confident and bravely risk-taking. He made Archie Banyon a breathtakingly huge amount of money, and he never, on some level, expected to see a penny of it.

And then suddenly, everything changed the day he met Peter, a spur of the moment appointment that Luther had allowed himself to be privately talked into by Thomas one unlikely Boxing Day at Archie's house. Peter had opened up a future, an actual one, not the fantasy ones he expected to evaporate at any precarious second. Peter ignited something – why not, let's call it love – deep down somewhere in Luther's dusty internal file room. Whether it worked out, whether Peter reciprocated, aside from being wished for, hoped for, longed for, was in some ways beside the point. In an instant, Luther remembered himself. In a second, he saw how past futures had failed to fall away as he had expected them to. In a moment, he realized how vicariously and almost post-humously he was living. In a day, he knew that he didn't want the future as it was now laid out before him. He woke up from nearly three decades of willful self-ignorance.

This was what he had to tell Archie Banyon before the spring board meeting next Wednesday, the board meeting where Archie was going to name Luther Acting Chief Executive Officer, responsible for all business of Banyon Enterprises until Archie Banyon's death, at which time the 'Acting' would be removed from Luther's title. What Luther realized, at long, long last, was that he did not want it, not any of it. He loved Archie Banyon dearly, would do almost anything for him, but that future was not his. It was a proxy future, a temporary one that had been allowed to run on too long.

The only problem with telling Archie that this future was impossible was that telling Archie was also impossible. And if both his choices were impossible, what was there to do?

28. Digitalis.

They were coming for her.

She couldn't open her eyes, but she knew they were in the room. She could hear them, almost like a breath, almost like   107 they could breathe. More, she could feel them, knowing their presence like she knew her own. These weren't the Lions. The Lions she could handle. These were something else. They wanted her. And they were here. Why wouldn't her eyes open? It was so much worse in the dark. A scurry across her bare foot. A twitch at her bare hip. A twinge on her oh God bare cheek. The rustling of their movements filled the room, and with just the slightest change in the air, they were on her.

Jacki finally thrust open her eyes but only appreciated the briefest moment of relief before she realized the nightmare had followed her. Numbers, black, filthy, crawling, clamoring, skittering numbers flooded the room and covered her body in a writhing, undulating mass. She leapt to her feet, barely able to keep her balance from the extra weight. The numbers stuck to her like frenzied leeches. She tried to brush them off with her hands, but they burst under her palms until she found herself covered in their viscera. She opened her mouth to scream, and the numbers poured in and down her throat.

—My God, what's wrong with her? Is it a seizure?

—Looks like it. Can you hear me, Ms Strell? Ms Strell?

The numbers crawled down to her stomach, up her nose, and into her ears. They had somehow gotten beneath her skin, and she saw their shapes pushing out from the palms of her hands. They wormed their way beneath her eyelids, and she could feel them making their way to her brain. I'm dying, she thought. I'm going to die in terror and agony. Help me help me help me help me. She reached back for a final scream and mercifully lost consciousness.

—Give her the water.

—Ms Strell? Can you take some water? I don't think she's awake yet. Ms Strell? Jacki?

Jacki was aware of some vague shaking at her shoulders. Something slapped her face. You've got the wrong one, she thought. Meg from the stables is the one who gets slapped.

—What was that? It looked like she was trying to talk.

—It was all slurred. I think she's drunk.

—High more like it. I mean, that *sound* she made, like she was seeing something horrible.

—Which one does that to you?

—Katzutakis? No, wait, I think Forum is the big hallucinating one.

—Katz is the one that makes you frantic. It must be Forum, but why would *she* be on Forum?

—Why do you *think*?

—Surely he can't make her do clips.

—He makes everyone do clips.

—But we've got the immigration thing. What would he have against her?

—That she's a Forum addict.

Jacki felt cold all over. She began to tremble, growing more violent as the seconds crawled on.

—Uh-oh.

—Should we call him?

—No way. This is probably somehow his fault. She needs a hit.

—Where in the world are we going to find a hit? I wouldn't even know what one looks like.

—If she's addicted, she's got to have some on her.

—She's naked.

—I mean check her desk.

Jacki could hear some sounds in the background, echoes wrapped in echoes. The numbers were gone, but she was so cold. Her vision began to go white.

—This has to be it. And here's a syringe.

—Give it to me.

—You're going to inject her?

—Look at her. She's going to die otherwise.
—Do you know how?
—No, but I can take a guess. Hold her arm still.
—Oh, my God.
—Here goes nothing.
—Oh, my God.
Honey ran through her veins, and she was warm again.

29. The Crash at the Pond.

While the others pushed past her, she stood and regarded her muddy footprint. This was it then, the final clue. It was too early for the grass to be bitter. It was too early for the air to smell so much of dust. It was too early for the eagles to have left their aeries for more verdant hunting grounds. And now, it was definitely too early for the water to have pulled back far enough for mudflats to emerge at the pond's edge. Drought was coming, was already here in the smaller places, poking its nose at the corners of things. She had lived through a drought when she was a calf, but even with the help of the cubes of dried grass and small stone ponds of water that had seemed to appear from nowhere throughout the city, she had watched many of the older herdmembers and a good number of the younger ones grow weak and finally die. It was a horrible time, the days filled with endless droning sun, the nights filled with the bleats and moans of herdmembers mourning both their hunger and their dead. Lean times had come and gone since, but nothing like that terrible season. Nothing, that is, until what now hovered on the horizon, poised to reach in its hot, dusty fingers and snatch the last blade of grass from them.

She looked out at the herd, squinting to see as they lowered their heads and drank, the water lapping at their toenails. Some of them, perhaps many of them, perhaps even herself along with them, would be dead by the end of the season. Hardship was natural, even drought was natural, yet still the burden on her was far from light, and deep in her crowded, instinctive brain, there was the unpleasant coldness of doubt. She walked slowly over to the water's edge to join the other herdmembers in a drink. Stopping, she sniffed the air and turned to look behind her.

Something grabbed her horn.

She jolted herself back and wrenched her head up into the sky. She heard a short cry as one of the thin creatures fell down into the shallow water, away from where its grip had been on her nose. She gathered herself quickly and looked down into its eyes, staring back up at her. She was not afraid, only startled. The thin creatures had never been any danger to the herd and especially not one this tiny. She brought her massive head down for a closer sniff. The herd nearby stopped to watch, all eyes on her, straining against their collective myopia, as she took in the smells of the thing. It was mostly sweet with a faint sickly odor of food too ripe, of mother's milk gone bad. It must be one of their calves, and a very, very young one by the smell and size of it.

(—*Melanie! Melanie, you come away from there right now! Right now!*)

Her ears rotated towards the sound of hoofbeats slapping on the mud. Another thin creature dashed towards them. She could smell fear on the second one as thick as sweat. It stopped short of where she stood and began squawking loudly in that gurgled way they had.

(—*Shoo! Get away! Get out of here! Get away from her! Melanie, you come here right now!*)

The first thin creature, the calf, reached its front hoof up   111 to her nose, holding it at a short distance. She didn't smell fear in this smaller one and allowed it to touch her nose lightly, even accepting a little gentle scratching.

(—*It's friendly, Mrs Carlson. See?*

—*Get away from it, right now, Melanie! They're dangerous.*

—*No, they're not. My father says*—

—*I'm not telling you again!*

—*You're going to scare them if you keep shouting like that.*)

A third thin creature had come up behind the second one. She began to feel uncomfortable. True, the thin creatures rarely involved themselves with the herd, but this proximity was too close, the sounds they were making too loud, and she could smell strongly that they were beginning to muddy the water. She inhaled deeply and brought her shoulders up, emitting two short snorts into the air. It was time to lead the herd away from this ruckus.

(—*What's it doing? Melanie, I'm going to count to three!*

—*You're upsetting them, lady. They're not going to hurt her.*

—*I'll keep charge of my own students, Officer, thank you very much. Now, would you please be useful and help me get her?*

—*All she has to do is walk away. She's not in any danger.*

—*You didn't see it knock her down. Oh, for God's sake, I'll do it myself.*)

The second of the thin creatures suddenly stomped over and grabbed the foreleg of the smaller one. The young calf yelped loudly. She swung her head back towards the thin creatures at the sound, accidentally brushing the flank of the taller one. It let out a startled cry and struck her on the side of her face. Defensively, she rumbled out of her chest, lowered her head, and gave a short hop forward on her front feet. It was a scare tactic, and it worked. The taller thin creature cried out again and dragged the calf quickly past the third creature and away.

Enough was enough. She turned abruptly and set off for the far end of the pond. By the time the herd had followed her there, the thin creatures were forgotten. She drank, but her mind turned once again to the certainty of hard times ahead.

30. It Always Comes Out Somewhere.

Peter took apart his motorcycle and separated the pieces – there were 183 distinct ones, so far – into rows on the stained red dropcloth. He cleaned each individual part with a blue rag and laid them out on an unconscious grid, placed randomly, he thought, but actually forming a neat criss-cross pattern. A tiny washer just here, a larger screw just there, a casing here, a foot pedal there, as if he were performing an especially thorough autopsy rather than just cleaning gritty motorcycle parts.

Four hours had passed this way, four hours since he had left Luther at the crack of dawn to return home. Luther pretended to be asleep, but Peter could tell by the patterns in his breathing that he wasn't. After a soft kiss in the curve of Luther's neck, Peter had gone straight home, where he had grabbed a banana shake for breakfast and set right to work on his cycle. He always did this when preoccupied which, given the lack of mental interaction offered by his waiter job and the necessity to block out mental interaction from his entertainment job, was rather more often than not.

The cycle was almost completely disassembled, save for the

battery cell-pack which he couldn't have put back together anyway, and still Peter didn't know what to do. He didn't even have any thoughts that weren't complete self-beration. The concept of his only chance vanishing fruitlessly swept across his mind every second or so, and he would push more furiously at the grease covering the bearings in the wheel wells, bearings which he would eventually have to spend a considerable amount of time regreasing later.

He paused while removing a handle grip. His face went tight. A smothering nothing of time passed.

—Goddamnit. Goddamnit! *Goddamnit*!

He smacked his fist against the floor, hurting it, and returned intently to the removal of the handle grip. He was self-taught at cycle mechanics, as he was self-taught at nearly everything else. His father had vanished when he was a young boy, his sister had her own friends, and his mother worked almost round the clock to keep the family solvent. He had been a solitary child, but this was different from being a shy child, which he was not. He was popular or at least well known at school, did passably at his studies, and generally earned the respect, if not exactly the friendship, of children his own age. He was polite with adults, a regular at his mother's church, and for one, brief, horrifying season, captain of his junior rounders team, a sport he finally realized he hated and promptly quit.

It was more a case of enjoying his own company than anything else. He was happiest with a book or word puzzle in the front window of his family's apartment. Or pretending to be on a solo reconnaissance mission around the swampy part of the pond down in Restitution Park. Or going on an hours-long walk by himself through the woods above The Roots, his hometown. Even on group activities, he oftentimes found himself alone without quite knowing how. Once at a church summer camp, he only realized at sundown that he had rowed his canoe what ended up being nearly six miles away from the other boaters on a trip across Loch Onnatonka. When he finally returned and was banished to his cabin for disappearing from the group, an occurrence he could barely remember happening (—I guess I just got distracted. —For seven hours?), he realized that after a week at camp, he still didn't know the name of a single cabinmate. If his mother was in a good mood, she called this solitary streak self-reliance. If she was in a bad mood, she called it self-obsession. Either way, he was an easy child to raise: a few vague worries in exchange for a minimum of disciplinary headaches.

He left home with few ambitions when he graduated. His mother, naturally, had wanted him to be a doctor or lawyer or priest or, in her more bilious moments, all three. But then she had suddenly succumbed to a vicious and hitherto unknown tumor on a heart valve, and Peter, after his grief – and to be honest, after a few years of shiftlessly spending his small inheritance on books and hiking gear – had turned his sights northward, as many an unfocused Rumour lad had done before him. He applied for a work permit and surprisingly, given his almost complete lack of specific tangible skills, was granted one.

Serendipity had seen to it that at the same time Thomas Banyon was looking to replace a recently murdered Rumour waiter at Hennington Hills Golf Course and Resort, preferably this time one who didn't ask so many bloody questions. Peter hadn't paused when Thomas had asked him to disrobe at the interview, nor even when Thomas had grabbed Peter's flaccid penis and said, —What I'm wondering here is if this does anything special.

A lack of investment was the problem. Peter had taken life as it had arisen, with very few questions and almost no complaints as long as he got time to spend with himself. He didn't care that Thomas treated him like a piece of meat because he figured that was what happened to immigrant workers generally in their first years, and besides that was just life, right? He had no real opinions on sex and sexuality, though he had dabbled with one or two forthright girls who found him attractive due to the fact that he was so oblivious to them. When Thomas asked to see what Peter's member looked like when it stood on end, Peter obliged without thinking twice.

—What I've said doesn't bother you?

—No.

—You understand what your place will be here?

It wasn't that Thomas cared that Peter understood, it was just unusual to find someone who accepted it all with no apparent misgivings. Whatsoever.

—I'll be having sex with people that you arrange for me.

—Yes.

—All right.

—This doesn't give you any pause?

—My permit says I work for you for three years. If that's the job, then that's the job. It's what newcomers do, isn't it?

—It's what they do *here*, yes. When they work for me.

—Fair enough.

—Let's go over this one more time.

A year had passed since, uneventful except for the occasional oddity here and there with a clip. He had two years to go on the permit, and though he doubted Thomas would let him go without a fuss at the end of it, he would deal with that when the time came. He would be twenty-nine then, still time enough to do whatever. He looked forward, on those rare times when he did look forward, to the two years passing without anything remarkable happening.

But something *had* happened. Something more than remarkable. Something that provided him with both investment and focus. Luther had happened, and now, for maybe the first time ever, Peter cared desperately about what would happen next. It couldn't be random chance that they'd met and clicked so well over what should have been a simple business transaction. There had to be something to the fact that Luther asked him back again and again. At last, Peter had caught a glimpse of a wished-for future, and now his present circumstances, his present actions, his present needs *mattered*. His relaxed attitude towards his own life was suddenly swallowed by the messy exhilaration and anguish of falling in love.

What do I do now? he thought. What do people do?

He set down a sparklingly clean coil on the red dropcloth, completing a perfect grid. Without realizing what he was doing, he picked the coil back up and began to put his cycle together again.

31. A Basic Question.

What does it all mean? thought Jarvis, turning over the dirt with a handrake. If it meant anything at all.

It was that second bit that nagged at him. Frankly, he would have liked to dismiss Mrs Bellingham's dream out of hand. He was a rational man, or at least that was how he had always viewed himself. Being a parish priest and seeing the day to day banality and wonderment of trudging and ongoing life would have taken the mystery out of him anyway. The miraculous happened in the first breath of a baby born to a mother thought to be barren, or in the soft scent of an unexpected bloom of amaryllis in his garden or even just in how the sunlight spoke its way in rows across the wooden floor of the older sanctuary. The glory and mystery of God expressed itself *here*, he believed. One needn't make it, meaning life and the world one lived in, *more* mysterious and miraculous by reading omens and prophecies in every ill-lit corner.

As for his parishioners, Jarvis had heard them talk of prophecies before, usually after the fact when hindsight performed its organizational magic and made everything seem as if it had all gone according to a pre-ordained plan. Premonitions were always so much more potent when remembered afterwards. Jarvis saw little harm in them, even approved of them because if all religion were in some part an attempt to explain the big mess of life, then this was just that function put to use at a basic level. If this was what some of his parishioners needed to explain God to themselves, well, then wonderful; most people never got an explanation of any sort. Prophecy also managed to fill the time of some of the more runaway control freaks in his congregation, those gray-eyed souls who liked to sail in on black clouds of foreboding offering 'divine guidance' on what the parish could do before its obvious and inevitable – and imminent – collapse; folks who seemed to want to do nothing more than place a reservation for an 'I told you so' later on. Theophilus Velingtham, of course, was grand champion.

Mrs Bellingham was different, though. She had never been given to the mystical and had even seemed embarrassed to speak of it in front of him. Moreover, he was convinced of her sincerity, her own deep belief in what she was telling him. This was no new convert offering proof of a supernatural schematic or an old eccentric gloomily predicting vague woes to come. Jarvis believed her because he could feel her genuine concern. And now, he found himself struggling with what in the world to do, what to make of it all, wondering what on earth did it all *mean*?

If it meant anything at all.

'*I'm a little girl again, picking haggleberries in the woods out by the stream behind my grandmother's church. I'm alone, but I can hear her voice talking to me. When the dream starts, it's just jibber-jabber, but then she starts to say, "He's coming, He's coming," and I can just tell, the way you can in a dream, that the He is capitalized, like in the Sacraments. "He's coming," she says, and then there are all these other voices that surround hers, whispers, all saying, "He's coming, He's coming" over and over again. I keep asking, "Who? Who's coming?" but they just keep saying it.*'

'*Is it malevolent, do you think? Is that what's bothering you?*'

'*It's hard to tell, Father.*'

'*Do you think you're being warned? Or that* we're *being warned?*'

'*I really don't know. I wasn't especially scared by the dream until last night.*'

'*What happened last night?*'

'*It was the same dream as usual, but after a while, my grandmother and all the voices started saying . . .*'

'*What is it, sister?*'

'*They said, "He's already there."*'

'*Meaning, in Hennington?*'

'*Yes. He, whoever "He" is, is here, and whatever that means makes me feel very afraid indeed.*'

Jarvis grunted as he tossed a handrake of sod into the compost pile. He was sorting through his dilemma by unearthing an unsuccessful crop of Hereford's tulips, piling up stubbornly unopened bulbs like old stones. He was, in fact, almost precisely where Mrs Bellingham had discovered him cajoling   119 his basil on the previous day. The sun was out. The sky was blue. Jarvis' mind was focused dually on tulip removal and prophecy comprehension when he put the first two prongs of the handrake through the soft tissue between his thumb and forefinger.

—Fucking hell!

He clasped his other hand tightly over the wound, not forgetting to glance around the garden to see if anyone had heard his epithet, the harshness of which surprised him momentarily out of his shock. Then the blood began to run through the fingers of the work glove, and he took off for his kitchen. With a yelp of pain, he peeled away the gloves and thrust his injured hand into the sink, turning on the cold tap. An astonishing amount of blood pulsed out in time with an ache that radiated up his whole arm. The handrake had gone all the way through; blood poured from holes on both sides. He began to chant the Samaritan's Catechism under his breath, not as a prayer but because it was short and repetitive and gave his mind something else to do besides concentrate on the sickening sight of his hand. He grabbed a white cloth towel from the sink and wrapped it tightly around the four bleeding holes. He felt dizzy. He slumped down into a chair, holding his hand up near his face, gasping out the Catechism.

— . . . *grant me assistance in my moment of need, give me strength to face my duties and commitments*, ow ow ow . . .

He was clearly going to need hospital. As hard as he held the towel, he was still bleeding through it. And my GOD, it hurt more than he could ever have imagined such a thing hurting. He stood to walk to the phone and nearly swooned. His mind raced with words, growing louder to cover the pain. I must not faint, he thought, I'm going to faint. He made it to the wall and leaned heavily for a moment to try to keep himself conscious. He uttered a short prayer.

—Lord, help me. Grant me clarity.

Behind closed eyes, he was suddenly witness to a picture of his desktop bathed in afternoon sunlight. Have I fainted? he thought. Am I coming to? The picture moved, making its way to his desk, coming to rest at his own well-worn copy of the Sacraments. Jarvis had, for the moment, forgotten his wound. There was such a direct feeling to this vision (was that what it was?), such a *vividness* that his mind was clear of everything else. The cover of the book opened, and the pages shuffled themselves along before reaching the final chapter, the Book of Ultimates, zeroing in on a set of verses. He read the two lines that had somehow insinuated themselves into more of the Bondulay and the culture surrounding it than nearly any other segment of the Book, the two lines that had sprouted an entire cottage industry that Jarvis both disapproved of and found obscurely frightening.

And in a time of sunlight, a dark wind will encroach,
  obscuring the truth,
And in the time of dark wind, a light wind will encroach,
  revealing the truth.

Oh, no, thought Jarvis. Not again. It couldn't be happening again. Could it?

32. Opening the Deal.

The church, thought Theophilus, is the only building which is never truly empty.

He leaned forward in the pew, elbows on the prayer bar, hands clasped together, lips pressed shut, eyes closed. He prayed rhythmically, silently, repeating the All Hail precisely 121 forty-one times, a decades-old penance for who knew what sin that had turned into a daily ritual, even though the penance prayers had been out of use for years upon years. Whatever slackening in principles the church had undergone in the name of so-called 'social change' – the dispensation with the penance prayers being only the most galling example – the Lord remained eternal and unwavering. Theophilus had been raised with the All Hail, and he would continue to use it, regardless of fashion or, worse, the laxity of the clergy.

—. . . *All hail to the Lord who rescued me from the desert of despair, all hail to the Lord who saved my soul from perdition . . .*

He wasn't explicitly aware of it, but as he sat in the cave-like quiet of an empty (despite his own axiom) sanctuary on a bright Thursday morning, Theophilus' body had settled into a rhythm, too. The length of each prayer took precisely two long measured breaths, and each breath comprised exactly ten heartbeats. After forty-one turns through the fourteen-line prayer, Theophilus' thoughts would fall silent, but the regular beats in his body would continue. His eyes still closed, he would push away sounds from the outside and any stray thoughts which chose to saunter by. The world would slowly soften away, and Theophilus' mind and soul would open up. For here in the Lord's place, in His house, attuned to (and by) the deep quiet of Theophilus' mind, here was where the Lord spoke to him. As clearly intentioned as a gun, the words would come, the words would come. Over a long, long lifetime, Theophilus had trained his body to move easily into the place where all he had to do was listen, listen for the words from the One True Lord, the words from the Almighty. Sometimes words of comfort, sometimes scripture references, usually encouragement to wait. Quite a bit of encouragement to wait, actually, until recently, when things took a turn.

The Lord had been doing rather a lot of talking of late, and He had been saying the most remarkable things.

—Holy sugar, Deacon! You scared the life out of me!

If this violent summons out of his meditation startled or even affected Theophilus, his face reflected nothing. He merely opened his eyes and turned his head casually towards the interruption. There even seemed to be a smile on his lips.

—Good afternoon, Martin. Doing some work today, are we?

Marty Farnham, church electrician, stood sheepishly a few feet away in the aisle, carrying a ladder and sporting a surprised grin.

—Yeah, there's some lights out in the baptistry. Nobody's usually here at this time.

—*I* am *always* here at this time.

—Well, I meant during the day.

—Which is, of course, what I meant.

Theophilus' smile broadened, teetering somewhere between friendly and garish. Marty Farnham hadn't the slightest idea how he should take it.

—I just meant that it was so quiet, I didn't see you there. I must normally come at other times.

—Yes.

—Are you praying for Father Kingham?

—I pray for Father Kingham every day, but why, pray tell, would I specifically need to pray for Father Kingham today?

—He hurt his hand. They took him to the hospital.

—'They'?

—Yeah.

—Is he badly hurt?

—I think he just cut himself with a tool whilst in the garden.

—Then I will be sure to offer up a special prayer for Father Kingham and his gardening injury.

—Yeah, well, anyway, like I was saying, I didn't think anyone was here. I just walked on in, and I was almost on top of you before I realized, you know, I wasn't *alone*.

—You're never alone in church.

—Pardon?

—I said . . .

Looking at this poor, simple man, Theophilus paused. His heartrate was steady, his breathing still cyclical despite the jolt of the interruption. His mind felt, yes, it did, it felt opened. Opened and ready. So this was where it started, was it? Well, why not? Hadn't the Lord Himself started out with the humblest of followers? One becomes two, two becomes four, and so on, but the miracle of zero becoming one must happen first. Here, at last, then. So be it, and praise be to the Lord.

—Are you all right, Deacon?

Marty shifted his hold on the ladder. The Head Deacon, who was always so intimidatingly *holy*, had gotten the oddest look on his face, as if he was listening to something, even though the church was so quiet it could have been the dead of night. And then he asked a very strange question indeed.

—Do you believe in the prophecy of the Sacraments, Martin?

33. Unsentimental Journey.

Jacki had faced disorientation upon awakening more times than she cared to remember, but this was really something. She seemed to be lying down in the back seat of a car. Scratch that, the back seat of a *moving* car. She was wrapped up in a dark gray blanket that covered her from feet to neck. Apart from that, she seemed to be completely naked. She stared upwards and listened to the hum of the car for a moment. This wasn't the usual disorientation where she failed to recognize familiar surroundings for a brief, terrifying span before her synapses started firing and making the proper associations. No, this time she really had no idea where she was.

The interior of the car was a drab blue vinyl with silver sparkles glimmering dimly here and there. Jacki could feel a broad cross-stitch design on the seat beneath her, with hard round buttons where the lines met. Everything smelled faintly of grease and soap. The back of the front seat was all one piece, stretching from door to door. So it was an older car, then. The sun pushed through clouds to shine into the back window, so that made it morning, at least. Nope. Nothing was signifying. Nothing was suggesting any sort of memory. It all remained stubbornly unfamiliar.

She could feel worry hovering off in the bleak, queasy distance somewhere, but she concentrated purely on naming things in her field of vision: wool blanket, blue ceiling, tree going by, Jacki, Jacki is who I am. She realized she could see the person sitting in the passenger seat. Her skin was a darker tan color, probably Rumour, and she had short, unevenly cut hair. She had a large raised mole growing out of the middle of her cheek. The sunlight glinted off a shiny layer of oil coating her broad nose. In a sudden coalescence – wham! – Jacki recognized her. For a brief, thrilling moment, she couldn't place whether this was a good thing or a bad thing. Curiosity was finally the engine that drove her to speak.

—Excuse me? Davis?

Her voice surprised and dismayed her. It was a croaking, rusty thing that squeaked her syllables up and down. Nevertheless, the brown head with the mole and shine immediately turned around.

—She's awake.

—Thank God.

Another voice. The driver.

—Ms Strell? How are you feeling?

—I'm thirsty. Yes, really thirsty and—

—We'll be at your house soon. We'll get you something.

—*My* house?

—Yes. Joanie and I are taking you home.

So. Joanie and Davis, the two custodians from Jacki's wing of Hennington Hills, were driving her home.

—Where . . . I mean . . . I don't remember anything.

Jacki saw Davis exchange a worried look with Joanie.

—We can talk about it later, Ms Strell. You've had a bad . . . shock. When you're feeling better, we'll talk about it then.

—Where are my clothes?

—We couldn't find them.

—Oh. Shit. Oh, my God.

Panic sat like a dust mote just outside of her range of vision. She couldn't see it, but she could tell it was there.

—Just hang on, Ms Strell. We're almost home.

—How do you know where I live?

—We found your purse in your office.

—I was in my office?

—We'll talk about it later. Please, just rest. You've had a bad shock.

—A bad shock.

It's the end, thought Jacki. The end of everything. This has to be the end. Am I dying? she thought, for the second time in two hours. Am I finally dying? Is this what I'm seeing? Panic crawled forward over her thoughts, and here at the end, Jacki could suddenly see, clear as day, where everything had started.

Thomas had invited her to dinner her third day on the job,

six years ago, on a Friday before a three-day weekend. Having grown up in Ottorongo, thirty-five miles southeast of Hennington, Jacki had never heard even a whisper about Thomas Banyon or Hennington Hills Golf Course and Resort. She moved to the city after her divorce as a way of starting over. Her husband had used a clever lawyer and Jacki's own mercurial attention span to gain sole custody of their preadolescent sons, which if Jacki were honest with herself was actually sort of okay. The boys, Morton and Tucker, had always baffled her, especially in their utter resistance to logic, almost like aliens placed in her life as a test. She struggled with a deep lode of shame these feelings caused her, but seeing her sons on weekends or occasionally for holidays was, when you got right down to it, preferable to the constant battles that their lives would almost surely have turned into. A fresh start was in order. Answering an ad, she had taken her skills and moved away to begin a new life. She had no idea what she was walking into when Thomas approached her one evening, his voice nearly a purr.

—This isn't a come-on. Just an informal thing to get to know my new accountant better as a person.

Saying no wouldn't have even occurred to her as a possibility.

—So why the move from the 'burbs into the big city?

—I've lived in the suburbs all my life, I guess. I just wanted something different. A clean slate, maybe.

—Are you running from something?

He smiled when he asked that, a smile that made Jacki feel like she was running from something even though she wasn't, a smile that made her *want* to be running from something.

—Only a marriage that ended with the same dull unpleasantries as any other.

—Nothing more than that?

—Afraid not. I'm just a strange mathematician who sometimes wears different shoes on each foot without realizing it.

Thomas laughed.

—Do you really?

—My head's in the clouds, as my ex-husband said. Over and over again.

—Would you like another drink?

—I think that might be nice.

—Has anyone ever told you how pretty your eyes are? Again, that's not a come-on. I'm just saying.

Flattery. *Flattery.* Of all the basest caprices, of all the simple-minded ruses that had been used to snare willing participants in the history of world seduction, flattery had pulled Jacki right in. Three drinks later, she was whispering to him about her breasts. Three drinks after that, she was back in his office, showing him how they worked, letting him take a suckle or two. Before she knew it, his hand was up her dress, his pants were down to his slightly bowed knees, and he was sticking his stout, stiff little prick up inside of her. And even then, she knew she wasn't all that drunk. Even then, pressing into his stocky body on the large, leather couch in his office, she knew that it was his words and the way he smiled at her and the way he just recognized that she was there, her, Jacki, of all people.

Lying there naked with her, idly brushing a last drop of come off the end of his cock, Thomas had said, oh so casually, oh so lackadaisically, —Did you enjoy that?

In a way, Jacki thought, in a way absolutely, but in another way—

—Yes.

—I've got something that you might find makes this whole experience even better.

128   —What is it?

—Just something special I thought you might like to share with me.

—But what *is* it?

—You're a very beautiful woman, Jacki.

Her big, bulky body blushed, almost from head to toe. She may not have been drunk enough to believe him, but when he pulled out the syringe full of high-grade Forum (—But just a taste for you tonight, Jacki. Just a little honey to make you feel warm.) she *was* drunk enough not to notice that after he had injected her, the needle never got anywhere near his own skin. By that time, though, waves of utter goodness were melting in her brain, and she no longer cared.

Looking back, Jacki realized for the first time that Thomas hadn't *needed* another entertainment. He had probably just started out the evening wondering if he could make her bend, but then she had told him about her breast milk and that had been the end of it. He was probably disappointed when she ran right into his open arms. After that, the equation was simple. He would bring her more Forum, though never quite enough, and she would do whatever he wanted. They never made love again.

She cleared her throat.

—Davis?

—Yes, Ms Strell?

—It's Jacki, please.

—All right.

She cleared her throat again. Her voice was abandoning her. She looked up straight into Davis' eyes, and when the image shifted, Jacki realized she was crying.

—Please don't take me home.

—What, Jacki? I can barely hear you.

—Please. Don't take me home.

34. A Shot Across the Bows?

—Good Lord, what did you do?

—What could I do? I sent him home. Told him to think about it good and hard and that I'd need an answer by Monday. Excuse me, more coffee, please.

—An answer? You mean a definite yes or no? No more for me, thanks. Has it gotten that serious?

—Did you see that sneer? She's just frittering away her tip. Yes, it's gotten that serious. I didn't plan for it to be. I thought I'd just scare him out of a daze, but lo and behold, he wasn't just brooding. He was serious.

—Well. Shit.

—No kidding. I mean, I hope his answer is yes, because—

—Because a lot of people have done a lot of work—

—Fundraising—

—And ass-kissing—

—And hand-shaking and so forth, but putting all that aside, it's better for everyone in the long run if we've got a candidate who actually wants the job. Could I get a little more cream, please, or rather *some* cream, since you didn't bring it the first time? Thanks ever so much.

—You're being unpleasant to the help, darling.

—She's not 'help', Albert, she's being paid, and she's acting like she has a cab waiting.

—So what do you think he'll do?

—I wish I knew. I'm just trying to let go, leave the results up to fate.

—You are not.

—I'm trying. I have no control over the matter.

—You could try counseling him some more.

—He's had as much from me as he can take, I think. I'm

surprised he hasn't told me to butt the hell out already. It *is* his campaign, after all, not mine.

—*Please*, Cora. It's been your campaign the whole time, and you know it.

—Well, of course it has, but I don't want it to look that way. At least I'm throwing myself behind a good man.

—A good, if indecisive, man.

—He's deciding this weekend. That's the whole point. Hi, what's your name? Jenny. Jenny, I could get you fired in the time it takes me to sneeze, so how about you stop being such a resentful little cow and bring me some cream already?

—You're not like this.

—I'm *agitated*. She picked the wrong time for subpar service.

—I thought you hated people who threw their power around.

—I do, but after twenty years I'm allowed a grumpy moment or two.

—Only one or two?

—I'm hardly an angel.

—Thank God for that or this marriage would never have worked. Speaking of . . .

—Oh, dear.

—There's a possibility down at the auction house who might be game.

—All the usual questions apply.

—His name's Kevin, dark hair, dark eyes, a bit short but in nice shape.

—Does he turn your way or mine?

—Mine, but he's got the right glint in his eye.

—I'll bet. Discreet?

—Darling, have I ever failed us before?

—Almost. Remember Pierre?

—Not my fault. One does not inquire if one's godfather is a High Court Judge.

—How close is he?

—Actually, I think the asking might be enough. He's got that sporting feel.

—Mmmm . . . all right. Might be fun to have a little recreation this weekend. After all, it's been quite a while.

—Almost three years.

—Really? To be honest, I don't think I even noticed.

—Interestingly enough, neither did I until this one showed up.

—We're getting older.

—Yes, and it's not nearly as frightening as I expected. It's turned out to be fine as long as I'm spending my time with you.

—Oh, Albert. What a thing to say.

—In the midst of all your crabbiness, I do still love you, you know.

—I honestly feel as if I might cry. You can still get to me, old man. Amazing.

—Thank you for walking me back, darling.

—How could I treat my beloved wife any less?

—Do stop, Albert. You're going to lapse into sentimentality if you're not careful.

—Warning heard and ignored.

—Afternoon, Lisa.

—There's a message for you, Mayor.

—Here? Why didn't you send the call in to Angie?

—It was a walk-in. Someone named Tybalt Jon Noth stopped by for you.

132 —What?

—Said he was an old friend. Said you'd probably know him by 'Jon'.

—Are you sure it was Jon Noth?

—Yes. He even spelled his name. He was actually very charming.

—Of course he was. What did he look like?

—Um, sort of light green eyes, short salt-and-pepper hair.

—The eyes I remember. What was he wearing?

—Okay, that *was* strange. He was wearing all black.

—That's Jon Noth. What in God's name did he want?

—I don't know. He thought you'd be happily surprised to hear from him.

—He's half right.

She turned to Albert.

—What could Jon Noth possibly be doing back in town?

—I don't know. It's been a long time.

—Nearly forty years.

—I can't imagine . . . Lisa, did he leave a number?

—No, he just said to say that he stopped by.

—Is he going to come by again?

—He didn't say.

—He just stopped by to say that he stopped by?

—Yeah.

—That sounds like Jon.

—Don't get riled up yet, Albert. We don't know what he wants.

—When has he ever wanted anything that caused our lives to be easier?

—It's been forty years. A lot can happen to a man. You just like being angry with him.

—As should you. You don't suppose it's a shot across the bows?

133

—What? In a new war to win my hand that wasn't even a war in the first place?

—He was always a stubborn one.

—A rival for your hand. How romantic.

—Not especially, Lisa. Thank you, that'll be all. Send my calls to Angie for the rest of the afternoon.

—Yes, Mayor.

—You going to be all right, Cora?

—Yes, of course, why should this upset me? It's a surprise, that's all.

—Call me later.

—Yes, darling. I will. Jon Noth.

—I know.

—What do you suppose he could want after all this time?

35. The Story of Cora, Jon, and Albert, as told to Eugene by Jon.

I was a history major in college, which in those days was even more frustrating than it is now. (—What was there to even study? —My whole point.) The Recent Histories were almost forty years *more* recent than they are now, giving us poor scholars of the period a whopping fifty years of material with which to write theses and dissertations. I can't tell you how many of us were working on projects about the lack of an oral tradition after Pistolet's destruction of the Prior Histories. You would have thought that an oppressed people would have passed *something* along to its grandchildren, but apparently not. (—He killed almost everyone over twenty in the Wars. —Very astute, Eugene. —And then he took nearly everyone else with him when he saw he was losing the Six Years' War and did that Grand Immolation thing. —Excellent. I'm heartened that someone your age has such an immediate grasp on the issue. —I heard all about it from my grandparents. —Proving how the oral tradition has at last reasserted itself.)

A saving grace was that history studies then also had the exciting facet of archeology. Today, we've recovered what?, maybe fifteen per cent of the Prior Histories, but when I went to school, there was almost nothing. The old computer codes hadn't even been discovered, much less any manner of putting them to use un-erasing anything that hadn't been completely annihilated. It was daunting, but it was also thrilling to be right at the start of the greatest recovery project ever undertaken. (—That we know of. —I'd be awfully surprised if any previous society had to spend decades unraveling even the barest facts of its own history.) Fully half of my class time was spent out in the Brown, among the mile-high dunes and the rock fields further north. The heat was unbelievable. We had to do most of our excavating at night under chemical lamps, but even then the desert gnats made it almost as unbearable. It was dangerous and exciting, just after the end of that idiotic Gentlemen's War. A great time to be a student. (—So this was at Mansfield? —Yes. —I wanted to go to Mansfield. —What happened? —I didn't.)

There were periods where I would be in the desert for weeks and months at a time. The school would truck in supplies and shelters, because we weren't just doing schoolwork; everyone, especially the government, was interested in what we might find. Everyone wanted to know where we'd all come from. Everyone wanted to know what their family trees looked like and when the cities were settled and where Pistolet had come from and who he conquered when he took over. All of that still to be found. Everything was amazing. *Everything.* Every day was full of hope and expectation, as if we could   135 discover the whole world, which in a sense was exactly true. I regret to this day that we couldn't find more of it, that Pistolet's policies were so devastatingly effective. It's impossible to know what could still be out there.

I was in the graduate program, and part of our requirement to the university, besides handing over any major discoveries we happened upon, was to teach the undergraduates they would drag into the desert and drop on us. As you might imagine, they were generally more trouble than they were worth, asking smartass questions and kicking up a lot of dust. You know Mansfield, what it's like, what it *was* like. Busloads of greasy-haired lesbians in tank tops and hiking boots and frat boys whose idea of high entertainment is urinating out of doors. Frightful. The graduate students had to teach them elementary things like Surveying 101, how to construct rudimentary history hypotheses, and, more or less, how not to die in the Brown. Tedious, but those were the requirements, and it was where I met a student named Cora Trygvesdottir, the future Mrs Albert Larsson.

(—Have you ever been in love, Eugene? —I think so. —Then no, you haven't.)

Cora was something quite extraordinary. She was a law student taking History & Archeology as an elective, but right away I could tell she was a different breed than the other students. Brighter, quicker to pick up the basics, and then more thorough in her understanding of even the esoteric aspects of our work. Beautiful, but not in that transient way of your average college beauty. She was a beauty that I could tell would last and only become more thrilling with age. And more than that, she had a presence, an assumption of the space around her, a way of making herself seen by everyone she talked to and a way of making yourself *feel* seen by her. Do you understand what I mean? (—No.) It's really no wonder she succeeded in politics. She was distant and formidable, but she was also the kind of person who was first in your mind when you needed a definitive opinion. Obviously smarter than everyone else but at the same time lacking a need to tell you that. The word that leaps continuously to my mind is 'impressive'. She was impressive. A cut above. Made from different cloth. You might disagree with her, you might even dislike her, but you would *never* not take her seriously.

She was under my tutelage for four weeks out in the desert. I taught her how to date archeological metal, how to test old circuits, and so on and so forth, but I also was able to teach her in the off hours. I showed her how to get water out of casque plants, how to keep the gnats out of our food when we ate, how to pick up a rattleback without getting bitten, every little trick that I had learned as a history digger. And the *talks* we would have about where we were from and where we were going, what made us happy, and what we had gone through, things that you only discuss with persons you hold dear. It was marvelous, one of the happiest times of my life. My, to be young again.

Foolish me, I fell madly in love with her, and like a lot of other young, dumb, idealistic twenty-somethings, I didn't say a word. (—Why the hell not?) It was the time of the New Man. Remember him? Of course not, you're too young. Shelbert Shelbert had just published *The Third and Final Chance* as a rebuke of the Gentlemen's War. This was five or ten years before he blew his head off. We were all trying to be better people, trying to recognize what we had, what opportunities we could make of the world with our whole history lost to us. It seems laughable now, but I was trying to attain some sort of pure higher ground, a kind of love on an intellectual plane, a meeting of the souls rather than just mindless physical pleasure that could be done with anyone.

(—You were scared. —I was *not* scared. I wanted something more. —Bullshit. You were scared. —I'm going out on a limb here for you, Eugene. Are you interested in hearing the rest of this story or would you rather I just be your boss? —All right, sorry, you say you weren't scared. —*I wasn't scared.* —Fine, I believe you.)

Cora went back to campus, I stayed in the desert, and we began a correspondence. Mail only came out once a week with the supplies, and I would receive a new letter from her and drop a new letter from me into it at the same time, so we essentially had two lines of conversation overlapping. These were not silly love letters. No snatches of bad poetry, no flowery language. This was pure cerebral engagement. We discussed philosophy, the reorganization of the government, the ecology of the desert, the backward reconstruction of precedent that her law studies were plowing through, all kinds of fascinating, living, life-of-the-mind things. A love was growing between us, unstated and unsullied by childish emotions, a true love, honest and strong and bright, an *impressive* love that I thought was suitable for her, one that lived up to her, one that was good enough for her.

And then she met Albert Larsson. On a nude beach. Where he had just finished having sexual relations with some man in the bushes. (—Did you know that's how they met, Eugene? On a nude beach? —I don't think I've ever cared, but it doesn't seem like that big a deal to me. I've been to that beach. The one down around the Point? If you're here trying to cause a scandal, I don't think that one's going to fly. —I'm not trying to make a scandal, Eugene. I was merely trying to point out what she forsook and what she accepted as love. —Have you ever heard of an 'Albert and Cora'? —No. —It's a legal term for a binding contract. —Doesn't matter.) I heard all about it in a letter I received one week. How he was the most honest man she had ever met. How he was a free spirit who cared nothing about crossing boundaries and blazing new trails. How she had immediately fallen in love with his purity of feeling. Can you imagine saying that to me after all the things we had shared? Every word of it without the slightest acknowledgment of what had passed between us.

I was hurt, of course. Who wouldn't be? But I decided to fight because, not to sound too jejune, a man fights for what he believes in. I sent her letters declaring my love for her. Not just letters, Eugene, epic expressions of myself and how I felt, wherein I poured out all the contents of my heart to her. I wasn't mistaken in what we'd shared, what we *still* must share. I think perhaps she was just too intimidated by it or it was just too big for her to handle at the time, and so she went for the next bright prospect that came her way. Simple transference. She couldn't express her love for me so she lavished it upon Albert, that frivolous, ridiculous man.

She answered my letters in the worst, most painful way possible. With *politeness*. She said she was flattered by my attention, that she thought I was a wonderful person, that it wasn't anything I had *done*. It was just one of those things. 'One of those things'. How could she say that to me? How could she be that cruel? How could she act so counter to her true feelings? Of course, Albert was an influence on her. How could he not pit her against me? But still I fought for her. I cared about her that much. I pleaded with her in person. I waited for her outside of her classes in order to talk to her. I talked to Albert, as a gentleman, to get him to release his claim, but of course he would have none of it. I finally even challenged him to a duel for her, to prove that his love wasn't as great as mine. He laughed in my face, and then when I struck him for laughing, he tricked me and left me savagely beaten. This was the final straw, the final slap to my dignity. 139

It was going to have to be enough that I knew I was right and that I knew what Cora and I could have had together.

(—And so you went away? —I went away. —Where? —Lots of places. It's not important. —And now you're back? —And now I'm back. —And you think you're going to convince her that she's been wrong for fifty years? —*Forty* years, and no, I'm not foolish. But in all that time I've never forgotten her or been able to set the matter to the side. *Something* must still be there. I just need to make her *see* that something. The results will be what they will be, but I think I've confessed enough today, Eugene. It's time to go. Get yourself together. —Where are we going? —There's someone else in this town I've been wanting to meet.)

36. Max and Talon Discuss the Ramifications of the Weight of Cultural Pressures and Also Buy a Dog.

—Thank you again, Daddy.

—Just a little ray of sunshine for a girl who's under the weather. What are you going to name him?

—Theodore.

—That was quick.

—It seems right.

—Yeah, I guess it does, doesn't it?

—Can he sleep on my bed?

—Of course.

—Can he eat at the table?

—No.

—Can he rescue me in a fire?

—I think he might be a little short to pull you anywhere,

but his barking would definitely wake us up. Plus, he won't
need to because there won't be a fire.

—Tiffany Hinchell's house burnt down.

—That was because the forest around them burnt down
first. We're in the city. We've got sprinklers. You and me and
Theodore are going to be fine.

—But aren't we going to move when you're Mayor? Theodore, down!

—I don't think I'm going to be Mayor, pumpkin.

—Are you going to lose? Hee hee hee hee, stop! He's
tickling me with his tongue! Ha ha ha ha!

—I don't think I'm going to run for Mayor after all.

—Really? Why not? What happened?

—Nothing happened. It's just not the right time, not the
right decision.

—But what are they going to do without you?

—They'll find somebody else. He's got your Margo.

—Bad, Theodore! You leave Margo alone. Can they do
that?

—Do what?

—Find somebody else.

—Of course they can. Remember how we talked about
democracy? They can choose anyone they want.

—I thought they wanted you.

—Some of them wanted me, maybe. Maybe even enough
of them for me to win, but that's not important. I don't want
the job.

—How come?

—It's hard to explain.

—You said you'd never say that to me.

—So I did. Fair enough. No, little puppy, over here. Uh-oh.

—I'll go get a rag. Keep talking!

—You just have to be friendly to a lot of people you don't   141 want to be friendly to. You have to make a lot of promises that you don't want to make. And I don't think you get to stay the person you want to be. Do you understand?

—Yeah, I guess so. Eeeew. But what about being the first Rumour? I thought that was important.

—It is important, and someday someone will be the first Rumour Mayor. But I can't run just for that alone. It's a good reason, but a bunch of not so good reasons outweigh it. Sometimes people think you *should* be something just because you *can* be, without taking into account whether it's actually a good thing for you or not. Like say you were a really good tap dancer—

—I hate tap dancing.

—Exactly, but what if you were really good at it and you still hated it? I wouldn't make you do something you hated just because you were good at it. I would want you to do something you love instead. Understand?

—Sort of. But wouldn't I automatically love the thing I'm good at?

—I hope so, but it doesn't always work out that way.

—What do you want to do instead?

—I don't know. I've had a few ideas, but sometimes that's okay, too. I *do* know I don't want to do this.

—What about Mrs Larsson?

—What about her?

—Isn't she mad at you?

—She doesn't know yet. Look, he's fallen asleep.

—You haven't told her?

—I've only just come to the final decision.

—She's going to be mad.

—She'll be disappointed but she'll understand. That's different from being mad.

142   —Better?

—Better but harder.

—Why harder?

—Because anger is usually temporary. It takes a lot of energy and then you get over it.

—That's true, isn't it? Did you hear that? He burped in his sleep!

—Speaking of sleep, maybe you should join him.

—Okay, Daddy.

—That was easy. Are you that tired?

—Yes. I'm ready.

—Well, then, get under the covers. I'll tuck you in.

—Good night, Daddy.

—'Night, sweetheart.

—Daddy?

—Yes.

—I don't mind if you're not Mayor . . .

—Yeah, baby?

—But what happens now?

37. What Happened Between Luther and Archie.

—Good God, Luther, you look stricken. Are you all right, Son?

—Archie, we need to talk.

—No good conversation has ever started that way.

—I want you to know this is very difficult for me.

—It gets even better.

—In fact, I don't even really know how to tell you.

—Just do, my boy. It's Archie you're talking to, not just anyone.

—I know that. That's what makes it harder. I don't know where to begin . . .

—Is this about that boy you've been seeing?

—Excuse me? How in the world—

—How could I *not* know, Luther? I have a network over the whole city. I find out stuff I don't even *want* to know. Like this. Your private business.

—Thomas?

—No, surprisingly enough.

—Then who?

—Jules.

—Jules? How the fuck—

—He used the boy's . . . 'services' once and got him talking. You know how Jules is. In another life, he would have been a great spy. This boy—

—His name's Peter.

—Okay, then, this Peter let slip that he'd fallen for you, I guess. He had no idea of the connection between Jules and you, and Jules didn't tell him. It was complete coincidence.

—How long?

—A couple of months. You know Thomas. He forces those people to work constantly. It isn't pretty, but it's his way.

—And you didn't mention it to me?

—You didn't mention it to *me*, confirming my feeling that it was your private business. You're allowed to have your own life, Luther. I'm not an ogre.

—I know you're not an ogre.

—So what's this all about? Does this Peter person have you in some kind of blackmail situation? Because I can take care of that.

—No, no, that's not it. It's nothing like that at all.

—Is it Thomas? Because I can fix that, too. He's a difficult one, but money usually settles things with him.

—No, it's not Thomas.

144   —Well, was it just telling me that this had gone on? Because

I don't really care about that either. I can't say that it wouldn't be a bit awkward if the new Chairman was in love with a hooker, but worse things have happened. The Board would get over it. Is that it? Are you in love with him and afraid to tell me? Because that's nothing, Luther. I don't care. I just want you to be happy. It sure as hell won't prevent you from following me into the Chairmanship if that's what you're worried about. I own the goddamn company. They'll do what I tell them.

—No, that's not it. Well, part of it, I guess. I do love him. That's where it starts.

—Then what is it? You're giving me fucking heart failure here, Luther.

—I can't accept the Chairmanship, Archie.

—What? Why not?

—There's more. I have to leave Banyon Enterprises.

—I don't understand.

—I quit. I can't take the Chairmanship at the next Board meeting. I can't stay in my current position. I can't accept the future as it's laid out now. I have to get out. I'm sorry, Archie. I'm very, very sorry.

— . . . God, you had me scared there for a moment, boy! Whew! Not a nice thing to do to an old man, let me tell you.

—I'm being serious.

—Of course you're not. It's nerves, Luther! Nerves, pure and simple. Everyone gets cold feet now and then.

—Archie—

—No, no, no, no, no, you're just a little intimidated now that the moment of truth is here. That's all. Nothing to worry about. Do you think I didn't have my doubts when I was moving up? I did. Big ones.

—Archie, I'm telling you the truth.

—Son, I know you think you are. You're under a lot of   145 pressure, and you've been handling it all so well. It's admirable that it's taken this long for you to crack a little. Nothing to worry about at all. Happens to the best of us.

—This isn't cold feet.

—Of course it is.

—Archie—

—I don't want to hear anything more, Son. Just take whatever time you need to adjust to things, and that'll be fine.

—Please don't make this harder than it is.

—I don't want to hear this, Luther. What you're thinking, well, you're mistaken. I know it seems right to you now, but you're facing a big decision and you're just blanching a little. Don't make it more than it is.

—I'm *not* making it more than it is. I wish I were.

—So what exactly is it that you're telling me here? Be sure about it, Luther. We're in unknown territory, and I don't like it.

—I know. Trust me, I don't like it either. I detest the fact that this conversation is necessary, but I have no choice.

—There are *always* choices.

—This is life or death for me, Archie.

—It's a job, Luther. It's not life or death.

—It's not who I am. It's not what I want to be. It's not what I want my life to be like.

—You're almost forty. Isn't it a little late to be deciding what you want to be when you grow up?

—Yes, but hopefully not *too* late.

—So you're saying to me you want to opt out completely? You just want to chuck it all based on some vague feeling of personal unfulfillment?

—It's more than that.

—Then quit beating around the fucking bush and tell me what you mean!

—There's nothing I can say that can properly express my gratitude to you. Nothing. You literally took me out of a desperate situation and became my father.

—You never took my name.

—I know, because I didn't want to forget who I was. And that's the problem.

—That you're going to forget the first ten years of your life?

—Twelve years, but yes.

—So what about the last twenty-odd? Have those meant nothing?

—Of course not. I couldn't repay you if you lived another eighty years.

—That's not going to happen. And you *can* repay me by doing what you've wanted to do all along. It's a simple thing, Luther. Don't let some misgivings fuck up your whole future. And mine. Let's not forget that I'm involved in this, too.

—I know. That's what makes it so difficult.

—You really want to quit the whole thing? You really want to just toss a lifetime of my care and love for you right out the window. For what? Some *whore*? Some entertainment who gives you the business?

—No. Peter is the catalyst. He's not the reason.

—What does that even mean?

—It means that falling in love with him finally let me let go of this rushing inevitability I've been trapped in.

—You haven't been trapped in it, Luther. You could have talked to me *any* time, but goddamnit, what's the meaning of coming to me now? Now, five days before I retire, when nothing can be undone, when the die's already been cast.

—I can't be you.

—I don't want you to be me.

—That's not true, and we both know it. I'm the son that 147

Thomas never was. I've tried to be, Archie, and frankly, I've succeeded. But I can't take over Banyon Enterprises for good. I can't. There's no going back from that. If I do, then I will have completely sacrificed any chance I had to ever make a life for myself, to ever fulfill what might have been when I lived in Tishimongo Fair.

—You don't think this is better than what you would have gotten growing up in a pisswater bordertown?

—It doesn't matter if it's better. It's not mine.

—What do you want then?

—I don't know. I just know that I don't want this.

—I don't understand you. Every boy in that town would have killed to get the chances you've had.

—But I didn't kill, and I didn't choose. It was chosen for me. When my parents died, I somehow just gave up my will to you, to circumstance, to the opportunities in front of me. I decided that I had to accept whatever happened. I was afloat on chance and whatever came my way was supposed to be my future.

—And you're saying that you've realized, just now, just this week when the most important event in the history of Banyon Enterprises is going to take place, you've realized just now when hundreds of people and billions of dollars are riding on you, you decide *now* that this has all happened to you rather than you having your own part in it? Because I just want to be clear here, Luther. You're fucking me because bless your little heart you would rather have been a humble blacksmith instead of the most powerful man in the city. Do I have that correct?

—Archie, it's not like that—

—You selfish whiny little prick. I'll say it again, I don't understand you. I don't know where this is coming from,

except that all of a sudden you seem to have given up a lifetime of levelheadedness to start thinking with your dick. You come in here and tell me that I can't retire, that all my great plans for you have to be canceled because you haven't been able to grasp some destiny that you can't even articulate?

—Archie—

—No, not another word. You've hurt me, Luther, where no one else ever has. I'm blindsided and dumbfounded. Everything is ruined now. Do you realize that? Do you realize the extent of this?

—Yes, I—

—No, no. I can't listen to you any more. Go. Get out. I have to think. I have to ... get out, Luther. I can't believe you've done this to me. I just don't believe it.

—All right, I'll go ...

—Luther?

—Yes?

—One question.

—Yes?

—Are you sure? Because there's no going back. If I say you don't want it, you'll never have credibility in this business ever again. If you say no now, it's no forever.

—I'm sure, Archie. I'm sorry, but I am.

—Then never set foot in this office again.

38. Maggerty on the Move.

Step. Step. Step. Step.

The sun draped its heat over Maggerty so that it felt like he was walking under a great heavy blanket. He'd had nothing to eat all day and had vomited up the muddy water he had taken at the pond in the Arboretum. Something was wrong. His head was a miasma of fever and hot visions that buzzed 149 with terrible colors. His wound throbbed, making him feel all the sicker. And this heat . . .

He was having trouble keeping up with the herd, sometimes losing sight of them as the last animal disappeared around street corners and behind buildings. He had been sick before, many times in his life, colds, flus, injuries from falls, a bout of Battery Pox which had nearly killed him until an angel in a white room had stabbed him gently in the back several times with the thinnest of knives. After a brief, cool, honey-like time of white cloth and bright sunlight, he awoke again, healed, surrounded by the herd in the fields just south of Hennington. Yet, save for that one occasion, he had never completely lost them. A part of him knew that he wouldn't now, but the fear that this could be, would be the first time he lost them for good drove him forward step by step by reluctant step.

In those rare moments when he could piece together a coherent thought, Maggerty suspected his current illness had to do with yesterday's walk along the Bracken River, northeast of Hennington. The Bracken was befouled, a perennially murky strip of water over loose, salty clay that had worked its way into the surrounding soil, killing all local foliage except for a few gnarled elms that grew out of the red landscape like angry plumes of smoke. From where the Bracken emerged at the edge of the Brown Desert to the small, violent delta where it met the sea, the surrounding land was essentially dead, a breeding ground only for the viciously biting desert gnat, otherwise devoid of both humans and animals alike except for members of either group who came near the Bracken only while in the process of heading for the other side.

But The Crash had not crossed the Bracken, and Maggerty was at a loss as to why they had even gone. The lead animal had walked them out of the city's northeast corner, through a suburban neighborhood of brightly colored houses and whitewashed fences. Maggerty sensed something unusual when they walked past the area's only park – a small, sandy place, but with some grass nonetheless – and headed on towards the river. He felt some uneasiness among the animals as well, though he had imagined such things before to no result. But when the herd reached the red, crumbly bank of the Bracken, he definitely heard some low moans among some of the animals waiting near the back of the group where he stood. The ground was not easy to walk on even for Maggerty, much less for the animals, some of whom approached four tons. It gave in odd spots, was alternately soft and hard, and filled with jagged agate stones that could cut through even the thick-soled feet of members of the herd. The air swarmed with inflamed desert flies, irritated that their underground nests were being trampled upon. Maggerty's hands worked in a flurry trying to keep them from biting his exposed skin. Why had she brought them here?

Then he saw the river. The shock of it momentarily flash-burned away the fog in his brain. The Bracken had somehow *shrunk*. More, judging by the change in the color of the clay, it had shrunk by nearly half. The briny, sick smell of it was even more pungent than he remembered, and the color was the ominous, slightly evil color of bloody pus, something with which Maggerty, through his ever-present wound, was thoroughly acquainted. A cloud of vague terror insinuated itself across his mind. There was some awful clue here that he was missing.

She led them away soon after, but not before Maggerty had been bitten almost beyond recognition by the desert flies. His face and hands swelled overnight, and the itching was enough to push the worry away for a while. This morning, he had begun to feel sick, something the gnats had passed along to, or taken from him in the blood they had sucked. Maggerty was friends with misery, though. He had been through worse, and now his only worry was becoming permanently separated from the herd. When they had awoken and set off for the day, he had struggled to keep up almost from the beginning.

(Dora McKinley sat in her idling car, the back seat stuffed with groceries, waiting for The Crash to pass. Turning up the air conditioner against the heat, she examined her fingernails and vowed for the third time that week to stop chewing them. She looked up and caught sight of Maggerty stumbling up the road. As she put the tip of her index finger to her teeth, she murmured to herself, —He looks even worse than usual, poor thing.)

As the sun beat down, he watched the last animal disappear yet again around a station wagon. He quickened his step, lurched around a streetcorner lamp, and saw with frantic relief that the animals were stopped in a small green park on the side of a hill, grazing on the green grasses that sloped up through a small grove of trees. Good. They would stay there for a while eating. He would have time to rest. Good. He had already forgotten the questions that had been bothering him. His only thoughts were to get out of this heat, lie down in the shade, and hopefully fall into some sort of feverish sleep. After a lifetime filled with steps, Maggerty yet again mustered the will to take the next one.

39. The Frustrating Aspects of Prophecy.

Jarvis closed his eyes and sighed. His hand, wrapped deep under bandages covering four frightening wound clamps, throbbed whenever he moved it too quickly. Dr Henreid had given him Pilonnopin, but after he had taken the first one and then slept for twenty-one hours, Jarvis decided that aspirin would be a little more practical, if markedly less effective. He had spent every spare moment since returning from the hospital reading and rereading the section of the Book of Ultimates he had seen in his vision or hallucination or whatever it had been. He opened his eyes and read again, many hours removed from the hundredth time.

> *And in a time of sunlight, a dark wind will encroach,*
> *obscuring the truth,*
> *And in the time of dark wind, a light wind will encroach,*
> *revealing the truth.*

The verses were infuriating and vague in the way typical of all of the Book of Ultimates. Decades of debate had never quite settled whether the Book even rightly belonged in the Sacraments, and no wonder. The Sacraments was one of the few texts that Pistolet had permitted to pass untouched, at least for a while. He had even used the opaque teachings of these very verses to justify the Great Immolation, associating it with the 'light wind' and thereby prompting murmurings that he had written the Ultimates himself, an idea vitiated only by the fact that, in his usual style, he then contradicted himself and placed the Sacraments, Book of Ultimates and all, on the list of things to be destroyed, which by that point had grown to include effectively everything that *could* be destroyed, including every man, woman and child who could be killed before Pistolet himself finally fell. Fortunately, his last gasp had not reached as far as he had hoped, and a few things survived into the Recent Histories, copies of the Sacraments among them. The survival of the Sacraments then came to be thought of as the 'light wind' that revealed the truth, and the stories of Pistolet's possible authorship, while still hovering in the background, were mostly put to rest.

For Jarvis, though, along with many of his colleges, the Ultimates never sat well. He found most of the verses obscure to the point of meaninglessness. If something could be interpreted to mean anything at all, then in effect it meant nothing. The Ultimates was rarely taught in the Bondulay canon, often being treated, certainly by Jarvis, as nothing more than a quaint addendum of suspect origin. The truths it contained were covered in better fashion elsewhere in the Sacraments, and any differences written there were evasive to the point of futility.

Which would be easy to dismiss, Jarvis thought to himself, if they hadn't caused so much harm.

And in a time of sunlight, a dark wind will encroach,
  obscuring the truth,
And in the time of dark wind, a light wind will encroach,
  revealing the truth.

—How can it mean anything when it means everything? What do you want me to see, Lord? What are you trying to show me? What's here that I'm not seeing?

At best, the verses were a *metaphor*, for pity's sake, and a murky, impenetrable one at that. History had shown over and over again the danger of taking these writings too literally. Pistolet. The Brandon Beach Massacre where all those poor dark-skinned sailors had been killed. Raymond Wittingham and that whole mess with the old government. The Rat Hill Battle of the Gentlemen's War. All those lives lost because this, this ethereal *poetry*, had been taken as fact.

154   Jarvis paused.

Maybe that was the reason behind the vision. Not the Ultimates, but the reaction to it.

Oh, dear Lord. That would be so much worse.

Part III.

All Bets May or May Not Be Final.

40. Considering Variables.

—Anyone seen Jacki Strell?

—She called in sick, Mr Banyon.

—Again? That's not like her.

—She said it's a bad flu.

Thomas turned and re-entered his office. No, it was definitely not like Jacki. He'd had to cancel two very disappointed clips for her and then when he called her at home, there was no answer. She must really be sick, and if so, she was about to get a lot sicker, since Thomas had calculated her supply of Forum to run out in two more days. That she hadn't called him about it was curious, but no matter, she would be calling soon enough, sick with the 'flu' or not.

He tapped his fingers on his desk. His laptop let out a whir and a beep as Tracy Jem-Ho logged in a mid-morning clip. He could hear a shrill birdsong coming through his sunlit window, followed by a dog barking, of all things. He tapped his fingers again. He picked up the phone and dialed Jacki's number. Ring-ring, ring-ring, ring-ring, Hello, this is Jacki, I'm not in right now. He hung up and dialed his secretary.

—Did you take the call from Jacki yourself, Rita?

—Yes, sir.

—Did she sound sick?

—Yes, sir. She could barely speak.

—She's not picking up at home.

—She said she wouldn't be, sir. She said her doctor told her to get rest and nothing but. She said to apologize to you specifically for the inconvenience and that she'd try to be in   159 tomorrow or the next day, but that she was feeling unwell enough to possibly be out all week.

—Maybe I'll drive over and drop off some flowers.

—She might be contagious, Mr Banyon.

—I'm as fit as a horse, Rita. Order some flowers and I'll take them over to her tonight after work.

—Yes, sir.

He hung up. Why was he taking her flowers? He hit redial.

—You might be right about the contagion, Rita. Just have some flowers delivered to her.

—What kind?

—Whatever kind, and put a note saying 'Get Well Soon' from me.

—Of course, Mr Banyon.

Enough of this. Time to get some work done. She had better come back to work soon or he would have to think of a way for her to cover her clip losses. He considered himself a big-hearted boss, but entertainment could only get away with so much sick time. He had a balance sheet to cover, accounts to pay, a business to run. His margin was more than enough to cover unexpected losses, but Jacki brought in so much money in fees, what with her special talents and all, that he didn't want her out for long.

Tap. Tap. Tap. Tap.

—Rita?

—Yes, sir?

—Never mind.

He pulled his laptop onto his lap top and began reviewing accounts. Tracy had finished up with a nice tip. Hartley Chevalier was scheduled to wine and dine the recently widowed Mrs Declan Butler this evening at eight. Peter Wickham had called in sick as well. Was there an epidemic? Johnson Partham, the boy with the affinity for wax, had two clips

160

scheduled for tonight. Ah, the stamina of youth. Meg Reubens. Jack Walsh. Veronica Wilby also had two clips tonight. A full schedule, a full slate of fees, a full complement of happy customers. Jacki wouldn't be missed. I wonder if it's really serious? Maybe I should send over my own doctor.

—Oh, fuck this. Who cares?

Thomas cracked open his drawer and pulled out a TB's Special Blend. He lit it and pulled the smoke down into his lungs. That was better. A musky calm flowed through him, allowing him to let go of all the bothersome details that buzzed around his head. Thomas believed strongly in enjoying the finer things that life had to offer, because what was the point of being the boss if you could never relax? Never any of that heavy stuff, though. Thomas looked down on addicts, because they had so completely surrendered their will to something as stupid as a chemical.

Even Jacki. He hadn't intended to give her the Forum. He'd actually enjoyed himself that evening, to his own great surprise. She was a woman his own age, kind of an odd duck, but all the more charming for it. If only she hadn't told him about her marvelous breasts and the intriguing thing they could do, if only she hadn't taken the Forum so willingly, maybe something could have happened. Who knew? But business was business, and Thomas wasn't about to let those magnificent lactating organs slip out of his grasp. Forum was the easiest way to convince someone like Jacki to work for him, and after that, well, who the hell wanted anything to do with an addict?

Puff. Puff. Puff. Ring-ring, ring-ring, ring-ring, Hello, this is Jacki, I'm—

He hung up and was ready to redial Rita when the phone surprised him by ringing first.

—Yes?

—You have someone here to see you, Mr Banyon.

—I'm not aware of any appointments.

—He says he's a fellow businessman who, I'm sorry, sir, what was that again? 'A fellow businessman who has long admired your own business acuity'.

—He's standing right there in front of you?

—Yes, sir.

—Why didn't front reception stop him there?

—I'm getting to the bottom of it, sir.

—'Business acuity'. Sounds like a bunch of bullshit to me.

Rita lowered her voice to a whisper.

—Indeed, sir, that was my impression at first. But perhaps there's more to it.

—You think so?

—My opinion would be one of further investigation, sir.

—Does he look like a lawyer?

—No, sir.

—Police?

—Emphatically not, sir.

—What's his name?

—Tybalt Noth.

—'Tybalt'?

—He says he goes by Jon.

—Never heard of him.

—Says he's a friend of the Mayor's.

—Then definitely not.

—What shall I tell him, sir?

Thomas tapped his fingers again once or twice. The cigarillo was putting him in a smooth sort of mood. This Noth character wouldn't be the police, that was true. Thomas kept close tabs on possible police activity through a dizzying array of informants, both inside and outside of the police department, some of whom informed on each other. Besides, half the force were customers anyway. He knew of no pending or potential lawsuits, either. One of the very few benefits of being the son of Archie Banyon was access to the veritable mini-city of lawyers who worked for Banyon Enterprises. If Thomas ever needed legal assistance – the constant threat of which was a hazard of his business – they were as available as air; Thomas could get a lawyer faster than it took him to inhale.

Once, just after he officially became Chairman of Hennington Hills Golf Course and Resort – his father had retained the title as honorary for an annoyingly long time – Thomas had hired a young Rumour girl. She looked eighteen, said she was fifteen, the legal age limit for a work permit, and turned out to be twelve. Thomas had set her to work as a waitress in the restaurant and as a general purpose, low-priced entertainment for some of his more blue-collar customers. Unfortunately, she also proved to be a prolific letter-writer to the folks back home. In less than a month, a team of liberal-minded child-labor lawyers had shown up in Thomas' office with the reluctant Chief of Police, the girl's weeping mother, and a camera crew in tow.

After Thomas' arrest and subsequent release twenty minutes later, he had selected the cream from his father's lawyer crop. A day later, he held a news conference, offering proof of the girl's deception. Within two days, he'd had all the charges dropped, the girl deported, an on-air apology from the television station, and a lawsuit filed for defamation of character against the child-labor lawyers and the girl's mother. Within a month, he had bankrupted the lawyers, sent the girl's mother to a poorhouse in the Rumour Land, and had added seven new clients to his portfolio, including the presiding judge and the male and female news anchors at the TV station. Maybe he shouldn't have come down quite so hard on a twelve-year-old girl, but let's face it, business was business was business was business. No, no, no, this Noth, whoever he was, couldn't possibly represent a threat to him. Thomas was comfortably untouchable.

—What the fuck, Rita. Send him in.

41. The Lonely Hunter.

Peter rang the bell again. A light had gone off in an upstairs window as he pulled in on his cycle, so he knew Luther was home. Luther never went to bed until after midnight, and it wasn't yet eleven. So why wasn't he coming to the door?

—Luther?

After finally making his decision, Peter had left his waiter shift at Hennington Hills early claiming stomach flu and had driven straight over to Luther's house. He wasn't confident in a response. He wasn't confident in *anything* to do with his presence here. He knew what he wished for, what he wanted, but he wasn't at all sure if this was what he *should* be doing, if this is what people in his position did, or if other people were even *in* his position. And then there were all those questions that declined to rest. Luther was a different class, a different league. He was a different age, from a different upbringing. He was even a different race. But none of that was supposed to matter anymore, was it? Although not to put too fine a point on the unmentionable, it was also true that Peter was the entertainment and Luther was his clip. That romantic schematic never worked anywhere except fantasy. It was all wrong. Peter being here on Luther's doorstep with a catch in his throat and an anxious knot in his chest was all wrong.

Yet here he was, ringing the doorbell a third time.

—Luther? Are you there? It's Peter.

A quiet eternity later, the door opened. Luther looked horrible. His eyes were puffed from crying, his clothes had clearly been slept in, and he had at least two days' beard growth. Peter momentarily forgot the whole list of things he wanted to say.

—What's wrong? Are you okay? Are you sick?

—You don't know? Well, of course you don't know. How would you?

—Know what? What's happened?

For a second, beneath all the mess, Luther looked genuinely curious.

—If you didn't know, why did you come?

—I wanted to see you. I have a million things I want to say, but what do you mean, 'if I didn't know'? If I didn't know what?

—There's no use.

—Of what? What's happened?

—It's over.

—What's over?

—Everything. All of it. I made the wrong decision, and now it's all over.

—Can I come in? We'll talk about it. We'll fix it.

The house was its usual immaculate self, all smooth, clear surfaces, white spaces, clean and crisp, save for the fact that Luther's desk looked like it had been ransacked. Papers were torn, drawers left open, the garbage can next to it overflowing with trash. It looked as if some of the papers had even been burnt. Somehow this one set of wreckage amidst the cleanliness of the house upset Peter more than if the whole place had been a ruin. Luther led him to the living room. Peter sat down next to him on the couch, putting an arm around him. Luther stared stiffly forward, only after a moment leaning his head on Peter's shoulder.

—Just tell me what happened. We can make whatever it is right.

—No, we can't.

—Tell me what happened, Luther.

—I let Archie Banyon down. I told him I didn't want to be Chairman of his company. I told him I didn't want this career, that I needed to quit.

—Why is that so terrible?

A dishonest question, asked out of shock.

—I've destroyed every plan he's ever laid for me.

—Can you talk to him again? Can you take it back?

—He won't see me. I don't think I could face him again, anyway.

—Why not?

—I understand what you're trying to do. Part of me is so glad to see you. It's wonderful. It's everything I wanted, but it's too late. It's too late. It's not your fault. It's mine. I should have said something earlier, but that's pointless now. I didn't know, and now it's too late.

—It's not too late.

—It is. Everything's over.

—No, it isn't.

—I can't see you again, Peter.

—Don't say that. Of course you can.

—I don't exist anymore.

—You're just upset now, Luther. Everything's going to be all right.

—No. One thing I can guarantee is that it's not going to be all right.

Luther stood abruptly.

—I can't do this. I'm going to go crazy. Please leave, Peter, and understand that this has nothing to do with you. I just can't be around anyone. I can barely stand to be around myself. Oh, fuck fuck fuck fuck fuck what did I do?

Trying to buy time, Peter changed the subject.

—Have you eaten anything today?

—I don't remember.

—Let me fix you something.

—Can you just please leave?

—Do you really, really, honestly want me to leave? If you do, I'll go, no more questions.

Luther's eyes met Peter's for the first time that night. A long moment passed. Peter held his breath. Luther finally whispered his answer.

—I want you to stay.

—Then I'll stay, and I'll make you something to eat.

Peter got up and went straight to business in the kitchen, cooking the first food that came to hand and trying to come up with something, anything to say that would help. He finally set a bowl of pasta on the table.

—The whole reason I came here was to tell you that I've fallen in love with you, and I know it'll never work for a million reasons, but how could I not tell you?

—I'm not sure that's going to be enough.

—It will be. Trust me, it will.

42. Refuge for the Weary.

Under seven wool blankets and a space heater that made the small bedroom swelter, Jacki was freezing. She huddled herself into a ball, but there was really no use and she knew it. The cold was coming from inside her, from a vibrating steel column that stretched from her stomach to her brain, sending cold pathways out from the center of her body. She shook and shook and pulled the blankets around her tighter.

—Is there anything more I can do for you at all, Jacki?

Huddled in her blanket cocoon, Jacki struggled to shake her head. Davis had opened up her home as a place to hide, for make no mistake about it, they all knew that hiding was exactly what Jacki was doing. After she had explained some of her history to Davis and Joanie, they insisted that she not go back to work. She obeyed, reporting a vague, open-ended illness. They had then gone a step further, bundling Jacki into Davis' home, into the vacated bedroom of a son who had left for college. Joanie had immediately called in a doctor, Dr Ketcham, an ancient Rumour who had been practicing medicine in the Rumour community for almost fifty years. He had spoken in a voice filled with sand.

—You don't have to worry, Ms Strell, Joanie's explained everything. No one will hear from me where you are.

—Thank you. How am I going to get through this without dying?

—Well, I won't lie to you and tell you you have an easy path in front of you. Forum is hard to kick but not impossible. The Recatur will help to wean you off. I'll show Davis how to give you the shots until you can do it yourself. You're going to be going through some pretty horrible things, Ms Strell. Your body is going to punish you for not taking the Forum, but it can be done. Try to keep as warm as you can, and rest as much as you can, too. I'll call every day, and I'll stop by often. You take care of yourself. You're going to make it. That man has ruined enough lives. He's not going to get yours. Not if I can help it.

—You know Thomas Banyon?

—I know that he's ravaged more than one young Rumour that's passed through my care. Some of the things I've seen would turn your eyes back in your head. If I can save someone from his grasp, I consider it only justice.

168

—Wait a minute. Is this the Rumour Underground?

Dr Ketcham smiled.

—Of course not. That doesn't exist, now does it?

Then he winked.

In no time, Jacki realized that taking Recatur was better than going cold turkey, but only just. It was like offering a communion wafer to a starving man: it served the minimal purpose but missed the point entirely. All Recatur did was satisfy the physiological demand that the liver developed for a certain chemical in Forum – and only half did that, because the point was to get rid of that dependency. It did nothing to satisfy the *brain's* physiological craving for Forum because that allegedly wasn't fatal, and of course, it didn't even try to satisfy the emotional and psychological dependency, because that was the thing you were supposed to let go of. Death was still the hard option but only by the slimmest of margins.

Despite the difficulties, despite the impossibility of getting warm, after three days of Recatur and plain old withdrawal she was starting to notice a difference, if only slight, and that gave her some hope. She wasn't shivering quite so badly this afternoon, and this morning she had almost eaten a whole banana. Her breasts were intensely sore, the milk from them having taken on a yellow sheen as it dribbled out in thoroughly unattractive spasms, but she was sure now that the withdrawal from Forum wasn't going to kill her body. It was her mind that was giving her the most trouble.

She craved Forum every waking second, in spite of every-thing, in spite of all it had done, she *craved*. This was different from wanting. She didn't want Forum, didn't want to be anywhere near it. Davis and Joanie had brought the rest of her small stash from her office because they were afraid of her dying, but in an act of brutal, terrifying will, Jacki had told them to pour it out and to smash the hypos. Her voice

169

had been so desperate and scary that Joanie had obeyed without a pause and had even taken the remains to a public garbage
can miles away just to be sure. Jacki regretted asking them even
before she said it, but there seemed to be two Jackis now. The
old one had lived for the drug, happily offering herself to
Thomas' services for the sweet metallic kiss of the needle. But,
it seemed, a new Jacki had been born in that moment of clarity
upon waking in the back seat of Joanie's car, thinking she was
dying and remembering how it all began. The battle was on.
The new Jacki was fighting tooth and nail to keep herself alive.

Davis, sweet, tender Davis, stood shyly at the door, waiting
to see if Jacki really didn't need anything more.

—It's okay, Davis. Come on in.

—I just wanted to tell you. Joanie stopped by your house
to check on things, and there were flowers on the doorstep
for you.

—Flowers? From who?

Davis licked her lips once and averted her eyes.

—I think you might be in some danger.

—Thomas.

—Yes. I only tell you because if he comes looking, we
might have to set you on the move. I think you're safe here
for now, but he knows things, Mr Banyon does. He finds
things out.

—Yes, Davis. I know. I don't want to put you at risk.

—Don't worry about me. You just concentrate on getting
well, but I wanted you to know that he's noticed you're gone.

—I bring in a lot of money for him.

—Used to.

—Beg pardon?

—You *used to* bring in a lot of money for him.

Davis' smile was small but heartfelt.

170   —Thanks, Davis. I hope that's true. I really do.

43. Max Has The Same Conversation.

—You know I'm grateful for all the things you've done for me.

—Oh, shit, it's a 'no', isn't it?

—Good God, Cora, don't I even get a preamble?

—Is there any real point to one?

—Yes. I want you to know I'm not a complete ingrate.

—I already know that, Max. It's in every bit of work you've ever done for me. You've been an invaluable friend and advisor. I'd have to be a monster to just forget all that at the first sign of disappointment.

—So you're really not surprised then?

—In a way. I was hoping it wouldn't be true, but I can't say that I honestly didn't expect it, especially after our conversation on Thursday.

—I am truly sorry to be doing this to you at the last minute.

—Better late than never, and looked at objectively, it's not even something you're rightfully doing to me. Ideally, you were running for Mayor and I was helping. In that case, I don't have any right to expect consideration.

—But we both know that's not true.

—To an extent. And I am disappointed, but I want to be clear on this. My disappointment is that I think Hennington is losing out on a great Mayor. I think you would have been terrific at the job. I think the city would have loved you, and I think you would have loved them back. Any other personal disappointment is pure hubris.

—Come on, Cora. This is all very reserved for you. I'd actually feel better if you yelled at me for a bit.

—What? And tell you that you dropping out is a huge

pain in my ass? It is. There's a part of me that wants to box your ears. But I'm not your mother, and even if I were, well, this is just one of those things that happens. Life deals you something, you gotta play it.

—Yeah, I guess so.

—Oh, shit, Max, are you sure this is what you want to do?

—What happened to playing with what you're dealt?

—It's a metaphor and a stupid one. An opportunity like this doesn't come along twice in a lifetime.

—I'm not turning away lightly, Cora. I really feel like it's the right thing for me, the right thing for Talon, the right thing for us to have a good life together.

—Do you know what you want to do instead?

—I've got some ideas. I've got a law degree that I've never used. I could do some good with it. Maybe formalize a job protecting The Crash, like when we handled the wheat blight.

—All well and good, but nobility doesn't always pay the bills.

—Neither does being Assistant Mayor, and there's more to life than money anyway, which you know.

—But you've got your daughter to think of as well.

—Of course there are questions, but I'm still convinced it's the right decision.

—Are you sure?

—Sure enough.

—Sure enough doesn't cut it. Are you sure?

—I'm sure.

—Then hell, that's all you really need. That and the bravery to go through with it.

—Yes, I guess so. I just need the flesh to agree with the spirit.

172   —I wish you luck then.

—I'd like to keep working here until I find another place, or at least until the next election.

—Of course, of course. Bloody *hell*, I'm going to miss the future you would have brought.

—*Could* have brought. If I didn't want the job, who knows what sort of mayor I'd have been?

—You would have been great, Max. Trust me on that. Despite all your doubts. You would have been magnificent.

44. The Crash and The Injured Calf.

Something was wrong with the thin creature that followed them. He – for, alone among the thin creatures, he was recognized as having a sex; they had seen it, pitifully small as it was, on the rare occasions when he shed his outer skin – he had taken on a new smell, a scent so powerful it was impossible *not* to notice if he was anywhere around. He had always been fragrant, especially to the sensitive noses of the herd, some of whom occasionally pushed him lightly to one side when he was getting in the way of their grazing. It was difficult to enjoy eating flanked by odors of old sweat, festering sores, and who knew what else. Lately though, this new, horrible, sour smell had found its way into the mix, strong enough for some of the herdmembers to react violently to it, snorting loudly at the thin creature to drive him back.

Nothing like this had ever happened before. He was a fixture of the herd and that was all, something to be ignored most of the time. She couldn't recall another period when the animals had so actively avoided him. Most of the time, they didn't even notice he was there. She usually kept an eye on him in a general way, but his new smell kept pushing in at the edges. Moreover, it didn't seem to be a normal sort of   173 smell at all. Bad scents inhabited the world just like good ones. They provided information. Eat this, don't eat that. That was all. The thin creature's smell, on the other hand, seemed purely aggressive, as if it only existed to offend. It was unnatural and, in some respects, unsettling, too.

She suspected he was sick, and whatever it was that caused the smell was also beginning to affect his behavior. This morning, for the first time in the twenty-five seasons she had been alive, he had tried to climb on her back. She was grazing quietly, twisting her ears to the buzz of the heat, when her nose suddenly filled with the new smell and something touched her side. Instinctively, she whirled her massive body away, but as lightly as possible. She knew he was no threat and took care not to hurt him. He landed on the ground with an oomph and sat looking at her, panting wildly. He gurgled out a strangled sound, slowly pulled himself up, and walked towards her again. She moved to face him, keeping her horn between them and allowing herself a better look.

(—*I'll be damned. Did you see that?*

—*What?*

—*That smelly sod who follows The Crash just tried to climb up on one and it threw him off.*

—*And?*

—*No 'and', just, I'd never seen that before.*

—*Do you know how hot it's supposed to get today?*

—*Well, yeah*—

—*Then quit jabbering about animals and get back to work. The roof's not going to fix itself.*

—*I was just*—

—*Shut it and work.*

—*Yes, sir.*)

The smell made her want to back away as quickly as possible, but as leader she needed to always be alert to the unprecedented, which this surely was. He continued his approach, waving his forelegs and emitting short, odd sounds. The stench was unbearable, and she instinctively began to step back. But no, she should not be the one who relented. This thin creature should recognize her greater size. He needed to be made to understand what his place was. He stepped forward and placed a hand on her horn. Holding her breath, she jerked her head sideways sharply, flinging his hand away and tapping him in the face. He fell backwards once again, and once again rose to his feet and stepped towards her.

She reared up her weight and made a short charge forward, bumping him full on with the flatter front of her horn. The force of the impact knocked him off his feet. He flew backwards, hitting the grass with a surprisingly hard thud. She watched him as he landed. For a full moment, he lay there, looking back up at her, in itself unusual since he never seemed to be looking directly at anything. He slowly drew himself back to his feet, holding his side with his foreleg. He seemed to take the hint and moved away, staring at her.

For the rest of the day, he kept his distance, until finally, as dusk was falling, he recovered a little, moving back into his usual muttering stance just beyond the edges of the herd. He sat leaning against a rock near where the field ended, making sounds to himself and touching his side over and over again. She walked slowly across the darkening grass towards where he sat, trying to see . . . what? There was no communicating with the thin creatures. Their calls were incomprehensible, and on the whole, they were intolerably frantic, loud, and bad-smelling. She had no idea how to gauge an injury on such a thing, yet still she walked, keeping her distance so as not to frighten him.

He didn't look up at her, and she took that as a good sign. He seemed to be back to what was for him normal behavior.

She didn't sense fear on him. He rocked a little back and forth, eating a handful of berries he must have picked somewhere. He was never calm, but this at least seemed a return to the usual. The offensive scent lingered, though. It was, perhaps, even stronger than before. She stood there, in the increasing shadows, watching him ignore her. Finally, she moved back to the rest of the herd, but not without the occasional glance backwards before losing sight of him in the falling night.

45. Class Reunion.

The intercom buzzed.

—Yes, Angie?

—Reception says that a Jon Noth is here to see you.

—He is, is he? What does he say he wants?

—An audience with you.

—Of course he does. It has to happen sooner or later, I guess. Tell Lisa to send him on up.

Cora stuck a pen in her mouth and nibbled on the end. There was no reason to feel threatened at all. It was a little unsettling, but then again, that was probably what he wanted. So she wouldn't be unsettled. There. He wouldn't achieve what he obviously wanted by this mysterious re-emergence. She wouldn't squirm, not for anyone, but especially not for Jon Noth. And yet why all this energy expended convincing herself?

Three knocks signaled Angie's entrance. She held the door open and, heavens above, Jon Noth walked past her into Cora's office. Older certainly, but also trimmer, shapelier, handsome still and moving like liquid. Her memory corrected for the spectacled dilettante he once was into the smooth older man he had clearly become. My, this was even odder than she had expected.

—Cora.

—Shit Almighty, if it isn't Jon Noth.

She stood and accepted a handshake and a kiss on the cheek over her desk.

—Have a seat. You're looking well.

—Thank you, and yourself, Mayor. Mayor Cora Larsson.

—So it would seem.

—How exactly did *that* happen?

—Somehow I just got all these votes. Interesting what life serves up, isn't it?

—I would agree one hundred per cent.

—So what brings you out of the past, Jon? To what do I owe the pleasure of this surprise?

—I stopped by here last week. Did you get the message?

—I did indeed. Also that you hadn't left a number or address if I wanted to contact you. It would seem that you wanted to just announce your presence and leave it ringing like a struck bell.

—It *was* rather power hungry of me, wasn't it?

—Not in any way that was surprising. In fact, typically annoying, I would say.

—You wound me, Cora. Sparring so quickly, are we?

—What *is* it about that smile that I can't trust? Oh, yes, I remember. History and precedent.

—That was a long time ago.

—A very, very long time, but unless you've changed even more than you appear, I don't imagine a trip down memory lane is why you wanted to see me.

—Actually, in a sense, that's exactly why. I wanted to see if you're the same Cora Trygvesdottir I knew forty years ago.

—Then I imagine you're disappointed. I'm forty years older and named Cora Larsson.

—I'm not disappointed in the least. True, you're a bit pricklier than that young bright girl in the desert, but that only somehow adds to your incandescent beauty. Don't roll your eyes, Cora. I'm speaking the truth.

—What truth? To whom?

—To you, of course. It *is* good to see you looking as beautiful and appealing as ever.

—Once again, Jon. I'm married. Happily. Of course you remember Albert Larsson, don't you? Shocking of you to have forgotten.

—Ah, the icicle spear of sarcasm. Of course, I haven't forgotten. I still haven't managed to explain it to myself after all these years.

—What? That I chose him over you?

—Now you're being deliberately cruel.

—And you've not answered my question at all. Every word out of your mouth so far has been smug and self-serving. I can safely say that you haven't changed a bit since college.

—Oh, but I have. More than you can possibly know. I'm a different man now, my love.

—How so?

—I've been through many things these past years. I've traveled, around the planet even, and you know how difficult that is. I've seen things with these eyes that would cause your heart to stop. I've changed, my darling Cora.

—You've been on a forty-year odyssey, and you've found yourself. How cute.

—I wouldn't have put it quite so deprecatingly, but more or less, yes.

178 —And now you've returned to Hennington for what?

Some kind of peace offering? What is it that you want to tell me, Jon? Why are you here?

—So admirable of you to cut right to the point. So invigorating and fresh. It's something I've always loved about you.

—You're avoiding the question. Why are you here?

—I've come to take you back, my love.

—Take me back.

—Take you back, yes, precious one.

—Take me back where?

—With me. Into my life. I'm ready for you now, my darling.

—Stop calling me that and have you lost your mind? 'Take me back'. There are so many things wrong with that, I don't know where to begin. I'm not bounty that can be taken, and what on earth makes you think I'd ever want to go? And go where? I'm not and have never been a prize in a contest. Really, Jon, you can't possibly have nursed a grudge for this long against Albert.

—True, he has proven a worthier opponent than I thought at first, but are you really satisfied with him? Are you honestly and truly in your heart of hearts a happy woman with that man? He's not worthy of you. Entirely too frivolous.

—You have the gall to walk into my office after forty years—

—Thirty-six, if we're exact.

—Shut up. You walk in here and think that you have the right to attack me and the man that I love, and let's be unambiguous about this, I adore Albert with my heart, soul, and body, you imagine that I would willingly sit here and listen to this? You're delusional, Jon, and that really proves that you haven't changed one bit. I'm dumbfounded.

—I expected you to be a bit surprised, but I don't doubt

you'll come around soon enough. I've come back for you, Cora. Here I am. For you.

—You've lost the plot in a fairly spectacular way, Jon.

—On the contrary. I've finally found it.

—Amazing. You amaze me. Do you know what I'm going to do tonight? I'm going to go home to my beloved husband, and after he greets me with his usual kiss and after we've settled down to the nice dinner that he's prepared for me, I'm going to tell him that you came into my office today and I'm going to tell him what you said. And do you know what we'll do then, Jon? Do you know? We're going to laugh. We're going to laugh at your presumption and ego and effrontery and audacity. We're going to laugh at the idea of a grown man nursing a college-age grudge for four decades, *well* past what any normal person would consider healthy. We're going to laugh at someone who would think he has some primogeniture on not only my time, but somehow on my affections as well. Not just my affections, it seems, my entire bloody life. We're going to laugh, Jon. We're going to laugh. At you.

—You don't even know how unhappy you are. Right now, right at this moment, you're in misery.

—Out. Now. Leave like a gentleman, or I *will* have you thrown out.

—I didn't expect you to understand right away.

—Well, thank heavens for that. Get out. The next action I take will be a call to security.

—Don't worry, I'm leaving, but you haven't seen the last of me.

—I think you just might be wrong there, Jon.

—We shall see, Cora. We shall see.

46. He *What?*

Thomas heard it from Hennington Hills' bartender Tracy Jem-Ho, once again proving herself as a source of reliable information.

—You're kidding.

—Nope. 'Personal reasons' and none of them can figure out exactly what the hell that means.

—I'll bet. Well, I'll be goddamned. I don't believe it.

—Believe it. Apparently, your father is having fits.

—I don't think my father has ever had a fit. I'll bet he's at work every waking moment, though. My God.

—Butterfield said the assumption is they had some sort of falling out, and the rest of the Committee—

—Board.

—Board, whatever, the rest of them are sitting tight, hoping it clears itself up.

—What else did Butterfield say?

—Not much. I had the ball in his mouth most of the time.

—What about during foreplay?

—Now who's got to be kidding?

—What about pillow talk?

—He's a sleeper. He shoots, he snores.

Thomas drained his cocktail, his third so far.

—So that was all you were able to get?

—Well, that and your father says he's looking for someone new to take Luther's place.

—Don't get your hopes up, Tracy. He most assuredly doesn't mean me.

—Why not?

—I was sent to Hennington Hills as banishment for being an incorrigible youth.

181

—Precisely, and you've proven yourself an effective leader and a great businessman.

—I could do with a little less ass-kissing, but thank you. My father might secretly like what I've turned this place into, it used to be a money pit, you know, but he could never publicly approve. And the Board would never have me.

—Why not? You're well respected.

—I'm well *known*. The respect of the Banyon Enterprises Board of Trustees is another thing altogether.

—But half of them are regular clips. I see three of them myself.

—Precisely. Would you want your entertainment-provider to be your boss?

—There are probably a hundred reasons why I shouldn't answer that question.

—But you see my point.

—You could at least *try* your father.

—And say what? 'Heard you were looking for a spare son? How about trying an old favorite?' Ain't gonna happen. Hey, did Butterfield say anything about a third party being involved?

—What? Peter Wickham? Doubtful. Too nice a guy to cause trouble, unless the old man flipped out over him and Luther.

—Not Peter. Another businessman, say.

—No. Why? What do you know?

—Just a new guy in town that I had a meeting with, hints that he's wealthy as the dickens.

—When do I get to meet him?

—You don't. He's not interested in joining up.

—That's odd.

—Exceedingly so. See what you can find out about him, a
182 mystery man from the Fifty Shores called Jon Noth. Says he's

an old friend of the Mayor's but they had some falling out.

—Sounds boring.

—Rich is never boring.

—Fine, I'll see what I can do.

Thomas took another drink.

—Tracy.

—Yeah?

—Do you like your job?

—Someone's getting a little drunk.

—Just answer the question.

—I'm one of the ones who doesn't mind, remember? Stephanie's going to the best prep school in this half of the country because of this job.

—That's what I thought. Give me another one of these.

—See what I mean about being a little drunk?

Tracy poured him another.

—Do you ask because Jacki Strell is still missing?

—You should quit trying to become my confidante, Tracy. It's not a good idea. For either one of us.

—Can't help it. Bartending tool of the trade.

—But this one could get you killed.

—Oh, big, big talk from a big, big boy. I know how to take care of myself.

—I'm sure you do. I've seen you with that whip.

—Practice makes perfect. Still no word on Jacki though?

—Not unless you've heard something.

—Nada. No one here knows anything?

—Not that I've been able to find out. Paul Wadstone says there's no clue at her place either.

—You sent that thug snooping?

—I couldn't very well call the police, could I? He said that some clothes had been packed, but I've had the house under constant surveillance since the day she called in sick. Nothing.   183

—Foul play? A clip that got a little too attached?

—I've been through every single one of her clips. Councilman Wiggins was her last one, and he says he left her that last night sleeping.

—Do you believe him?

—No reason not to. He hasn't changed his story under various pressures. Plus, she called here three times after that to report in sick, and no one thought anything strange.

—Did you ever talk to her yourself?

—No, and that's what smells funny.

—I thought she'd at least come in for some hits.

—You'd think so, wouldn't you?

—Any ideas?

—None. She doesn't have any *reason* to hide.

—Doesn't she?

—She was happy here.

—Whatever you say, Thomas.

—She *was*. Anyway, it doesn't matter. If she's hiding somewhere, I'll find her. I can guarantee you that much. She's too valuable to this company to just leave without even giving a reason.

Thomas patted his pockets for a cigarillo. When he found one, Tracy lit it for him. Without asking, she refilled his glass.

—Are you going to try to sweet-talk her back?

—I'm not going to try anything. I'm concerned about her wellbeing is all. She could be hurt or in trouble. I want to save her from all that.

—Maybe she doesn't see it that way.

—I can make her see it that way. She's part of our family now. She'll come back.

—You sound so sure.

—I am. We haven't seen the last of Jacki Strell. She's out there somewhere, waiting to be rescued. Oh, and Tracy?

—Yes, boss?

He winked at her.

—I'm not as drunk as you think.

47. In Which Much News Is Confirmed.

—Cora, there you are. Is it correct, what I'm reading in the papers?

—Depends on which papers, Archie.

—That Max has dropped out of the race?

—I wasn't going to officially announce it until tonight, but—

—This is now a fundraising dinner without a candidate?

—In a word? Yes.

—How in the hell did *this* happen?

—He dropped out. That's all there is to it.

—And this is the first I've heard of it?

—You've been impossible to get a hold of lately. I finally just assumed you weren't returning my calls on purpose.

—Oh. Well. I've been busy.

—So it would seem. Is it true what *I've* heard?

—What?

—That Luther's left Banyon Enterprises?

—Albert! Thank God! Please say you brought drinks.

—Do you honestly think I'd arrive without them?

—Cora tells me that we're now in a horse race with no horses.

—Looks that way.

—And Archie was just about to confirm or deny the rumors about Luther Pickett.

—That he left?

—Bloody hell, does everyone know? 185

—So it's true?

—Yes, unfortunately, but how did everyone find out?

—How did the papers find out about Max? They just do. The world has ears.

—Fuck the world and its ears.

Albert raised his glass.

—I'll take that as a toast.

—What are you going to do, Archie?

—I'll live. The more important thing is what are *you* going to do about this campaign?

—You want an honest answer?

—No, but let's hear it.

—Hell if I know. We've got just under four months until the election and not a single legitimate candidate. The ballot's going to have weirdos and felons and 'None of the above', and 'None of the above' is going to win.

—What would happen then?

—I'd stay Mayor until we had a special election. Somebody serious would have to run eventually. The problem is who. I was hoping to have someone to announce tonight, but so far nothing.

—What about the City Council?

—Marian, Jim and Marcus are all retiring next year and aren't interested. Wiggins may be but his wife's divorcing him and that's going to bring up all sorts of dirty laundry. David barely won his seat last time, and his popularity's only gotten worse since the DUI. And those are the most credible of the lot.

—Johnson?

—No one's heard of him.

—That could change.

—Yes, for the worse when they do.

—Henley?

—Lesbian and too liberal. Not in our lifetimes.

—Mornington?

—Incompetent.

—Incompetent good or incompetent bad?

—He's called me 'Clara' for the past six years.

—What about Rushford?

—Are you kidding? The woman's so right-wing even her staff don't turn their backs to her.

—Not one potential candidate on the entire City Council? That's disgraceful.

—Tell me about it.

—You could run, Albert.

—Oh, I think I'd rather swallow my own vomit, thank you.

Archie stirred his champagne with a slightly trembling yet clearly annoyed finger.

—Well, *shit*, Cora. What are we going to do?

—Before I heard the news, I was actually thinking of approaching Luther Pickett.

—He'll certainly have the free time.

—Ouch, Archie. What happened?

—I don't want to talk about it.

—When you do—

—So why are all these people here if we've got no candidate?

—I was going to make a speech about the current situation. Obviously they want to hear it or they wouldn't have shown up after the article in the paper today.

—You don't expect to get a candidate from this group, do you?

—I shudder to think. Most of these people see being Mayor as a step *down*.

Thank you all for coming tonight. I want to especially thank Louis and Betsy Prompter for graciously opening their lovely home. Let's give Louis and Betsy a hand, shall we? Great. I might as well get right to the question on all your minds. You've all probably read in today's *Times* that Max Latham has dropped out of the Mayoral race. I can confirm, to my regret, that it's true. It was for the simple and honorable reason that he didn't feel he could be both an effective Mayor and an effective single parent. I tried to persuade him otherwise, but he stuck to his convictions and you have to admire him for that. He has elected to take up a new position in City Government, that of Crash Advocate-General which, pending City Council approval, you'll all be hearing more about very soon. But this does pose an interesting dilemma. With Max out of the race, we are currently lacking a credible, talented candidate for Mayor of Hennington. Let me take this opportunity to assure you, my friends and past supporters, that we will not be in this position for long. A search is underway and we have some very tantalizing possibilities. So I urge you to keep the faith and keep your money at the ready. Ha ha. As for tonight, please enjoy the food and entertainment and the hospitality of our gracious hosts. And as they say on TV, stay tuned.

Albert held a glass in each hand and smiled at her.

—Well, that was . . . perplexing.

—I've never needed a hard drink more in my entire life.

—Way ahead of you.

—I knew there was a reason I loved you. I used 'gracious' twice, didn't I? Damn.

—So 'tantalizing possibilities' was pretty much a complete lie.

—Think anyone noticed? Where'd Archie go?

—Home, I guess.

—And you let him go?

—You can't force an octogenarian to do anything. There was nothing for him to do here, so he left.

—Without even saying goodbye? I wanted to talk to him about Luther.

—I don't think he was in a talking mood.

—What do you suppose happened there?

—Hard to say. From what I gather, Luther Pickett has always been something of a closed book.

—But Archie thought he was the sun and moon, everything that Thomas never turned out to be.

—Thomas is as astute a businessman as his father.

—Except his father probably won't end up in jail—

—Good evening, Cora. Albert.

—Oh, shit.

—It's Jon Noth, isn't it? Well, I'll be damned. Come to make a nuisance of himself in the flesh.

—A gentleman as always, Albert. You've never been able to open your mouth without betraying how common you are.

—'Common'? Does anyone even *say* 'common' anymore? Cora intervened.

—You're not welcome here, Jon. You shouldn't have even been allowed in.

—Fortunately, they must have been looking for some sort of lunatic to breach security, which of course allowed me to slip in quite unnoticed. You do me a discredit by barring access, Cora. I come as a friend and admirer.

—If you don't leave this instant, Jon, I will have you escorted out as roughly as is legal.

—Are you sure Albert wouldn't want to do the honors himself?

—I've just had a manicure, little man, and wouldn't want to scuff a nail flicking off a flea.

—Time's up, Jon. Security!

—Stop it, Cora. I'll leave peacefully, I just wanted to—

—I don't care what you wanted. I won't listen to a single further word.

—All I wanted to say was—

—Yes, ma'am?

—This man is here without an invitation. Please escort him from the premises.

—Cora—

—Get him out of here now.

Albert raised his glass again.

—Goodbye, Jon! Lovely seeing you again.

—How can you . . . Ah!

—I'm dreadfully sorry everyone. Someone had a little too much to drink it seems. Ha ha ha ha ha. You know how unfortunate and embarrassing a little misplaced rowdiness can be. Go back to your conversations. Enjoy your evening.

She turned back to Albert.

—We're leaving here at the first polite opportunity.

—Just what I was going to suggest.

—What could he possibly have wanted to say?

—Probably something we're better off not hearing.

48. Jarvis' Sermon About the Brandon Beach Massacre.

I was not yet born when Brandon Beach happened. Even our most senior churchmembers wouldn't have been more than children, but we've all heard the story through our grand-parents. We've read the books. We've had the school lessons.

It's a tragic moment in Hennington history that we all, by rightful necessity, have learned about so that we may be ever watchful not to repeat the ugliness of the past. Brandon Beach is especially painful for the many, many Rumour members of our church. It is, as we all know, a lesson about racism, about the lengths people will go to out of fear, about mob mentality. But the lesson I draw for you today about Brandon Beach, a lesson that has been on my mind for some weeks now, is one for us all, Rumour and non-Rumour alike. It is the lesson of the abuse of the Sacraments.

You all know the story. The economy of the world, and of Hennington itself, had finally blossomed twenty years after Pistolet's death, and the sun was beginning to shine again on all of our grandparents and great-grandparents as they went about reassembling the world. The tooth-and-nail fight for survival had finally seemed to ebb, and society had seemed to reform. But then a wheat famine struck the Rumour Land. Hennington tried to help as much as it could, but the times were merely good, not exceptional. Things took a dark turn. Good people who could still remember the brutal rationing of the post-Pistolet years began to hoard food in collectives. Whole neighborhoods and communities began to set up private commissaries. A black market reappeared, trafficking in basic staples and foodstuffs.

We know now, of course, that this was an over-reaction, that food stores would turn out to be sufficient, but lest we feel too condescending to our forebears, understand that the world then was a shaky, unstable place. We have ninety years of history behind us. That's not a lot. Remember, though, that they had merely twenty years and many of them had managed to survive in that impossible time before the start of the Recent Histories, under the thumb of Pistolet's madness. We can and should forgive them if they acted too hastily   191 in the face of what they thought was their world collapsing all over again.

What is harder to understand, yet still perhaps no less important to forgive, is the breakdown in the relations between Rumour and non-Rumour. What had for two decades been a full-fledged partnership to put life back in order, disintegrated virtually overnight because of the wheat famine. When starving Rumours moved north in large numbers to join families already settled in Hennington, resentments, as they have a way of doing, began to form.

Fanning those resentments was, of all people, a Bondulay minister, a Rumour. Merrill Eycham.

Sunday after Sunday after Sunday, Merrill Eycham railed against the influx of people from the Rumour Land. Moreover, there are tapes existent of his appearances on public service television shows, complaining about the drain on present-day resources, selling the idea that the immigrants would forever damage the fragile growth that Hennington had managed to achieve. His message was typical demagoguery, a man seeking to cement his own power across the backs of others, in this specific instance conjuring up the supposed 'difference' of the Rumours who were immigrating, making veiled references to skin color and so on. The only surprise here is that the people of the day allowed such a man power in the media. You would have thought the fear of a new Pistolet would have caused the people of Hennington to turn a deaf ear towards him. But again, I remind you that these were fragile times that seemed to be taking a turn for the worse, and in difficult hours finding someone to blame can be a dark comfort.

There is of course the matter of Eycham being Rumour himself. History has often wondered why he quote-unquote 'turned against his own people', especially by making the matter one of race against race. I do not know the answer to this. Perhaps he considered himself different from the immigrating Rumours because he had been born in Hennington, perhaps it was a cynical and shrewd use of his own race to stoke the fires of racism. If a Rumour is saying awful things about other Rumours, then like-minded non-Rumours could feel okay about agreeing without having to run counter to the unpleasantness they felt towards overt racism.

I do not know Eycham's justification, but I do know his motivation. I've read his sermons.

And in a time of sunlight, a dark wind will encroach,
    obscuring the truth,
And in the time of dark wind, a light wind will encroach,
    revealing the truth.

The Book of Ultimates, Chapter 19, Verses 43 and 44. The last words in our Sacraments. We've all heard these words before. We as a church have always touched lightly on the Book of Ultimates, primarily because it is so open to interpretation. We do this to avoid division and schism among our own congregations. In this, we have been successful. I know personally this is the first sermon that I have preached since seminary that has focused on the Ultimates, a span of over twenty-five years. You all know this. It is accepted Bondulay doctrine.

But I put it to you today, my beloved brothers and sisters, that perhaps we have been mistaken in skimming over the Ultimates. Not for the reasons you might think, not to look for prophecy, but to learn the lesson of *misunderstood* prophecy. I put it to you that Merrill Eycham started his crusade not just because he was power-hungry, not just because he coveted the spotlight, but also because he interpreted these   193 verses in such a way that inflamed the fears of an already worried community, that tragically led to violence and to the one hundred and seventy-nine deaths at Brandon Beach.

Picture it if you can. The *Dulcinea*, a fishing boat, one of those big ones, four or five stories tall, more than two hundred meters from stem to stern. They had been at sea for more than four months, pulling in the huge summer catch, storing it in the refrigerated decks below, a catch that normally would have been exported but which was intended that year to help alleviate the famine in the Rumour Land. See in your mind's eye an enormous ship, packed to the rafters with food intended to help the hungry and filled with fishermen who hadn't set foot on land for four full months. Now picture if you can their despair when one of the ship's engines fails and the ship has to limp into Hennington Harbor for repairs so it can make the now-relatively-short ocean journey southward to where hungry families await. Now imagine how that desperation multiplies when the other engine fails under the strain and they realize that the *Dulcinea* won't even make it to the port inside the harbor and instead strands itself irrevocably on Brandon Beach where, in one of history's horrible coincidences, the Reverend Merrill Eycham just happens to be holding a tent revival on a sweltering summer's day.

Now imagine yourself in that tent. Imagine sitting in a crowd of people overheated on both humidity and rhetoric. The *Dulcinea* beached itself at around three in the afternoon. The revival meeting had begun at seven that morning. Imagine having listened to Merrill Eycham rant about the prophecy of the dark wind for eight hours. Imagine hearing doom foretold with salvation only coming later from an unnamed 'light wind'. Imagine the sweat making your church clothes stick to the sides of your body, even here on the seashore where the sea breezes seem to have died. Imagine turning your head at the great crashing sound of the *Dulcinea* hull plowing its way into the clay seabed, slamming great walls of mud out of the ground before coming to rest with a lurch up on dry sand itself. Now imagine seeing the dark tan skin of the Rumour fishermen scrambling around on deck, frantically trying to minimize the damage and do what they can to save the catch if at all possible. And now in this moment, you think to yourself, it's the dark wind. And at the same time, your neighbor thinks it and his neighbor thinks it and his and his and so on and so on until it reaches the pulpit where Merrill Eycham stands and he says the words out loud: 'It's the dark wind'. And as if by silent command you stand. And you reach for something heavy to carry, your chair, a hymnal, even the Sacraments.

There were one hundred and twenty-one fishermen on the *Dulcinea*. There were more than one thousand churchgoers in that oven of a revival tent. History reports to us that thirty-eight fishermen were bludgeoned to death right there on the beach, eleven were forcibly drowned, and the remaining seventy-two were burned alive when the wreck of the *Dulcinea* was set afire by the mob. Fifty-eight revivalists were also killed; at first it was thought by fishermen fighting back, but that seems to have happened in only eight or nine instances. The fishermen were overwhelmed so quickly that they barely had time to fight at all. No, the bulk of the revivalist deaths were caused by other revivalists, settling old scores perhaps, getting caught up in the heat of the moment. There are even reports of revivalists being killed when trying to shield some of the fishermen from attack. So there were brief flashes of humanity even amidst that crowd, but that humanity was rubbed out along with the fishermen.

Blame the massacre on the economic climate of the day. Eycham's light sentence afterwards would seem to be proof 195 enough of that. Blame it on the shakiness of society itself at the time. Blame it on a generation not yet quite removed from the purges and violence of Pistolet's reign. Blame it on simple fear that the life they had built was going to shimmer away. Blame it on a deep-seated, inflamed racism. Blame it on the heat of that sweltering afternoon.

Perhaps it was all of these things. Certainly they each played a part. But the blame for those deaths, along with those of countless others who needlessly starved because the shipment never reached them, the *real* blame, I think can be rested squarely on the shoulders of Merrill Eycham who believed he was following the final words of the Sacraments, who built himself up to such a degree that he thought he was the vessel meant to fulfill a vague, obfuscatory prophecy, who ventured where he should not have and brought about the deaths of one hundred and seventy-nine people.

I offer no further comment on this cautionary tale except the obvious. There are parts of the Sacraments that are vague, sometimes impenetrable, as here, but this was done, I believe, so that they could be all things to all people who seek Our Lord. Our Lord is a loving Lord who has given us the Sacraments as a way of finding Him, as a path to His never-ending love, but this is not a gift given without attendant responsibility. Any use of the Sacraments that does not further this purpose of bringing ourselves closer to Our Lord is an abuse of His Gift to us. We must be ever-watchful that we do not twist the Word of Our Lord into what it is not, into what we would rather hear, into anything that takes power away from the Sacraments and places it into the hands of a man. We have seen the potential for disaster. If we keep our eyes open, it is my hope that we will be able to keep it from ever happening again. This is my hope and my prayer.

49. An Unexpected Intransigence.

As difficult as it had been to have Archie tell him not to come back to his office, Luther had held out hope that their relationship was not completely severed, but as time passed, he kept not having the courage to visit, not having the strength to face Archie's fury and hurt. Of course, the longer it took, the harder it got. Somehow, two weeks went by, then three, the days and nights piling weight onto his immobility. On an occasion or two, he had called Archie but had only gotten machines or Jules, who was surprisingly sympathetic but similarly unable to get Archie to the phone. Luther leapt every time his own rang, but it was only ever Peter.

Peter. Lovely, lovely Peter. It was just possible that Peter was the only reason he was still alive. Certainly, the physical contact they shared was enough, once in a while, to remind him that he wasn't alone, and Peter fed him and clothed him like a convalescent child, which in a sense was exactly right. All of the burdens that were supposed to have been lifted by making this decision had instead gained in gravity. Luther was wrong, totally, utterly, completely, absolutely wrong to think that he had a right to do this to Archie, and the painfully obvious results bore this out. Instead of solving his problem and giving himself a life filled with options and possibilities, he had destroyed his past in one fell swoop and left himself unable to enjoy or even greet his future.

Peter, naturally, disagreed.

—This is only a challenge. That's all, nothing more. A big challenge, yes, but I know you. You can face it.

—You don't know me, Peter.

—I learn more about you every day.

—I've ruined everything.

—If everything was ruined, I wouldn't be here. I love you. I know you don't quite believe me, but if we ever had a chance, here it is.

The thing was, despite wanting to do so quite badly, Luther *couldn't* believe him. He loved Peter, it was true, there was a small part of him that rejoiced at Peter's presence, but that too was sullied and blackened by his destruction of Archie. Even taking the smallest joy from Peter seemed almost obscenely selfish. They had sex, of course, but Luther could barely bring himself to come and was often impotent. Some nights, he would have Peter fuck him and not even get an erection, doing it more for the pain at the beginning than for any pleasure that might come later. Not surprisingly, Peter caught on, and now he just held Luther when he couldn't sleep, which by now had become every night.

Finally, late into one evening, Peter wore him down.

—You can't go on like this. Some change has to be made or you'll die.

—What if I want to die?

—You can't talk like that either. This is just a period of time. It will pass, and you'll feel better. But you have to do something about it.

—I can't face him now. It's been too long.

—That's not a choice you can make. You have to see him. You can't move on without a resolution one way or the other.

—Maybe.

Which all eventually led to here, now, a shaved and showered Luther standing like a penitent before Jules' desk and sweating waterfalls into a clean shirt that Peter had pressed.

—Land o' Goshen, look who's here.

—I need to see Archie.

—I think that's a terrific idea, but I'm not sure he'll agree.

—Could you tell him I'm here, please?

—Yes, and for all of our sakes, I hope it goes well.

Jules rang Archie in his office. Thomas heard Archie's voice crackle over the speaker.

—Yes?

—Mr Banyon?

—What is it, Jules?

—Um—

—Spit it out, I haven't got all day.

—Luther's here to see you.

—Luther.

—Yes, sir, shall I send him in?

The weeks, for Archie, had been nearly as bad. He told the Board Luther had departed for 'personal reasons' and then steadfastly refused to elaborate. There was no worry, he told them, he would merely stay on as Chairman for a bit longer until he could find a suitable replacement. He knew this didn't wash, the *Board* knew this didn't wash, but they also had never seen Archie so forcibly cheerful before, so terrifyingly *large*, a remarkable achievement from a man who had made a career out of largeness. They let the matter rest and privately speculated that the two men had had a falling out, one that, given Archie's hot temper and Luther's cool demeanor, had probably been a long time in coming and would work itself out sooner or later. Until then, they were resigned to curious watchfulness.

A work tempest then commenced wherein Archie demoted fourteen different people; researched, initiated, took over, dismantled and sold a small car dealership conglomerate at a 34 per cent profit; changed the investment strategy for Banyon Enterprises Pension Funds twice at a .015 per cent loss; switched the name of his line of salad dressings from Green Valley Gardens to The Delighted Palate, against the advice of his Marketing Department, all of whom he summarily fired; and started a foundation in memory of his mother to help provide sporting equipment to financially strapped local schools. He was in the office late every night and every day on weekends, avoiding a house that was suddenly oppressive. Sitting there on his own, he could do nothing but think about Luther, and he just wasn't ready to have any of that. God only knew when, but not yet.

He knew exactly why the whole situation bothered him: he had no idea what to do. Fate had reared back and walloped him before – the deaths of his wives and daughters; the casual cruelty of his son; the surprise adoption of Luther – but he had been able to take all those in his stride. The things you couldn't see coming were what made life life. For his wives and daughters, he had grieved. For Thomas, exile to the Country Club, where hopefully the damage he caused would be minimized by the smallness of his universe, a hope that hadn't quite panned out. For the adoption, delight at discovering an able, bright replacement for Thomas who could be groomed and loved like a normal son. But this decision of Luther's, this wasn't fate, this was caprice. This was selfishness and misjudgment and egotism.

Or was it? Was it just willful blindness on his own part to ignore in Luther what he hadn't wanted to see, to choose to believe in the future that would suit Archie best? Which was it? Was Archie wrong or was Luther? What was the right course of action? Should he try to bring Luther back, or should he cut him off completely? What was he supposed to do? What was the answer? He had no idea, and it scared the daylights out of him. Archie's waking hours were spent in alternating anger and grief, and he couldn't foresee an end to the cycle. He tossed and turned, turned and tossed, giving up sleep entirely in his inability to gather even the faintest notion of the next move. He began to wonder whether he was finally too old to handle it all. Which confusion made him give the wrong answer, the answer that would haunt him until the very end of his days, the answer that would make him long for the finish to come even sooner than it eventually did.

—I told him I don't want to see him.

—Don't you think it's time, sir?

—I'll be the judge of that, Jules. No, it's not time. Not now. Maybe not ever.

Jules looked at Luther. Luther could hear every word, including the last ones he ever heard Archie Banyon say.

—Tell him to go away. He's not welcome here.

50. A Tentatively Happy Bleakness.

It was a simple split, really, almost laughable if the stakes weren't so high. One Jacki, the new one, the seemingly (fingers crossed) stronger one, wanted to quit Forum, wanted to leave the clutches of Thomas and the whole impossibly degrading entertainment industry. The other Jacki wanted things back just the way they were, a thoroughly unpersuasive and obviously wrong argument, but this older Jacki was not without weapons, foremost among which were replays of the few positive seconds of Forum plus that old stand-by, hopelessness. The old Jacki knew she would never get out of this alive, so why not just give up, go back to Thomas with sincere apologies, and get what enjoyment there was (and there *was* enjoyment, can't you remember?) out of the time she had left.

This was the Jacki that didn't want to take the bath. Fortunately, the odor of detoxification sweat was almost like an extra presence in the room, and the new Jacki reached in the tub to turn on the tap.

Davis tapped lightly on the door and leaned her head into the bathroom.

—Are you doing all right in here?

Jacki nodded slowly. She knew what sort of a sight she was presenting, naked on the toilet seat. She had transformed in a few short weeks into a line drawing of her former self. She had lost nearly fifty pounds, and Dr Ketcham had been forced to put her on intravenous liquids to keep her kidneys from failing. She was covered in bruises as her blood vessels, angry at the disappearance of Forum, burst furiously at the slightest touch. Her breasts were empty pouches, weakly lactating a foul-smelling yellowish ooze instead of the rich milk she had produced for almost her entire adult life. She had also started a near-constant menstruation and was wracked with crippling stomach cramps that at times prevented her from breathing until she was on the verge of suffocation. Just this morning she had noticed that her hair had begun to fall out in handfuls.

And yet when she nodded at Davis' question, she also managed a smile, meek but definitely present.

—That's good. That's so good. I'm so happy for you, Jacki.

Jacki nodded again.

—You're looking better.

At this lie, Jacki nearly laughed, but it turned into a cough. Davis stood at the door with a questioning look on her face.

—All right, I'll let you be. Give a knock if you need anything.

She was unbelievably grateful to Davis. She had to stay *somewhere*, and this was the most anonymous place she could think of, a place that might hold Thomas at bay for a good while, maybe even forever. That Davis, and Joanie, too, were putting themselves at such risk – for make no mistake, the risk was enormous – seemed inconceivable. Jacki had entertained the idea of the Rumour Underground, as both women were Rumour, but her questions were laughed off. Still, their willingness both puzzled and touched her. She only met Davis and Joanie rarely in the hallways at work. She knew them well enough to say hello, but that was about it, the very fact that protected her here. If *she* would never have expected to be taken in by more or less perfect strangers, then certainly Thomas wouldn't suspect them either. At least not for a while. She felt safe, that's what it was. For the first time in who knows how long, she felt safe, no matter what danger she was in.

Jacki filled the tub with water as hot as she could stand, then lowered her malfunctioning body down into it, wincing as it seared her skin. She liked it that way, especially now, when reminders of being alive were at a premium. She reclined back, slipping deeply under the clear surface, relishing that peculiar quiet of hot baths.

The steam condensed heavily on the walls. Turning slightly, Jacki ran a slow finger across the scar where she'd had her caesarian when Morton was born. He had come out of her side feet first with the umbilical cord wrapped around his neck. There had been a few panicked minutes when the doctors had been unable to get him to breathe. Having slept through Tucker's birth, she had elected to be awake for the surgery, a new procedure at the time, and she could remember asking, 'What's wrong?' while being told repeatedly to hold still, a ridiculous request since the epidural had paralyzed most everything from the neck down. When they finally gave her Morton, wailing away at the top of his lungs, her husband cried with relief, but she remained strangely unmoved, wondering, as she had done with Tucker, what in the world this little wet alien could possibly have to do with her.

Guilt came like a punch, not merely for being so cold at

the harrowing beginning to Morton's life, but also because she realized she had forgotten his birth completely until this moment, that she hadn't seen either of her sons in almost two years, that it had been at least a year since she had even spoken to one of them on the phone, and that right until this second, right until just now when she looked at the scar, right until this hot bath for her ravaged frame, it hadn't even occurred to her that any of those were bad things or even anything that required a second thought. Regret and love and pain flooded into her, as if she had accidentally tripped a porthole below the waterline. She closed her eyes and gripped the sides of the tub until it subsided.

They must hate you. Of course, they don't hate you. *You* would hate you. There's not enough time. There is. You can't go back to them. But you can move *forward*, and they'll be there. As if they'll ever want to see you now that you're such a pathetic mess. You won't always be this way. You've hit bottom. Yes, and now things can only move up.

She waited until the voices stopped pinging off one another inside her head. She felt blessed to be so tired that the future didn't quite matter yet. These arguments she had with herself weren't relevant right now. They were just reflected noise as the battle raged on. She tried to concentrate on the bath and was pleasantly surprised to find that she could do so. She inhaled the steam slowly so as not to bring on a coughing fit. Eyes still closed, she flattened her body, trying to get as much of herself under the water as possible. Morton and Tucker, Tucker and Morton, soon but not just yet.

There was a light knock on the door, and Davis poked her head in again. She looked worried.

—Jacki? I'm so sorry to interrupt. It's just that—

She stopped. Jacki sat up further in the tub. When Davis didn't go on, Jacki reached for her towel.

—I'm sorry, Jacki. This will be a shock. It looks like he's close to finding you. We don't think he knows yet, but he interviewed Joanie for a second time today and it looks like he wants to talk to me again tomorrow. We're the only menial employees he's talked to twice.

—He knows something.

Jacki's voice croaked out in a timbre at once her own and someone else's.

—It looks that way. My brother is coming here to take you to our mother's. She lives out in Foster Downs. You'll be safe there. I shouldn't come with you in case he's having the house watched. We're going to sneak you out the back.

—Oh, Davis, I can't ask you to take that risk for me.

It was the most she had spoken in weeks.

—The risk has already been accepted and taken. We wouldn't bring you this far just to abandon you. You can be sure of that.

—But, Davis—

—No, don't you worry. My mother knows the whole story and will take good care of you. Me and Joanie will visit you when we can, which I hope will be often. I brought you some clothes, and I packed up the rest of your things. I've got food in the kitchen that we can eat until my brother arrives. It won't be long now.

—How can I possibly ever thank you?

—By surviving this, Jacki. By beating him. That will give us all hope, and then we'll be the ones thanking *you*.

51. Post-Coital Powwow.

—Hand me that washcloth, will you, darling?

—One second. Here.

—That was invigorating.

—'Invigorating'?

—All right, how about 'fun'?

—'Fun' will work.

—Didn't you enjoy it?

—I absolutely did. The boy is energetic.

—I'll say. Could you grab some more soap?

—I'll get the floor all wet.

—*Lean*, Albert. I know you can reach. I've seen you do it.

—Almost. There we are . . . Shit, I dropped it.

—Just get out and get it. It doesn't matter if the floor gets wet. That's what tile is for.

—Here. Hold on, I need to rinse.

—Do you think we should have invited Kevin in here with us?

—Why? He turned us down all the other times.

—Still, it's polite to ask.

—He's young.

—He's not *that* young. You said he was thirty.

—Younger than us, my love. I think he's still of an age where he likes to sleep in his own spunk. It's kind of sexy, actually.

—'Spunk'?

—What?

—Where did you hear a word like 'spunk'?

—All the cool kids are saying it down at the high school.

—Picking up teenagers again, are we?

—I think I heard it on television, actually.

—They can say 'spunk' on television now?

—You should probably write a law, darling.

—I probably should. Hand me a towel, please.

—My God, even with the air conditioning, it's still torrid
in here.

—We just got out of a shower.

—But feel the vent.

—It's the heat wave. The weather center says we're probably going to end up having a drought.

—Well, we're already doing our part by showering together.

—Kevin should be doing his part.

—Oh, you liked him that much, did you? I haven't seen you this randy in a good while, O horny wife of mine.

—You know the thing is, his, whatever, manhood doesn't *seem* all that big, but once it's, you know—

—Yes.

—It sort of—

—Seems a whole lot bigger?

—Yes. How does he do that?

—Enthusiasm.

—And that Y-shaped thing he does—

—Tell me about it. I was chafing terribly and I still didn't want it to stop.

—How do you learn something like that?

—I hardly think our dear Kevin is an angel.

—You don't think he turned clips, do you?

—Maybe. I think he hinted that's how he got through college.

—He went to college?

—Yes. A Mansfield alumnus even. Art history. He worked in galleries before we hired him down at the auction house. Why so ashen all of a sudden?

—Hearing 'Mansfield' reminds me of Jon Noth.

—Cora, my sweet, this is hardly the time to be thinking of Jon Noth.

—I know that, but I just can't forget what he said. And that *look* on his face. Smug and triumphant. Did I tell you he said I didn't know how unhappy I was?

—Yes.

—I mean, the *nerve*. It's nearly forty years, for pity's sake. Who does he think he is?

—I'm sure I don't know. Now, dear—

—As if I would just drop everything. And then turning up at the fund-raiser, too. Why can't I just let go of this? Why can't I just brush this off?

—Probably because you once cared for him.

—I'm almost *obsessing* over it. This isn't the last of him, I can assure you.

—I wasn't doubting.

—He was always tenacious.

—No, he wasn't. I fought him once, and he disappeared for thirty-six years. Maybe I'll just have to fight him again.

—Don't joke. I'll bet that's what he wants.

—Darling, we've just had the most delightful sex with a charming, handsome young man who seems to genuinely enjoy our company. We've never gone three occasions with *anyone*. Not many people involve themselves so uninhibitedly and joyously with a married couple without also seeking a cash payment. And if history has taught us anything, it's that this shower was probably for naught because our man Kevin is in there right now working up that marvelous prick of his in order to stick it into one of us all over again while the other of us does something equally wonderful to him. How many other couples nearing sixty do you know who have this much fun? I *forbid* you to bring Jon Noth into this.

—What if he's dangerous?

—You've had lots of threats as Mayor, and you've never worried before.

—But—

—No 'buts'. Honestly, Cora. Put him out of your mind.

You've instructed the staff to keep him at a distance like all the other crackpots. That's all he is, another crackpot.

—But that's just the thing. He's not.

—He *is*. Just because he once knew you doesn't mean anything. Quit worrying.

—I wish there was some way I could just get him out of the city, out of my *life*.

—He's not *in* your life. He's a gnat that you've swatted away. He won't be back.

—If only you could have seen him when he came to my office—

—Cora—

—What are you two doing in here?

—Just cleaning up, Kevin. My word, hard again already?

—The night is still young. There's plenty more we can accomplish before dawn. You're becoming an upstanding citizen yourself there, Albert.

—We're being summoned, Cora.

—Yes, Cora. I'm summoning us all back to bed. Come and come.

—Why is someone like you still single, Kevin?

—But I'm not single. I have the two of you.

—But surely—

—Tut, tut, now. Not another word. I like my freedom is all. Besides, why limit myself to one when these evenings with two as handsome as you are so enjoyable? I do hope Albert constantly compliments you on your smile, Cora. It dazzles.

—It certainly does, darling.

—Here. Take my hands and off we go. All worries forgotten.

—Did you hear that, Cora? All worries forgotten.

—I heard. All right, let's go.

52. A Casualty.

The drought had taken its first.

An ancient female began to bleat early in the morning sunshine, and they all knew that when this particular bleating began, death was inevitable. The high pitch meant that the cow's throat was nearly swollen shut from lack of fluid. Even if they could have gotten to water immediately, which they very nearly did, there was no way for the old cow to squeeze more than a drop or two into her stomach. The herd knew she was doomed, and the poor cow knew it, too. Her bleatings increased in intensity until the air was filled with the cries of herdmembers answering her long, slow death song. By noon, heat and exhaustion had caused the cow's knees to buckle, and she collapsed. The rest of the herd kept close around her all through the night, offering gentle nudges of comfort and concern as her sounds became gradually quieter. Finally, she laid her massive, aged head down onto the grass of the small field and softly moaned until dawn broke, at last quietly dying just as the sun touched her massive, wrinkled face.

She watched the cow die and felt at fault. They hadn't been away from water for all that long, only two nights and a day, but the grass they had been eating had been increasingly dry, robbing them of extra moisture that had apparently been more precious to some than she realized. None of the other animals had shown signs of excessive dehydration. She was aware of her own thirst, but even so, the death of the cow was an unpleasant surprise that could have been avoided. She should have known that the amount of water a good-sized, healthy herdmember like herself could survive on was considerably less than the frailer and older members needed.

They didn't seem to blame her, though, glancing at her

sadly but without accusation, and indeed, they had a point. The cow had been extremely old and perhaps unable to eat enough to keep her alive even if greener grass were underfoot. Maybe some other, unknown condition had merely accelerated an already imminent death. Herdmembers died. It was sad that it had to happen. That was all.

And yet. What if the worst was true? What if the old cow had died because of her neglect? Though she had not slept through the night as the cow had slowly passed, and had led the herd with considerable vigor all day long to the greenest, wettest spots she knew of, she was still wide awake well after dark. What had she not seen? What could have happened differently? *Was* there anything?

When she was a calf the leader was a stout bull with dark creases under his eyes. He had once led the herd in an attempted fording of a river that was nearly in flood. Four of the first five animals crossing had been washed away and drowned, excepting only the leader whose immense weight alone carried him safely to the other side. A shaky, tenuous period followed, but the chastened leader was slowly forgiven and allowed to retake a firm, if increasingly cautious, grip over the herd. The lead position depended entirely upon the faith of the members of the herd being led, and it was true that there seemed to be no question of her losing that. Still, she didn't want to lose any others, even from natural causes, even from the inevitable additional deaths that the worsening drought would certainly bring. It was an impossible goal, but in striving for the impossible, she might accomplish the improbable.

As if this wasn't enough, there was also the whole matter of the thin creature. His behavior was becoming more erratic, if that was possible. His awful sick sour smell hovered about like a swarm of lazy bees. He had not made any further 211 attempts to bother the herdmembers physically, but he had taken to yelping at them from up in the trees. Some of the more sensitive among the herd were becoming unnerved by his presence and had begun chasing him off if he ventured too close. She was concerned not only for the safety of the herd but, distantly, for the thin creature himself. What if his strangeness increased? He had never been a threat to them before. How could she keep him from molesting them without hurting him? What if he died of whatever illness he was suffering from? He had been with them since before she and most of the rest of the herd were born. What would happen to them after he was gone? Of course the herd would continue just fine, but even so, that sort of change was unwelcome.

Her ears turned back as she heard him pass by some distance behind her in the dark, a low gurgling coming from the underbrush. What was to become of him? What was to become of *them*? As tired as she was, it was still a long while before she could manage to sleep.

(*Agnes Derwent was deep into her morning constitutional when she heard the buzzing. Her gnarled hand raising her walking stick-cum-cane, she strayed from her set path, whacking away a few low palm leaves in search of the sound's source. She had done this walk in varying forms for years, dwindling from a stroll along the beach in the early days down to the current widowhood version of three turns around her (admittedly very large) back garden. She had never enjoyed it, which was the point. Exercise should be unpleasant, boring, and difficult, otherwise how would you know you were doing it properly? So when she heard the buzzing of the flies through the trees that led to the lawn bowling green, she was annoyed. She grew even more annoyed when she saw the carcass of a large rhinoceros baking under the morning sun. The day was* 212 *hot, again, which annoyed her even further. She scowled even though there was no one to see her but the flies and the dead beastie.*

—Now who do you suppose is going to clean that *up?*)

53. Fallout.

As soon as Monday had dawned, a daisy chain of visitors began appearing in Jarvis' office and continued with surprising persistence as the week dragged on.

Sally Nottingham: 'Maybe I'm being oversensitive, Pastor, but I couldn't help thinking you were talking about me. I mean, I know I sometimes get a little over-enthusiastic about what I let my children do and don't do, but do you think that's wrong? I realize there was some talk when I wouldn't let Melinda wear trousers to school, but to me, the Sacraments are very clear on what a woman should wear. And if I don't think that either her or Daniel should date until they're twenty-one, well, I'm sorry, but that's just the way I feel. I'm just trying to be a good Bondulay and follow the Sacraments exactly as I read them. Am I going too far? Is that what you were trying to say? Was it about me?'

Rackle Minneham: 'Couldn't agree with you more, but it won't do any good. *I* understood you, but for the rest of the sheep in there, it's just in one ear and out the other. You got them old biddies who started reading the Sacraments when they were eight years old in Bondulay School and haven't come up for air since. Now about that loan I was hoping to get from the church. It would really be a help to this business I'm starting up. Listen . . .'

Jerry Bish: 'Was that a warning since I'm not Rumour? Am I in some sort of danger?'

Jessica Hickham-Dearth: 'I for one am really tired of this   213 left-wing propaganda coming from the pulpit of my own Bondulay prefecture. Your job is to instruct us and uplift us with teachings from the Sacraments, not pass along this nonsense fairy tale. I've never seen any convincing evidence that the sailors didn't bring the punishment on themselves, or for that matter whether this supposed "massacre" ever even took place. Let's face it, it's a fiction started by bleeding hearts like yourself to add yet another chapter to the persecution sweepstakes. I mean, really, Pastor, I expect more from the head of my church than historical lies.'

Amos Oham: 'I once went out on an ocean-going fishing boat, back in the days just after the Gentlemen's War. I remember it like it was yesterday. The sun beat down from a pink, morning sky, shining on a young lad of thirteen . . .'

Lorna Wyndham: 'Forgive me if this seems paranoid but were you alluding to anything in particular? Do the prophecies say there's something coming? Is it the end of everything? You know me, Reverend Kingham, I'm a bit of a worrywart. Is there something I should be keeping an eye out for, something I should be preparing my family for? Or am I missing the meaning of it all, maybe? Is it happening soon?'

Jameson Drossham and Wil Huffham: 'We've been speaking with some of the other Deacons and some of the parishioners, and frankly, some of us are a little offended by the, shall we say, *hectoring* tone of your sermon on Sunday. Some of us sort of feel that this type of thing is a bit too much of a *sermon*. Do you know what I mean? There's a feeling that your lesson was too much of a *lesson*, rapping us on the, so to speak, *knuckles*, a feeling that you maybe treated us a bit too much like, as it were, *children*.'

Germaine Pelham: 'This bad reaction to prophecy or misuse of the Sacraments or whatever it is you were talking about, how will it affect the Spring Cotillions? Because my parents have put out a lot of money, and if we need to change venues, we need to know that now. Do you have any idea how cutthroat it is these days?'

And on it went. The most heartfelt, passionately directed sermon of his life, and it was like rubber bouncing off stone. Even his friends smiled politely and shook their heads. Somehow, in some way that he couldn't see and that continued to astonish him, he had stepped wrong. Why was this so unpleasant for them? What had he said that had been so difficult to hear? Jarvis was nothing if not a thoughtful man, and he searched his mind and soul to see if and where he had gone wrong. He was coming up empty. If he knew this little about his parishioners, then how could *any* of his sermons have impact? At least, he thought, the week was almost over, and there could hardly be another week's worth of uproar over his upcoming sermon on generosity of spirit. That one would just bore them.

But then half an hour before Jarvis left for the day on Friday, his office door opened without a knock and in walked Theophilus Velingtham.

—Greetings, Brother Kingham, on this fine, warm summer's day.

—Fine *hot* summer's day, some might say, Brother Velingtham.

—I'm not one to question what the Good Lord has chosen to bless us with, Pastor.

Theophilus wore his ever-present smile. The best Jarvis could muster in response was a tight-lipped grin that he knew made him look as if he was bravely suffering through pain, which, come to think of it . . .

—What can I do for you, Theophilus?

—A friendly visit, Pastor. A friendly parishioner-to-preacher chat is all. No agenda.

—That's good to hear.

—Though I have been going over your latest sermon in my mind in the past few days.

—Ah.

—Listening and learning from it with much prayer and reference to the Sacraments, as I do with all of your sermons.

—That's very flattering.

—I do not intend it to be so. Flattery leads to pride, which the Sacraments tells us is a venal sin. I refer to the story of the King and the shoemaker wherein—

—I'm familiar with the story.

—Yes, of course you would be. I'm merely a parishioner. Who am I to venture instruction to my own most reverend Reverend?

And still the smile. Jarvis fought down thoughts of putting his hands around Velingtham's throat.

—Was there anything in particular about my sermon that you wanted to talk about?

—No, I can't say there was anything 'in particular' about your sermon that I wished to go over with you. There is, however, something in *general* that struck me as worthy of further discussion.

—And what would that be?

—May I be candid?

—I would hope for nothing less.

—I think perhaps you are misguided.

—In what?

—In your interpretation of what the Sacraments have to teach us.

—You mean my feelings on the Book of Ultimates.

—Yes, precisely. I wonder if your distaste over the admittedly horrible goings-on during the Brandon Beach Incident—

216   —Massacre.

—Yes, 'Massacre', I wonder if your feelings of revulsion at that episode, natural as they are, of course, have colored your opinion of the wonderful things the Book of Ultimates contains, the information it has that adds meaning to our lives.

—Well, as I hope you know, my whole belief in the Sacraments is based upon the meaning I feel they can add to our lives.

—Except, it would seem, the Book of Ultimates.

—I don't dismiss the Book of Ultimates out of hand—

—That's good to hear, since I may have misunderstood that exact viewpoint from Sunday's sermon.

—Theophilus. I understand the appeal of prophecy—

—Prophecy is a gift from Our Lord.

—But surely you must admit that the writing in the Ultimates is so open to interpretation that we must proceed with the utmost caution, if we proceed at all.

—I admit only that the Sacraments, the Book of Ultimates included, are the divinely given word of Our Lord. It would be dangerous to presume that one can ignore them at will.

—It would also be dangerous to presume we understand their meaning without reservation.

—Don't you think that Our Lord took that into account? How can you know His mind and His plan?

—How can *you*?

—I can believe that He planned full well the words in the Ultimates. I can believe that He would have His believers act as their hearts tell them based upon our interpretation of those words. And I can believe that whatever the outcome of that interpretation, however unpleasant it may be, it must follow as a part of His plan, and therefore His will.

—Brother Velingtham, if I may say so, that's the road to chaos. To madness. First and foremost, Our Lord gave us free will with which to avoid debacles like Brandon Beach.

—But He also has a destiny for every man. Who are you to say that Brandon Beach was a debacle? Yes, on the surface, it's terrible, but how do you or any of us know that the deaths of those sailors was not part of Our Lord's plan?

—I think you're veering dangerously close to blasphemy, Theophilus.

—Am I?

—With what you're saying, any action whatsoever, no matter how debased or violent, can be justified.

—Who are we to get in the way of Our Lord's plan?

—I don't know what Lord you're speaking of. Certainly not *My* Lord. The deaths of innocents come when the hand of man contradicts what Our Lord teaches. Destruction comes when man misinterprets the word and name of Our Lord for his own selfish purposes. These are the things the Sacraments teaches. At least, the Sacraments that *I* read.

Theophilus' smile broadened. An empty moment of time passed before he spoke.

—Very passionately presented, Pastor. I respect your position immensely, and though we disagree on this one small point, I thank you for your willingness to talk my ideas through with me.

—Did I change your mind?

—Does that really matter so much? We now know where we all stand and that's before Our Lord in worship. I'm grateful to have a man as ardently committed to the Sacraments as I am at the helm of our little church. Our disagreements are as nothing in His eyes. Good day, Reverend Kingham, and may Our Lord bless you.

With the smile still stretched across his face, Velingtham left without another word. Jarvis leaned far back into his chair with the frustrated sweat of a man cut off just before the culmination of a difficult task, a stumble with the finish line in sight. Theophilus had always been zealous and officiously pious to the point where Jarvis wanted to kick his teeth in, but today seemed to point to a depth of blind faith that almost wandered into the unsettling. Jarvis was surprised to find himself agitated on a very basic level and not a little frightened. Where was this all heading? He exhaled deeply and tried to figure out just how it was that he had managed to venture so far into unknown and possibly dangerous territory.

54. Max and Talon and The Emu.

—I don't see him.
　—Look beneath that stretch of bamboo.
　—Where?
　—There.
　—Where? I can't—
　—Follow along the tops of the shrubs and stop just under that bamboo.
　—Oh, I see. Not doing much, is he?
　—It's hot. He's probably taking a siesta.
　—What's a siesta?
　—It's a nap in the middle of the day to prepare yourself for the evening ahead.
　—Can a tiger really get that tired in a paddock?
　—Probably not, but it *is* pretty hot out here.
　—Okay, so *then* what did Mayor Cora say?
　—That the City Council had approved the title and passed a budget making it a separate office.
　—What's the title again?
　—Crash Advocate-General.
　—I still don't understand exactly what you'll be doing.　219

—Well, you know how sometimes The Crash walk on people's lawns and accidentally knock down fences?

—And smash cars.

—I've never heard that.

—Jamie Lewis' father had to turn his car to miss them and he hit a bus bench.

—Then that's more Jamie Lewis' father's fault than The Crash's, huh?

—I guess so. What's that?

—A vole.

—Never heard of them.

—Says here they're mainly in the desert. They're rodents.

—Like mice?

—Exactly.

—They're bigger than a mouse.

—Takes all sizes, honey.

—So what about The Crash?

—You know sometimes people complain about them, right?

—Yeah.

—And you know that the city has laws protecting them, right?

—Yeah, everybody likes them.

—Not everybody, and even the ones that do sometimes get annoyed with them when they trample gardens and knock down fences.

—So you're going to protect them yourself?

—If I can. Cora's agreed to give The Crash separate legal representation. Me.

—You're going to be their lawyer.

—I see it more as being their public advocate. They can't talk for themselves, so maybe I can do their talking for them.

220   —What about Maggerty?

—And where did you learn *that* name?

—School. Everyone tells stories about him.

—Well, you stay away from him if he ever comes around, okay? He's probably harmless, but he's not all right in the head.

—But doesn't he already look after them?

—Maybe he thinks he does. Who knows?

—Could something bad happen to The Crash?

—Don't worry, little one. I don't think anything's going to happen to them anytime soon, but they might as well have someone to defend them if it does.

—And that's what you're going to do?

—Yep. What do you think?

—These monkeys smell.

—Let's keep going then.

—That one's picking up poop and throwing it.

—Come on, Talon. Let's go to the aviary.

—The aviary's boring.

—How can you say that?

—You can't do anything with a bird.

—Birds are amazing. They can fly.

—But you can't pick up a bird. You can't pet them or sleep with them in your bed. They just stare at you with those crazy little eyes and scream all the time.

—I had no idea you felt so strongly.

—Tara Wiser has a cockatoo, and all it does is scream.

—But there are more birds in the world than cockatoos. Come on. You'll see all kinds of things.

—Daddy—

—Come on. You won't regret it.

—All right, but so why The Crash though?

—Remember when we put out food for them when there was that wheat blight?

—Sort of.

—You were very little, but that was something my office did.

—And you liked doing it?

—Very much. The Crash sort of seem to exist outside of us, you know? In their own separate little world with their own separate little destinies. I like the idea of being the one who makes sure they're allowed to keep on doing that. Understand?

—Yeah, I guess so. Aaaaah!

—That's an emu. They're pretty much harmless.

—'Pretty much'?

—You don't have anything to worry about.

—It's huge.

—You wouldn't want to climb on it, but it's not going to hurt you. Look, it just wants some seed. Here, go get some out of the dispenser and see if it'll let you feed it.

—No.

—It won't hurt you. Come on, I'll go with you. Here. See, just put a little in your hand. Now, hold it out.

—Daddy! It's pecking!

—Of course it's pecking. That's how they eat, but it's not hurting you, see?

—Oh. It's got a funny neck.

—I know. Like a rubber band.

—It'll be neat to tell people you help The Crash.

—Good.

—Will it pay enough?

—We'll be fine, honey.

—I hope so. I like that job.

—Me, too, pumpkin. On to the giraffes?

—Yeah, giraffes.

—Here, take my hand. The exit's on the other side of the emu.

55. Sometimes It's Just Sorrow.

This is it. The moment of my death.

Physically, Luther had gone completely haywire. He put his head between his knees to try to keep himself from vomiting again. No good. He rushed to the bathroom and only made it to the door before heaving pink bile onto the floor. Since Archie had refused to see him, a sort of progressive deterioration had taken over, hand in hand with an emotional doom that overwhelmed him. He didn't see how he could go on living, and his body apparently agreed. Chest pains began to keep him awake at night. He perspired constantly, and no matter how much water he drank, his urine remained a stinging, burning sun color. When he did physical exertion of any kind, including something as simple as walking to the mailbox, he was split by muscle cramps that ultimately kept him from going anywhere without something to lean on. And for the past three days, he had been unable to eat any food but somehow threw up anyway.

It can't always be like this.

Peter assumed that Luther had a bad flu, but Luther knew otherwise. This was a spiritual sickness that was so poisonous it was killing him. Archie had provided a second life for Luther for so long that when Luther cut it off he wasn't able to subsist on what was left. He was going to die. He knew this, felt it through every heaving, ailing, feverish cell in his body. He was the parasite that killed its host, only to have nothing left to live on.

But I was more than a parasite.

Which of course is what makes it so much worse.

How can this be? Where did I lose my grip?

He had to get Peter safely away before he died. Peter would

be hurt (*which is all you seem to be able to do*), but Luther was afraid that if he didn't get Peter to a safe distance he'd take Peter down with him. His head ached so bad now it was affecting his vision. He fell to his knees as spasms rocked his diaphragm. He coughed up bright red blood onto his shirtfront. How would he be able to convince Peter of anything in this condition? He had to, though. It had to be done now, today, because he knew whatever it was that was killing him would finish the job soon. He would be dead, and Peter had to be gone before then.

It's your own fault. No one to blame but you.

He struggled getting to his feet and had to rest on the counter to catch his breath. He felt his bowels loosening and rushed to get his pants down in time. Black, evil-looking liquid spilled into the toilet. The smell made him retch again, this time splashing more blood onto the increasingly covered bathroom floor. He noticed through the mucus that his nose was bleeding, and suddenly he knew.

He was afraid. Now, for the first time. Now, when it was too late, he realized. He didn't want to die. The mistake wasn't fatal. It was just a mistake. It could be rectified, and if it couldn't be rectified, it could be lived with. No. No, this is wrong. No. He vomited again and then again. The violent heaving threw him to his hands and knees. The bathroom floor was slippery with blood and bodily fluids. There was no way he could stand, but he had to get out of the bathroom. He forced his arms to move, forced his legs and knees to push forward. He tensed his stomach and torso as tight as he could to fight off further vomiting. He had to get to his phone. He had to somehow get himself to a hospital. Peter was on his way over for what was to be the final separation, but suddenly it didn't have to be that way. Peter could help him. It really could happen.

224

I can be saved. I can. I'm going to make it.

Peter let himself in carrying a takeaway noodle soup dinner he had picked up on the way home. He took it into the kitchen, grabbed some silverware out of the cabinet, and opened up the boxes of food. He called out Luther's name. He transferred all the food to real plates and bowls. He folded two napkins for them to use and turned the coffee maker on to brew. He called Luther again. He picked up one of the bowls of soup and headed upstairs.

Somehow, before he reached him, before taking the six steps from the bedroom doorway over to the bathroom, before dropping the soup onto the carpet, he knew that Luther was dead. Holding Luther's body in his arms, oblivious to the blood and the mess, Peter decided. It was that quick. He was able to lock away the grief, the unbearable pain, if only for a moment. The next actions were in front of him, and with every passing second they became clearer.

There was no question. It was obvious. He knew what he had to do.

56. And What of Eugene?

Sitting in the Bisector waiting for Jon, Eugene cleaned his fingernails, an obsession that had begun the instant he had given up chewing them, or rather, was forced to give up chewing them when he was eight by a mother with a will, some cotton balls, and a bottle of tobasco sauce. He trimmed them once a week with an extremely sharp clipper (replaced every three months) that he kept attached to his keyring. He took each clipping away in a single piece, then he filed down the rough corners with a set of three emery boards that flipped out from the clipper, the first for the big corners working down to the smallest one which buffed the edge to a smart, shiny tip. More than one girl had mistaken his valuable fingernails for a personal fastidiousness that promised perfect boyfriend things like flower-buying or apt performances at dinner with mom. More than one boy had mistaken his perfect fingernails for an attention to preening and awareness of himself as a sexual object that promised a cultivated night of sweat.

Neither could have been further from the truth. Eugene was obsessed with the condition of his fingernails, and that was the beginning and end of it. It didn't even cover his cuticles, which he still chewed and peeled and which still bled most of the time. Any girl who succeeded in getting him undressed quickly noticed an unwelcome but easily recognizable smell coming from the sweatier corners of his body. The few who summoned the courage to go through sex with him, steeling themselves to call his body odor 'manly', had often had that same courage fail them when discovering what lurked in the folded corners of his foreskin. No boy, of course, had ever gotten that far, poor Eugene being too clueless to notice the pale-skinned schoolmates who laughed too loudly at his infrequent jokes. He would have been too mystified to act on the interest even if he had ever suspected it anyway, and besides, as he freely pointed out, that wasn't his bag.

Which is not to imply that Eugene was a virgin or in any way inexperienced with the grander passions of what those around twenty choose to call love. The still-nagging scaly chrysalia was proof enough of that (though mercifully it was on its way out, thanks to Jon's surprising offer of health coverage, a perk that had also helped to clear up Eugene's purplish acne to a point where he could almost shave without having to sop up blood afterwards). His last girlfriend, the one who had left him for that bastard non-Rumour No

Margin surfer with the blond curls and small waist that Eugene thought made him look like a ballerina, *that* girlfriend had liked to have sex in the shower anyway, so it didn't matter. The times they did it in bed, she would often come equipped with a Q-tip which he thought was her kinky way of getting him hard. She hadn't been perfect, a little wide about the backside, a little too flirty with his friends, but all in all, she was a catch that Eugene felt lucky to have. Until she met the surfer. Well, if that's what she wanted, someone tanned, muscular and brainless, then fuck her, let her have it.

He realized while digging out a piece of red lint from deep behind his thumbnail that he hadn't thought about suicide once in the weeks that he had been working for Jon. Jon was a good guy. He treated Eugene fairly and, more importantly, like an adult or even better, a friend. Jon paid well, more than the Solari anyway, and Eugene actually found himself looking forward to coming to work. The guy *was* kind of nuts. This whole fixation on the Mayor, for one thing, and what was with all the black clothes? But otherwise, there was nothing too weird. No strange groups Eugene had to join, no bizarre midnight journeys to destinations unknown, no stray hands on Eugene's knee, though there was a very small part of him that wondered *why* he (Jon) never put a hand on his (Eugene's) knee and what he (Eugene) would do if he (Jon) ever did. No, Jon was definitely a good guy. Half the time, Eugene couldn't believe his good fortune at falling into a job this cushy and one that seemed to promise so many connections and future opportunities.

Who would have ever thought a guy like him had any luck left?

—To Hennington Hills, my boy.

—God! You scared the crap out of me!

—Pardon me for tearing you away from your manicure.   227

You know, if you put even a tenth of the effort into the rest of your personal appearance that you do your nails, you'd have the girls knocking down your door.

—Nah, that's not true.

—You'll talk none of that self-flagellation in my presence, Eugene. In fact, you know what we'll do? I have someone I want to see at Hennington Hills, but after that, why don't we get you a haircut?

—A haircut?

—Yes, and some new clothes. I have standards for my associates, and I've been letting you lag. We'll get you all cleaned up and sharp-looking.

—For what?

—'For what?' For the sake of itself. For the simple fact of looking good. For the way you'll feel. Has no one ever taught you this?

—No.

—Obviously. It's settled. I don't know why I didn't think of this before.

—I don't really have any cash on me.

—My God, Eugene. Do I have to hit you on the head with a block of wood? I'm paying, of course. Now, drive.

—Thanks.

—Don't mention it, and I mean that. Don't mention it. The tiny amount of money it will take could hardly be called generosity. It's the least I could do. Trust me. I'm not a bad person, despite what others may tell you.

—No one's told me anything. I haven't even met anyone else who knows you.

—But of course not. Why would you? Still, I want you to believe that, Eugene, no matter what happens.

—What's going to happen?

—Nothing. Certainly nothing to worry about, but maybe

things that don't reflect on me too well. I'm not exactly sure yet.

—Okay, I'm not really following you here. You're asking me to forgive you in advance for things you may or may not do? How is that possible for anyone?

—Once again you surprise me, Eugene, by calling me out. I'm going to have to get used to that one of these days. You're correct, of course, I can't ask you any such thing, especially in these vague terms. So, I'll try and clarify. What do you know about revenge?

—Fucking someone who fucked you.

—In an astoundingly blunt phrase, yes, in a way, fucking someone who fucked you.

—Or is it someone who *didn't* fuck you?

—Meaning?

—You're mad at the Mayor.

—Mad doesn't quite get the flavor of it.

—You're not going to kill her, are you? Because if—

—Good heavens, no! Kill her? Are you mad? What sort of person do you take me for?

—You said not to think bad of you no matter what happened. What else could you have been talking about?

—Surely not murder!

—Well, what other kinds of revenge are there?

—You are so very, very young, aren't you? I am a gentleman, and I shall have a gentleman's revenge.

—So that's, what? A duel?

—I told you I'm not going to kill her.

—With her husband, then.

—Mmmm, yes, well, no, of course not. I'm not going to shoot anyone.

—You could use swords. Or, what are those things? Rapiers?

—I'm not quite *that* old-fashioned.

—So what's a gentleman's revenge then?

—It's elegant, first of all, and refined. It doesn't kill them, because, to put it brutally, where's the fun if they're dead? It needs to hurt them where pain would be felt the most acutely. It must be done, of course, perfectly legally, because who wants to end up in jail? The target must know who is doing it to them and, here's the real clincher, be completely power-less to stop it in spite of that knowledge.

—Sounds impossible.

—Difficult, yes. Impossible, no. And the difficulty only makes it that much more satisfying when it's completed.

—But why even bother? Why go to all that trouble in the first place? Why not just let the Mayor have her life?

—Because I haven't told you the last step. Truly brilliant revenge ultimately ends in the target recanting and capitulating completely.

—So you're going to hurt her to get her back?

—In a sense.

—Why would you ever think this would work? She'll just be more pissed at you than ever.

—You'll have to trust me.

—But still—

—One day, if you're lucky, you'll fall hopelessly in love. If you're unlucky, that love will be taken away from you. That day, and that day only, will you truly understand. She will see the error of her ways. She will see how much I love her, how right I am for her. She will. You'll see. She will.

—It's when you talk like this that I kind of stop listening.

—Never mind, then, Eugene. You'll see how it will all work out.

—When is this going to begin?

230   —Starting today, if we're lucky, and I expect to be lucky.

—It starts here at the country club?

—Yes.

—How?

—Patience, my boy. Patience. Wait for me. I'll be back within an hour, and then we'll go and get a whole new you.

57. Fever Dream.

They were after him.

(*Were they?*)

They had seemed so welcoming up until now, his big gray friends with their hardy hides and warm 'hellos'. (*Or had they ever even said that? There's a mistake here, but which side?*) And now they had turned against him. They were merely biding their time. Why was it so goddamned hot? Why did they bring the sun out? What had he done to them?

They were on him. (*No, wait.*) They were on him. Stomping and cheering, calling out his name as they pounded him into the ground. He could feel his body flatten, even his voice when he tried to scream. Then they were laughing, laughing at poor, flat Maggerty, melting into the mud. (*This wasn't right.*) Grass shot up through his flattened body, and they grazed on him, pulling bits of his flesh away with each mouthful, the caress of their soft, full lips followed by a horrible, painful snap. Then the worst came, the worst of it all. After they had eaten him, pulling him to bits, his bones in rubble, they turned away. They left. They left him behind.

Maggerty woke, or at least he thought he did. He *hoped* he had. It was hard to tell lately. His head felt like constantly boiling soup. Some days he really couldn't figure out where he was, knowing only that he should stay as close to the animals as possible. Other times he would emerge from a   231 purplish-orange haze and have no idea what had gone on since the previous day. Once he had opened his eyes to find himself waist deep in a bog with the herd grazing onshore. Another time he was somehow near the top of a tree, two pine cones in one hand, apparently ready to drop them on the animal resting below. Each time, he had rescued himself from his predicament slowly, trying in vain to retrace how he had gotten where he was.

This was worse than his normal cloudiness, much worse. Losing himself in a haze was one thing, but to disappear completely, so much so that he vanished into his own mind for hours at a time, was a different story altogether. His lucid moments, which had never been dependable, were now plagued with fear every time he reached them. A cycle had begun where he either didn't know what he was doing or was worried about what he had done. He couldn't even remember where or when all this had started. It felt like it had always been this way, now until forever. During the brief moments of awareness, when he wasn't too stricken by fear to move from a huddle close to the ground, he did his best to fill his stomach with grass or berries or water. He was terrified that he might die in one of the hazes, and by forcing himself to eat as much as he could, he somehow hoped that he could stave off an unknown, unseen death.

It was a wretched existence, even relative to what he had lived before, and he didn't know what to do. He had tried communicating his troubles to some of the animals, including the leader. He knew this wouldn't work, even *he* knew that, but it felt at least like he was doing something, anything to stanch the flow of panic, to try to at least act like he had control over what was happening. It was all so exhausting, too, which was another thing. When he was lucid, he couldn't sleep, and he didn't think he slept when he was away from his senses. There *were* times, like just now, when he felt like he had woken up from a nightmare, but he couldn't have even said with certainty that he had been asleep then or was awake now.

This must be insanity.

(*But I'm as sane as anyone.*)

He ripped up a handful of grass and stuffed it in his mouth. It was bitter and juiceless, but he chewed slowly just the same, grinding it into a mulch before swallowing. He pulled another and had it halfway to his mouth when he realized that the herd was moving on, wandering out of the park onto a street behind. How had he missed that? He tore up two more handfuls and got up to run, forcing as much grass as he could down his gullet and trying not to lose the rest in the jostling. They couldn't be leaving him behind, could they? Was this still the dream?

He ran as fast as he could, but the fatigue that had hugged him tightly for what seemed like weeks now slowed him down. The muscles across his chest began to cramp with the effort, and without realizing it, he let out a strangled series of coughs, green saliva drooling down his chin and across his cheeks. He ambled after them, finally reaching the street in time to see that they had stopped in a group, waiting for individual animals to file through an opening in a wooden fence. He fell to his knees, gasping loudly. And then, before he even noticed it, his grip on himself vanished. He disappeared from his own consciousness, blacking out, consequences be damned.

Waiting at the fence, the herd heard the long cry first. The more curious amongst them near the back turned to see where it came from. They could smell the thin creature's approach more than they could see it, their noses noting a shocking odor, their eyesight barely registering a growing form. The first herdmember who was hit was more surprised than hurt. It was difficult for the tiny front foreleg of a thin creature to make much of an impression on the massive hindquarter of one of the herdmembers. But when he hit her again and then again, the middle-aged female swung around to take notice.

The thin creature jumped back to avoid being hit by her horn and with another cry began slamming his forelegs against another member of the herd, flinging himself indiscriminately, trying to strike whatever he could reach, jumping out of the way of an ever-increasing irritation of lunging horns. He hit eyes and mouths and rumps. He kicked under to less-protected stomachs and genitalia. He shouted the entire time, and his stench was almost blinding to the olfactories, throwing some of the animals into confusion. One animal accidentally punctured a neighbor's side by thrusting blindly into the smell. It was this cry of pain that alerted the leader, standing patiently on the other side of the fence, waiting for the herd to make its way through.

There were gaps in the wood, and when she turned around sharply, she could see that something was happening at the rear of the herd. The sickly sweet dying smell of the thin creature reached her nose. She pushed into the oncoming line. The herd thundered out of her way as she forced herself back to the small opening they had all been walking through so peacefully. She gently, yet hurriedly, pushed a small juvenile male out of the opening and made her way to the other side.

A chaos of sight, sound and smell surrounded her. Animals ran in all directions, some of them clearly panicked at the overwhelming sensory attack. A cloud of his odor hung in the air like a lingering poison. It took her a long, tense moment before she could sort any of it out, before she could even find where he was in that writhing, movable shock that caused the ground to tremble with shifting weight. At last, two members of the herd parted, and she saw him standing between them, forelegs held high, running after a youngster. She was instantly, instinctively at a run, shoulders dropped, horn low, all four feet leaving the ground at the high point of the step. She saw him see her coming. She saw him stand his ground. At the last second, she turned her head slightly, hitting him with the broad flat of her nose rather than the lance of her horn. He flew off of his feet, and for a brief moment, they were together in momentum, him against her, moving across the pavement at a frightening speed, before she slowed and he separated, tumbling into space. He hit the concrete very hard. She heard a distinct and unmistakable snap as he rolled across the ground in a heap, turning end over end, until finally coming to rest halfway under a thin creature carrying-box.

Maggerty opened his eyes to find himself in immense pain and also upside down, both of which were disorienting. He tasted blood and realized he had somehow bitten through his tongue. He couldn't move his arm, and the jabs of pain coming from his elbow were what cleared his head enough to notice that he was sprawled up against a parked car. He felt blood pooling beneath him. Pains in his chest kept his breathing shallow. He didn't have the strength to get up, barely enough to move his head to look for the herd.

He saw the leader standing a little way from him, snorting loudly and pacing back and forth in what seemed like agitation, although he wasn't sure. After a moment, he heard her let out a low grunt in his direction, and then he watched her turn and walk back to where the rest of the herd seemed to be standing in isolated groups. What happened? Where was he? A grayness started permeating his thoughts. He realized, at last, that he was passing out, really passing out, not disappearing to somewhere else, and as he closed his eyes, he was grateful for the chance to rest.

235

58. A Most Delicious Proposal.

—And somehow here he is again.

—Surely you don't mind, Thomas? Am I interrupting something?

—Only my wonderment at your ability to appear here repeatedly, this time without even a warning from my secretary.

—I'm afraid I didn't give her a chance. You'll have to forgive me. I *have* been accused of being over-driven. I'll use the proper routes next time.

—Apology accepted.

—I don't recall apologizing.

—You just—

—I've got something you might be interested in. Are you busy?

—Would it do any good to say yes?

—No. If you wanted me out of your office, you'd have me out. I recognize that I'm here as part of your good humor.

—Appealing to my vanity doesn't hurt either.

—Shrewd. I knew there was a reason you were the right man for me.

—Right man for what?

—Do you remember my disclosure of my relationship with the Mayor?

—An old flame, if I remember correctly.

—You don't remember correctly. I never said any such thing, but your inference is smart and your way of putting it even smarter. The Mayor is an 'old flame' of mine, an old flame around whom I swirl not an abundance of nice feeling, if you understand my meaning.

236

—I'm guessing you're either looking for some kind of revenge or trying to win her back.

—Both, actually.

—Both? This I've got to hear.

—Leave that part up to me. All I wish to share on the matter is that I've got certain feelings toward the Mayor, and I've got a plan, a plan that requires you and one that would bring you many, many benefits.

—All right, but let me say right at the beginning that I don't know much about the Mayor, but what I *do* know, what *everyone* knows, is that she ain't leaving her husband. Have you ever heard of a 'Cora and Albert'?

—It's 'Albert and Cora' and yes, I'm quite sick to death of hearing it, thank you. I reiterate that the plan is mine, and the consequences, pro or con, are up to my calculations. I merely ask you to get involved because your involvement could help us both immensely.

—Fair enough. What do you imagine my involvement to be? Understanding of course, that I'm a very busy man with many irons in the fire. It would have to benefit me in a very large way indeed in order to pique my interest.

—Hear me out.

—By all means.

—The Mayoral election is coming up in four months.

—The one without any candidates?

—So you've heard that Maximillian Latham, the presumptive winner, has dropped out.

—I do read the papers, Mr Noth. I know what's going on in the city.

—Then you might also know that there is speculation that Mayor Larsson will run again?

—It's only speculation. I don't see it happening.

—Why not?

—Four terms. She's nearly sixty. She wants to retire. The most she'll do is be caretaker until a new election is scheduled early next year.

—I happen to agree with you. So you are aware then of the peculiar power vacuum in which Hennington currently sits?

—Ye-ess. I think I see where you're heading.

—Do you?

—Yes. You want to run for Mayor against your former girlfriend, showing her, well, showing her God knows what, that's your affair, and you want me to help you do it.

—You've got it exactly wrong.

Part IV.

Commodities.

59. The Foster Downs.

Katherine Tcham, Davis' mother, was nearly two feet shorter than Jacki and couldn't possibly have equaled more than a third of Jacki's body weight, yet somehow she managed to get Jacki out of bed, into a bath, out of a bath, and to the breakfast table every morning with only the faintest help from a strengthening but still emphatically wobbly Jacki.

—How in the world do you do that?

—I had five children in four years. It got to the point where I could carry them all at the same time if I had to. Willpower, I guess. It has to be done, and so you do it.

Then she smiled, a smile at once more sly and sanguine than Jacki had expected, much like the Downs itself. Jacki had heard only that it was a housing development for low-income families. She had immediately translated this to 'slum' and filed it away, never expecting the subject to arise again. Stepping out of Davis' car, though, the first thing she noticed was the flowers. In every corner of green area, in every windowsill, in every pot on every flat public surface, wave after wave of flower upon flower upon flower. Irises, tulips, roses, primroses, tuberoses, peonies, hayslips, zenias, azaleas, parenzans, rhododendrons, philodendrons, bougainvillea, dewlaps, blue cowls, morning glories, violets, even a rack of hanging orchids thriving under hot mist, and heaps upon heaps of the light blue fosters which gave the Downs its name. Somehow, in the midst of a drought, the air lived in a shimmer of sunlight, bees and butterflies.

Wow, Jacki thought. Just, wow.

The apartment buildings were all gorgeous aged brick,

recycled from ruins discovered in the Brown and peaking in flying black roofs, a row of chimneys buttoning the top ridge. Each set of apartments surrounded a brick-inlaid central courtyard, these too swarming with flowers and sunshine. Between each building were broad brick walkways leading to a massive green field behind the development. Children's football games were in progress, with teams of little ones in matching jerseys running up and down the grass. The first thing Jacki ever said to Katherine was,

—Holy moly.

—What do you mean?

—I had no idea it was this nice. No offense. Sorry.

—None taken. It didn't used to be. It was always livable, but it didn't get really spruced up until the Mayor started that bond investment cycle about twelve years ago. It's gotten better and better since then. I'm Katherine Tcham.

—Jacki.

—I know. I've got a room all ready for you. I hope you're not allergic to flowers.

She smiled. Jacki immediately felt better and then fainted. She woke up on a sunny bedspread in a sunny room with sunny wallpaper.

—Tell me if the cheer gets a little oppressive. It does to me sometimes. I've got darker rooms we can put you in.

Jacki shook her head slowly.

—Obviously, the first thing we need to do is get your strength back.

Jacki nodded her head equally slowly.

—Sleep now. We'll see if we can get some of my cooking into you a little later.

Jacki was unable to leave her room for over a week. The simple twenty-five minute car ride to get Jacki into the Downs had proved to be enough to sap every ounce of strength she had managed to gather. Katherine, who insisted she had never been a nurse but who Jacki believed must have been, if not in this life then somewhere in reincarnation's datebook, didn't even require Jacki to move to the bathroom, providing a chamber pot that looked like it pre-dated Pistolet. In fact, it wasn't until the ninth day of her stay, and going on a month of qutting Forum, that she was able, with help, to walk to the kitchen table, at which point she discovered to her astonishment that she was not the only invalid in Katherine's care.

—This is my grandfather, Reginald, and his sister Rhona. Papa, Auntie, this is Jacki, who I've been telling you about.

The two oldest people Jacki had ever seen nodded and waved their greetings to her. Jacki did some mental arithmetic. Even if Katherine was younger than she looked, say fifty-two instead of fifty-seven, and setting the variable of the mother's age at a low seventeen, then these two must be—

—I'm one hundred and four.

Off by eighteen years. The chamber pot wasn't the only thing that had outlasted Pistolet. Reginald smiled at her through strong, white teeth that couldn't possibly have been his own. He pointed to Rhona.

—She's a hundred and seven.

Rhona looked up, more alert than before.

—What? What's he saying?

Katherine placed a steaming tureen of creamy potato soup on the table.

—They're the oldest living brother and sister on record anywhere in the country.

—My goodness.

—I'm one hundred and seven.

—Yes, Auntie, we heard.

—Will you be here long?

—I don't know.

—What was that?

—Let's not tax Jacki too much, Auntie. She's not well, remember?

—What?

—She's not well!

—It's not contagious, is it?

—Of course not. Eat your soup before it gets cold, Papa. You too, Jacki. Just ignore them if they get to talking. It's a bottomless pit, trust me. After you turn a hundred, that's all you ever talk about.

—Katie! A terrible thing to say.

—Hush, Papa.

—Don't you listen to her, Jenny. You can talk to me all you want.

As Jacki took her first sip of the potato soup, and as the slight taste of rosemary caressed its way across her tongue, and as it worked its warm way down her throat into her stomach, and as Reginald intently watched her eat before picking up his own spoon, Jacki felt herself smile, actually smile from actual happiness for the first time in, well, who *knew* when?

60. How to Serve Man.

Thank you all for coming. This turnout surprises even me. I have more connections in this great city than I thought. Or maybe it's my infamy that's so large. Ha ha ha ha ha. I'm digressing and I haven't even started. Ha ha ha ha ha. Seriously, though, thanks to all of you, members of the press, trusted colleagues and members of Hennington Hills, my friends in high places, ha ha. Well, get out your pens and dictaphones, because I've got a surprise for you all, hopefully a pleasant one, definitely a brief one, ha ha.

I am here today to announce my candidacy for Mayor of Hennington.

Okay, calm down, calm down. Quiet, please, give me a chance to talk.

Thank you. I know what you're thinking. Now, why in the world is Thomas Banyon, a man with no political experience and one of the cushiest jobs in the city already, ha ha, running for Mayor of Hennington? It's simple, really. I love this city. Love it with all my heart. I was born here, attended school here, made my livelihood and my business here. And it's no secret that I've thrived. Some might say that I've thrived on my father's coat-tails, but I can assure you, *he* would be the first one to deny that. I'd be the second, ha ha. I took Hennington Hills from a decent golf course and turned it into a center for city commerce, as well as *the* spot in the city for that most important factor to quality of life: *relaxation.*

But this is not a commercial for Hennington Hills, though I've got membership application forms with me in case anyone wants to join, ha ha ha ha ha. I merely point to it as a measure of my success in business, in management, and most importantly, in giving back to this great city of ours.

There is a power vacuum in Hennington. You know it, I know it. Since Max Latham took himself out of the race, for honorable reasons as I understand it, no one has stepped forward to assume the stewardship that Cora Larsson has held on this city for the past twenty years. More importantly, no one has stepped forward with a promise to be more than just a standard-bearer. No one has stepped forward with a vision for the city, with a will to push us forward into new avenues, with a burning desire to make Hennington even better and brighter than it already is, and what's more, with the power, influence, and talent to make that all happen.

That is, no one has stepped forward until now. 245

I will admit to you that the idea of running for Mayor has not been on my mind for long. In fact, I, like the rest of you, was expecting a stay-the-course Mayorhood by the competent Max Latham. It was only when he dropped out and when a trusted advisor of mine suggested that I might be the man to take his place that I began to consider the possibility. The more I thought about it, though the idea shocked me as much as it did you today, ha ha, the more sense it made.

I am the one to take us forward. *I* am the one with the vision. *I* am the one ready, willing, and most importantly, *able* to help Hennington and her citizens fulfill every ounce of potential we have inside us. *I* will reinforce our business community and add to it to bring a new boom to our economy. *I* will work with the police force to drop our already low crime rate to proportions so infinitesimal as to be non-existent. *I* will increase funding to our public schools so every child, non-Rumour and Rumour alike, has the best opportunity to advance in the world at large. *I* will knock down the taxes that we over-pay, the taxes that we then have no say over how they're spent. *I* will do all of these things and more. But these promises are just the beginning.

As I've said, it's early yet. I've only just begun to look at how I will reform this city and create a better place to live. And make no mistake, reform *is* needed. No one will argue with the fact that Mayor Larsson has done a good job. I'd be a fool if I tried to run on *that* platform, ha ha ha. But perhaps four terms has taken some of the steam out of the Mayor that we've all grown to love and respect. Perhaps that's even why she herself is retiring when it's obvious she could easily win re-election in a landslide. New blood is needed. A new outlook is needed. Mayor Larsson has served us well, but she herself realizes that it's time for a change, time for a reinvigoration of government, time to sweep out all the stagnation and usher in a new vitality.

I welcome all challengers to my candidacy. I am confident that what I have to offer is what the citizens of Hennington want in a new leader. However, even if I end up running unopposed by legitimate competition, I do not expect a coronation. I am a leader, not a King. I will work harder than I ever have in my life to bring Hennington to a permanent place in the sun. And I hope you'll work right alongside of me.

It is the right place. It is the right time. And I, Thomas Banyon, am the right man. Thank you very much. No questions.

61. Ambushed.

The phone calls were quick to manifest.

—Where the hell did that come from?

—Don't ask me, I'm only his father. He hasn't told me his plans since he was eleven.

—You don't think he's serious?

—He wouldn't have done it if he wasn't serious. Thomas isn't exactly known for his sense of humor.

—The impossible bastard.

—'Bastard' might not be the best pejorative in this circumstance, Cora.

—Sorry, Archie. Can he possibly stand a chance, do you think?

—Running unopposed? Trust me, he's got enough friends and terrified underlings to beat 'None of the above'.

—Shit. I mean, just shit fuck shit, if you'll pardon me. What's he thinking? I mean, it's obvious what he's thinking, 247 but I thought the book on Thomas was that he was happy in his Hennington Hills cave.

—Maybe he's outgrown it. And it's not a cave. He's turned it into quite an enterprise.

—Don't turn disingenuous on me, Archie. He's an untouchable there. The police won't arrest him and the courts won't prosecute him. There's no paper trail of any kind and no one's talking. I don't like it, but I can't change it. I've just had to live with it, and it was mostly fine as long as he kept to himself. We've managed to spend twenty years avoiding each other's toes, and now, out of nowhere, *this*, a disaster of epic proportions.

—It's hardly *that*—

—But aren't you as appalled . . . of course not, he's your son.

—Yes.

—So what *do* you think?

—I think he'd be a highly functioning, thoroughly efficient, completely amoral Mayor. I think Hennington would run like clockwork but would be corrupt at its core. It might survive a Thomas tenure, but it would end up as something altogether more ghastly and unpleasant.

—So you're with me that we have to do something?

—I'm not sure I'd go that far. I wasn't the best father to him. If this is what he wants to do, I'd feel like a fink standing in his way.

—But surely for the sake of the city—

—He's flesh and blood, Cora. He's never gone out of his way to hurt me. On the contrary, Hennington Hills has a profit margin unparalleled in Banyon Enterprises, and I'm assuming that's *after* he's fixed the books. He didn't buy that mansion with his *salary*. It may be for the good of the city, but who would I be if I crushed my own son?

248

—I'm not talking about crushing, Archie—

—He's made too public an announcement to step down without an all-out battle. He's far too tenacious and bloody-minded.

—Are you saying you can't help me?

—I don't know what I'm saying. Luther's not speaking to me, and I've no idea where he is. If I step in front of Thomas, where does that leave me? I'm old. Do I really want thwarting my only biological son to be my last action as a man? Who am I if I do that? He'd be an absolute disaster as Mayor. I think Hennington would become a fairly frightening place to live—

—But?

—But I'll be dead soon.

—Not *that* soon.

—Do you really think I've got another five years in me?

—Yes, I—

—I'm eighty-eight, Cora. Can you see me at ninety-three?

—You don't expect me to believe you'll give up on the entire future of our city just because you won't be around to see it?

—It might not be that bad.

—You just said yourself—

—I know what I just said, but maybe it won't. Maybe he's got better motives. Maybe it's a new leaf. How do we know? No one's even talked to him yet.

—Archie, with all due respect, you're whistling past the graveyard. You know how highly I think of you. You know how long I've respected you. Don't take this the wrong way, old friend, but I also know that you're a shrewd businessman. Do you honestly believe that if *you* were Mayor, you'd be able to practice enough restraint to keep all ten fingers out of the cookie jar? Do you honestly think that you'd be able to keep from utilizing some of the hidden, less-than-ethical perks of office? There's no disrespect intended here at all, Archie, but if *you* couldn't—

—I should tan your hide, but I see your point.

—Exactly. My private line's ringing. It's got to be Albert.

—He probably just heard. Go on, go talk to him. Jules just walked in anyway looking like someone ran over his puppy.

—I'll try to understand the quandary you're in, Archie, but *please* think it through. Your help would be invaluable.

—I'll give it my best.

—Thank you. Call me soon. Albert?

—Armageddon has arrived, and it's wearing a pinstripe suit, of all things.

—I know. I just got off the phone with Archie.

—Any insight?

—None, and I'm not even sure he would help us defeat Thomas.

—Why not? I thought they never got along.

—Not getting along is different to destroying your son's ambition. Plus, this whole schism with Luther's got him completely befuddled.

—Kind of late to become paternal. Can he at least help us with Jon Noth?

—What's Jon Noth got to do with it?

—So you didn't actually *see* the press conference?

—I was just pulling into the office. I heard most of it over the radio while sitting in the parking garage. I called Archie as soon as I got upstairs.

—You didn't call me first?

—Not now, Albert, the world's coming to pieces. What about Jon?

—He was standing off to the right when Thomas gave his little announcement. They left together at the end.

—I . . . He . . . Holy shit.

—It sort of makes sense in a screwed-up kind of way.

—I don't believe it.

—I believe he'd do such a thing, I just never would have believed he'd pick Thomas Banyon, the least palatable candidate in the city.

—Where the hell did they even meet?

—I'd like to have been a fly on *that* wall.

—You don't think—

—That somehow this is to get back at you? Only the scale of the endeavor makes it questionable.

—He's odd, but he's never been out-and-out crazy. Or malicious.

—You're forgetting the duel.

—He was a college student then, full of stupid overwhelming passions. But how can he still, after all this time . . . I don't believe it. He's up to something.

—Obviously.

—No, more than that. This is a ploy. Maybe he *has* gone off the deep end, but there's something more going on.

—An alliance with Thomas Banyon to take over the city?

—Like you said, it's only a question of scale.

—But why? I love you heart and soul, petal, but do you really think he'd go to these extraordinary lengths just to spite you? Although, having said that—

—I don't know, Albert. This is unbelievable. There's more here than we know. Was there anyone else at the press conference?

—Just Thomas, Jon, and a bunch of Hennington Hills flunkies from what I could tell. A distinct lack of VIPS. No one who might have even hinted at an endorsement.   251

—Which would suggest that it was thrown together quickly.

—It would seem. You'd think he would have had *someone* there to give him credibility, having none on his own. The man's a criminal.

—That doesn't mean he won't get elected.

—Some dirty laundry will have to come out in the campaign. It could all get very, very uncomfortable for him.

—It can't if he's running unopposed.

—*Somebody* will run, especially now. We can't be the only ones who know what a bad idea Mayor Banyon would be. What about Max?

—He's out of the race.

—Maybe he'll change his mind due to altered circumstances.

—This might make him want to stay out even more. Can you imagine running against Thomas Banyon?

—I hope *you're* not imagining it.

—My God, what if it came to that?

—It won't. We'll think of something.

—I'm going to call him.

—Thomas Banyon?

—Jon.

—Do you think he'll talk to you?

—Yes. If this is all some plot to get my attention, well, then he's got it.

—Be careful.

—He can't hurt me over the phone.

—You know what I mean.

—What's he up to? Why has the world suddenly gone crazy?

62. Maggerty in Purgatory.

The room heaved with an angry whiteness, even when he closed his eyes. He struggled against the fever, stopping only when the pain in his chest and head were too much. One hand was bound to the railing of the bed, the other in an arm-shaped box that he couldn't move away from his body. Every few minutes, he forgot and tried to touch his wound for comfort, failing every time. Whenever the pain and the fever cleared, he would suddenly panic because he was in an all-white room, tied to a bed, with the herd nowhere in sight. Then he would disappear again into the angry whiteness, only to re-awaken in the same room, beginning the process once more.

Maggerty had no idea how much time had passed, was passing. Often, he couldn't even tell what was real and what was a nightmare. Once, a white angel with a red face had forced knife after knife into his arm, draining all the blood from him. He had fought as hard as he could, but the room reared up and joined in. The nightmare swirled on in a twisting white-and-red spiral until he awoke again. The room had stopped moving, but there was a knife in his arm attached to a tube. The angel had won.

She caught herself looking for him.

After she struck him, the herd had moved away again, but it was soon apparent something was off. Each herdmember kept looking around in pensive turns, and few of them slept that night. Suddenly, it all seemed too quiet, too still. No thin-creature calls, no thin-creature smells. There was a small feeling of relief, but it was overtaken by a faint feeling of the world gone askew.

253

They missed him. So did she.

He had vanished once, years before, only to return a short time later, but this time was different. She had expelled him herself. She had been justified, but still. The next day, she had led them back to the place where it had happened. How would she treat him if she saw him? How would he react? He had proven himself a danger to the herd, a fact that was unacceptable. Expulsion had been the unambiguous and clear option. Yet somehow, the herd didn't feel quite right without him. He was small. He couldn't possibly prove more than a nuisance, *none* of the thin creatures could. Maybe he had learned his lesson. Years of calm shouldn't be thrown out because of one negative action. He would be welcomed back, chastened, injured maybe, but still welcome.

He wasn't there. The spot was empty. Only a faint remnant of his smell remained. She followed a brief trail of it, but it soon vanished altogether, as if into thin air. The herd shuffled behind her. It was a long while before they moved on again.

(—*It's going to take awhile for it to get completely through his system, but we're pleased with the results so far.*

—*So he's responding?*

—*In fits and starts but with observable progress, which is more than can be said for the gash on his torso.*

—*Still not healing?*

—*We've cut away a remarkable amount of dead tissue and the stitches are holding, but there's no real clotting. It's bizarre.*

—*Any ideas?*

—*I'd like to try him on the steroid-antibio combination we talked about.*

—May as well give it a try. Nothing else seems to work. Shame he can't tell us what it feels like.
—Story of his life, I'm guessing.)

On and on the limbo went until the most startling feeling of all. It took him a moment to realize what had happened. He was awake. And he knew it. He was *sure* of it. He knew it the whole day long. When the white angel with the red face came to him, he recognized that the angel was cleaning him. When he was tired, he took a nap and woke up again in the same white room where the same angel with the same red face was gently changing the tube in his arm.

He knew.

And then for a time he didn't know. The room bent towards him, the walls curving, the ceiling bending down. He curled up as best he could against the restraints, wrenching his eyes shut to prevent the room from getting inside him, but it didn't work. The white insinuated its way underneath his eyelids, forcing them back, forcing him to see see see. But then the angel returned and changed the tube in his arm again. Before long, everything was clear once more. He wasn't even concerned about the herd. He wanted to get back to them, there was no question of that, but for now it was all right to be here, under the care – for care was what it must have been – of the angel who could make the white step back to where it couldn't touch him.

He dreamed. And he was conscious of the dream. He was a boy again on the great farms to Hennington's south. It was the barely-remembered time before the goat, before the wound, before his life became whatever it had become. A trail engulfed in cherry trees rooted its way through a grove that sat like an island among the plowed fields. Maggerty's father

255

was buried there beneath an already decaying stone tablet. The trail twisted around the grave without ever quite reaching it, and for many years, Maggerty hadn't even known it was there. All he knew was that his father had just disappeared one day. In the dream, though, the trail changed its geography, and the grave became its terminus, a grassy circle bathed in sunlight even though this was where the grove was at its thickest. Maggerty sat there on the gravesite, eating fat, luscious cherries by the fistful. He was alone, and the silence, save for the sound of smacking cherry consumption, was both comforting and complete. A rustling sound started to float in faintly from all sides. Maggerty smiled to himself. They were coming. The rustling grew louder. Maggerty dropped the cherries he was holding and clapped his hands together. He heard twigs breaking and the sounds of bodies pushing their way through tightly packed trees. He could hear breathing, snorts, grunts, a call or two as one of them became momentarily stuck. The ground began to tremble in an awesome low rumble. Maggerty turned to one side and then the other as he caught sight of something moving, of branches bending, of trees swaying. He saw shadows moving around the circle of the grave, tantalizingly out of reach beyond the border of trees. He leaned his head back and yelled a call of welcome. Come, come, come to me, here I am, come to me, I'm ready.

Maggerty opened his eyes. He recognized the room again. He felt the soft whiteness of the sheets. He saw the angel's back as it left, surely after providing care for him, just him. He was mending. He was healing. It felt like the right idea. He would be back with the herd soon. That was what the dream meant. He would be there with them again. He would feel that feeling again. They would welcome him as one of their own again.

He had never felt happier in his life.

Which, as has already been observed, just couldn't last.

63. The Reasons Why We Do Things.

—Mr Banyon? Your father is here.

—Tell him ... tell him hold on for a second. Don't tell him that. Tell him I need to wrap something up, and I'll see him in just a quick moment, okay?

—Certainly, sir.

Archie wouldn't like to be kept waiting, but for one of the rare times in his life, Thomas Banyon was unnerved. He had expected a call from Archie about launching his Mayoral bid, had welcomed it, in fact, with a deep curiosity as to how his father would take it. Not well, that was for sure, what with his longstanding friendship with Cora Larsson, but there was a part of Thomas that knew Archie would be proud of his audacity. Grudging acceptance was an emotion Thomas liked to inspire in people. The call, however, had taken hours to come, and the Mayoral bid had been dealt with in one sentence.

—Thomas, I need to talk to you.

—I thought you might.

—No, the Mayor's office, whatever, I don't care. I need to talk to you about something else, something much more important.

—What?

—I can't talk over the mobile phone. God knows who's listening.

—How many times do I have to tell you? No one can hear—

—I can be over there in fifteen minutes. Do you have time to see me?

—Of course, I do, but what—

—Fifteen minutes.

The only real likelihood was a problem with Luther. Thomas had never really gotten to the bottom of the split between the two. Neither had anyone else, as far as he could tell. Maybe there were shady goings-on that Archie, no slouch at shady goings-on himself earlier in his business career, needed Thomas to look after. Which, frankly, was annoying. He resented being Archie's clean-up man for the other side of the law, if that's what it was about.

But there had been something else. For years, Archie had treated Thomas with a polite and distant deference. Thomas guessed it was out of guilt at the banishment to Hennington Hills and maybe hidden pride that Thomas had made something out of it anyway, despite the lack of expectation. They hadn't talked much over the years, especially as Luther ascended, and perhaps they hadn't even really liked one another, but there had been no violent break, no battle to establish position, just year after year of calmly going about their individual lives, doing their level best not to intersect except when absolutely necessary. So for Archie to call with such, what was the word, such *need* was extraordinary and had managed to shake Thomas to the extent that he needed a moment to compose himself before seeing his father. First rule of business, family or not, composure was king.

He drummed his fingers along his desktop. He inhaled and exhaled audibly. He was pissed off that he was this nervous about a meeting with anyone and began to grow even angrier at Archie. He shook his leg up and down, tapping his foot testily on the floor. He punched the page button so hard it almost hurt.

—Send him in, Rita.

A pale Archie sloped through the door, keeping his gaze aimed downwards, even when he collapsed into the chair facing Thomas.

—You all right, old man?

—Luther is gone.

A breadth of silence opened up. Thomas had no response. Archie seemed unwilling or unable to go on. Thomas' annoyance grew steadily. The thought occurred that there was no way Archie would get this upset if it was Thomas who had 'gone'. The only thing that tempered the feelings around the thought was the lack of surprise accompanying it. If Archie had ever made this sort of desperate fuss over *him*, Thomas would have been among the amazed.

—What do you mean, 'gone', exactly? Did he leave town?

—No.

—Was he kidnapped? What?

Archie, clearly struggling to maintain his composure, set about methodically straightening his tie. Holy shit, was he *crying*?

—It didn't really hit me until now. I was fine until I got here. He's been murdered, Thomas.

—*What?*

—The police called me over to his house this morning. His blood's all over the bedroom, well, it *was* all over his bedroom, but someone tried to clean it up. And some idiot neighbor finally reported someone dragging a body out of the house.

—A body. Are you sure it was Luther?

—Who else could it be? And I know who did it. It was that little Rumour bastard he hired from you to fuck him.

Even in his various levels of surprise, Thomas read checked anger in Archie. So there was blame in this, too.

—How do you know that?

—It's the only scenario that explains everything. Have you seen this Peter Wickham in the last week? Has he been in to work?

—No. He's been taking some vacation time.

259

—You see? You see? There's your answer. The police won't listen to me. All this shit about searching for 'possible suspects'. They won't even admit that he's been murdered. 'No body', they say. I mean, the dumbfuck neighbor saw someone dragging out a body a week ago. A week, and the moron only reported it now.

—Why would someone wait a week to report a body being dragged from a home?

And now having to fish out the old man's exaggeration. This was getting more aggravating by the second.

—They said they thought it was just someone helping a drunk friend.

—Which it very well could have been.

—Goddamnit, Thomas, help me! You're the only one who can do this without screwing everything up.

—You want me to get you Peter Wickham before the police do.

—Yes! Yes, yes, yes. Find him, assuming he hasn't fled already. Find him and bring him to me. Find Luther's body—

Archie halted his speech, took a deep breath, and began a steady, almost stately weeping. It all fell into place. Archie didn't care about Thomas' run for Mayor because he needed Thomas' help to find his precious favored son, and if there had ever been any lingering doubt about *that* exact status, it vanished now forever. As Archie wept on and on, something Thomas had not seen since the death of his own mother and sisters so many years ago, a final break occurred, without anger, without even much disappointment. Any connection between himself and his father disappeared like so much ether. A cold purposefulness moved in its stead. If this was how it was, then this was how it was. Business was business was business was business. He would put his private detectives on the hunt for Peter Wickham. It would mean diverting some of them from the hunt for Jacki Strell, but so be it. There would be a price to pay, for everyone involved, but so be that, too.

So be it. So be it.

—Rita?

—Yes, sir?

—Please have Mr Banyon's chauffeur come in and help him to his car. Mr Banyon is feeling unwell.

—Certainly, sir.

Thomas looked at Archie, still hunched forward, still crying.

—Go home and stop worrying. I'll find Peter Wickham for you.

—Thank you. Thank you, my son.

Archie held out his hand. Thomas declined to take it.

64. Rest.

He could not, would not think, 'Luther's body'.

Luther was dead, no question about it, but that was not the end of the argument. There was a fantasy, an old wives' tale, an absurd metaphorical fable out of the Sacraments. There was his grandmother's solemn, sworn word to the truth of it all, a legend heard from a friend of a friend, a tale woven and passed along by the invisible They, 'They say . . .'. There was an ancient story that any priest would deny ever existing or ever having survived Pistolet, but if you asked five times on five different occasions, that same priest would reward your persistence with a quiet wave inside and relate whatever hearsay still clung to the Church's misty past.

Peter refused to entertain, even for a second, any of the doubts, any of the utter, empirical impossibility of it all, 261 because he knew, without knowing how, that his faith would have to remain unwavering. It would never, ever work, it was completely impossible, it was perhaps blasphemous, even dangerous, but these conditions had to be disregarded. He shut out all doubts. In that moment of complete devastation, of thorough-going grief, he had sealed his decision and would, from here on out, act on faith.

Death is the end. Almost always. What had filtered through the Bondulay for generations, never confirmed, was the rare case of the soul who had not left for the greater beyond but who had been filled with enough grief to be unable to live in this world, whose spiritual pain took their life but didn't push them any further. Theirs was not death, it was a rest from grief.

And they could be called back.

Peter didn't know how, but he would find out. Luther was the rare case. He would call Luther back, and when Luther was rested, Luther would return. It was preposterous, it was impossible, it was outside the realm of sane thinking, and Peter knew it would happen beyond a shadow of a doubt.

There were logistical problems. He could only stay at his own flat for a short time because it would obviously be the first place any authorities would look for him. He didn't doubt they would be looking either. It was only a matter of time before someone started investigating the trail, and he would have to use the brief interval wisely. He had decided that first night to take Luther to his own house anyway, allowing what little time he had there to think of the next move. He had taken Luther's car, driving it down the darkest streets he could find. He took Luther up to the bedroom and drove the car back to Luther's house. He got back on his cycle and sped home.

That night he went online to find some practical information. It was most important of all to keep Luther in a condition of rest, so that when he returned (which was inevitable, only a matter of time), he would have an undamaged vessel to return to. Peter found what he was looking for and went and purchased the entire waxseed oil stock from five different all-night markets and returned home. He removed Luther's clothes and coated every inch of him with the brown, viscous oil. He kept his mind on the business in hand, ignoring the lips he had kissed, the body he had stroked, the hands he had held. He took clean sheets and wrapped Luther tightly, legs bound together, arms bound to torso. By eight in the morning, Luther rested peacefully on Peter's bed. The oil was only a temporary solution, but it would do for now. Peter sat on a chair in his room and finally drifted off to sleep. He would decide what to do later.

And then time had just kept passing without a decision. A day, then two, then almost a week. Peter had called in with vacation time and then never left the house, never left Luther's side. He prayed with long-forgotten words from his childhood, asking (who?) for both guidance and for the safe return of Luther. He did more research on the computer looking for Bondulay teachings that might be helpful. He dusted off his own long-forgotten copy of the Sacraments, reading it cover to cover. He even got the name of the local Bondulay minister, one Jarvis Kingham, but somehow never got the courage to allow another person, and their inevitable doubts, into the mixture.

But he was becoming more and more concerned about staying in the house. Someone would start looking soon. Luther couldn't go missing for long without someone noticing, estranged father or not. But Peter also became *less* sure of what came next, of what to do, of where in the world he could take Luther to keep him safe until he returned.

263

On the seventh morning, waking up for the seventh time in the chair in his bedroom, for the seventh time looking immediately to Luther still prone on the bed, Peter realized something. He blinked into the morning air, already baking hot. He let out a long breath, feeling alert and completely awake. Within a moment, he was sure. He went to Luther, touching him firmly, tenderly. A second later, he grabbed his helmet, ran to his cycle, and took off into the burgeoning day.

65. I'm Begging You.

Even before Cora opened her mouth, Max knew what she wanted, but that didn't mean he was going to make it any easier for her.

—Maggerty's coming along well.

—That's great. Max—

—He's responding really well to the Thoraxin, too. He still can't hold a regular conversation, but he no longer seems to be perpetually terrified.

—It still bothers you, doesn't it?

—I don't like the idea of trying a new medicine on him without his assent.

—He can't give his assent, and your new job gives you legal power of attorney. You specifically asked for it, remember? Now—

—But that doesn't give me the right to treat him like a guinea pig.

—Stop whining, Max, you made the right decision. You've circumvented his free will but made him an immeasurably happier person. Let the philosophers figure out the right and wrong. Listen—

—I still wish we knew what happened. No witnesses. No sign of The Crash. It's strange—

—Would you just shut up for a goddamned second? I'm trying to talk to you.

—I'm not running, Cora. I don't care how awful Thomas Banyon is. The people in this city aren't stupid. Someone will run against him, and he'll lose.

—But what if that doesn't happen? He's got more influence than you think, Max. He could win.

—Then the voters would have the man they wanted. It's democracy, Cora. If Thomas Banyon wins the election, then he wins the election. End of story. This isn't a monarchy with rungs of ascension.

—That's evasion. You know what a disaster Thomas Banyon would be.

—*I don't want to run.* I haven't had a single second thought since deciding to drop out of the race. I'm not even ambiguous about it anymore. Besides, how in the world did the options boil down to just me? It's not like I could step into the race and somehow automatically win.

—You're the best candidate we have. Do you honestly think they'd choose Thomas Banyon over you?

—Yes, as a matter of fact. The man's got power, money, and influence.

—So do you.

—A fraction of what he has. And what if I *was* a real challenge? Do you have any idea how ugly a race against Thomas Banyon could get?

—What about how ugly Hennington would become if he actually won?

—Oh, for heaven's sake, Cora. It's just Mayor. No offense, but it's not like we're electing a god to control our destinies. He implements a few unpleasant policies and cuts a few   265 ribbons. He'd have one term tops. Someone would get riled during his term, someone *viable*, and would run against him in five years and win. I think maybe you're over-reacting.

—And I think maybe you're *under*-reacting.

—That's not a word.

—Shush. You yourself admit that he's got the consolidated power to win. Why then do you think he wouldn't use that power to *stay* in office and ruin the city?

—You're overdoing it. How many times have you complained to me about lacking the authority to do something? Or your frustration over the Council watering down a perfect piece of legislation so badly that it manages to make whatever the problem was *worse*. That's the way things go. It's just government. Most people don't care. And you know *why* they don't care? Because government doesn't touch them.

—You're going too far the other way. You know government affects them. I've tried to *make* it affect them in a positive way. The Mayor sets direction. The Mayor *initiates*. The Mayor sets the tone of how the City runs itself. In the hands of someone like Thomas Banyon—

—You're giving him too much credit. Some bad leaders are just bad leaders. Some oily politicians are just oily politicians. Just because he's venal and rough-and-ready with the law doesn't mean he's evil. He's a bully, not a demon. There's a difference. His father will probably keep him in line anyway.

—I don't think Archie Banyon will have much say in the matter. Plus, there's more that you don't know. Thomas Banyon is being supported, might have been *recruited* for all I know, by an old nemesis of mine.

—'An old nemesis'? Are you a superhero?

—You're just looking for a slap, aren't you? Someone from my past named Jon Noth has suddenly re-entered the picture after forty years. Frankly, he seems to have turned into a complete loon in the interval. I had to have him forcibly thrown out of a fundraising dinner because he more or less threatened me and Albert.

—Oh, *him*.

—Yes, and guess who's suddenly standing with Thomas Banyon when he announces for Mayor?

—You're kidding. How?

—Trust me, I'd love to know. Suddenly the man who veritably stalked me at public functions won't return my calls and has disappeared from sight. Something's going on. I don't know what it is, but it's more than just Thomas Banyon running for Mayor. Jon Noth has something up his sleeve. If Thomas Banyon wins the Mayoral race, I have no idea what that means for Jon's plans.

—That explains the paranoia, then.

—I am *not* being paranoid.

—You're certainly not acting yourself.

—Neither are you. You're playing devil's advocate because you don't want to run for Mayor.

—I'm playing devil's advocate because my saying I don't want to run clearly isn't enough to convince you of the fact that *I don't want to run*!

—Why are you making me beg you?

—Are you even listening to yourself? If it's so all-fired important that someone run against Thomas Banyon, then why don't *you* run?

—I can't run.

—Why not? There's no law. Everyone's mourning your retirement anyway. Seems like a no-brainer to me.

—Besides the fact that I don't want to—

—Sounds familiar.

—I can't run.

—Why not?

—Because.

—'Because'? Even Talon doesn't let me get away with that.

—Because I think it's exactly what Jon wants, that's why. It's just a hunch, but for some reason, I think he wants me to run again. He's gotten some bizarre scheme into his head.

—That doesn't make any sense.

—Nothing he's done so far has. But I just know, I *feel* it in my heart, that running would be playing right into his hands.

—And that would necessarily be a bad thing?

—Oh, my dear, I don't think any of us have any idea how bad.

—You've no proof of this?

—Only that it's the one explanation that holds everything together.

—It's the one explanation that holds everything together that you *know*. It's also mightily self-centered.

—I have my reasons.

—I can't change this decision based on a hunch. I can't upheave my life again based on a feeling.

—But you might if I found out more?

—I didn't say that. I was just pointing out the faults in your argument to convince me.

—Then I'll find out more and convince you.

—I *said*—

—I know, but I need to find out more anyway. I'll tell you when I do. I don't think I'm wrong, though. Something bad is on the horizon. I can feel it. Ever since I saw him again, I felt it. Something's in the works. Something that needs to be stopped.

—You're talking like a superhero again.

—Oh, Max, if only I *was*.

66. Young Man's Fancy.

—I'm telling you, she *is*.

—No, she isn't.

—Are you blind? Watch the way she looks at you.

—She's just being friendly.

—Take it from someone much older and much more experienced. She's interested.

—Why would she be interested in me?

—Why *wouldn't* she? Look at how handsome you are. You've cleaned yourself up. You're dressing better—

—Thanks to you.

—Your skin is clearer than I've ever seen it, and you've gotten rid of that awful gauntness that made you look half dead. She thinks you're attractive. It's obvious to everyone in the restaurant.

—Give me a break.

—I'll do no such thing. Here. Miss? Miss?

—What are you doing?

—Is everything all right?

—Perfectly, but I do think we've got a potential case of missed opportunity if I don't say something.

—Jon—

—What's your name, miss?

—Jill.

She tapped her nametag. It read 'Jill'.

—So it is. Jill, I'd like you to meet Eugene.

She turned and smiled at Eugene, but all she could see was the back of his head as he stared down into his plate. He mumbled something to his dessert.

—What was that, Eugene?

—I said hello.

269

—He's going to require the patience of a saint, my dear girl, but I assure you, he's worth it.

—Is he your son?

—Yes, why not? Tell me, marvelous Jill, provocative Jill, where are you from?

—I was born here in Hennington.

—Ah, a native! So is Eugene.

—Really? Where'd you go to high school?

—Cascade.

—Me, too! When did you graduate?

—I dropped out.

—Only to follow his dream, dear Jill.

—What dream is that?

—Bass player in a band.

—Cool! I play drums in a band down at the Hive on Tuesdays.

—See, a match made in heaven. What are you doing tonight, percussive Jill? Because I know for a fact Eugene has the night off.

—I'm free tonight.

—Perfect. When does your shift end?

—Seven.

—Then he'll pick you up here at seven. Sound good?

—Sounds good to me? What about him?

—Yes, Eugene, what about you?

Eugene's response was a blush so crimson both Jon and Jill thought for a moment he might be choking. His response was a whisper.

—If it's okay by you.

When he pulled up six hours later in the Bisector, he was still blushing. Before he could get out, she opened the passenger door herself and hopped in.

—Hi!

—Hey.

—This is okay with you, isn't it? I mean, you can just give me a ride home if you want. Your father kind of forced the issue, and I mean, I think you're totally cute and that shyness thing is really attractive, but you know, I'm only fine with it if you're fine with it, okay?

—No. No, I want to.

—What'd you say?

—I said I want to.

—Then the first rule is you have to actually look at me once before we go anywhere, okay?

She had a short, black bob of hair that framed an open, smiling face. Her nose was small, perhaps a bit too small, throwing her enormous green eyes into even greater relief. The green was the color of dark moss and gave her a literate air that contradicted the way she smacked her chewing gum. She wasn't outrageously beautiful. She was better. She was *accessibly* beautiful.

—Sorry.

—Nothing to be sorry about. You're just shy. This car is incongruent with known reality, you know? I mean, I see it, here it is, I'm sitting in it, and I still don't believe it exists. It's like a carnival or something, all on its own.

—So that's . . . good?

—Oh, yeah. Points already on the car alone, but trust me, I'm not that shallow. I mean, I am, but there's depth below the shallows. Where are we going?

They went miniature golfing. By the seventh hole, Eugene had only produced forty-three words of conversation.

—I counted. Look, it's only a certain amount of fun to do all the work, then it just becomes plain work. You're cute and all, but I could have this much fun at home with my hand and a mirror, all right?

271

Eugene took his putt between the swinging arms of the giant wooden gorilla before he answered.

—I'm sorry.

—The eleventh time you've said that.

—I'm just ... You're just ...

—Ye-esss?

—So much prettier than the girls I usually go out with.

—Oh, your first full sentence and you hit the bullseye.

She smiled at him, and for the first time, it was a pure smile, without bluster. It was even almost bashful. She looked away from him.

—I'm not that pretty.

—What are you talking about? Have you even *seen* yourself? *I'm* the one who's a pain to look at.

—Are you high? You're totally handsome. I didn't think in a million years that you'd even show up tonight.

—You're kidding. I didn't think *you'd* be there.

—And yet here we both are.

—I know. So this was all—

—Bravado and girly stupidity. I thought I could brazen my way into a good-night kiss and then you'd never call again.

—I thought you were only coming on the date because Jon asked you to and you were too nice to say no.

—I wouldn't waste a whole evening out of politeness. I'm not dumb. *I* thought your father would make you come because otherwise I'd be stranded. You call your father by his first name?

—He's not my father.

—He said he was.

—He's my boss. He does stuff like that.

—So we're both here despite the fact that we each think the other is here only out of courtesy?

—Or that we're giving each other a pity date.

—How desperate is that? Shit, what does that say about us?

—That we're both kind of pathetic?

—Or that we're made for each other.

—I don't think it's a pity date. I think I'm lucky that you were there when I pulled up.

—And I think I'm lucky you pulled up.

They stood staring at each other, holding the gaze long past where it should have been uncomfortable. The gorilla's arms went slowly up and then slowly back down. Eugene held up his club.

—I don't even like miniature golf.

—Neither do I.

—Want to go get something to eat?

—And talk for a bit, now that you've got your tongue back?

—Yeah.

They didn't even take the equipment back to the clubhouse, leaving their clubs and balls at the seventh hole, joining hands as they stepped back on the path. The gorilla swung its arms in silent protest as they disappeared into the night.

67. Old(er) Man's (and Woman's) Fancy.

—Ooh.

—Oh, my heavens.

—With ... ouch ... with those—

—What was that?

—Shh, just let it happen.

—There, yes, there, *that*.

273

—What?

—Slowly now.

—Who ... No ... right there ... *there*. Who am I touching?

—Me?

—Then who is this right here?

—Me again.

—Good Lord, the *flexibility*—

—I've got it—

—Hold on, I want to—

—Up, up, up, up, up, up.

—My *God*, that feels ... so—

—Here, take hold here.

—Okay.

—And you grab onto here—

—All right, now let's all of us—

—Moving—

—Slowly, don't lose it.

—With the ... Oh!

—Nice, isn't it?

—Good God.

—Albert?

—I'm dumbfounded.

—I told you.

—Wow, in fact ... in fact—

—Go ahead, it's what we're here for.

—Cora?

—Please, Albert, yes, please, I'm ready whenever you—

—Aaaaaahhhhhhhh!

—Yes! Very nice.

—Very nice indeed.

—I'm ... wait ... I'm going ... Unnnnnnhhh!

—Hold her head. There we go—

—Oh, goodness.
—Just—
—With—
—Here—
—Come on—
—Excellent!
—And Kevin makes three.
—Man, oh, man.
—That was—
—I know.
—With the—
—I know.
—Hold on, my arm—
—Where?
—Darling, could you—
—Yes, here.
—Thank you.
They lay breathing.
—I think I'm going to have a cold glass of water.
—What, *now*?
—Yes, anyone want anything?
—Just a moment's rest is all.
—I'm with her.
—You two. You're going to wear me out, and that's saying something. I'll be right back.
Kevin smiled that warm smile of his. As he walked away from the bed, they both watched his naked backside, so smooth and compact, with the delightful pattern of hair creeping up his thighs. He turned to them as he went out of the bedroom, smiled again, and closed the door.
—Quite something.
—Isn't he, though?
—For kind of a little guy, he's got real oomph. I mean,   275

what *was* that? Where does someone even learn to do something like that?

—Who cares as long as he does it again?

—Do you think we're giving him any pleasure?

—I think it's obvious, isn't it? Why would he keep coming back?

—You would just think he'd have other, you know, people to meet.

—What does that mean? 'Other people to meet'. He's not a public service, Cora.

—Don't laugh at me. You know. People his own age. People who could give him more than we can. More quality time. More of the things of a proper relationship.

—Oh.

—Surely you concede he deserves it.

—I see what's going on.

—What?

—I see where you're headed with this.

—What are you talking about?

—You've got a little crush on our dear Kevin.

—What? Well, *of course*, I do. Don't you? He's different from the ones we've had before. He's kind. He's generous. He has a brain *and* a decent job.

—Which he's really good at, by the way. He'll be the auction house's senior art appraiser by year's end, you just watch.

—And he's good-looking, too, in just the right way, without being boring about it. I can't figure out why he's not setting hearts afire citywide.

—You're afraid he's going to dump us.

—Aren't you?

—No.

—You'd be willing to see him go?

—Of course not. I'm not afraid because I don't think he's going to.

—It has to end eventually.

—Why?

—What do you mean 'why'? You know good and well why.

—Tell me.

—We're twice his age. Our attractiveness is only going to stick around for a little while even to the most generous of eyes. Plus, we're a couple. Two's company and three's a crowd. Jealous alliances always happen with *trois*. It's only a matter of time before someone gets hurt.

—Those are all nonsense reasons.

—Not all.

—Just conventional wisdom, nothing more. And if we had ever believed conventional wisdom at any point in our lives, then you and I wouldn't be together either.

—You're not suggesting—

—I'm not suggesting anything. I'm only telling you that, yes, I'm terribly fond of him as well and I don't want this to end, but that I also don't see why it has to any time soon.

—But—

—No 'buts', my darling bud. We've come all these years and years without sticking to rules and we've thrived. Why should we adhere to them now? Why not live in each pleasurable moment instead of forecasting the end? You'll have more fun that way.

—Life is just getting too strange lately.

—All the more reason to take what pleasure you can.

—I suppose, but it does tend to wear me out.

—I repeat, all the more reason—

—I heard you the first time. He does help one to forget, doesn't he?

—Rather thoroughly.

—I wonder what we're helping him forget.

—Oh, really, Cora, do we have to help him forget *anything*? Why can't you take this at face value? Maybe, and here's a radical idea, maybe he fancies us. Maybe he so enjoys our times together that he actually looks forward to the next one.

—But all we do is . . . you know.

—Do you really think that's all we do?

—Meaning what?

—We talk together, and we sleep together. I mean, actual sleep, not the sex. We eat meals together. We share each other intimately, in more ways than just the obvious physical one.

—But it's not sharing a life together.

—Is that what you want?

—Is that what *you* want?

—I told you. I'm very fond of Kevin. I very much like having him as a part of our lives. *Our* lives, not my life. And yes, I want what we have to continue with him. I want him to keep coming back to us as long as possible. But that's future. Right now, I'm enjoying him being here when he's here. I enjoy the pleasure he gives me. I enjoy the pleasure he gives you. I enjoy the pleasure we give him. He's a bit of fun that's turned into a gift, my love. We should cherish it for what it is, not what it might or might not be at some unspecified future date, *especially* with how strange the world seems to be getting.

—Well, I'll agree with you there. If Kevin can make me forget 'Mayor Banyon', then I'm all for that.

—But that's not going to happen.

—It might.

—It might, but Max'll run.

278   —He told me no.

—He'll come around. Luther Pickett's disappeared. Things have gotten serious. He'll run.

—I wish I could be as certain.

—Then you'll just have to trust me, on this matter as well as on Kevin.

—I wish I could speak with Jon again.

—And accomplish what?

—If I'm his aim, then I'm the one who can get through to him.

—Then go see him.

—I thought you were opposed.

—Only on the grounds that it was what he wanted, but if you think you can resolve this by seeing him, I'm all for any means of getting him out of our lives for good. I for one am sick of discussing petty little Jon Noth.

—I love you, Albert.

—Oh! Well, I love you, too, beautiful one, but where did that come from?

—Just . . . nowhere. 'Petty' is a good word that suddenly makes it all feel a little better.

—I'm glad. A little bit in love with Kevin, too? It's okay if you are.

—A little bit in love with Kevin, too.

—Good. Me, too.

—I'll make it unanimous.

Kevin walked back towards the bed from the hallway.

—How long have you been listening?

—Long enough to assuage any fears. I'm happy as the proverbial clam when I'm with the two of you. I'm not planning on going anywhere any time soon.

—Glad to hear it.

—I'll second that.

—Good. Are you rested up? We can sleep if you want, 279

but if you're up for it, I've got something else I've been
wanting to show you. Yes? Terrific. First, cross your arms
like this, then using both feet . . .

68. The Prodigal.

He fell asleep and didn't dream. When he awoke, he was
somewhere else.

Maggerty was first aware of wetness under his back. He
opened his eyes. The ceiling had turned blue, a light, faraway
blue with white –

Clouds.

He was able to sit up, free of restraints. The heavy bandage
was off his arm. He felt strange. The sun hung low in the sky,
and the air carried the clarity of morning, early morning. It
was quiet, extremely so. His mind, he noticed with curiosity,
felt as sharp as the waking breeze across his face and out-
stretched hands. The distant panic was gone. The awful suffocating colours that had swooped in on him so much lately
weren't even in sight. He felt as good as he had in years. *Still.*
Yes, he felt that way still.

He reached into his shirt and ran his fingers along his
wound. It wasn't the mess it usually was, but there was still
an ache there. He let out a sigh of relief. He wasn't dead,
then. What did this all mean? Had the room with the angel
been a dream? It hadn't felt like one, and now for the first
time in a long while, Maggerty felt sure that he could tell the
difference. He had a full stomach. His clothes were clean. His
wound had been washed. Yet not a dream. Where had that
been, then? And where was this now?

He looked around slowly. He recognized the high lea on
the upper end of the Arboretum, a flat, green rink of grass

surrounded by trees, perched on a hilltop away from the main paths of the park. The sound of twigs breaking leapt suddenly from the dreamworld of his father's gravesite into this real one. A low rumbling came from the downhill edge of the lea. If this was all real, which it *must* be, then that meant the herd was either coming into or moving away from this place.

He pulled himself to his feet. His legs were stiff, and he cramped after only a few steps. The snapping, rustling sounds continued but seemed to be getting quieter. The normal panic of losing the herd filled him (or was it a bit less?). He forced himself forward through the pain, hopping on one foot to try to shake out a charley horse. He made it to the edge of the lea and plunged downward into the trees. A rack of ferns tripped him up, covering the knees of his pants in dirt. He stood and took a moment to brush it off before the oddity of the action stopped him. He pushed his way out of the ferns and headed back down the hill. Rounding two large trees, he hopped over a fallen log, and entered a small clearing. And there they were.

They were indeed making their way down through a thickly wooded part of the Arboretum, towards a small reservoir hidden away near the back, an arduous trek for animals so big, through densely packed trees and formidable underbrush. He could remember following them there only a handful of times. Yet here they were heading for it again. Maggerty remembered the briny river, remembered the mud at the edge of the lake, remembered the disappearance of the eagles. He couldn't quite put it together in his head, but it all must be related somehow.

He caught up with the herd easily. Some of the older animals were having to roam far to the left and right to find easier openings to pass through and soon he was walking among them, slipping through small passages, keeping out of 281 the paths of the animals. He reached the front of the herd, somehow passing the lead animal without seeing her through the greenery. The sound of rustling and breaking twigs was behind him. He had grown thirsty from the exertion and wanted to get to the reservoir before the animals muddied it with their feet. This was also a new thought, maybe even a new sensibility, and the distraction nearly caused him to stumble into the water as he came through a thick wall of ivy. He walked around the water's edge to get to the other side before the animals started wading in. He lowered his face and began taking a long, deep drink. He heard a snapping of wood. He looked up briefly as the lead animal broke through the edge of the woods and took her first steps into the cool water.

She froze when she saw him there, catching his eyes once and watching as he continued to drink. She immediately noticed his new smell. Or rather his lack of one. She inhaled deeply. The sick sweetness had disappeared. So had the normal rankness that was his usual accompaniment. Instead, a smell that was almost *clean* drifted lightly from him. She inhaled again to make sure she had scented right. He made no move towards her or any of the other members of the herd as they made their way knee-deep into the pond. Instead, he simply carried on drinking. She could hear the slurping of his mouth on the water, could actually smell the satisfaction flooding through his body.

He had left and returned somehow different. He still made no move as the rest of the herd finally crowded their way in, churning up dirt and debris, turning the water brown with motion. She waited until the thin creature had fully satiated himself, watching him sit back quietly. Slowly, she took her gaze away from him and began to drink. The conflict of the thin creature rose in her head once more, his sudden presence confusing her feelings as much as his sudden absence had. He *was* different somehow, but that didn't mean he wouldn't endanger them again. She welcomed his return, especially given the new smells and the calm she could sense in him, but actually seeing him in the flesh, she knew he would have to be watched. Welcome or not, another attack and she wouldn't turn her head.

Maggerty leaned against a tree near the water's edge. He felt the sun hot and clear on his face and the coolness of the water still swishing around his feet. He decided that he truly *must* be happy, because he couldn't imagine feeling any better. It was all so new. There were so many things he would have to get used to, so many new thoughts that seemed to keep popping up. He felt something strange on his face, a weird pull of muscle. He leaned forward to try to catch his reflection in the water.

He was smiling.

69. Want.

Look at him there. Just who does he think he is?

Mistrust was natural, of course. How could someone who had appeared out of nowhere with an offer too good to be true ever be considered trustworthy for anything? Thomas was no fool, as he had proven on occasion after occasion, particularly in creative ways to those who had considered him such, and he wasn't taking any chances with Jon Noth, no sir. Jon was being very helpful in the campaign, had footed a surprisingly large amount of cash, and had unexpectedly turned out to be a wizard at building an office from scratch, seemingly pulling volunteers out of thin air. He continually insisted that his only desire was the defeat of Cora Larsson and that since Thomas was the man to do it, Thomas was the man he would help. This lack of pretense to be Thomas' friend was reassuring, but still, Thomas eyeballed Jon's every move. He would have been a fool not to.

Right? Thomas watched him across the room, cajoling a plump female volunteer to inject a little more enthusiasm into her scripted phone pitch. He certainly had, was it *charisma*? The word felt right. He was handsome enough, had certainly kept himself well-groomed for his age. He was the kind of man that young college girls fell for: older, intelligent, experienced, attentive. In unpleasant, unguarded moments, Thomas himself felt flattered by Jon's attentions, but he usually spat the feeling away and lit up a cigarillo. He had to admit, though, this man had *something*. He watched the plump volunteer's face positively beam when Jon spoke to her, watched her whole body language change pleasurably when Jon put a hand on her back. When he stepped away from her, she picked up her phone and in under a minute had pulled in a thousand-dollar donation from a cold call. Jon squeezed her shoulder and walked away while she was already on to the next unsuspecting voter.

The search into Jon's background had proven interesting yet inconclusive. No apparent family. A degree in history from Mansfield, of all places, that he seemed to have disregarded the second he left school. Went overseas towards the Leeward Side to an as yet undetermined land for nearly eight years. Arrived back in the Fifty Shores under the name Aaron Sevillian, an alias he dropped six years later with as little explanation as that which had accompanied it. Founded a shipping business between the Fifty Shores and Chamberlin that thrived and thrived and thrived until he abruptly sold everything nearly fifteen years ago. And for that fifteen years, there was exactly zip to be found on him. He might as well have sailed off the edge of the world but for his sudden reappearance in Hennington. There were some faint whisperings of a religious conversion that happened, was abandoned, then refound, but nothing more than that. There was also a vague if nonsensical story that he had wandered the Leeward Coast for that time as some kind of vagabond. Thomas was running low on reconnaissance manpower, though, what with the concurrent investigations for Jacki Strell and now Luther. He'd had to pull back while still being without a concrete picture of this stranger who was now exhorting the young girls folding leaflets to fold even faster.

From all available information, it also seemed that Jon Noth was almost immeasurably rich, perhaps even more so than Thomas' own father, but both men, as with all the wealthiest of the wealthy, had secreted most of it away in differently named corporations and God only knew where else. When Archie finally died, Thomas expected to spend at least a decade tracking down all of the family wealth, even more so now that it looked like Luther had been murdered. Or disappeared. Or whatever the fuck had happened. Which of course was now yet *another* headache to add to the list, along with just where in this Piece-of-Shitville Jacki was hiding. How could one woman, seemingly alone, though Thomas had his doubts about that, keep evading his men? And again, why did he even care? Fuck her. If she had quit Forum – and it seemed she had, all the dealers could only comment on her absence – then she was worthless now anyway. Ex-Forumheads were notoriously members of life's rubbish heap. And why was he even bothering to think about this now?

He glanced down to the papers in front of him. He had lost his place again. Oh, yes, a speech. Another fucking speech. About agriculture. Who gave a shit about agriculture?

—Hey, Jon?

285

—Yes?

—Who gives a shit about agriculture? This is a city. All the farmlands are outside city borders.

—Half the members of Hennington Hills give a shit about agriculture. Agriculture is how they pay their substantial membership fees. Don't be bullheaded, Thomas. You know that.

—Of course I know that, but what I also know is that money from Hennington Hills members is not something I have to be too worried about collecting.

—But you'll get twice as much if you show an interest.

—I know these people a lot better than you do.

—True enough, but I know *people*. Trust me on this one. It's not hard, just a bunch of general statistics that'll make it look like you care. You'll thank me for it. Hell, *they'll* thank you for it. With a large check.

—All right, fine. Another thing. When are we going to move to a campaign headquarters where I can have my own office? This communal we're-all-in-this-together thing isn't working for me.

—Well, *make* it work for you. It's how campaigns are run. People vote for you because you're one of them, not because you're their boss.

—People will vote for me because I'm the only one running.

—So far.

—I'll win regardless.

—Are you familiar with the lowland hound?

—Pardon?

—The lowland hound. A wild dog that hunts in the desert.

—What does that have to do with—

—The lowland hound is a brilliant hunter. The only known wild dog that doesn't hunt in a pack, and that's because it doesn't need to. It can reach speeds up to seventy-five kilometers an hour and has a jaw that can literally crush a steel pipe. They've been known to decapitate desert antelope so thoroughly and quickly that the poor antelope's body still runs another fifty meters before falling.

—I don't believe that.

—Doesn't matter. I bring it up because the lowland hound is also one of the most spectacularly lazy animals on the planet. They only hunt when pushed to the brink of starvation. Their prey don't fear them because they know they can't outrun the hound if it wants to hunt, but that they probably won't need to because it probably *won't* want to hunt. Herds of antelope will sleep within sight of a lowland hound without concern.

—But he can eat whenever he wants to.

—I'm not yet to my point.

—Well, hurry it along. I'm busy.

—The lowland hound is also noteworthy in that it does one intensely stupid thing that has caused much amazement in the zoological world.

—This would be the point, then.

—The lowland hound never starves to death in times of famine because obviously conditions will drive it to use its hunting prowess for survival.

—But?

—Quit interrupting, please. The lowland hound never starves in times of famine, but it quite regularly starves in times of excessive plenty. Surrounded by prey that it could easily catch, the lowland hound will wait to hunt because it knows it could get food any time it wanted. It will wait more and more, until it has nearly collapsed from starvation. Then, seeing all the prey within easy reach, and this is the important part, Thomas, it will wait *still*. When the hunger has finally gotten so intense that it can barely move, only then will the lowland hound rouse itself to hunt. But, of course, by then it hasn't the energy to hunt. The antelopes can easily outrun it. No heads go flying off bodies in mid-stride. The lowland hound whimpers along behind, unable to catch up. Surrounded by plenty, it lies down and starves to death.

—And yet somehow, the lowland hound survives.

—That's not the point.

—Sounds like the point to me.

—Don't be obstinate. The species may live, but the individual dies.

—You still haven't quite grasped the balance of power around here, have you? This is my campaign, not yours. Your help is appreciated. Your illustrative anecdotes are not.

Jon waved his hand dismissively.

—I don't have time for this. I'm working too hard to get you elected, despite your best efforts. Learn the goddamn agriculture speech or don't. All I'm telling you is that you'll double your contributions from rich farmers if you do. If you need me, and you *will*, I'll be at my own office.

He turned on his heel and walked off before Thomas could say another word. Thomas pondered calling after him, almost did, but then thought better of it. He frowned, breathing heavily out of his nostrils. In his mind, he very loudly thought of the angriest songs he knew, sustaining some extremely ferocious guitar solos before finally reaching into his pocket for a TB's Special Blend. Some relaxation was definitely called for. He lit up and drew a long, silky cloud into his lungs before slowly, grudgingly turning his eyes back to the speech. He kept reading even when the smoke made his eyes water with deliciously narcotic tears, finally drawing a languorous smile that seemed suspiciously large and lengthy for someone reading a factsheet on local agriculture.

288

70. The Worm, Aching to Turn.

Cora sat in the underlit reception area, angrily pondering its opulence. An office conjured seemingly from nowhere in a building she knew for a fact had no new rental space available. Yet here it was, all white marble and shadow, hard lines diffused by the organic curves and greens of tall plants emerging from recessed vases. It was beautiful, if too damn dark, much nicer than her own office, and irritatingly improbable. The receptionist, a dark, handsome boy of about twenty, had shown her where to sit, pressed a single button which was allegedly a summons to Jon, then went back to talking to his equally dark, handsome girlfriend, who was slouching forward over the front of the reception desk, her face close to his, her ass roundly up in the air like a new planet. They bantered back and forth in an irritating chatter too soft to be understood but too loud not to be heard, smiling deeply into each other's eyes with the velvet intimacy of those who seem to be just marking time between sexual encounters. Cora stared at them unabashedly, for there was nothing else in the waiting room to look at, not even a magazine. It wouldn't have mattered anyway. They were so oblivious she could have danced a striptease and been left to finish it unobserved.

Gradually, she noticed that her first impression had been slightly off. The boy was a little less handsome than at first sight. Acne scars dotted his face here and there. His hair, though obviously expensively cut, had not been further attended to by hands that knew what to do with an expensive haircut. The girl, too, was slightly girthful in the legs, and Cora noticed the reddish eczema of a worker's fingers when the girl caressed the boy's face. A certain amazement also accompanied the movements of both, as if neither of them could believe that the life that was happening to them hadn't been delivered by mistake. The easy intimacy seemed to also include a measure of huddling, as if separating, even for a moment, might be irreversible. Cora felt herself soften towards the two young lovers, even saying a silent blessing, wishing them well.

Jon strode into the room through a door that had opened soundlessly. Cora stood. The boy and girl didn't bother to look up.

—Cora. What an expected non-surprise.

—We need to talk.

—Perhaps, though I warn you now might not be the best time.

—No. Now.

—Then if you insist.

He ushered her into his office with a mysterious grin. He motioned her to a seat. When she remained standing, he shrugged and took the chair behind a lavishly understated wooden desk.

—What are you doing?

—What could you possibly mean?

—Don't fuss me about, Jon. Thomas Banyon for Mayor? You think you can swoop into Hennington out of nowhere, install the worst Mayor possible and that this will all somehow result in wooing me?

—Cora, Cora, Cora. Why would I want to discuss anything at all with you after the way you've treated me? Why should I even entertain this visit?

—Because someone needs to get through to you that you're off your rocker.

—Compliments like that do *so* much to keep up my good graces.

—It's never going to happen, Jon. Understand this. It's *never* going to happen.

—Have you grown so calcified that you actually believe you have power over 'never'? Even your anger has grown old, Cora.

A misstep. A slight one, but a misstep nonetheless. Cora blinked. Was that it? After all this hullabaloo, was that really it? Had it really been that ordinary this whole time? She regretted that it had taken her this long to understand that Albert was right, that 'petty' was the right word, regretted, for a moment, that now they weren't even going to be able to have a proper row.

—You don't really want anything, do you?

Jon looked surprised.

—I beg your pardon?

—You don't want me back.

—But of course I do.

—No. No, you don't. You want to hurt me, that's all.

—Cora, my darling, my love, that's exactly what I *don't* want to do. I would stop all this right now with a single word from you. All of this, I'm doing for you.

—Wrong. You ask me for the impossible and now you're using my refusal as the justification for your real aim. You want to hurt me, to hurt Albert, to satisfy some wound that you've been nursing for all this time that the rest of us have forgotten about, one that any sane, rational person *would* have forgotten about. That's it. That's the beginning and end of your agenda. You want to demonstrate how powerful you are. You don't want me. That was just a pretense. You knew all along that I would never say yes to you. It's actually kind of disappointing in a way. It's so *usual*.

—It most certainly—

—It is, whether you can admit it to yourself now that   291 you've come this far or not. Fortunately, that makes things a good deal easier for me now.

—Meaning what exactly?

—Here I thought you were some ghost from my past come to haunt me with insane claims of ownership, throwing the world into chaos to get your way. It was almost mythological. But you're just a small, *petty* man, nursing a small, petty grudge, another schoolboy who's managed the appearance of adulthood without ever assuming the mantle.

—Oh, but you're wrong, my love. You couldn't be more wrong.

—I don't think so.

—I'm on a *mission*—

—You're not. You're throwing a tantrum.

—Funny, but that's how powerful women always try to de-fang powerful men. By calling them boys.

—I should have said yes to you on that first day in my office just to watch you scramble.

—You're making an enormous mistake in underestimating me, Cora.

—Ah, now you're just flailing.

—I suppose we'll have to see who's right.

—And the predictable threat of ominous, yet un-named future recrimination. Good grief, Jon, I've been a lawyer and a politician for my entire adult life. Do you honestly think you can hold any surprise for me now that I know what you are?

—You'll be very sorry for this, Cora. It hurts me, this course of action you're forcing—

—Blah blah blah. Your next line should be a threat for me to 'leave this office at once!'. I'm stunned that I didn't see it before. Stunned. You're nothing special at all, are you? You're merely a man. Nothing more, nothing less.

—Is this all somehow supposed to send me home with my tail between my legs? Now that you've made this alleged grand discovery, I'm supposed to just run screaming into the night?

—Irritatingly, your type never do, do they?

—You're making a huge mistake, Cora. Bigger than you can imagine.

—Haven't you already said that?

—Cora—

—No, listen to me, Jon. Listen with as much attention as your navel-gazing egomania can allow. I suggest you quit what you're doing, this idiotic alliance with Thomas Banyon, this whole farce of 'winning me back'. Get out of Hennington. Leave. Today. Because know this, I've cut you slack because I thought you were a special case, a misguided pain in the ass, but at least interestingly so. Now I see that you're not. You're just a miserable old man looking for a scapegoat for some imagined wrong. You're a dime a dozen. Hell, half the City Council used to be filled with you, but guess what? *I know you.* I know how to fight you. Moreover, I know how to *beat* you. So bring out your big guns, Jon. Go ahead. I'm calling your bluff. Let's see your best hand. But consider this—

She leaned over his desk, pushing her face towards his, stopping uncomfortably close as he refused to give ground.

—Maybe you're the one who's underestimated his opponent.

71. Paradise Interrupted.

A change could come so quickly, so unfairly.

Jacki shook quietly where she lay, still barely awake, under 293 a pile of woolen blankets in the back seat of the laundry truck, heading off in unknown directions under cover of just-breaking dawn. The weight of the blankets caused her back to sweat while her front reeled from the cold of the truck's metal floor. She was exhausted, groggy, terrified, and her stomach was pulled into a queasy tautness from hunger and nerves. She had probably been under here less than a half hour, bumping along as the truck sped towards ostensible safety, but in the dark, with only herself and the itch of the wool, she felt trapped in a nightmare that had followed her into wakefulness, a nightmare set aflame by the strong possibility that this escape might not work.

The Jacki with the annoying nihilistic tone tried to convince her that it was her own complacency that had gotten her into this mess, a sense of untouchability in her weeks in the Foster Downs that had caused her to drop her guard, that had caused her to dare to imagine a world without Thomas Banyon, a world that included, maybe, just maybe, her own two sons, Tucker and Morton. But the new Jacki fought back. Who *wouldn't* have grown complacent in a setting as compactly bucolic as the Foster Downs, with the endless sunny days, the forests of flowers, the warm hospitality of Katherine? It was circumstance, perhaps inevitable circumstance, that of course she would eventually be caught out by Thomas. Nothing more, nothing less.

Indeed, days and nights had passed with such graceful steps that Jacki had begun to feel almost outside of time, as if the world had accidentally left her behind on its relentless march forward, leaving her to rest in that small stone walkway of paradise. Katherine filled the house with the scents of good cooking, insisting that Jacki tend her tired, withdrawing body as it adjusted to life without even the Recatur to help it along anymore. Under blue skies and the eccentric company of

Reginald and Rhona, Jacki started to feel better, then actually to feel *good*, a sensation so alien that Katherine had to explain it to her.

—As if, after the sun sets tonight, it's a sure thing it'll come up again tomorrow?

—Yes.

—Like you can anticipate what's for dinner and actually enjoy the waiting?

—Exactly.

—Darling, that's happiness. Tentative, maybe, and there's a whole lot else going on inside you, too, but happiness has definitely shown up to the party.

—How do we keep it from leaving?

—By letting it be. Here, have a muffin, I just took them out of the oven, and then you rest. We'll get you in the habit of happiness, and you'll find yourself not wanting to break it.

But if it were really that simple, then happiness wouldn't have such a high price tag on the open market, now would it? Because isn't that what Thomas sold? And if you could get it for free, then what was the point? And where had it been all this time? Just 'showing up to the party' out of nowhere; uninvited, really. *Crashing* the party, more like it. And what if, in its apparent fickleness, it just decided to up and leave? You wouldn't count on a friend who did that, would you? Jacki?

And yet.

One day she lifted herself out of the bathtub with her own strength. The next, she got through the whole of the daylight hours without taking a nap. The sags in the pulling skin around her belly and buttocks were showing signs of filling in again, if not in an especially attractive way, nevertheless filling in as if she were actually moving away from being a sick person. She spent an entire sunny afternoon basking in the glow from the marigolds and reading a Joan Reachpenny novel (the one with the funny uncle in uniform at the funeral). Reading for pleasure. An event which hadn't occurred since at least before college, if even then. Some nights she almost cried with relief before drifting off into a still-bumpy but increasingly nourishing sleep.

Reginald began to eye her suspiciously at meals.

—I want whatever you've been giving Jenny.

—Beg pardon, Papa?

—Look at her. She's fattening up like a hog headed to market. I want to have whatever she's having.

—She was sick, and now she's getting well, Papa. Don't be rude.

—I want it.

—There's nothing to have. I told you. There's no secret, except she's eighty years younger than you.

Jacki spoke up at this.

—Seventy-three actually.

Katherine raised her eyebrows.

—Really? Maybe you *are* getting a bit younger, then.

—'No secret', huh? Can't give an old man a helping hand.

—Quiet down, Papa. He's determined to outlive Rhona by at least three years, you see, and then he can be the oldest one.

—Did someone say my name?

—No, Auntie. Eat your dinner.

Jacki finally convinced herself to allow some warmth into her brain and heart, maybe even soul, a tiny pinch of the Downs' omnipresent sunlight beaming into her black insides, illuminating dusty surprises covered by years of mental drop-cloths and nearly forgotten. Her boys, for instance. Almost men by now. They had gone to live with their father, and she had dropped out of sight, moving down the spiral from bad mother to drug addict and prostitute. How did something like that happen? And so quickly? Was it just the drugs? Had she just lost track? What the hell had happened?

Morton and Tucker had always seemed strange to her. She knew she loved them (she was pretty sure) because that strange, quick worry had to be love, didn't it? But if that was so, why would she have let the estrangement happen so resolutely, with so little interference and even worse, with so little regret? Or rather, so little regret until now. Maybe it wasn't only Forum she was recovering from. As the new Jacki gathered strength, maybe she was aiming for the gold ring. Now there was a thought.

Certainly a new epoch must be beginning because her breasts had upped and stopped working. She'd had down times before, during illness and, perversely, pregnancy, but she had never stopped lactating completely; an unpleasant dribble was their lowest ebb. But as her body regained some of its former shape and as her muscles allowed her a normal day, there was still no word from her breasts. They, too, had reformed some, gathering a smallish fullness that wasn't at all bad looking, but not a drop of milk, or indeed of anything. To her surprise, Jacki found herself mourning just a little the disappearance of the milk, but if nothing else, it was the best representation of the line she had crossed. If this was the price for not turning back, besides providing her with a new uselessness to Thomas Banyon, then the milk could be left behind.

True, these were breathless thoughts, and frightening. She was becoming a new person, a new person whose identity and formulation was still unknown, but here in the Foster Downs, she could face it. Even, perhaps, imagine a future. Even, maybe, possibly, one that included seeing her boys again.

Then all of a sudden a flick of the light and the voice of Katherine saying those three words, 'He's found you'. Maybe it was too much to ask. There hadn't even been time to pack any clothes or say goodbye to Reginald and Rhona. Katherine pulled her out of bed, took her through a dark house, and hid her in the thicket of marigolds.

—Stay here.

—But how—

—Somehow he found out and went to Davis' house.

—Oh, my God, is she all right?

—No. He tried to force her to take him here to the Downs, but she fooled him and took him to her brother's. When Thomas realized what she'd done, he broke her jaw.

—Oh, no—

—Somehow he got the address out of her, then he left her there on the front lawn.

—Shit. Oh, my God, shit. I'm so sorry—

—Listen to me. Thomas Banyon is the one causing all this trouble, not you. My son took her to the hospital. She was able to write out what happened, and they just called me to tell me he's probably on his way.

—How can he get away with this?

—Because he always has. We've no more time. I'm trying to get you somewhere I know, but I'm not sure it'll work. It's going to be touch and go. Wait here until I come get you.

—What if he comes? Will you be all right?

—He broke my daughter's jaw. He's the one who should be worried about finding me alone, the bastard. Stay here.

Jacki had shivered in the darkness under the flowers, wrapped only in a bedsheet, her feet bare, her hair getting wet from the dew, until Katherine returned with a pair of shoes and a coat. She hustled Jacki to a waiting truck, kissed her once on each cheek, and shoved her in.

—But where—

—No time. Be safe. My prayers will be with you.

—And mine with you.

Katherine touched a hand to her cheek and was gone. The doors to the truck closed, and Jacki covered herself in blankets. She didn't even know who was driving, much less where she was going. Why didn't Thomas give up? Why this relentless pursuit? She closed her eyes against the darkness and tried to think of her sons, hoping that the future led out of this nightmare and somehow made its way to wherever they were.

72. The Swinging Gates of Opportunity.

Despite certain severe aspects to his personality, Theophilus Velingtham took pleasure in a nice long soak in the tub, almost (but only almost) luxuriating as steam filled the room, his long frame in water so hot he occasionally had to gasp for air. With perhaps a few alterations in the gene pool, a cozier life history, and a more attentive focus on personal appearance, Theophilus might have approached handsome. But the chromosomes had been fickle, his life history was very scarred indeed, and Theophilus Velingtham felt himself too much of a sinner wasting time in a bath to ever commit the further sin of vanity. So it was that he remained not ugly, but worn.

His hair was cut short against a towering scalp, offset by ears so large that even from a distance he seemed to be eavesdropping. Surprisingly, he had an easy smile, but it always combined with an involuntary raise of his eyebrows, undermining whatever sincerity might exist. He was tall, having to bend his knees quite high to fit into the tub, and he was thin, the thin of a body that seemed to have worked every muscle every day of its life. Even under the water, he looked made of nothing but sinew and bone. Hairless, except for a modest plume of curls surrounding a cock that was long and hardy but seldom ever used, it seemed impossible to tell his age. He could have stretched anywhere from thirty to sixty without much argument, and that the truth lay outside even those wide boundaries wasn't difficult to believe. He did seem to have always been around, didn't he?

But this bath was cut short. He rose quickly out of the water, wrapped a thin white towel around his waist, and moved efficiently and quietly into the bedroom. His clothes were only either shades of gray or shades of brown, and after a moment's thought, he decided on brown. He dressed in practiced movements, covering a body that he had long since forgotten to look at, tucking away his prick without a pause, unused again for yet another day. He pressed his hair flat with his hands, then buttoned his shirt all the way up to the collar. He fastened his cuffs tight, drew a belt around his midsection, and pulled on long brown socks that reached up to his knees. He moved into his living room, glanced briefly at a clock, then took a seat in a hard, wooden chair with a straight back. He placed both hands on either thigh and raised his head slightly.

And waited. Motionless.

Who was this man, that he could sit here so still, so almost *inert*, waiting for whoever it was that was going to arrive, this man who lived alone without radio, stereo, television, or pet? There wasn't a single person alive, besides himself, who knew his middle name. The question is pertinent once more: How does something like this happen? Carefully, as if by plan, he seemed to have become known to everyone, yet known by no one. What stirred him? What occupied his thoughts? Who, for that matter, was he waiting for, a man whose neighbors had not seen a single guest enter his house for at least the past fifteen years, and who knew how long before then?

One question, at least, had an answer.

A knock sounded from the front door. Theophilus was already on his feet and seemed to open the door in the same motion. He proffered a hand to the figure standing on his doorstep.

—Welcome, Brother Noth. Please, do come in.

And what of this man, in his black trenchcoat (in this heat?), his black boots, and black hair with gray speckles sparkling in the sun? What goes through *his* mind when he shakes Theophilus' hand, feeling the grip that seems to be nothing but cords and bone approximating a greeting? And what does his smile conceal, so thin in his jaw, so small it draws just two elegantly cut lines on his cheeks, yet definitely there, definitely signifying *something*? When Theophilus steps aside, what does this man feel as he enters the domicile of one for whom guests are anathema, almost a puncture in this dry, airless (yet thoroughly dust-free) space?

Whatever the answers, it is doubtful they contain anything encouraging.

—Pleasure to see you again, Brother Velingtham.

—So glad to hear you use the proper address, Jon. So many of the young among us have begun using the first name in the initial greeting. I find that a bit too casual for our Blessed Sacraments. Don't you agree?

—I defer to your expertise, Theo. The breadth of your knowledge of the Sacraments has always been unparalleled, even among the preachers of this parish.

—You flatter me, Jon, but you've been away a long time. 301

—It *has* been a while—

—And now you've returned. As the Sacraments themselves might even have predicted.

—Well . . .

—Always the doubter. I remember the doubts from when you were but a pup.

—You've always been a great friend, Theo.

—Friendship has nothing to do with it. I recognized potential in you, and now you've returned to prove me right.

—I've *returned*, at least.

—And now you require my help?

—Always right to the point. Is small talk so much of a sin?

—Why waste time when there's so much to be done?

—And what work would that be?

—The obvious.

—Clarify for one student still stumbling around in the dark.

—What else could you need but believers?

—Believers.

—Yes. I've been doing The Lord's work, spreading the Word among those who would hear.

—Are there many who would hear?

—It is a powerful message, the one Our Lord has given us. It works its own wonders. One becomes two, two become four—

—And pretty soon—

—Pretty soon there are enough to set a great idea spinning. The key is never sheer numbers. The key is the correct catalyst. A pebble can start a landslide and the boulders have no say in the matter as they tumble down the hill.

—I think we understand each other, then.

—'Each other'? I recall asking nothing of *you*, Brother

Noth.

—The benefits would seem manifest in your own actions.

—Would they, now?

—Don't tell me the pure-living Theophilus Velingtham has some sort of price?

—I said nothing of the sort, my friend. Merely that so far this is a one-sided exchange. That is all, nothing more.

—So there will be an outstanding balance due sometime?

—'Let no man be made foolish by charity'.

—Book of Aramea?

—Book of Josefina, Chapter 9, Verse 11.

—You won't be made foolish, old bird. You can count on that.

—That was not my point, Jon. I have no intention of being made foolish. I merely remind you that your end of the discussion must be fulfilled as well.

—Oh, it will be, Brother Velingtham, it will be. I'm looking forward to it.

The brief conversation ended. Jon stood and Theophilus showed him to the door. They exchanged handshakes and parted. And then, on either side of the closed door, each man smiled to himself, Jon's firm and small, Theophilus' gracious and eerie, as if, somehow, each had the other exactly where he wanted him, which, surely, couldn't simultaneously be possible.

73. A Rush and a Push and the Day is Ours.

After so much lengthy agonizing, the final decision, the reversal of that decision, and the making of a new final decision happened almost absurdly fast.

Cora and Albert:

—So what did Jon say then?

—Nothing. I left before he had a chance.

—That's the Cora I know and love. I think a thump on the head is the only thing that man understands.

—Precisely. Which is why I have to call his bluff.

—Uh-oh.

—It's the only way, Albert.

—You can't be serious.

—I'm hoping that it won't be for real.

—You're going to run again.

—No one else seems to want to, and *someone* has to. That's all there is to it.

—Oh, my love, are you sure?

—That I have to run? Yes. What happens after that is anyone's guess. I'm hoping calling his bluff will be enough.

—You want to enter the race long enough to get Thomas Banyon to withdraw?

—I want to enter the race long enough to get *Jon Noth* to withdraw.

—I'm not sure I see how that's going to work.

—I don't really, either. It'll probably mean that I'll end up as Mayor yet again. Maybe I can retire halfway through the next term this time. Appoint a successor. Or something.

—Aside from not being particularly fair to the voters—

—Don't start. I see no other recourse. He wants a fight. That's all there is to it. I've looked, and I can't seem to find a way to avoid one.

—But dearest—

—Albert, I know. I know, I know, I know. All of it, I know. But he seems to think that he'll either get me or the city. He's not going to get either, and this is the only way to do that, especially since viable candidates haven't exactly been crawling out of the woodwork. I'm it. No one wants to run against Thomas Banyon. This is the only way. I wish it wasn't, but there it is.

—Well, I'll be right behind you, of course. Anything you need.

—Thanks, darling. If that smarmy little bastard wants a fight, then he's got one.

The next morning, Cora and Max:

—You're *what*?

—Tell me another way. At least you'll know you've got the Crash Advocate job for the next five years.

—But, Cora—

—Read my lips, Max. I. Don't. Like. It. Either. But trust me, I know this man, and he's not kidding.

—What about the retirement you so wanted?

—It's gone now, isn't it?

—I can't believe this.

—Neither can I. Now, what can I help you with?

—Screw that. Just another batch of medicine for Maggerty. It all seems to be working finally.

—Good. Easily approved.

—But what about—

—I don't want to hear it, Max. I'm not blaming you. I know you have your reasons and they're good ones and I respect them. Such as it is, though, no one else is going to do it, and I'm the only one left standing who can beat both Thomas Banyon's money and Jon Noth's bile. That's all there is to it. I'm running again. I have to. I announce on Thursday.

—That's not much time.

—One good thing about my experience, I can do this with my eyes closed.

305

—You seem so angry about it, though.

—How the hell else am I supposed to be? Some crazy man from a life of mine long since forgotten shows up, and despite my best efforts and despite the fact that such a thing should be impossible at my age, he completely disrupts my life. I wanted retirement. I was thrilled to bits with it. I've been Mayor for twenty years. I wanted to water plants and take walks with Albert, but here I go again, now don't I?

—Are you sure that's—

—If you say one word about being good for the electorate or having passion for the job, I swear to God, I will break your neck.

—But—

—No. No. I'm not angry at you, Max. I'm just angry, and if you stay here, I'll take it all out on you. More medicine for Maggerty? Great, fine, approved, done. Now, please go, or I'm not responsible for my actions.

That night, Max and Talon:

—Honey, do you remember when we talked about destiny?

—No.

—Remember? About how you plan for what you can, but that sometimes destiny comes along with its own ideas of what you're going to do?

—No.

—It was when we talked about whether I'd run for Mayor again.

—Um, okay.

—Anyway, my point is that destiny might have come along with a different plan for me than what I'm doing now.

—You're going to run again?

306   —Certain things have happened—

—Wow.

—Certain things have happened that may mean that I should get back in the race.

—Are you going to?

—I wanted to talk it over with you first.

—It's up to *me*?

—No, no, no, little pumpkin. I just wanted to talk it over with you because it affects you, too.

—Like what you said before about having less time and all these commitments?

—Yes. I hope that I'll be able to control some of the time I'll have to spend doing campaign stuff.

—Isn't that what Mayor Cora said before?

—Yes, so we'll see if she's as good as her word.

—Do you think she will be?

—Why? Are you worried about not seeing me?

—Well, yeah, but I'll be okay if it's not forever.

—Believe me, it won't be forever.

—But what about your new job?

—I'll keep doing it until the election, then after that, the job exists. It doesn't only have to be me that does it. The Crash will always have someone in their corner.

—But I thought you liked doing it.

—I do, but sometimes destiny demands things of you and you have to take it.

—Oh.

—So what do you think, darling? Can you put up with me working long hours for a few months? I promise on my heart that I'll make plenty of time for you anyway, and afterwards, if I win—

—You'll win.

—*If* I win, then I'll just throw my weight around and make my own hours.

—I think you're going to win.

—Nothing's guaranteed, Talon. Remember, I didn't think I would even run.

—But you said that we should still plan and dream anyway, didn't you?

—Yes, I did—

—Then I'm planning and dreaming that you'll win.

—Thank you, honey. What should you never forget?

—That you love me.

—Correct, sweetheart.

—I love you, too, Daddy.

—Don't forget *that*, either.

—I won't.

And finally, later that same night, Max and Cora.

—I'm in.

—Are you sure?

—As I'm ever going to be.

—I didn't do this to force your hand, you know.

—Yes, I know.

—It's going to be tough.

—I'm prepared.

—Oh, Max. Max, I just—

—I know. I'll call you in the morning.

And that was the proverbial that.

74. Banyon Enterprises.

Archie sat outside Thomas' office, kept waiting again. His hair was rumpled and mussed, the shocking whiteness of it made more so by its unchecked roller-coaster swoops. His clothes were only clean because of Jules' insistence on dressing him every morning. The assistant now lived in Archie's home, having moved there when it became clear Archie was unwilling to take care of himself in all but the most basic sense. Archie allowed himself to be dressed and fed, but he couldn't stand the thought of being bathed by someone so young and efficient, even though Jules had done it before when Archie had been laid up with a broken hip a few years back. It all seemed so much more pointless now. Maybe that was it.

Jules, at least, kept the company running, though quite how was beyond Archie. He suspected that Jules used his name rather more often than Archie might have liked to keep things moving, signing memos and so forth, issuing proclamations to the Board and press releases to the papers, transferring money around so it looked like business was being done. It would only work for a while. The Board would have to be faced sooner or later, but for now it was fine. Whatever happened was fine, really. Jules could appoint himself Chairman for all it mattered now.

Archie slipped another small yellow pill out of his pocket, a tranquilizer Jules had gotten for him but which only pushed away the torment temporarily. He popped it in his mouth, swallowing it without water. He wondered why he had been kept alive this long, and now, when his pain was at its most acute, he would have to *stay* alive to get his answers. A cosmic bad joke, of which Archie Banyon was at last the punchline.

Thomas opened his office door and motioned Archie inside.

—Sorry to keep you waiting. Busy with the campaign and all. You understand.

—Is there any word?

—None yet.

—There *must* be. It's been almost three weeks.

—I know, but—

—How can you not have found anything?

—Let me speak. He's Rumour. They've got a close-knit community. Trust me, I've had other reasons to find that out this week. I suspect he's being sheltered.

—Who would shelter a murderer? The Rumour Underground is supposed to be a myth, a *benevolent* myth.

—Maybe, maybe not. You can't trust them. You know that.

—He has to be out there somewhere.

—He is. I'll find him. Trust me.

—I've trusted you for this long and you've given me nothing.

—I realize you're upset, so I'll overlook that.

—I'm sorry, but what of Luther's body? What if he's not dead? What if he's just injured and this Peter, this horrible bastard is keeping him alive for some insidious purpose?

—Don't let your mind get carried away. You won't be surprised that I've had to deal with this sort of thing before in running the country club. Crimes usually end up being exactly what they appear. The banal motive is always the most likely, and the boring explanation is always true. Luther is almost certainly dead. As hard as that is to swallow, imagining bizarre horror-movie scenarios isn't going to help you.

—Do you have any leads at all?

—No.

—No?

—Luther isn't the only person who's disappeared lately. I've only got so much manpower, and right now, it's split down the middle.

—Well, unsplit it then.

—I won't. I'll find Peter Wickham for you, and I'll find what I'm looking for as well. You're not thinking rationally now, and I can understand that. But remember, *you* came to *me.* I'm willing to help you, and I'm as good as my word. I'm not out of line in asking you to trust me to make my own decisions and use my own judgments.

Archie sighed.

—I apologize. It's just—

—I know.

—I've been—

—I know, but you have my word that I'll do what you ask.

—You'll tell me as soon as you find anything?

—The second I know anything, *you'll* know.

—Thank you.

—You're welcome.

There was a heavy pause. Here it comes, thought Archie.

—Now. You know Max Latham has re-entered the race?

—Saw it in today's paper.

—He doesn't stand a chance, you know.

—Others might disagree. I state no opinion, Thomas, but others might disagree.

—I know that. I can beat him. I *will* beat him.

—He's got Cora Larsson on his side.

—And you, too, if I remember correctly.

—Yet to be decided.

—I can beat Max Latham, no matter what the circumstances.

—But?

—But those circumstances could be made a bit easier.

—You want me to withdraw my support?

—Support is irrelevant. I can't stop your thoughts or your mouth. It wouldn't be my place to ask. It *would* be advantageous if you withdrew your help.

—My help.

—Your money. Your contacts. How embarrassing if your 311

friends and benefactors were forced to choose between Max Latham and your own son. I would hate to see that happen. I'm only thinking for your sake.

—Are you now?

—Do what you choose. I'm only stating the possibility of removing potentially awkward situations which would also have the effect of making my campaign for Mayor that much easier. It doesn't matter to me if you do it or not. I'm merely saying.

—You're merely saying.

—Yes.

Archie looked down at his hands. Old now, wrinkled and spotted with time. Even two months ago, the skin had been tighter, the grip firmer, more imposing. Two months ago. When he had played tennis three times a week with Luther. If this was Thomas' price for finding Luther's murderer, after all that had happened, it didn't seem quite so high after all. His real son was dead. What else mattered?

—I see your point, Thomas. Wouldn't want to cause any awkwardness, strain any sympathies between father and son. Bad for business, difficult for friends. And all in the best interests of family.

—Yes, the best interests of family.

—I'll withdraw my help from Max Latham.

—Very generous of you, Father.

The last word floated in the air, unable to find an accurate footing anywhere in the room.

75. Listen.

The week was steadfastly refusing to get any less baffling for Jarvis. Things weren't going well in the parish, and he couldn't quite trace where he had lost his influence. It seemed to spring from the Brandon Beach sermon, but if that was true, if reaction to it was the reason his parishioners had disappeared from his office, if that was the reason attention at his sermons (rather than attendance, which stayed steady out of decades of familial guilt and habit) had seemed to drop off to nothing, then *that* particular truth was just a little too awful to bear just now. Because if reaction to what Jarvis considered an essential and strongly believed set of tenets was that disinterested, even adversarial, then, well, there really wasn't any point at all, was there?

He did his best to avoid self-pity, but he was also sure he wasn't imagining things. The after-sermon fellowship, the hand-shaking at the door to the sanctuary, the enthusiasm on the charity committees had all noticeably waned to the point where he had asked some of his friends in the church – trusty old Mrs Bellingham; Matthew Badham, the church organist; even Stella Maritain, the staunchly unbelieving church janitor – if something was amiss, something he had failed to notice, some action of his that had set things so strangely, had made things so chilly and formal. No one knew or at least professed to knowing. Jarvis tried to convince himself that everything, human behavior especially, waxed and waned. This was just a cooling trend, maybe without a reason at all, and if he waited it out, things would warm up again.

And then a young man named Peter Wickham, whom he had never seen before in his life, had shown up in his office and things went from strange to downright impossible.

—I need help with a resurrection.

—Excuse me?

—I've got someone who qualifies. I know this is something the Bondulay Church used to do.

—Someone who, I'm sorry, 'qualifies'?

313

—Yes. This man. That I loved. He, well, he didn't *die*. He had too much grief to stay in this world.

—Oh, my son.

—No, no, no, please don't do that. I know what you're going to say. That I'm just mourning in an unhealthy way. I'm not. There's no reason why he should have died. None. He only had a broken heart. He wasn't sick, just in pain. That's all.

—Son, Peter, that story is a myth. A lovely one, a sad one, very sad, but a myth nonetheless. It's dangerous to take the Sacraments so literally. It's meant as a metaphor—

—Yes, I know, a metaphor for dealing with grief. I'm not stupid. But that's not the case here. I've been keeping him with me.

—You've *what*?

—No, listen to me. I've been keeping him hidden away—

—Oh, son, your grief has made you not think clearly—

—No—

—You have to . . . You can't just—

—Listen—

—What about his family?

—*I'm* his family. His other family is why his heart broke. He thought he had failed his father and that made him think he was so worthless that he couldn't even love me or anyone or *be* loved by anyone. And that hurt him so bad that he died, except he *didn't* die.

—I know that's what you want to believe—

—It's what's true.

—It's what you want to believe. Of course, it is. This person's death has obviously been horrible for you. But, son, you can't do what you're saying. You can't.

—I know how I sound, but hear me out. I've had him
314 with me for a while now. I've wrapped him in waxseed

oil and bandages. I've kept him as clean and safe as I could.

—Oh, my God.

—Please, just listen. I may be in a strange frame of mind, but I haven't totally taken leave of my senses. I know how it looks. I know the risk I'm taking. I know how crazy it makes me seem. But listen. Even with the waxseed oil and bandages, there are things that should have happened by now that aren't. I know I'm right about this, Father. I have proof.

—How can you possibly have proof?

—He's not decomposing. Even with the care I've taken, *something* should have happened by now. Some smell, some natural course of death. I know that. I was prepared for that, I was hoping it wouldn't happen, but I thought that it would and my worry was how to keep his body in good enough shape for his return to it. But listen.

—I'm listening.

—I waited. It was foolish, but I waited. I didn't know how the return would happen, so I just waited. And prayed. Nothing happened. I should have spent that time searching you out instead of waiting, but then I saw his body wasn't changing. At all. I realized I had to *do* something. I had to come and see you. And I know how this looks, but I know I'm not crazy. Or maybe I *am* crazy to believe this, but I do believe it. And I'm right. I have proof. His body is waiting. It's not breaking down. It's waiting for his return to it and it's waiting for me to help that return.

For a second, Jarvis wavered. He had seen plenty of crazies come through his door, but despite what this young man was saying, none of the usual alarms were ringing. It wasn't that he sounded truthful – all of the mentally unstable believed they were telling the truth, and they were, a truth that was all their own – but there was a clarity here, along with an ounce of genuine bafflement, the same mix that had made him   315 listen to Mrs Bellingham's dream. Impossible. And yet. The world was quiet, and Jarvis made his fateful choice.

—Tell me, Peter. Tell me everything that's brought you here. Make me understand.

—You won't judge until I'm finished?

—You have my word.

And so then the trip the following night to a house buried in the suburbs, safe in its own anonymity, to see what remained of poor Luther Pickett – quite a lot, it turned out – which, why understate things, had shaken every belief and non-belief Jarvis thought he had ever held. After viewing himself as a rational priest offering common sense and the good graces of a genial, half-understood Lord, here was incontrovertible proof of a miracle. On the surface, that is. Jarvis told himself over and over again that just because *he* didn't understand it didn't mean that it wasn't understandable.

But what to do? Even dealt with on a moment-to-moment basis – what should he do right *now*? – the impossibility stuck like a parasite. Should he turn Peter in? For all he knew, Peter had *killed* Luther, for there was no question Luther Pickett was dead, and maybe Peter had then lapsed into some sort of quasi-religious ecstasy out of guilt. That seemed the likeliest possibility, and so Jarvis' duty was clear. But what if? The young man's veracity seemed as solid as terra firma, and as for the body . . .

The body was the whole other disturbing bit that had quite promptly set to monopolizing Jarvis' dreams. There were the few obvious certainties: It was definitely a dead body with no heartbeat and no breath, but it was also 1) warm and 2) giving off a strange, barely-there *hum* that Peter hadn't noticed until Jarvis pointed it out. Jarvis had performed eighty-one funerals in his years in the parish, a macabre personal tally that every priest knew by heart and wished they didn't. He knew what a dead body looked like, even shortly after death. It didn't look like this. Luther was flushed, decidedly odorless, easy to move, giving off the mysterious hum, and yet dead, dead, dead.

Jarvis didn't believe in miracles as anything but illustrative allegories in the Sacraments. Honest-to-goodness ones never appeared in real life and certainly none that were so obvious. The blind were never healed except through limited science; limbs were never reattached except imperfectly and without their full usage; and the dead never returned to life under any circumstances. And still. And yet. Unless.

Unless it was a miracle.

Because how could it otherwise be explained? His rational mind told him to turn Peter over to the authorities, but there was a voice, too, that also questioned him. What if this were the one time he was presented with the miraculous, and his only response, as a clergyman, as a righteous, believing man, was to turn a blind eye? What if the one time he was offered a glimpse of the truly holy, he refused to see?

—Whose house is this?

—A foreclosure. I saw the address in a want ad.

—I don't understand.

—Hennington Hills is full of all sorts of local thieves and things. Some truly not-nice people work there. You pick this kind of stuff up. Bank forecloses, family is evicted, then months go by while the bank and the government work out the sale. The house stays empty until then.

—But you've no idea when anybody might come back?

—No.

—So you're not really safe then?

—Not really, but what choice do I have? I have to keep Luther hidden. I have to. That's my only option. People are going to start looking for me soon, if they haven't already. I 317 don't have much time anyway, but I have to try. I have to be here to bring him back.

—I'll tell you what I'll do.

—Yes?

—I'll return on Monday. That's four days. If nothing else has happened to Luther, if the body is in the same state, well, we'll go from there. I'll help you. But if he *is* changing—

—He won't. He hasn't.

—If he *is*, then we'll have to start talking about other things. Call me every day. I'll come back on Monday.

Jarvis left with a sick feeling in his stomach, a knot of doubt, confusion, and yes, a faint faith. Things got worse. When he returned home, the television news greeted him with a public appeal to find Peter Wickham, wanted fugitive connected with the disappearance of Luther Pickett, beloved foster son to multi-billionaire Archie Banyon. What had he done? A probable murderer had sat in his office and he had let him go free without a single word of counseling to turn himself in. He had ignored the horrible experience the family of Luther must be going through, and for what? A miracle? Who was he kidding? What had come over him? How had so many years of loyal service and devout worship failed him so utterly?

All this, and the pinnacle of the week had yet to come.

—Father Kingham? If I may.

—This isn't an appropriate time for an announcement, Brother Velingtham. If you wouldn't mind waiting until the end of the sermon when we have some time set aside for church business—

—But this is so much more important than mere 'church business', Father. I think it might be too important to wait.

—*After* the sermon, Theophilus.

318

—I'm afraid not, Jarvis. I need to speak. Brethren and Sistern, hear me.

—Theophilus—

—The time has drawn nigh.

—Time for what?

—The light wind has encroached.

—*What?*

—I've spoken to some of you already. I've heard your murmuring. There is a man among us.

—Sit down, Theophilus. Now.

The congregation rose up.

—Let him speak!

—Let Brother Theophilus speak the truth!

—It's the time of the light wind!

What in the wide green earth was this? Theophilus stood in his pew with an infuriating, smug grin that Jarvis had to quell an urge to punch.

—Theophilus, what is the meaning of this?

—Only what any good parish priest would know if he'd had his ear to the ground, if he had been listening at all to the voices of his flock. That very section of the Sacraments that you railed against so passionately a few weeks back is coming true. I say again to you good people, the light wind has encroached.

All became clamor. Voices shouting, one on top of another. Jarvis could sense that not everyone was following what was happening, which was good, because he was completely lost himself. Through it all, Theophilus accepted the support, the accolades, the questions, even the disagreements, with the same inflated, magnanimous smile and a look in his eyes that, despite the heat, made Jarvis shudder.

76. An End and a Beginning.

She stepped heavily across the pavement, raising clouds of dust with each round footstep. There was a field further up this street that they rarely grazed upon, the grass being so short it was difficult for them to grab even with their wide, strong lips. Still, it was a field, and one that stayed green no matter what the weather. She reached the spot and headed for a break in the fence. She led the herd across grass that changed color and height in stripes, into thicker grass along the edges. They interrupted the walking of four of the thin creatures, but she took no notice of them. What concerned her most was the sound the grass made under her feet. It crackled. Grass that crackled was not too dry to eat, but it was close. She walked until the crackling quieted and then finally ceased. It was a longer walk than it should have been.

Maggerty wavered outside the fence after the herd entered. There had been trouble on the golf course before, trouble which he could not quite put his finger on. He seemed to remember that he had been roughed up here, and he had a vague idea – its vagueness a plonking, ugly thing in this time of new mental sharpness – that he had been told not to trespass again. He could remember bowed legs and big, beefy arms, but try as he might, he could not get the images to coalesce into a bigger picture. Oh, well. It was hot, and he didn't want to lose sight of the herd. He stepped through the open slats and stumbled after the drifting animals.

(Thomas sat on his perch in the golf cart more for the sake of an escape than any current business necessity. If he was really honest, he was also here for a boost in confidence. From this seat, he had dazzled and cajoled Hennington's finest, accepting the money that he had managed to convince them

320

was a mere gift for the treats he could offer. Stealing money was easy. Having your victim willingly, even happily hand it over was one of life's great pleasures. But these recent months had filled him with unease. Jon Noth was turning into a more and more difficult wild card, Jacki Strell was still – still – missing, and his father, once so formidable, had fallen to pieces at the loss of the one son he loved, the son that wasn't Thomas. Here in the golf cart, patrolling his greens, the greens he had personally supervised the building of, the greens where he had conquered and vanquished, he felt the rush of return of the old Thomas, the Thomas that brooked no bullshit, the Thomas who made enemies quiver, the Thomas who was either feared or respected. He lit a cigarillo to aid the mood's revival. As he put the lighter away, Thomas saw Maggerty follow The Crash across the course.

A slow, ugly smile spread across Thomas' face.)

Maggerty had been right in his recollections. He had once before been thrown out by Thomas Banyon. On facts alone, no one could quite blame Thomas for his actions. Maggerty had used a sand trap as an opportunity to defecate while The Crash grazed. What one *could* object to was the vigor and seeming glee that Thomas had taken in grabbing Maggerty by the neck and thrusting him onto the pavement outside. Even the richest of Henningtonians agreed that, after the horror upon horror of Pistolet, necessary punishment should be meted out grudgingly with a stern face and serious demeanor, not a laugh and a smile. Maggerty's nose had been broken, but it had been broken so many times in his life that he didn't even notice the pain. The same with the cuts on his elbows and palms which were so scarred he barely even bled. He had very much noticed, however, the pain in the cut under his arm, the stab in his side that seemed to go all the way to his heart, a bayonet into an enemy soldier.

He paused for a moment to catch his breath. His fingers ran their familiar years-old path to his wound. For a few seconds, he actually thought he couldn't find it. He ran his hand up and down his side feeling for the suppuration, the infection that had always been, if not an old friend, then a familiar acquaintance. Concerned now, he pulled his shirt open and then all the way off. He lifted his arm into the air, pulling back loose skin, searching for it. Then he saw.

It had healed over. Where the wound had always been was now a bright pink scar, tender still, now that he knew where to touch, but definitely there. No smell came from it, no blood or clear liquid. Just a frightened little scar that seemed to shrink from the bright sunlight. Maggerty touched it tenderly, with awe, even. He traced the smooth edges with the lightest brush his suddenly trembling fingertips could manage. He held his breath out of sheer disbelief.

Healed.

He brushed his fingers over the spot for the millionth and last time when he saw the ominous approach of Thomas Banyon in his electric cart.

Maggerty ran.

She smelled the approach of the thin creature long before she saw him. The smell grew stronger by the second. She heard the stamping of running feet along with an electric whine in the background somewhere. Then the smell, which had so briefly been tolerable, clogged the air, changing into the most ancient smell of all. Fear. Her nose filled with the dank, dirty scent of another's fear.

(*Thomas yelled with a jolly smile as he drove his cart towards the fleeing Maggerty. This was an unexpected pleasure. He was feeling better already.*

—Come back here, you flea, you vermin, you shitrag!)

322   Though physically stronger than he had ever been, Mag-

gerty ran with a sort of anti-grace that it hurt the eyes to see. He had fear on his side, though, and he was fast. With unconscious purpose, he ran beseechingly into the herd, his friends and protectors for so long. His arms were out, and he made a terrible moan for sympathy. He saw the lead animal and ran straight for her.

She heard the rumble of feet as the members of the herd shifted, startled once again as the strange-smelling thin creature ran wildly through them. She heard his lighter, faster steps as he ran towards her, finally catching sight of him rounding two of the larger males. The smell grew rapidly. She took an alarmed step back.

Maggerty unknowingly chanted a desperate whisper as he ran.

—Help me, help me, help me, help me.

(*Thomas steered his cart wildly to avoid the animals in his way, driving Maggerty farther into the herd.*)

Too fast, too fast, *too fast*. She thrust up with her horn, the instinctive reaction to threat.

—Oof.

(*Thomas slammed the brakes of his cart, nearly lurching forward out of it at the sudden stop.*

—*Sweet God Almighty.*)

The smell of blood was danger. She shook her head violently to get the weight off, and then she ran, three thousand pounds at thirty miles an hour. The herd thundered after her at full gallop, not knowing exactly what had happened except that when she ran, it only meant they should follow without hesitation. She could not see. There was blood in her eyes. She simply charged. She didn't miss the fence opening by more than ten feet, but the wood was no match for her momentum. She tore out a section without even slowing her stride. The rest of the fence collapsed as the full force of the herd rammed through it. They disappeared down the city streets into a rising cloud of dust.

Maggerty lay on the ground. Such pain in his abdomen. From what he could see by raising his head, he could tell that his body was not shaped the way it should have been. He tried to lift himself up but failed. He slowly moved his right hand to his left side, his fingers at last failing to find the wound or even the scar. He saw Thomas Banyon drive up alongside him in the golf cart. Everything took on a terrible grayness.

(Thomas Banyon lifted a – still, despite all the years and pain and money – bowed leg out onto the green. He looked toward Hennington. The cloud of dust swarmed up into the blistering sun. Thomas did not hear Maggerty die because even if there was a sound, it was too quiet to hear over the machinery that was suddenly whirring away in his brain.)

Part V.

Hopeful Campaigns.

77. The Furniture Cave.

When they lifted the blankets off her and she squinted into the afternoon sunlight, Jacki was surprised that there were two of them, a shorter one with cropped hair and a mustache and a taller one with sideburns and a potbelly.

—Did you both drive?

The shorter one grinned.

—Not at the same time.

—She just called you and you came?

—Yes.

—She has that much stature?

—Not in and of herself. There are others, too, who we would help. And we are but two among others who would help as well.

—So a whole network of you?

—I can't really say.

—But—

—Please. It keeps our danger level down, ours *and* yours, if you know less. We'll leave you here, but we'll return. You'll have food and water. And you're safe here for now.

—For now?

—I'm sure you'll be moved again if there's danger. Whoever you are, you'll be protected.

—Yes, all right. That's fair enough.

They wouldn't tell her where they had brought her. It was obviously some kind of warehouse, but that was all she knew. Fine. The illusion of safety was easier to embrace if danger could be imagined at a distance, accurately or not. They also didn't tell her their names, which was perhaps less fine, but she could understand their caution. If small, gentle-featured Davis had received a broken jaw at the hands of Thomas Banyon, a man three times her size, there was ample reason to believe that he saw himself as being outside of the normal boundaries of propriety. If Thomas found her, then, for better or worse, she was the only one who would bear the brunt of his wrath, not these friendly, anonymous men.

For the best part of two days, she remained alone in the little clearing they had made for her in a large room with access to a small bathroom and sink. The rest of her new home was filled with piles of furniture, very *nice* furniture, hidden underneath tarpaulins or in towering stacks that reached a ceiling almost eight meters up. All kinds of burnished, polished chairs, tables made of heavy, dark wood, a whole delicate maze of mirrors twice as tall as herself. The warehouse was large but not huge. She wove her way around, wandering between rows of beautiful couches, armoires, ottomans, even bedsteads and sinks. At first, she assumed they were hiding her away in the warehouse for a furniture store, but a persistent feeling of déjà vu dogged her until, late on the second day, she realized what was causing it. She recognized the furniture.

—I'm in the winter storehouse, aren't I?

The shorter one had returned alone to refresh Jacki's food and water stores. Jacki's face was so fierce, her voice husky with a tensile fear so pure that he answered her immediately.

—Yes.

—How could you bring me *here*? Didn't they tell you who I was running from?

—Yes, that's why this is the safest place.

—Have you lost your mind? It belongs to the man who's hunting me!

—It's the dead of summer. Hennington Hills won't be

wanting this furniture for the winter makeover for another three months. History has proven that the best place to hide is right under your enemy's nose. He won't think to look here because he won't think anyone's foolish enough to hide here. Plus, the place is guarded. He won't think we could get past the guards.

—How *did* we get past the guards?

—They're on our side.

—All right. Okay. All right. I'm calming down. I guess I can see your point. No one bothers the winter furniture until November. By then—

—By then, you either won't be here or the situation will be resolved however it's going to be resolved.

—I can't imagine it being resolved at all just now. Isn't that something?

—Everything's going to be fine.

—And you can promise me this how?

—We've gotten others away before you.

—There've been others?

—Yes.

—What others?

—Ma'am, please, the less you know the better. For everyone. Trust me, you're safe here. I don't mean to be shifty, but you really don't have any choice other than to trust me anyway.

—I suppose.

—It's true.

—I have one more question.

—All right, maybe.

—How did there get to be 'sides'? You said the guards were on our 'side'. How did that happen? How did I end up on a 'side'?

—I can't really explain. Things just happen. Over time, they accumulate. Bad attracts bad. Good attracts good. 329

Eventually there are sides. The members flux, sometimes the boundaries are gray. Good and bad are sometimes not the point. It happens. For now, concentrate on the fact that you're safe and that you'll get out of this.

—Because I will.

—Because you will, yes.

He left her a surprisingly large number of sandwiches and a slightly less generous pile of fresh bananas and sweet lemons, as well as another cask of water. Time passed quietly, and she had only her thoughts for company. Maybe what the shorter one had said was all true. It made a certain amount of sense, and the hints that all this had happened before with success was also a surprising and welcome addition. She was part of something larger, that was clear. Where had this food come from? And the two men? Then again, if fortune had decided to step in and grace her with some good luck, then maybe it was about time, right?

The lights in the storehouse cast most of the room and furniture in stark shadows and sometimes plain blackness. She munched a banana. Somehow strength had sneaked back into her body, and she realized that several days had gone by without a single thought spared for Forum. She toyed with the desire in her brain, testing its potency. It was still there, still lurking, and she didn't focus on it for long. But still, a bunch of days in a row.

She threw away her banana peel and pulled back a few tarpaulins. All the stacked tables and chairs made a terrific ad hoc playground. Kids could have a grand old time let loose in here. She tried squeezing herself underneath a table, making a cave out of it, but even with all the weight she'd lost, she couldn't quite get deep enough to hide, deep enough to pretend she was spelunking miles away from the world outside. This is a pastime for a child, she thought. A child. She allowed a thought to germinate and take hold in her mind. Could fortune stand a test? How much luck was presently available? If she grabbed for some more, would it be there? On the run from a dangerous man who was spending an unseemly amount of resources to find her, suffering life-threatening withdrawals from a life-threatening drug, out of a job and any discernible future: for God's sake, fortune owed her one.

When he arrived again, she was ready with her request.

—Can you get me a phone?

78. Letter To The Editor.

To the Editor,

I write not, as you might expect, as a Candidate for Mayor of Our Great City of Hennington, though unlike my opponent, my stake in my Candidacy has never wavered due to personal doubts, nor did I re-enter the Race when I found it personally expedient to do so. I have remained in the Race since declaring my Candidacy because I intend to win by standing on my Principals [sic], by showing fortitude in this Contest, and by addressing the Issues and Concerns of the People. Not for me the hem and haw, should I or shouldn't I, back and forth that might bring into question my Character and my Dedication. No, I have stated my intention to run for Mayor, and running for Mayor is what I'm doing without reservations.

No, I write to you and to this fine newspaper as a Citizen of Our Fair City of Hennington, as a Tax-Payer, as someone with an active interest in the Future of Hennington. I write because it is my duty as a Citizen, not as a Candidate, to participate in the Civic Activities of my Chosen Home. In   331 this instance, I write to you because of my deep, deep concern about an Issue that has plagued this City for years, an Issue about which there has been much disagreement, an Issue that because of recent Events now needs a resolution more than ever.

I write to you about The Crash. I write to you because it is my deeply felt Belief that the time has come to control these wayward animals, to protect the Citizens of Hennington from what has now proven to be a menace and a danger to Our Beloved City, to place the right to Safety of our Citizens over the 'concerns' of a handful of City Officials for the so-called 'autonomy' of a herd of three-ton rhinoceros. As a City, we have given them free rein to wander in and out of whatever avenues and byways, private and public property, fields and roads that they choose. It is my opinion, and I believe the opinion of many of the other Citizens of Our City, that the time has come to end this freedom in the interests of the Public.

I am not a fool. I know this is not a Popular Issue. I know the risk I take to my Candidacy by demanding that something be done, but I am also a man of Integrity, a man of Probity, a man who is willing to Sacrifice Secular Ambition for my own Personal Convictions. If this costs me the Mayoralty of Hennington, then I rest in the knowledge that my Conscience will at least be clear because I will have stood up for what I believed to be true.

I ask my Fellow Citizens to hear me out.

Everyone knows by now about the death of harmless Maggerty the Rhinoherd on the horn of what is generally acknowledged to be the lead animal of The Crash. I had the terrible personal misfortune of actually bearing witness to the events of Maggerty's untimely passing. The whole action unfolded on the southern golf course at Hennington Hills Golf Course and Resort, a facility of which I am lucky enough to be President and CEO. I was taking my normal drive through the grounds, making sure they were up to the professional standard that we like to uphold at Hennington Hills, when I saw that The Crash had wandered deep onto the tenth green and were grazing away.

Because of Current Hennington Law, as any home- or business-owner in the City knows, I was unable to perform any action that might move The Crash off of my property or frighten or disturb them in any fashion. If such a law had not been in place, I might have been able to prevent the tragedy that followed. If I am lucky enough to be elected Mayor of Hennington, the General Public can rest assured that no one in the future will have to be put in my position of having to watch senseless slaughter without being able to intervene.

With no provocation whatsoever, the lead animal in The Crash suddenly charged Maggerty, catching him with its horn and tossing him callously to the ground. The animal then went back to eating the grass while poor Maggerty lay dying a painful, bloody death on the ground nearby. It was then that I must admit I broke the law regarding non-molestation of these pests, and I drove my golf cart loudly through the herd, trying to scare them off so that I could get Maggerty whatever help might have saved his life. The animals were belligerent and hostile to me as I shouted to try to get them to move away. The lead animal even attacked my golf cart. I was only saved by turning at the last moment and avoiding the charge. Finally, I was able to drive the herd off of my property, but as we all now sadly know, it was too late to save our poor, beloved City Mascot, Maggerty the Rhinoherd.

The next step should be obvious. The Crash are a menace, plain and simple. Who's to say when they'll strike next? Will it be you or your family who are gored? Will it be your property next to be destroyed? Will your rights be trampled upon in the name of 'Crash Autonomy'?

I call upon Max Latham, the self-styled 'Crash Advocate-General' – a position he invented himself when he decided to pull out of the Mayoral Race – I call on him to solve this problem, to do something that will put this Public Menace to an end, once and for all. If Max Latham has chosen to take up the cause of The Crash, then let him take the responsibility for keeping them in line. If he declines, then I call for his resignation. Something must be done. Someone must be held accountable. I say Max Latham is that person in his current position.

There's something more I'd like to add about Max Latham. My parents were both City Councilmembers up until my mother's untimely death, may she rest in peace. My father is still a Man of great standing in Our City, through both his civic-minded efforts and through the millions and millions of dollars his businesses generate. He has been a longtime supporter of Our Current Mayor, Cora Larsson, both financially and actively, and rightfully so. Mayor Larsson has proven herself a dedicated and effective Leader for the past twenty years.

Now, Max Latham has taken up the banner of Cora Larsson, running on her coat-tails and with her support and endorsement. I know many of you have assumed that Archie Banyon would automatically throw his support behind Latham. I write to you today that, because of the issues I have raised here and others, my father cannot and is not supporting Max Latham for Mayor of Our Towering City.

You know Archie Banyon. You now know how he feels about Max Latham. Now I have called upon Max Latham for action against an obvious danger to this, Our Magnificent City. This is a test right now of what kind of Mayor Max Latham plans to be. How will he handle it?

The ball is in your court, Max. This is an Issue that we as Citizens can't afford for you to be wishy-washy on. I and the rest of Hennington await your answer.

Proud to be a Citizen of Hennington,

Thomas Banyon

[Editor's Note: All capitalizations *sic*]

79. The Inevitable Disappointment By Those We Love.

And again, the phone.
     —Is what he said true?
     —Which part?

—I know all that bullshit about The Crash is lies, but have you withdrawn your support from Max?

—I would have put my endorsement of Thomas in less warm words than he did himself, but yes.

—Oh, Archie—

—Cora, please. I can't take your disappointment, too. I know the ramifications of my actions, but he's finding Luther's killer for me. And he's my son. In my position, you'd do the same.

—I guess I can't really say that I'm altogether surprised, but really, Archie, where have you been? Why couldn't you have told me yourself?

—Everything's different now. I'm sorry. I know I'm letting you down. I'm letting a lot of people down. But Luther's dead. He's dead.

—You don't know that. I thought there was still some question—

—Don't be consoling, Cora. You're a warm woman, but condolence has never been your strong point. It's almost unseemly in my picture of you.

—I'm not sure I know what that means.

—I've always loved you for your strength.

—And I've loved you back, Archie.

—That's not what I mean. I've *loved* you. Do you hear me? But I've always redirected my love in a friendly way. I was your good friend.

—You still *are* my good friend.

—But not your lover, or even your husband.

—Archie—

—None of that matters now. That's the only reason I'm saying any of it. It doesn't matter. The only thing that matters is finding Luther's killer.

—The police are doing all they can—

—Thomas is the only one who's going to be able to find him, and you and I both know it. Now, when nothing matters, please at least be that honest.

—You're frightening me, Archie, how you're talking.

—There's no point in beating around the bush. There's no point in saying anything that's not the truth anymore. It doesn't matter. Nothing does.

—Of course things matter. You've got your friends, your business—

—Who cares about that? I'd already lost one son, and now I've lost another. How can I possibly put any more energy into something as trifling as Banyon Enterprises?

—When can I see you? I want to see you in person.

—There's no point.

—Are you in your office now?

—Yes, but—

—Will you see me?

—Cora—

—As a friend, I ask you this favor. See me. I can be there in twenty minutes. Yes?

—All right. What can it matter? Yes.

It only took fourteen minutes, and she chewed her thumbnail the whole way. That bit about love troubled her. They had skated away from it, but it hung around her mind like an unannounced houseguest. Love, he said. He loved her. Had loved her this whole time. She smiled a little crazily behind the thumbnail. She had loved only one man in her entire life and that had been good enough for forty years. Now, all of a sudden, when most women her age were thinking about retirement, when *she* was thinking about retirement, suitors were falling out of the sky, and in the most unseemly ways. One was trying to destroy the city, the other offered up his devotion as an apparent prelude to death. Why couldn't this have happened when she had more energy for it?

He looked even worse than she had feared.

—Heavens above, Archie. Have you seen yourself lately?

—I don't need a lecture, Cora.

—You've lost Luther, I know, your son in all the most important ways, but—

—In my mind, I never counted him as anything but my son. Do you know how much it hurt when he didn't take my name? And then *still* didn't when he grew up? My heart ached over that, but did I say anything? No, because I loved him as my son.

—Archie—

—I asked the fates for a son and got Thomas. Some bargain, huh? Thomas isn't a son, he's a *limerick*. The richest man in town blessed with five daughters, but is that good enough for me? Of course not. I want a namesake. So here comes little Thomas. My pride and joy. Until he took his first independent action. Which was guess what? Pouring boiling water over the family bird. A childish accident, perhaps, but I knew even then I'd been fooled. Tricked. I'd wanted a son and had gotten an imp. Gotten a punishment.

—But—

—But was that enough? Enough punishment for Archie Banyon? Rich, successful Archie Banyon? Oh, no, not by a long shot, because here comes an earthquake. An earthquake! In Hennington! Never felt before or since and down comes my house, taking every woman in my life and leaving me with Thomas. Me and Thomas, what a treat.

He paused, but she didn't interrupt him again. The terrifying glint in his eye, the cracking force to his voice. I haven't watched him closely enough, she thought. I haven't been enough of a friend.

—So fate intervenes again. This time for the good. I'm delivered a wonderful, smart, sensitive, strong, *good* son, who loves me back, who works hard, who takes guidance, who brings me *joy*. Here's my reward, I thought. For all the heartbreak. Fate has realized that it's over-stepped and has taken measures to set things right. Luther. My beloved Luther. I'm even able to make a peace between the three of us, me, Thomas, and Luther. I'm even able to see Thomas flourish and become successful in his own right. I'm able to be happy at last.

His face hardened, his teeth clenched. His next words were punishments of air.

—And then what do I do with my happiness? Luther comes to me, comes to talk to *me*, in his moment of greatest need, as vulnerable as one person can be before another, and what do I do? I throw him away. My God, my God, my God, I throw him away. *I* did it. It wasn't fate this time. Fate had made amends for its errors and given me my greatest happiness, and I threw it away.

—Archie, please. Torturing yourself does no good. None. You're still in shock from the grief.

—I need to find his killer, Cora. That's it. That's the only important thing left. I need to find him.

—And then what? You can't—

—Then it will all be over.

Cora was nearly swallowed by the hole in his gaze as he said it again.

—Then it will all be over.

80. How Things Add Up.

—So, Daddy, I don't think I understand.

—That's because it doesn't make a whole lot of sense, pumpkin.

—I thought people *liked* The Crash.

—They do.

—Then why does Thomas Banyon say that people want to be protected from them?

—It's an old political trick, Talon. He thinks that most people are neutral about The Crash and—

—What does neutral mean?

—That they don't feel strongly for them or against them. Thomas Banyon is betting that most people don't really think about The Crash all that much.

—How can they not? The Crash is around all the time.

—Precisely. They become so common that people stop thinking about them. I think he's wrong. I think people care for The Crash even if they don't think about them constantly.

—But he thinks they will? I mean, won't.

—I think he thinks he can convince them that The Crash are some sort of threat. He's thinking that if most people are neutral then they'll be swayed by someone with a stronger opinion on the matter. Unfortunately, his strategy is usually right, but I'm hoping he's wrong this particular time. I think he is. I think he's making a mistake.

—So that's a good thing if he is?

—It is and it isn't. He's trying to tell everyone that he's on the good side and I'm on the bad side. It makes me waste time saying that it's not true.

—But that still doesn't make any sense to me.

—That's because you're a thinking individual.

—Is that a compliment?

—Of course it's a compliment. Move your feet. I'm trying to tuck you in.

—Will it work, what he's doing? Can I let Theo under the covers?

—Hold them up. I hope not. I don't think so. It's another old trick, too, to attack first, so I have to spend my time defending myself instead of telling people about my own ideas for the city.

—That's not fair.

—Yes, but if he kept the fight fair, he knows he would probably lose. Let him out if he wants, honey, he's probably hot under there. Let his head stick out.

—So he's cheating.

—Technically, no. He may actually believe what he wrote, though I doubt it. The problem is that he'll *claim* that he feels that way, so if I attack him then he'll be able to get upset that I'm calling him dishonest.

—But I thought he *was* dishonest.

—It's complicated, honey.

—No kidding.

—*I* believe, though, that people are smart enough, like you are, to see through what Thomas Banyon is trying to do. I think it'll backfire on him.

—But, okay, what about this? The Crash killed Maggerty, right? The kids at school are saying how bloody and gory it was, that they stuck a horn right through him.

—We don't really know what happened, little one. All we have is his word for it because he says he's the only witness, which is very bad luck indeed.

—'He says'?

—People with money can sometimes make witnesses suddenly very forgetful.

341

—Kids at school are daring each other to go near The Crash.

—I think that's a bad idea until we find out exactly what happened. I don't want you going near them.

—Do you think they killed him? Why would they do that?

—I think they did, yes, so do the doctors, but more could have happened than we know. Maggerty could have threatened them. The medicine we've been giving him could have worn off or he could have had a delayed negative reaction to it.

—But why would they attack him so *bad*? Why wouldn't they leave him behind?

—I don't know. The Crash have never hurt anyone, and they've been around longer than anyone's been alive. I just can't believe they did it without being pushed to it, and I think most people think that, too. I think most people want to know more. I hope they do. There are still questions here that need answering.

—Theo, stop it!

—Don't shout at him, Talon. He's just a puppy. He doesn't know any better.

—Who's going to answer the questions?

—Which ones?

—The ones that need answering.

—My office is investigating. That was the whole point of setting up the Crash Advocate post. Nobody expected something like this to happen. Which I guess only proves that this is when they need us most.

—Kids at school are saying The Crash should be shot.

—That's why kids aren't in charge of decisions like this.

—They're saying what they'd do if The Crash started attacking them. They're saying they'd fight back with guns and bazookas and tanks.

—And where would they get those?

—It's just kid-talk, Daddy.

—So it is.

—Daddy?

—Yes, pumpkin?

—Are you going to win?

—No one knows for sure. But I think I will. I believe it.

—Even with what Thomas Banyon is doing?

—Even with what Thomas Banyon is doing.

—But it's going to be harder.

—To win? Yes. It's going to be harder. You've got that one right, darling.

—I don't want it to be hard for you.

—Don't you worry about anything. Sometimes things are hard, but if they're worth it, you don't mind working for them. Now. It's time for bed. Look, Theo's already asleep. Good night, sweetie.

—But what's going to happen next?

—If we knew that, life would be boring, wouldn't it, pumpkin?

81. The Smell of Blood.

They wandered for days, and still she couldn't shake the smell from her horn. It was illusory, it had to be. She had shoved her nose into the musty peat in the southern bogs, rubbed it along bitter-smelling tree bark, coated it in piquant rotted fruit, even dunked it in the festering briny marsh to the north. Yet the smell remained, drifting lightly as smoke from her horn to her nostrils, delicate but persistent. There were times when the lingering scent drove her to a frenzied run, as if she could outpace it, pushing against her lungs harder and harder. She only slowed when she heard the thundering hoofbeats of an exhausted herd behind her, trying to keep up, her duties as leader never leaving her, never seeming heavier.

She had led them blindly at first, following no set path, heading towards no destination. Equally frightened themselves, the members of the herd made no complaint of hunger or thirst as they tromped a random path through streets and woodlands, fields and farms. Food had been scarce before, but now they didn't even seem to be looking for it. They stuck close together, walking in tight groups, sleeping when they could, piled almost on top of one another. Nothing like this had ever happened before. There had been deaths in the herd, of course. Death was part of life. But not ever a thin creature, and never by action of a member of the herd. They were used to certainties, used to routine, yet somehow they had gotten lost beyond some border of their normal pattern. When she was among them, she could hear small calls of fear and anxiety.

And they looked to her to set it right. She could see their eyes on her as she walked past, as she paced around them while they slept – sleep having eluded her since, since, since – as she tried to figure out what to do. But the blood, the smell, the horrible presence that wouldn't stop hovering around her nose, made it hard for her to listen to instinct, to sort out panic from the necessities of life and leadership. They looked to her. She had to lead them. That was the way things were. Those were the only facts that were important. But the smell . . .

They had to hide. They had to get somewhere away from the thin creatures and their shouts and jagged odors. Somewhere she could gather herself and put the herd back together
again. Breathing heavily, putting all her energy into move-

ment, she pushed them hard into the woods behind the hill of fields, deep into the thicket. Grass was sparse, but they could eat fallen leaves. There were brooks hidden, too, under the shadows of the dense trees. It wasn't comfortable and there were no easy places to sleep, but it was quiet, away from the hardened stink of the city. The herd settled in, uneasy, exhausted.

What now?

She paced. If large, future decisions weren't to be had, then the smaller, at-hand ones would have to suffice. She made a circle around the herd again and again, keeping them to a small area of woodland between two arms of a small stream. It wasn't difficult. None of the herdmembers wanted to go anywhere anyway and seemed more than happy to at last have a place to stay still, cramped though it was. The air of tension slowly deflated among the members of the herd as she began to act like a leader again, keeping them here, communicating to them where they should stay and what they should do. She could feel their relief, palpably so as some of the wearier members dropped quickly to the ground and went right to sleep.

As she flowed again into the duties of leadership here in the glade, she found herself more than once looking around for the thin creature that followed them. It was then the smell of blood, *his* blood, was the strongest. She shook it off, quickened her step, and was grateful for the opportunity to direct some of the younger ones over a tricky pile of rock. She led them slowly down the embankment to the rest of the herd, carefully guiding them on flat, inflexible feet that were the worst in nature for climbing.

And so what *now*? Never had she felt so exhausted and lost. After a rest here, she would move the herd on. But to where? And why? Why couldn't they stay here? Because a hiding place was never permanent. And why the need to hide? 345

Because instinct told her so, and instinct had gotten her this far, had gotten the herd through hard times before. But here now was where they were, safe for the moment. (Safe from what?) At last, three days without sleep caught up with her, and she barely had the strength to kneel rather than fall to the ground. Darkness was setting in. As she lay in the peat, the unwelcome smell persisted in her nose, as if the sky, so stingy with rain, was instead shedding sheets of blood down onto her and her alone.

82. The Hard Bit.

—Well, I've looked, and it's not encouraging.

—I know. I've looked, too.

—There's no written doctrine, surprise surprise, so all we've really got to go on is what others have done before, and the books aren't exactly busting at the seams with those stories either.

—I know.

Jarvis took another look around the room. Apparently, foreclosure meant you couldn't take your furniture with you either, and the presence of sofas, appliances, pictures, even books and magazines made the house seem less under auction than abandoned in a hurry and forgotten. The air was tense, but Jarvis assumed it was him. As if the whole business with Theophilus wasn't enough, how did he also manage to find himself sitting illegally in an abandoned, or rather, foreclosed house with a possibly crazy young man and a body that was both dead and not? He sighed.

—Are you sure you're safe here, Peter?

—No, but—

346   —Right, right. We've talked about that.

—I appreciate your help, Father, but I don't have much time.

Jarvis looked over the face of Peter Wickham once more. Weary wrinkles had appeared around his still-young eyes, eyes filled to the brim with a heartbreaking mixture of hope, belief, utter exhaustion, barely handled grief, impatience, and back around again to hope. Jarvis doubted Peter was over thirty yet his eyes were those of a soul containing lifetimes, lifetimes which had probably only been lived in the past few weeks. Almost reflexively, Jarvis offered up a silent prayer for this young man which was almost a warning. Save this one, Lord. Somehow, however this works out in the end, save this one. Save *this* one and his pure faith.

—So what do I do?

—From what I can tell, there's not a whole lot of *doing* involved. You pray.

—I have been.

—You keep Luther safe.

—I've been doing that, too.

—And you keep your faith that what you're doing is right.

—That's all?

—My dear boy, isn't that hard enough?

—But I feel I ought to be doing something. Go on some quest. Avenge his grief. Something grand, something big.

—The Bondulay teaches that we're all responsible for ourselves. Your part in this is to keep your faith, which, though you're doing admirably well, is and will become more difficult than you can imagine. Whatever Luther's grief is, the resolution to it will have to take care of itself with no input from you.

—I don't understand.

—Faith is rarely ever a journey, Peter. It's more like keeping a fire stoked in a rainstorm. The benefits and warmth are

347

obvious, but it's so much easier just to not do the work, let the fire go out, and use reason to bundle yourself up against the rain.

—With the rain being what? Doubt?

—Well, yes, I guess. The analogy doesn't quite hold that far, but I think you see my point.

—All I want to know is what I have to do, and when Luther will come back.

—I don't know. No one knows, and *that's* your challenge.

—But the Sacraments—

—The Sacraments say more or less nothing. You said you've looked so you should know that. Book of Aramea, Chapter 4, Verses 3–5, '*But the death of Sarah was not a death but a resting place away from her grief where she stayed until Antony came to fetch her*'. Sarah and Antony aren't mentioned again in the entire Sacraments. Book of Songs, Chapter 41, Verses 12–14, '*Rest from your grief in the place twixt life and death, until your former beloved calls you back, and life returns anew*'. That's it, Peter. That's everything. In a 900,000-word text, those are the only two mentions of your situation, and neither of them are much to go on for hard instructions.

—What about the Apocrypha? Meredith and her son.

—My, you *have* done your homework. Yes, Meredith dies, or seems to, when she learns incorrectly that her son has died in battle. He returns, declares that he will bring her back from a fruitless death, fasts for a month, builds a new church, drives out the quote-unquote 'forces of avarice' in his town, until finally, when he's on the verge of actually dying for real, Meredith returns to life.

—Well?

—Well what? Are you going to build a church and drive out the forces of avarice?

348

—It sounded allegorical to me.

—Ah, see, there you're right. It *is* allegorical. The whole story is. It's about how Meredith failed to deal with her earthly grief and was lucky enough to have a son to bring her back. However, the story also implies that death can be circumvented through good works, which is why it's in the Apocrypha and not in the Sacraments. The dogma is all wrong for a faith that believes in the divine cleansing of the soul. You do good works in service of your Lord because he's washed you of your sins, not vice versa.

Peter exhaled in frustration.

—So you have nothing at all?

—I'm telling you, everything there is still amounts to next to nothing. There are old tales, but they vary so much they're worthless for practical steps to take. Myth, speculation, half-heard whispers that contradict each other. There've been breakaway factions from Bondulay who have concentrated more on this type of mysticism, but even their literature contains not one clear example of resurrection.

Peter was quiet for a moment. He looked at the floor.

—You don't believe me either.

—I believe that *something's* happened, *is* happening. I don't have the certainty of your faith in the exact nature of it, no, I'll admit that. But we're in unknown territory here, Peter, and there's nothing to guide you. I think *that* may be the point, which is what I was trying to say before. Your mission, so to speak, the steps that you can take are praying, keeping Luther safe, and not losing your faith in the face of no evidence, in the face of no supporting material, in the face of only contrary opinion and doubt, including mine.

Peter cocked his head to the back room where Luther, Luther's body, still lay on a bed. The hum that emanated from somewhere around him could still be heard, even from the next room. No-man's-land. Jarvis was right about that. Peter had skipped some boundary somewhere, had jumped some line into who knew where, and Jarvis was saying that he was alone there. No, not alone. He had Luther. If this was love or if it was obsession, it no longer mattered. The only way to go was onward.

—I can do it.

—You'll be faced with doubts of a magnitude unimaginable.

—I can do it.

—I'll help you when I can, but I can't do anything illegal. I can't save you if you're caught, and I can't stop the police from looking.

—I can do it.

—I believe you, Peter. That's why I'm helping. Because despite everything, and there's a lot going on that you don't even know about, somehow I believe I'm in the presence of a miracle. It scares the everloving shit out of me, but I believe you.

83. Re-linking.

A phone was easier requested than provided. It took the shorter one three full days to find a mobile he could sneak to Jacki, and that was only after she had explained in long, convincing detail why she needed it.

—I still don't think it's a good idea.

—I know the risks. I'll make sure you're not involved.

—You can't make sure of that.

—But you still brought me the phone.

—Your reasons are good.

—I certainly hope they are. Is the phone safe?

—There's no problem with the phone. The problem is in letting someone else know your location.

—I won't tell them, I promise. No one will be able to trace me, right? Would someone have done that? Tapped my kids' phone or watched them or something?

—This phone will cycle as a mobile, so no one will know where you're calling from, and the mobile account is in the name of a dead person. What I'm worried about is putting out to the world that you're here, that you want to contact someone. That's a weakness that could be exploited. Plus and yes, your sons are almost definitely going to be watched.

—My ex-husband isn't going to let them be in any danger.

—It's not for your ex-husband to say whether they're in danger or not. He probably won't even know. Look, it's a big risk. I still advise you not to take it.

—But, well, see, have you ever had a feeling that you know is absolutely right, no matter what the externals are or how they tell you to do something else? That you've got to do this one thing because it's the *right* thing, no matter what?

—No, but I'll believe that you feel it. Just be careful. Don't over-use the line, don't talk too long or try to call too often. Tell absolutely no one where you are, and try to get them to keep even the fact that you called a secret.

—I might not even get through. It's been a long time.

—Be careful.

—I will. Wish me luck.

—Good luck.

—Jacki. It's Jacki. Say, 'Good luck, Jacki'.

—I wish you hadn't told me. It's better if I didn't know.

—Too late for that. Say it. You're the only human contact I've had in ages.

—I don't know—

—It would mean a lot.

He laughed. Her persistence was becoming an expected pleasure.

—All right, all right. Good luck, Jacki. Happy?

—Blissful. And nervous.

—Then definitely 'good luck'. I'll be back in the morning with some more water.

She spent the next hour walking the same circle through the storehouse, trying to talk herself into it, trying to gather enough nerve from her frayed system to actually push the buttons. The facts: two years was a long time not to see your sons and an unforgivable length if it was voluntary. Worse was the full year that had passed since the last phone call, and she couldn't really remember what it was even about. Probably nothing but embarrassed nonsense. She was deep in the grip of Forum then, and so many things were blurred.

But also factual: though she still occasionally pissed blood, though her heart still raced in odd fits and starts, though her temperature could skyrocket and plummet with no warning, she had kicked the Forum habit. Somehow, in all this mess, there was this miracle to hang on to, there was a reason to go forward, there was a reason to do this, yes?

But then the questions, too: why motherhood so suddenly? Or was that just a question from the old Jacki, the mean one, the harpy (so Jacki had taken to envisioning her) who wanted the needle? Was this too much too soon? Was she just feeling good again, and thought that automatically meant that all the trouble she'd had with being a mother to two boys was just going to vanish? Was she giving in to simple irony that now that she'd stopped producing milk then that must be the signal to start feeling maternal again? And why would her boys even give her a chance after she had behaved so badly? What in blazes was she doing? Was she so far out on a limb that she was willing to try anything? Or did being on a limb free her? Which was it? Was there a right answer after all?

When the moment finally came, she didn't think about it, finding herself suddenly dialing, and then doing everything she could not to pass out while it rang. She squatted down on her haunches and tried not to hyperventilate. Ring Ring. She was equally desperate that no one be there and that someone answer. Ring Ring. Maybe no one was home. Ring Ring. She could always call back, but the thought of gathering this courage all over again seemed momentarily unbearable.

—Hello?

Oh, my God.

—Hello.

—Yes?

The voice seemed out of breath.

—I'm sorry. Am I interrupting?

—No, it's fine. I was out back. Who's speaking, please?

Phrased politely, so it had to be Morton, the youngest, who would be what, fifteen? Sixteen? When was his last birthday? Her heart chilled in the few seconds that it took her to remember. She should have known immediately.

—Is that Morton?

—Yes. Who's this?

Still friendly, still welcoming, still persisting in the question, one that opened up a landslide of answers. Mom? Jacki? Jacqueline Strell? Former prostitute, former drug addict, former slave to Thomas Banyon? Who was she now anyway?

—It's, um . . . It's—

—Yeah?

—It's someone you know.

She winced. A stupid answer. You can't get to the finish line and then stall, she told herself. Shit or get off the pot. A   353 phrase, unbidden and unwelcome, that her ex-husband used to say with a cheeky grin on his face, waiting for someone to laugh.

—Who? I don't really have time to guess. I'm doing yardwork.

Morton doing yardwork. Her sweet, sensitive youngest out in the yard with his flowerbeds and his vegetables and his shrubs and trees. A world that perplexed both brother and father, but one they nevertheless were a little in awe of as Morton coaxed all kinds of amazing beauty into their tiny yard. Jacki was suddenly overwhelmed with love for him. She placed a hand on the floor to steady herself. Whatever happened was whatever happened. She would move forward no matter what.

—Morton, it's Mom. It's your mother.

84. Triumph of the Will.

—You know, for someone who's done precious goddamn little for this campaign, you're sure throwing your weight around a lot.

—'Precious goddamn little'? Have you paid attention to *anything*, Thomas?

—I'm just saying your pushiness is getting a little boring.

—All I said was that you should have let me read the letter first before you sent it.

—It's been a huge success. We're getting a shitload of supportive phone calls.

—Phone calls mean nothing. All they reflect are the opinions of those crazy or lonely or annoyed enough to call. They are only tangentially connected to reality or how the city actually views you.

—It's a success, Jon. The only reason you can't see it is because you didn't think of it.

—I didn't think of it because it's a *bad idea*, you overgrown bullock.

Thomas smiled. You were winning an argument if you could lower your opponent to name-calling. In fact, this whole exchange was turning into a great pleasure. A good opportunity to get out some aggression. He still didn't have his own campaign office. He still had to memorize idiotic facts about idiotic subjects to impress slack-jawed crowds of idiotic voters. He was still spending copious amounts of money while this extremely rich pompous twat opposite him prattled on with his *advice*. It was time for someone to feel some heat, and if it was Jon then so much the better.

—I apologize for the name-calling.

Thomas frowned.

—You do?

—Yes, it was juvenile. We're grown men. We should act like it.

—Fair enough.

—Also fair enough would be to run things by me, at least for an opinion, before splashing it before the eyes of every voter and, more importantly, every donor in this city.

—We've pulled in almost forty thousand since the letter ran.

—Thirty-seven thousand of that was already pre-arranged. By me. The remaining three thousand could be counted under regular daily donations. It proves nothing.

—It was more of a symbolic gesture. I was taking a stand.

—A suicidally unpopular stand.

—Now, there you're wrong. Unpopular, yes, but it shows I've got guts. Plus, The Crash did kill that smelly pile of shit. I saw it happen.

355

—The trauma is obvious.

—Could you possibly come down from your superior tree for just one short conversation? It's an unpopular stand. No shit. The Crash are an institution. But now they've killed someone. People aren't going to know how to think about that. They're going to wonder what to do. They're going to wonder until someone *tells* them what to do. I'm there first. If we change their opinion, then Max, who is Crash Advocate-General, that fucking fake job he made up, he's right in the cross hairs of public discontent. Check and checkmate.

—I'll admit that the idea has some appeal—

—*Thank* you.

—But I don't think it's that clear-cut. You're not absolutely sure you can swing the opinion.

—No one said it wasn't a risk.

—My point is I could have helped you make it better if you'd had even the common courtesy to show it to me before you had it printed. And that was it, wasn't it? You had it printed because Banyon Enterprises owns that paper, if I'm not mistaken.

—And your point?

—My point is that you looked like a buffoon.

—Now you go too far—

—No, Thomas, wrong. You looked like a half-literate moron in that letter, like an anti-intellectual jackanapes trying to stampede his way into power with all the finesse of a lovestruck buffalo.

Thomas smiled again. This was more like it.

—Why? What was wrong with it?

—Where do I start? How about the runaway capi-talization?

—Emphasis.

—If you emphasize everything, then it just looks like

you're screaming. Plus, do you even know what a split infinitive *is*?

—No one gives a shit about split infinitives!

—Not consciously, but on some level, deep down, they can see that they don't have to take you seriously.

—Wrong. Deep down, they can identify with me because they split fucking infinitives all the fucking time.

Oh, yes, this was turning into good fun. Jon's face was apoplectically red. Thomas had never seen him this upset.

—Why do I even offer my help to you if you won't take it?

—What do you mean not take it? I take your advice when I deem it worthwhile. You are an advisor on this journey, Jon, not the captain. That you keep forgetting is an unpleasantness that's wearing on my patience.

Jon took a long, angry breath.

—I only want you to win, Thomas. Then you can do whatever the hell you like as Mayor. It's only important to me that you win.

—Why? Why is it so important? We've come this far and you've said nothing except, 'Oh, I have my own blessed reasons'. Well, out with them, Jon. Out with your bloody blessed reasons if you want to stay here and help me, Mr It's-Only-Important-That-You-Win.

—My reasons are my own. My help, which is more valuable than you can possibly understand, is what I offer.

—'More valuable than you can possibly understand'. Do you know how intolerable you sound when you say that?

Thomas leaned slowly back into his chair and reached into his pocket for a cigarillo. Before he got it to his lips, Jon smacked it to the floor.

—And quit smoking those goddamn things! You can't be stoned and run a campaign!

357

—It's a mild narcotic, *Jon*. Are you suddenly my mother? Because I've got news for you. She's dead.

Jon cocked his head and was silent for a moment.

—I think this is just about enough, really.

—I beg your pardon?

—You'll either win or you won't. I no longer have any influence here, even though later on you'll wish I did. I'll still do what I can to see that you win, Thomas, even though you don't remotely deserve it. But enough of this bullshit.

He stood from his chair.

—What do you mean?

—What do I mean? I mean you now command this boat alone. I'd wish you well if both of us didn't already know that I wouldn't mean it. Good day, Thomas.

Six brisk steps and he was out of the office. Thomas was astonished, and then he was pleased. What a nice day this had turned out to be. He couldn't stop smiling even as he got down on his knees to look for the errant cigarillo.

85. Getting to the Bottom.

—I think I know what it is, Pastor.

—Come in, come in.

Jarvis was unnerved by both the ashen look on Mrs Bellingham's face, a look he had only seen the once before when she related her disturbing dream to him (a memory that stirred up its own unsettling chain of thoughts) and by the fact that he had no need to ask her what 'it' she was referring to.

—Unburden yourself, Sister.

She looked surprised.

—That seems awfully formal, Jarvis.

—Sorry, Mrs Bellingham. I'm just on edge.

—And you think I'm not?

—Of course, of course, I—

—Forgive me, I'm wound up. I'm very upset.

—Tell me what's bothering you, Sister.

She sighed deeply, as if she had at last found a place of rest after a long run.

—My friends Tova Kikaham and Evelyn Tottenham, you know them.

—Yes.

—Well, they paid me a visit this morning, which was unusual.

—Why unusual?

—Friends don't really 'drop by' anymore, do they? You call on the phone. You see each other at church or out shopping or visiting someone on a birthday. You don't 'drop by'.

—I can see that.

—Can you? Good, because it didn't feel right to me and I thought that was the reason. All I was sure of is that it felt strange.

—So I'm guessing it wasn't a straight social call?

—I'm getting there. I'm sorry, that was curt. I'm just out of sorts.

—Take your time.

—I *am*. Sorry. Tova and Evelyn came by just after breakfast. They just knocked on the door, and when I answered it, they stood there like they were salesmen or something. It was very strange. I've never even had Tova Kikaham over to my house before, come to think of it. I just know her from church and that's it. Evelyn's been to a few dinner parties, I guess, but not for a while. Yet there they were, on my doorstep like they were going to offer me new carpeting. They had this look, this kind of eager look that I couldn't figure out. This

359

strange thing in the eyes, kind of spooky. I almost didn't let them in, it shook me so.

—But you did?

—Of course! I couldn't just slam the door on them, could I now? They sat on my couch, right on the edge, not leaning back, not relaxing at all. They wouldn't take any coffee or cake that I offered, which was even stranger because you know Evelyn eats like a starved hyena. They just looked at me with their eyes all wet and sparkly, and I began to wonder who was getting married or having a baby. Then do you know what they said? They said, 'Please sit down, Sister'. Sit down! Like I was visiting *them*.

She wrung her hands together tightly, and her eyes darted around the room. She seemed to be getting more upset as she went along.

—Can I get you something to drink, Mrs Bellingham? Coffee? I've got a teapot still warm from lunch.

—That would be nice, Father. I can't believe how much this has unsettled me.

—I can tell. Sugar?

—And milk, yes. Thank you.

—Now slow down and just tell me everything they said to you. Take your time.

—Right. After they invited me to sit down like a guest in my own house, they started talking about Theophilus Velingtham.

—Ah.

—Yes, I know. I've never cared for the man either. Wields his faith like a blunderbuss, that one. No joy whatsoever.

—Well put, Sister.

—For the first ten minutes, it was Theophilus this and Theophilus that, like they were converts to a new Theophilus religion.

360

—That might not be too far from the truth, unfortunately.

—And then things got even more ominous. They started talking about 'the dark wind' and 'the light wind'.

—The Book of Ultimates.

—Yes, even though you'd preached that wonderful sermon about it, it seems Theophilus is doing exactly what you'd warned against.

—The ruckus in church.

—Yes. There's more. There's someone else.

—Someone else?

—Apparently, Theophilus believes, and has gotten a bunch of other people to believe as well, that there's someone in Hennington who is the prophesized 'light wind'.

—You're kidding.

—I wish I was. To see my own friends brainwashed or whatever it is that's happened, talking like they've joined some terrifying cult, which I'm afraid is exactly what they *have* done.

—Theophilus believes that the light wind prophesized in the Book of Ultimates has arrived in Hennington as a man?

—Yes, the prophecy that you don't even believe in. That *I* don't even believe in. I agreed with every word of that sermon you did on Brandon Beach.

—Does Theophilus give a name to this person?

—It took Tova and Evelyn forever to get around to it, and they weren't going to tell me even then, but I played along and finally got it out of them. It's someone named Jon. They didn't know his last name, but they know he's working with Thomas Banyon to get him elected Mayor of Hennington.

—That's . . . I can't believe it.

—Do you know anything about this man? Have you heard of him?

—No, but *Thomas Banyon?*

—Yes.

361

—After all the awful things that man has done to the Rumour community?

—I know.

—All those lives destroyed at that horrible, souped-up brothel?

—I *know*.

—And Theophilus is saying that someone close to Thomas Banyon is the light wind that people should follow?

—There's something worse than wrong about it. It's almost evil. You should have seen their faces when they were talking. I tried to tell them exactly that about Thomas Banyon, but apparently Theophilus is hinting that it's a front, that Thomas is the dark wind that this Jon person is going to blow away.

—I'm dumbfounded. I thought Theophilus was such an obvious lunatic that—

—It's worse than we thought.

—They wanted you to . . . what? Join up?

—Something like that.

—What did you say?

—I said I supported the teachings of the pastor in my parish, like every good Bondulay parishioner should. Then I threw them out.

—Goodness.

—I was so upset, I came straight here. I had to tell you.

—Thank you for that, Mrs Bellingham. Thank you so much.

—Do you remember that dream I told you about?

—Oh, yes. The one where your grandmother told you about someone or some force coming to Hennington, right?

—Yes. It seems she was right.

—I wish it weren't true, but it looks like it is.

—What do we do, Pastor?

—First we pray. After that, I wish I knew.

86. The Debate.

[Selected excerpts from the official transcript of the Hennington Mayoral Debate, moderated by Charles Jackson Foster, broadcast live from YYX3 Narrowcast Studios in St George, Hennington, 28 August, 7.00 p.m.]

Charles Jackson Foster: Opening statements, please, gentlemen. Mr Banyon?

Thomas Banyon: Thanks, Chuck. My Fellow Henningtonians. I stand before you tonight as a candidate for Mayor of our fair city. The Banyons have been residents and active members of Hennington society since the beginning of the Recent Histories. You all know the great achievements of my illustrious and respected father, Archie Banyon. Heck, half of you have worked for him at some time in your life. *[Scattered laughter]* Many of you have asked why I'm running for Mayor. It's simple, really. I believe we're at a turning point in the history of Hennington. Our Mayor is stepping down after twenty years in office. I'm sure you all join me in wishing her well. I hope you'll also all join me in seizing this opportunity to put our city on track for a fresh start. The rigmarole is the same. You know it, and I know it. Our taxes could be lower, the government could be more efficient, unemployment has held steady at one rate for years and could be lower. These are all issues you know, and issues that I promise to tackle head-on with vigor. My opponent has been endorsed by Mayor Larsson and has worked all of his professional life in her office. What he promises, now that he's changed his mind for a second time and decided to run, is more of the same. The same has been fine for twenty years now, but don't you think we can do better? I do. That's why I'm running for Mayor. With your help, I can make our great city even greater. Staying the course is no longer good enough.

CJF: Mr Latham.

Max Latham: Thank you very much, Charles. My fellow citizens, I believe in fate. I believe that sometimes destiny, or whatever higher power you individually choose to believe in, has plans for us that we shouldn't question. It's true, I had severe doubts about running for Mayor. As Mayor Larsson, my mentor and good friend, finally told me, if your heart isn't in it one hundred per cent, then do the voters a favor and don't run, because all of you out there deserve a Mayor whose heart and soul are committed to both the process and to the job. For a time there, mostly out of consideration for my ten-year-old daughter Talon, who I'm raising alone since the death of her mother, my heart and soul were *not* committed. So I withdrew, a decision I stand by as right at the time. I withdrew and waited with the rest of you to see who would come forward to run to replace the great Cora Larsson. It was only when Thomas Banyon became the sole entrant into the race that I reconsidered my position. The people of Hennington deserve a choice. You deserve a contested election that will pit different visions of our city against one another. And it is because I believe in my heart that my opponent's vision for our city is so completely wrong, so much the antithesis of what has made Hennington great, that the fire in my heart and soul were rekindled. With the support of my daugh-

364

ter, who wants me to 'win win win!' *[Scattered laughter]* and with the support of Mayor Larsson, I chose to re-enter the race. I intend to race hard, and if elected, I intend to be the kind of Mayor that Hennington can be proud of.

TB: Implying that I'm not?

CJF: Mr Banyon, please. We'll follow our format of question and rebuttal. The candidates are to have no direct argument with one another, lest chaos reign. *[Scattered laughter and faint applause]* Now, to begin. Mr Banyon, you've taken quite a controversial position recently on the issue of The Crash . . .

. . .

TB: . . . All these reasons I've stated before. The Crash is a public menace. It's obvious to me. It's obvious to all of you. The only person it's not obvious to is my opponent, who considers the matter still 'under investigation'. *[Scattered laughter]*

CJF: Mr Latham?

ML: It's clear that my opponent doesn't have an actual real opinion on this matter. He's merely stirring up public dissent. It's cynical. It's unpleasant. And it has no place in this campaign.

TB: I resent that remark.

CJF: Mr Banyon, please. You'll have your own time for rebuttal.

TB: He's calling me a liar.

CJF: Mr Banyon, please—

ML: May I continue?

TB: Why should I put up with being called a liar by someone whose decisions are made for him? Someone who—

CJF: Mr Banyon, enough! You'll have the opportunity for a follow-up answer. Now, we'll let Mr Latham finish. Mr Latham?

ML: Thank you. My current job title is, of course, Crash Advocate-General. That means I speak for The Crash on city matters, both legal and civil. My office is in charge of investigating incidents like the tragic death of Maggerty, and that investigation is ongoing.

TB: They killed him! They bloody killed him right before my eyes!

ML: So far, we've only got your word for that, Mr Banyon.

TB: He's calling me a liar again. Why am I having to put up with this?

CJF: Mr Banyon, please be quiet and wait your turn! And Mr Latham, may I remind you that you are to direct no comments at Mr Banyon.

366   **ML**: Of course, my apologies. I'll merely say that The

Crash have existed in Hennington since longer than anyone alive can remember. They've always been a treasured part of city life. Now, obviously, *something* has gone wrong. We don't know what, but it's unprecedented. Until we know the details, it's my opinion, and I think the opinion of any intelligent Hennington voter, that we give The Crash the benefit of the doubt until we know what's happened. That's my opinion, one that I strongly feel is the most rational. *[Scattered applause]*

CJF: Now, Mr Banyon, your follow-up rebuttal.

TB: I've reconsidered, Chuck. I'm going to take the high road here and refuse to participate in the kind of character-impugning that my opponent has chosen. The people of Hennington deserve better than that. I stand by my position on The Crash, and I just hope it's not the life of one of Hennington's children that proves me right. *[Moderate applause]*

. . .

ML: . . . And I call on my opponent to tell us just who exactly his supporters are. *I* have nothing to hide. My support comes from right here in our fair city. Just who from the outside does Thomas Banyon have funding his campaign and what do these people exactly want in the way of promises if he's elected?

CJF: Yes, Mr Banyon. There has been press speculation on the identity and background of one Tybalt Noth, who has been seen very publicly as a part of your campaign. Care to answer Mr Latham's charge?

367

TB: First, I'd like to say I resent the implication that I can be bought by this so-called 'funding' of my campaign. I can assure everyone here that I have enough personal wealth to fund the campaign myself if need be, but otherwise I've broken no fundraising laws and have acted in no way that has been different from my opponent, who, I might add, is dependent upon donors to fund his campaign and therefore considerably more beholden to them than I would ever be. As for Mr Noth, he is merely a friend and advisor who provided only a small amount of administrative start-up money to the campaign and has in fact recently left his formal capacity in the organization.

CJF: So he's no longer working for you?

TB: He's provided tremendous help, but as an official advisor, that's correct, he no longer works in the campaign.

CJF: So what is his background, then? Now that you've said he's provided tremendous help, perhaps you can shed some light on Mr Noth.

TB: As he is now a private citizen, it's really not my place. You'll have to ask him, I'm afraid.

CJF: Mr Latham. Follow-up?

ML: Mr Banyon's answers are disingenuous in the extreme. Mr Noth had to be forcibly removed from a party hosted by Mayor Larsson—

TB: A misunderstanding, I assure you, and a typical over-reaction from the Mayor.

CJF: Mr Banyon—

ML: Mr Noth has openly declared to the Mayor that he's obsessed with seeing her lose, and suddenly he pops up as your closest advisor. What are we to make of this, Mr Banyon? Your answers are not sufficing.

CJF: Mr Latham, I'll not have—

TB: You're grasping at straws, Max. You're angry because my father has endorsed my campaign and not yours. Jon Noth has only ever expressed support for me winning this election, not for Cora Larsson losing. She's not even running, for Pete's sake, so why is this even an issue?

ML: You're dodging the question.

CJF: Gentlemen, please! You will both stick to the groundrules—

TB: And you're sniping because you and Mayor Larsson can't stand to see me win. Why is that, Max? Why this overwhelming hatred for me? Don't you think the people of Hennington deserve an explanation? Are you so bankrupt of your own ideas that your only platform is 'Don't Vote for Thomas Banyon'? That's hardly what I would call leadership—

ML: Your so-called vision for Hennington is based on personal vanity and power-grabbing. You're widely known as a corrupt strongman—

TB: I'd watch what I was saying, Max, if I didn't want to end up in court. I've never once been successfully accused of corruption. You've got no evidence what-soever—

ML: Claiming I've got no evidence is different than say-ing you're not corrupt, Thomas. Is it so hard a question to answer?

TB: How dare you talk to me that way? I ought to—

ML: You ought to what? Is there a threat coming? Let the people hear it, Thomas.

CJF: That really is enough! Unbelievably, we've now come to the end of this mockery of a debate. There isn't even time for closing statements, which may actually be a blessing to those at home who are still tuned in after this disgraceful display. *[Strong applause]*

[Thomas Banyon is seen to smile. Max Latham is frowning. The two do not shake hands. Copies of full transcript available from YYX3, send SAE to '28 August Debate Transcript', 34 St George Square, Hennington, North 17–LR2.]

87. Old Love.

The older couple walks down the path in their gray jogging suits, deep in discussion but keeping a brisk pace. They are handsome, and not 'for their age' either, but truly handsome, attractive not simply physically but because of a certain alert-ness to their features, a certain concentration to the glance, a certain awareness of the world around them. It's obvious, look, there, him automatically steadying her back as they walk around the rock, that they are deeply in love, a gentle touch to the elbow, a leaning stance of the upper body. Habits long understood and taken for granted, yet somehow never managing to lose their electricity. See the way she takes his hand, not a grasp for balance or reassurance, but merely because she wants to. A laugh even though her brow is creased. A bow of his head to catch her gaze. A problem being dealt with inside the confines of an unquestioned love. How staggering when love finds its perfect match, how heartachingly tender, and how much a sense of exposure is felt for something so beautiful. Turn around, look behind you, scan the horizon, watch for the danger that must be on its way. Can something so miraculous remain invulnerable for very long?

—The thing that upsets me is that I've always been a woman of action, of forward motion, and somehow in this whole goddamn thing I'm just ending up reacting and defending. I *hate* that.

—My dearest darling love, you coached Max as well as you could. The strategy to let Thomas Banyon hang himself with his own obvious shortcomings was a good one.

—But who knew he would embrace his shortcomings with such glee?

—Precisely, and who knew that laconic Max Latham would lose his temper? He's got to shoulder most of the blame, Cora. It was his debate.

—How did we end up here? How did Thomas Banyon turn being a megalomaniac into a campaign plus? I've never heard of *anyone* who actively sought to squash voter turnout as a formal strategy.

—If it works, you're going to see it a lot more often, unfortunately.

371

—I just feel so helpless, Albert.

—Look, petal, Max threw you a curveball by withdrawing, then Jon showed up and inexplicably got Thomas Banyon to run for Mayor. I'd still like to know how that happened. The reason all you're doing is reacting is because even you can't be expected to foresee the future, particularly one that has made as little sense as this one.

—What if he wins?

—We'll deal with that when and if it happens. Until then, we keep working to make it *not* happen. Finally, in the long run, we'll just live our lives like we always have. I've been wondering how much of this is because you're worried about Thomas Banyon becoming Mayor and how much is difficulty in handing over the reins to anyone.

—Now don't you turn on me too.

—'Turn on you'? Like milk?

—Hush. Of course part of it is the retirement thing, but less than you might expect. I did – could you help me over this mud, thank you – I did a lot of thinking before I retired. You know I was ready.

—True.

—But then all this other brouhaha erupted and suddenly I had to think about Max dropping out, then about Jon going off the deep end, then I had to throw all my retirement preparation away because for a day or two there I was running again, until Max again surprised me by dropping back in. It's been exhausting. I don't know which end is up. Can we rest here?

—There's a nicer view about sixty feet further along.

—Still.

—All right. Water?

—Thanks. Look at those surfers. They're going to get killed.

—It's No Margin. All the rage with the under-twenty set.

—Youth is a form of mental illness. A weird thing happened today. You remember Lisa?

—The front desk receptionist?

—Yes. I came in this morning and she was reading the Bondulay Sacraments at her desk.

—She doesn't strike me as the religious type.

—To put it mildly. She sort of hid it away when I spotted it. I didn't ask her about it. Her business. And now Archie's gone all weird, too. I'm actually worried that he might be suicidal.

—That bad?

—That bad. I can understand his situation, I suppose; anyone would feel forlorn and just unhinged with mourning, but there's a resignation there that's frightening.

—And the unspoken, unrequited love for you, although that really didn't come as much of a shock.

—Yeah, I know, but it was the *way* he said it, as if it didn't matter anymore.

—Well. He'll either pull through it or he won't, darling. You do what you can, but this one's up to him.

—Oh, I know that intellectually, but the poor man.

—Absolutely, the poor man. And there's been no word at all about Luther?

—None. The whole police force is out looking, and Archie apparently has Thomas' army of private detectives out looking as well. I can't believe that nothing would turn up. *Something* has to happen.

—So you think that's why Archie's backing Thomas in the Mayor's race?

—That, and that he just doesn't seem to care anymore.

—You sound so down, my love.

—I just wish I knew how things had ended up so messy.   373

—Not everything's messy. Or are you still a little up in the air on Kevin, too?

—No. Actually, no.

—So what do you say to the idea of him moving in, then?

—We're on untrodden ground, Albert.

—I know. It will be very strange, very new. I have my own reservations.

—Like what?

—The expected. Jealousies. For him and you, for him and whomever. He'll have to have his freedom.

—I know.

—I'm also afraid of being hurt. I'm afraid of *you* being hurt.

—But every relationship has that fear.

—True, but it sounds as if you're willing to go ahead?

—We don't even know what he'll say.

—We won't know until we try. Should we try, my love, my darling? Untrodden ground, indeed. I get nervous and excited just thinking about it.

—Like we were teenagers again. I think we should ask.

—And I agree.

They smile at one another, seated on a rock sixty feet below the main ledge, sharing an intimacy, sharing a secret. He takes her hand, and they gaze out over the bay below them. She leans into him, and they kiss. They're still safe, for now.

88. The Immobile Journey.

The abandoned backyard was where the house's long vacancy showed most. Weeds, both banal and colorful, made a dwarf jungle from the cracked concrete patio back to the cracked wooden fence. On his third day here, Peter had seen an obviously pregnant fox find her way back through the brush and disappear into a den hidden among the taller weeds in the corner. Even now, there was probably a little fox family there, keeping itself cool from the sun.

Peter sighed, his breath hanging only for a moment against the windowpane. Doing nothing as a plan of action left much to be desired. He had searched the abandoned house from top to bottom, finding little of any use, save for an enormous stash of canned foods, including more soup than he thought one family could have eaten. Probably katzutakis addicts. An especially stupid drug originally designed as a horse tranquilizer, it numbed all feeling but also rotted your gums at an alarming rate. Homeless katz-heads were easy to spot: they were the blissed-out toothless ones. If the previous owners were indeed katz addicts, that would explain the soup, the abandonment of the property – either through arrest or through losing the way home and not caring – as well as the surprising number of empty pill bottles. Yes, probably katzutakis. One mystery solved, and who knew how many days ahead.

He wandered back to the front of the house, checking the street through the windowblinds, an action in danger of becoming compulsive. There was nothing to see there anyway; never was. Other yards, much better kempt than the living fire of brown grass that had taken over this front lawn; sometimes children playing, today only a gray sedan parallel parking. He let the blinds slide back into place.

Money was beginning to be a problem. He had cleaned out his bank account the day after moving Luther to his own house, but even though his savings were impressive, they weren't going to last forever. Right now he only needed food and replacement dressings for Luther, but he was also going to need a substantial amount to be able to take care of Luther whenever he returned. There was no telling what state he was going to be in, whether they would even be able to stay in Hennington, or whether Luther would be able to reclaim any of his own money. Peter thought it would be best to just disappear when the time came, and that would require all the money he could keep around.

He walked down into the basement bedroom where Luther lay wrapped in the waxcloth.

Peter sat down on the bed next to him. He refrained from touching Luther except when absolutely necessary. Best to leave him be, he thought. Peter sat in the silence of the house, closed his eyes, said a prayer, opened his eyes, looked at Luther again. From nowhere, from the quiet maybe or the lack of company or possibly just the never-ending heat, doubt appeared like the first inklings of a cold stinging the inside of his nose. For the first time since it all began, Peter was caught unaware by questions that now multiplied like an angry virus.

What if this was all for naught? What then? All this trouble, let's be clear, all this criminal *trouble would amount to nothing, except a jail sentence or worse at the hands of Thomas Banyon. Even the Hennington Police and whatever fate they might bring would be better. And forgetting all that, what if Luther was actually dead? What if this was just the fantasy that it seemed to every observer except me? What if I'm wrong? What if I'm wrong? What if I'm wrong? It couldn't be this easy to lose faith, could it? At once, just gone? No. I believe. I do. I've come this far. I've believed successfully up to this point, and I'll continue to do so. Luther's body's warm, and that strange hum –*

He couldn't hear the hum. He leaned down close to Luther, but there was nothing. It had been there this morning, hadn't it? It had been there only a few minutes ago, right? The sound was so familiar that he had stopped noticing it. Now, when

376

it was most definitely gone, he struggled to remember when he had last heard it. A wave of panicky fright took him. What did it mean that the hum was gone? Was Luther coming back? Or was it –

Peter slumped to his knees, placing his elbows on the bed and resting his head on his folded hands. The words were frantic, a rush of sentences.

—I don't know who's out there, but I believe. I believe that Luther isn't dead. I believe that it's only a matter of waiting. I believe, I believe, I believe. Don't take him from me. Not now, not because of a few seconds' doubt. Bring him back to me. Bring him back to me safe and sound. I'll take care of him until then and for as long as I need to afterwards. I believe, I believe. I do believe. I have faith. I believe. Please don't take him. Please don't take him.

On and on he prayed. Minutes ticked by, then an hour unnoticed, until he had worked himself into a kind of rhythmic trance, the prayer repeating again and again, folding in upon itself. He lost himself in the prayer, in the chant of belief, his voice cracking from the repetition and finally disappearing into a whisper. It was then that the sound registered.

The hum. Insistent and present. Quiet but strong.

Outside, the sun continued its blast, the fox protected her newborn kits, and the gray sedan remained parked across the street from the house and stayed there for a very long time without anyone getting out.

89. The Schism, Arriving on Schedule.

—My sermon today is about false prophets, and this topic is not a coincidence. I've heard disturbing reports of members of this congregation turning to certain individuals who claim to know of fulfillments to Sacramental prophecy. I know not why and I know not how this all exactly came to be. I only know that members of this flock are being led astray, away from the true teachings of the Bondulay, away from the words of the Sacraments, and apparently away from rational, individual thought towards a kind of cult-like mentality, the spirit of which seems to benefit no one except those requesting such adulation, fulfilling only the agendas of those who wish to assume and then consolidate power. You are being hornswaggled, my good people. You are being fooled by those who would play on your fears, on your rightful pursuit of holiness, and on your quest for spiritual sustenance. You are being used as pawns in a game where your own personal wellbeing is the interest of no one.

Jarvis paused. The parishioners stared at him in stony silence. Even Theophilus Velingtham, sitting like a king in the front row, seemed stunned. Good. He was bluffing some, making guessed exaggerations, but they needed to know he meant business. He wouldn't give up his congregation without a fight.

—You must forgive me for my strong language, brothers and sisters, but it is only an indication of the depth of my feelings on the matter. I've noticed a drifting-away among members of the congregation for some time now. At first, I assumed that it was merely the normal fluctuations of parish life. I have since learned that my good faith was misplaced, that there is an active contrary hand vying for guidance of this church. I have learned that you are being swayed and cajoled by those who would usurp the power of this parish, this church of longstanding that has helped and cared for you for so many years. This church which *still* helps and cares for you. This church which aches to see you so misled. My good people, I beg you to hear me—

—Pastor, if I may—

—You may not, Theophilus. You may sit back down, and you may listen. That's all you may do.

—But, certainly, Pastor—

—You seem to have fallen under the mistaken impression that my sermons are actually debates. They are not, Brother Velingtham. This is my church, and I will give my sermon without interruption.

Theophilus arched his eyebrows for a moment and then smiled.

—Very well, Brother Kingham. You may continue.

Jarvis took a long moment to silently pray away his anger. When he spoke again, it was with a flat calmness of which he was actually quite proud.

—You forget, Brother Velingtham, that I do not require permission to speak in my own church.

But then, a slip of the tongue. He couldn't stop himself.

—Or has your arrogance grown so enormous that you now see yourself as spiritual leader of this parish?

And he lost them, that quickly, that easily – perhaps they were gone already. The faces in his congregation began to frown, all except for Theophilus whose smile remained, perhaps even increased. Murmurs spread throughout the assembled group. Jarvis saw Mrs Bellingham look around with some alarm as the words swirled past her. Someone towards the middle of the pews rose, someone, Jarvis realized, that he had never seen before in his life.

—How can you speak to Brother Velingtham that way? He's the one showing us the true path!

Shouts of assent surrounded the stranger, and more voices joined in.

—You would lead us away from the truth!

—Where were you when the dark wind arrived?

379

—The light wind is here, and you're telling us to ignore it!

—You're the arrogant one!

—You're the one who would lead us astray!

—You're the power-hungry one!

Jarvis instinctively held up his hands for quiet and got no response. He would just have to shout over them.

—Listen to yourselves! Abandoning all that you've held true for your entire lives for the ravings of one man! The Sacraments teach us intelligent faith with good works and humanity based on a belief in God, not submission to the vision of one earthly man!

The shouts swelled now, an ocean threatening to crash over the tidal breaks.

—Who do you think you are?

—One lying sermon after another!

—You self-serving, faithless wretch!

Jarvis could see individual faces among the screaming parishioners who were just as frightened as he was becoming. So it wasn't unanimous then, at least. Small consolation.

—What has happened to you, my beloved congregation? Why do you attack the Bondulay like you are? Just think of the things you are saying, of the anger you're displaying. How can any of this be the work of the Lord? Again, I ask you, listen to yourselves!

The shouting continued, until first one parishioner, then another, then a row stepped from their pews into the aisle. They headed towards the front of the church, towards Jarvis. Involuntarily, he took a step back, and with a rush it seemed as if the entire church were on him. Hands grabbed him from either side, forcing him downward while they held his arms behind his back. Someone kneed him in the stomach, a hand belonging to Widow Mitcham grabbed his beard and pulled hard. Other faces, other hands, many that he didn't recognize, threw him to the floor. Vaguely, he could hear the faint shouts of Mrs Bellingham and one or two others of the few who were on his side, but these were ineffectual. Jarvis felt pummeling on his back, feet and fists digging into his kidneys and neck. He tried to call out, but a kick to the side robbed him of his breath.

—Enough.

One word, said quietly, almost conversationally, and the ruckus ceased, though Jarvis was still held against the floor. He could see the crowd part to make way for a single set of legs. He didn't need to look up to know who it was.

—I think, Brother Jarvis, that the congregation has spoken.

Quiet assents passed through the crowd holding him down.

—I think what they're saying, my dear Father Kingham, is thank you for all the work you've done for the parish, but we are no longer in need of your services.

At some signal Jarvis couldn't see, the hands lifted him, arms still behind his back. He felt blood trickling from his nose and a pain in his side. He looked up into Theophilus' still-smiling face.

—There is no happy ending for this victory of yours, Theophilus.

—I wouldn't worry about me, Jarvis. You shouldn't fret, though. You gave it your best shot. It was just woefully inadequate, that's all.

Theophilus looked up at the crowd.

—Any who disagree with what we're doing, I suggest you leave now.

He tilted his head towards the side exit door. The handlers immediately dragged Jarvis towards the door, opened it, and threw him to the concrete walkway beyond. In the long moment it took for Mrs Bellingham to reach his side, Jarvis 381 spat the blood that now filled his mouth and said a hopeless, angry, lost prayer.

I trust that whatever you have in mind for me, Lord, it is worth all this.

90. Cracking Skulls.

Thomas drew in such a long drag that his much-practiced lungs were finally required to cough. He closed his eyes and tried not to lose any of the smoke until the tremor passed. None of this was helping his mood any. He spoke again through watery eyes.

—What I fail to see, and what you are continually failing to illuminate for me is just how not one but two separate fugitives, one of them practically a giantess, the other quite possibly carrying around a dead body, can continue to elude your capture? I thought you were the best, my friend. That's what I heard anyway. And would you take off those goddamn sunglasses?

Paul Wadstone's expression declined to change, no matter what level of abuse Thomas hurled at him, a character trait Thomas both respected and loathed. Even as he removed the sunglasses, the face of the director of the best private security agency in Hennington betrayed nothing.

—This is not a fantasy story, Mr Banyon. The real world rarely ever agrees with the linear narrative that you seem to expect. People disappear. We do what we can to find them, but sometimes they stay gone.

—You mean you can't give me a guarantee of success? Give me one good reason why I shouldn't take my business elsewhere then.

—Of course I cannot guarantee you success. The reason is

that I am not a liar. You are always welcome to change security agencies if you are unhappy with our level of service, Mr Banyon.

—Anyone ever tell you you talk like a fucking robot? Ever hear of contractions, Paul? Fantastically efficient little things.

Paul said nothing. Thomas took another long drag, burning his fingers before he realized the butt was too short.

—Fucking fuck!

He stomped out the ember on the carpet where it had fallen. He opened the top drawer of his desk, fingered through his cigarillo box, and pulled out another. He bit off the end, lit it, and inhaled three more great lungfuls before he addressed Paul again. The narcotic seemed to be losing its effectiveness lately. Thomas would have to have words with the agribusinessman who supplied them. He was having to smoke so many to feel any sort of buzz at all that he suspected those around him were getting very expensive passive highs.

—Just tell me why you haven't found them. That's all I'm asking.

—There are very few trails to follow, Mr Banyon. Ms Strell disappeared from the Foster Downs through avenues as yet unknown to a location as yet unknown. The trail for Mr Wickham was already a week old when we began our search. We have investigated some avenues and have narrowed down possible surveillance sites. We also have reason to believe that either one or both of Ms Strell and Mr Wickham are receiving help from the Rumour Underground.

—I thought that was a myth.

—Myths have a way of perpetuating themselves to sometimes useful effect.

—How do you know all this?

—It is my business—

—To know these things. Yes, I've seen crime movies, too, Paul. How long? Just tell me how long.

—As I said, we have narrowed down surveillance for Mr Wickham to a few abandoned houses—

—Why?

—It is a fairly common practice for anyone not wanting to be found to hide in houses that have been foreclosed. There are a surprisingly large number of them in the city, hence they are difficult to keep track of. Again, through process of elimination, we have narrowed down our surveillance to a few—

—But you don't know if he's actually *in* one of these houses?

At last, Paul Wadstone sighed. Thomas smiled behind his veil of smoke. Give me enough time, I can get to fucking *anybody.*

—It is the most logical path of pursuit, Mr Banyon. I will, of course, let you know if it yields results.

—And Jacki?

—I was coming to Ms Strell. We have placed the house of her former husband and her two children under surveillance—

—Won't do any good. She doesn't talk to them anymore.

—Nevertheless, we have placed them under surveillance. Phone records indicate a high number of calls from a mobile phone number that turns out to be registered to a deceased person.

—Really. Meaning what?

—Meaning, of course, that it is something to keep an eye on. Perhaps Ms Strell is contacting her children and—

—But you don't know for sure?

Paul Wadstone slowly replaced his sunglasses. After a long moment, he reached down for his briefcase and stood.

384   —Where the hell are you going?

—Perhaps it would be best if I kept you aware of developments from the field.

—And why 'would it be best'?

Thomas puffed out a cloud, then involuntarily tried to huff it back in.

—Because clearly, Mr Banyon, at the moment, you are chemically indisposed.

—I beg your pardon.

—We will contact you as soon as there is anything to report.

—Wait a minute. I'm not—

The door clicked shut behind Paul Wadstone. It took a few seconds for Thomas to register the surprise, then a few beats more for anger to boomerang its way in.

—You fuck! You fucking fuck! *Nobody* fucking ... You fuck! Fucking talks to me! Fucking tells me. Tells *me*. Stupid fuck. 'Chemically' fuck! Fuck!

He angrily stubbed out the cigarillo butt in his ashtray and didn't notice he had lit another one until he was already well into it.

91. An Invisible Threat, Real Nonetheless.

She lifted her head.

What was it?

Something had awakened her. A sound, maybe, but one that didn't follow into wakefulness. The herd slept, scattered deep among the foliage in the shade of the trees, each member resting in whatever niche or nook they could carve out of this crowded bit of woods. The sun poked through the leaves, low in the sky. Morning, then, still early by the crisp smell in the air. The scent of dew and of chill being lifted. And something else. She sniffed deeply. At first, she only detected what should have been there, the greenery, the fruits on the trees, the slumbering members of the herd. She drew in another long breath through her great nostrils. Something evasive was there. Yes. Evasive but definitely present.

A crackle. Her ears spun to the sound on the slight hill above them. A rustle bigger than a usual forest animal in the bushes to the left. The evasive smell became stronger, a smell of the forest but too strong to be natural, too powerful to be the actual forest, and there, just underneath, another smell. But what? She slowly raised herself on her front legs, confused that the smell revealed only nonsense information. Something was there but was not offering itself up. And it followed that what didn't offer itself up in the otherwise democratic palate of forest smells usually had a reason for wanting to remain unknown. A bad reason. Her anxiety tightened, quickly as a flexed muscle.

Thin creatures.

She hadn't even breathed out a few seconds of her warning call before the first crack unfurled. It was so loud and sharp that there was no telling where it had even come from. A hundred drowsy heads snapped up at the sound and then turned to a sudden, strangled, terrified yelping coming from a young male near the top of the small hill. The herd watched as he struggled to his feet, stepped forward on wobbly legs, then pitched over on his side with a moan. The smell of his blood reached them even before they saw it spilling in an alarming flood from a wound in his side. And another smell, too. A burning odor that drifted down the hill with lazy malice.

A long second of impossible silence, and then the air
erupted.

They were on their feet and running before any of them knew what was happening, chaotically fleeing in all directions from the sounds that seemed to be coming from everywhere, as if every tree in the entire forest was falling at once. Explosions flowered from all sides, sometimes accompanied by the wail of a member of the herd, sometimes by a horrible thud as a running animal fell to the ground.

She ran with them, squashing her own panic and trying to bellow above the incomprehensible din. Herdmembers were running everywhere, and she was among them. The herd must not divide. The herd must not divide. She stumbled as a large male in front of her fell to the ground, blood pouring from a horrible gash between his eyes. The herd was dividing, and she was powerless. She bellowed as loud as her lungs would carry but the sound seemed ineffective and small, buried beneath the roar of the forest tearing itself to pieces. She had no choice. The herd must not divide. She stopped in her tracks, fighting every instinct to flee, and raised her head in an extended yell.

An explosion rocketed near her ears, and almost simultaneously her head twisted hard to one side, nearly throwing her to the ground with a grinding twist of her neck. A terrible soreness filled the end of her nose, as if something had tried to rip her horn off her body. Foggy eyes watering, she tried to squint through to the source of the pain. An alarming section near the front end of her horn seemed to have blown outward. The tip was still there, but the hard keratin around the outer curve was a mess of splinters and fragments. She coughed at the smoke that seemed to be coming from everywhere, and her nose throbbed at the motion.

Enough. Enough. The herd must not divide. Enough.

She opened her jaw as wide as she could, and a new sound issued forth, this time fear accompanied with pain and a

387

newfound rage. And again. And again. A pause opened in the explosions, and she could hear the sounds of thundering feet, now getting louder as the members of the herd began to respond to her call. She bellowed again, and for the first time, she heard answering calls from all around her in the forest, increasing in volume as the first animals broke through shrubs and undergrowth into her presence. Then came confirmation. An enormous female burst through the branches with a thin creature caught on her horn. The female shook it off and continued her panicked run towards the leader. The thin creature was trampled quickly under her stride and by three and more members of the herd coming through the thicket behind her.

It *was* the thin creatures, then. Was this the answer to the smell of blood she'd been unable to shake? Was this the price?

No time. She bellowed once more. The racing animals answered. She turned, forced her way through a fallen, dead log, only briefly noticing another thin creature running to get out of her way. At full gallop, forcing as loud a call through her throat as she could manage, she stampeded forward, onward, away from the explosions that were only now resuming behind them. More animals answered her call as she plunged through the brush. She heard cries of pain as animals fell near the back of the herd, but they were getting away, they were gaining distance from the chaos.

She headed for the edge of the forest. Another explosion just above her head caused her to swerve, but three more steps and she was through to the lea in the hill of fields. She turned her head slightly as she ran and bellowed, watching as the rest of the herd smashed through the wooded border, leveling small trees, and driving smaller forest animals in front of them. As she led them further from the woods, further across the lea, heading towards the open hills just across the northern edge of the city, she noticed that less than two thirds of the herd was following her.

How many animals killed? How many more wandering alone, lost and terrified in the forest? Sorrow mixed with her fear now, and a deep, ferocious fury. They were beyond all borders now, past all sense and history, past all precedents, all rules forgotten.

She bellowed again, and they followed her, running, running, running.

92. Not the Highest Bid, but the Earliest.

Archie's grand office had degenerated into squalor. Papers were piled everywhere. Half-eaten food decomposed on dirty plates. The garbage can overflowed. The breakdown didn't stop with the main office, either. Archie had turned off the ice rink and drained the water. The tennis court was dusty with lack of use. And the grass on the driving range had actually begun to sprout weeds, although how weed spores could have found their way into the for-all-intents hermetically sealed penthouse was beyond both Archie's knowledge and interest. The small living space, intended only for single overnight stays, was in even worse shape. Archie had only left the penthouse on three occasions in the past two months, all of which were brief visits to Thomas. Jules had finally insisted on bringing a maid service into at least the bathroom and bedroom, once even locking Archie in his office so the fleet-footed team could dispose of age-old clothes, change ripe sheets, and vacuum up alarming piles of detritus. Jules had worried about pulling such shenanigans on Archie, then had worried more when Archie had shown no response at all.   389

—I think you're in danger of falling into such a deep hole that you won't be able to get back out again.

—That'll be all, Jules.

—The Board are at their wits' end, sir. The individual companies can more or less run themselves for maybe a little while longer, but without a captain at the wheel—

—I said, that'll be all.

—Disaster is just waiting to happen.

—Leave now if you don't want to be fired.

—If you haven't made good on that threat by now, you're never going to. I'm merely telling you the facts.

—I'm aware of the facts! And despite your flitting and fretting, I'm handling the problem.

—You are?

—Yes.

—How?

—Who are you to ask me how?

—The one who's been running Banyon Enterprises singlehanded for months now, that's who.

—Don't worry, Jules. You'll be taken care of.

—Oh, shit, meaning what, exactly?

—Leave. I'm taking care of things. I told you. Leave. Oh, wait, yes, get that maid service in here again. I need the office cleaned up.

—You what?

—I have a meeting at 2.30.

—It's 2.10 now, Archie. I can't possibly get a crew in here between now and then.

—Oh, well, forget it then. Just call me when he's here.

—*Who*?

—The only one who'll show up by 2.30. Now, please go and wait for him.

390   Archie was indeed expecting a guest. A call from nowhere.

References and financial securities offered with a reassuring quickness. And now to actually meet the man and seal the deal. That his last deal should also be his easiest was a comfort. The office should have been cleaner, though. Simple good practice, that was. Archie was still a businessman, goddamnit. There was a way you did things. At least, there used to be. At least, that was what he tried to tell himself. At the very least, he supposed a cleaner office would have maybe made him feel a little better. Maybe. Maybe not. Who cared anymore?

He had stopped wondering how he had gotten to this point. He would find himself making a movement in his chair and discover he had been sitting there for hours. No matter. Somewhere a line had been crossed, some irretrievable boundary, but if so, fine. He had learned to not look back. Always move forward forward forward. Keep your goal in sight and don't bother with what's gone on before or what will come after. Eyes on the prize, as they say. And when you got the prize, because you always did sooner or later, you just went looking for another prize. That's all this was, he told himself. This whole meeting was a way to make it easier to get his hands on the prize, that of finding his dear son. Looked at that way it even seemed part of the process. Yes, he could live with that.

His announce light came on. Jules' voice came through the speaker.

—Your 2.30 is here.

—Send him in.

—Do you really think—

—Just send him in.

Archie clicked off. He closed his eyes and waited for the sound of his door opening. He kept them closed as the man stepped firmly into the room and made the long walk to   391

Archie's desk. There was a silence as the man waited for Archie's attention. Archie opened his eyes.

—It's a pleasure to finally meet the legendary Archie Banyon in person.

Archie reached forward, extending his hand. Jon Noth, new owner of Banyon Enterprises, shook it firmly.

93. What We Wish For.

—You don't understand, I *have* to.

—I'm sorry, Jacki, but the risk is just too high. You go see them, you get snatched up by Thomas Banyon, and then what?

—All right, answer me this. Do you think my chances of getting out of this mess are all that high?

—I think you stand a fair chance—

—A fair chance isn't good enough. It's also a lie, isn't it? My chances are pretty damn low.

—We've gotten plenty of other people away from—

—But not anyone that he was looking for quite so strenuously, right? Not anyone that he'd punch a poor little woman for, right? Not anyone who he would dig so deeply in the Underground for, right? If he finds me, he'll kill me. I know that. Either he'll kill me straight out or force me back onto Forum and then I'm dead anyway.

—Jacki, look—

—So he grabs me when I see my kids. That would be horrible, but if he's going to grab me anyway, at least I will have seen my kids that once. At least someone will know that I've been grabbed. At least—

—He could grab your kids.

—Not if we do it in a public enough place. Besides, they won't even know I'm there. I've got a plan—

—Listen to yourself. You're purposely putting yourself *and* your kids in danger that you don't seem to be aware of. There are some weird things going on that you don't even know about.

—Like what?

—Strange rumblings in the air. People who you wouldn't expect are finding religion all of a sudden.

—Religion? What does that have to do with anything?

—Something's at work, but nobody quite knows what it is yet. It might even be more of a risk than you think.

—I want to see them before I die.

That stopped things, at least for a moment. Jacki knew every argument the shorter one, whose name she still didn't know, was throwing at her. She knew the risk, but she knew her chances, too. She also bet that Thomas was far too smart to ever drag her kids into it. Jacki could be painted as a whore, a drug addict, and who knew what else. She could be disappeared; her kids couldn't. He would only want *her*. She had to see Morton and Tucker, even if it meant Thomas finding her. Because, because he wouldn't stop until he did.

If the shorter one could only understand what it had been like to talk to them again. Just to hear their voices, just to have them acknowledge who she was, after all this time. It was like throwing yourself out of a plane only to discover that the ground was a few feet away. Gathering the courage to jump was the hard part, the rest fell into place like a dream.

—Mom? Is this a joke?

—No, Morton. It's Mom.

—Oh.

He said it again.

—Oh.

—I know it's been a long time, and I can't tell you how sorry I am about that.

—Where are you?

—I can't tell you that, Morty.

—Why not?

—I, uh, I'm in a bit of trouble.

—What kind of trouble?

—I can't really go into it, but I'm safe for now. I just wanted to call—

—Where've you been? It's been like two years.

Apart from anything that could bring them danger, she had decided on complete honesty right from the start.

—I've been fighting a drug problem. That's only an explanation, not an excuse. But I'm better now. I've kicked it as good as I ever have.

—Is that why you're in trouble?

—Yes. I had to kind of run from a situation, making some people unhappy, but I'm doing it to rescue myself. Listen—

—We were worried about you. We thought you might be dead.

—I'm not.

I was, she thought, but I'm not now.

Amazingly, everything just got easier and easier. Morton and Tucker, savvy teenagers both, turned out to know about drug addiction in more intimate terms than Jacki frankly felt comfortable with, but the result was complete acceptance that in no time whatsoever transformed itself into an almost pushy curiosity. Arguments and resentments might come later, but for now, there was only shared relief. To her horror, being a Forum addict almost made her a heroine.

—How much did you take a day?

—Usually three or four hundred ccs.

—Holy cow, Mom! That's enough to kill people.

—I had to work my way up to it.

394 —Did you shoot or snort?

—I shot. Morty—

—Like where did you buy the stuff?

—Morton, is your father around?

—No. Where did you shoot?

Greg had been a more difficult hurdle. She had managed to get Morton that first time and then Morton and Tucker on the second call, each time asking for her ex-husband. Jacki found herself struggling to even remember his face. Had they really been strangers that long? He answered himself on the third try.

—Hello, Greg.

—Jacki. So the rumors are true.

—They like to think so.

—I didn't know what to say when Morton and Tucker told me that you called, and you know what? I still don't.

—I've been—

—I know. Drug heaven. I'm not sure I appreciate that kind of talk to my sons, Jacki. They're at an impressionable age. It's hard enough to keep them away from bad elements without their mother emerging from the past as a cool junkie.

—I'm drug-free now.

—So you say, but for how long?

—I've risked my life to do it. I'll either succeed, or I'll die. Either way, doubt shouldn't be an issue for you.

—That's all very melodramatic, Jacki, but surely you understand—

—Of course I do. I'm in trouble, Greg.

—Why am I not surprised?

—Big trouble. I may not come out of it with my life. I'm not exaggerating to win your sympathy. Those are the facts, and believe me, I wish they were different. That's what I'm facing. I had to call the boys. I *had* to.

—So let's see where we stand, Jacki. You turn invisible,   395 vanish right off the face of the planet, returning to us in rare, garbled phone calls and in the occasional grapevine report of drugs and even worse. Then you vanish completely, leaving me to explain to your sons why you've disappeared though I don't even know myself. Two years pass and now you're back? Out of the blue. In trouble, surprise surprise, but now drug-free and ready to be a mother again? You'll have to forgive my incredulity.

—I have no counter-argument.

—So why should I act any differently than any other sensible person in my position would?

—I have no legitimate reason that I can reasonably expect you to believe, except to say that what I've told you is true. I'm in danger. Thomas Banyon is after me. If he finds me, I'm probably dead. This literally may be my last chance to talk to my sons. Literally. I had to take the risk, even the risk of you saying no.

—You didn't ask me first. You've talked to them already.

—I wouldn't expect you to act any different if the situation was reversed.

—The situation would never *be* reversed, Jacki.

—Nevertheless.

—Why is Thomas Banyon after you?

—It's too long and degrading to explain. Please, Greg. I'm at your mercy. Please don't put an end to this.

A long pause, another obstacle jumped or not.

—I trust that your maternal instincts are sharp enough not to put them in any danger.

—That would never happen.

And it wouldn't, a point she was trying to make again to the shorter one, whose resistance she could feel weakening. Morton and Tucker wouldn't even know she was there. She would go to their school and wait. She would look for them as they arrived or after they left. She would question them lightly during their phone conversations about their school activities to find out the best place to watch. She would see them from a distance.

—And that's all.

—The risk you're taking—

—We can make it so the risk is all mine.

—There's no way to do that.

—Just get me a car—

—And have you drive how? Crouched down in the driver's seat?

—You could get me a disguise.

—Our resources are hardly unlimited. Don't forget that. We do what we can, but we're not miracle-workers.

—Look, please. Please. Think of this. I may never see them again. *Never.* It's that serious, and as optimistic as you are, I know you know I'm right. This could really be it. It's a risk I'm willing to take.

He looked at her for a moment, and she knew she had won.

—I'll see what I can do.

94. A Cold Dish.

He called Theophilus from the Bisector on the way back from the meeting.

—What we discussed has come to fruition, Brother Velingtham.

—I expected that it would, Brother Noth. So no one now needs to vote for our dear befuddled Brother Banyon?

—No, thank heavens.

—Don't worry, my friend. We are more than happy to help you drive out the dark wind.

—Yes, of course, the dark wind. The election's only six days away. Are you sure you have enough numbers to actually make a difference at the ballot box?

—My people have been on a mission, acting on the prophecies they've received in the Sacraments, spreading the word around the city. You don't need to concern yourself with my methods. As I've said, it only takes a small catalyst to spark a big change. The message is being disseminated.

—So you've gone beyond the one church, then?

—In the true sense, no. We have established the one true Church and new followers come to us every day. Answering the spirit of your question, though, yes, the message has spread to other congregations, and we anticipate many more in the coming days. By the time election day arrives, you will have no worries about the size of your assistance in driving out the dark wind.

—And there's no trouble with the preacher you kicked out?

—He's finding difficulty in getting our local, devout police force to listen to him.

—I'm guessing then that it was your people who orchestrated the attack on The Crash.

—Again, are methods so important to know? Isn't it the ends that both of us are after, that both of us *have been* after since we met so very long ago?

—It's only that I wonder if attacking The Crash doesn't play right into Thomas' hands.

—Whoever it was that might have attacked The Crash could very well be hoping that the kind of extreme reaction to Thomas Banyon's view on The Crash might in fact be exactly the kind of backfire that Thomas Banyon so foolishly doesn't expect.

398 —I follow you. If a few people react to him in this way,

everyone else will be too scared of what he's capable of.

—I also think that whoever it was that might have attacked The Crash would be foolish to discuss that attack over a mobile phone.

Jon paused. Theophilus was right, of course. There was something here he didn't like though, something odd, something *off*, out of his control, something that made him uncomfortable enough to ignore basic caution, apparently.

—Theophilus, look, these phrases you use, 'driving out the dark wind' and so forth. I've assumed all along that you've meant them metaphorically, like you said.

—Ye-e-es?

Theophilus stretched the word out to several syllables, and even over the mobile, even over the noise and honks of the traffic around him, Jon could still hear the taut smile in it.

—What exactly do you mean?

—Read the Sacraments, my dear boy. All will be revealed to those who believe.

—Of course, of course, but how are you able to spread that belief so rapidly? How are you going to be able to muster the numbers? You cover yourself by your Sacrament-speak, and I understand and respect that, but brass tacks, Theophilus, there's a lot here that I'm not seeing and I'm not comfortable with it.

He heard a long sigh over the phone line.

—Your faith was always a worry for me, Jon.

—I still have the faith—

—I don't think you do, but even now, that is perhaps not so important. What will happen will happen regardless of your faith. You cannot avoid your destiny even if you may not acknowledge it. As for my methods, speaking the Word is easy, because the Word is truth, the Sacraments are truth, the message is truth. People believe because it's truth. Things 399 accumulate. Disseminating the Word is easy as well. Don't forget that you are not Rumour, and we have ways and avenues that you don't understand.

—The Rumour Underground.

—I can neither confirm nor deny.

—But I thought that was just a—

—A rumor, yes, you wouldn't be the first to take a stab at the pun.

—No, what I meant was that I thought it was purely a charity thing, a benevolent organization, if organization is even the right word.

—Let's put it this way. A phone signal is merely a means of communication. It is neither benevolent nor malevolent. It merely is.

—I don't—

—All I can tell you is what I've already told you, dear Brother Jon. Have faith. Prepare yourself for the times to come. They're coming whether you're prepared or not, so think how much easier it will all be for yourself if you are.

—The time for what?

—Goodbye, Jon. I'll do my part. Make sure you do yours.

He clicked off. Jon sat back against the car seat. The attack on The Crash happened *before* Theophilus knew for sure that Jon was buying Banyon Enterprises, and therefore before he should have known that the plans to elect Thomas had changed. Why would Theophilus have acted before confirming it with Jon? And why had Jon not been able to ask that question? Was it really that easy to lose control? What was going on?

For the first time since he had set foot back in Hennington, Jon was worried.

LATHAM PUTS CRASH UNDER CITY PROTECTION

UNPRECEDENTED MOVE IN RESPONSE TO 'SHOCKING ATTACK'

HENNINGTON – Crash Advocate-General and Mayoral candidate Max Latham announced a plan last night to bring The Crash, Hennington's wandering herd of rhinoceros, under city protection following the discovery yesterday of the bodies of three men and twenty-two rhinoceros in the densely wooded area behind the Hennington Arboretum.

'The scope of this massacre,' said Latham, 'the deaths of the three men and so many animals, is shocking and horrible. I am, therefore, with the support of Mayor Larsson, ordering the Bering Zoo to assist the city in bringing the remaining animals in the herd into a protected paddock on zoo property. This will protect The Crash as well as allay any fears the public may have about their own safety.'

All twenty-two animals had been shot at close range, and the three deceased men – identified as Roger Norwitcham, 30; Alexander Kolbe, 41; and Fulton Lewis, 23 – were all found wearing hunting gear with rifles nearby. Norwitcham and Kolbe were apparently gored to death and Lewis was trampled. Authorities believe because of the number of animals killed that the three dead men were not working alone, though no other suspects have as yet been apprehended. Latham would not speculate on the reason for the attack, but there have been calls to City

401

Hall regarding the safety of the public following the as yet unexplained death of so-called 'Rhinoherd' Maggerty.

'I think the citizens of Hennington will agree,' continued Latham, 'that regardless of whatever safety issues might arise from The Crash's behavior towards Maggerty, this sort of attack is unwarranted and heinous. The death of Maggerty is still under investigation, and I ask everyone in the city to keep calm until that investigation is complete.'

Mayoral candidate Thomas Banyon was also quick to comment on both the incident and Latham's response to it.

'I would never condone such an attack on The Crash,' said Banyon, 'but I am also interested to see that Mr Latham seems to care more about the deaths of a few animals than the deaths of three citizens of this city. My thoughts and prayers are with the men's families.'

When asked if he thought his actions would affect his campaign, Mr Latham responded by saying he thought it was 'unfortunate that any action, rightly or wrongly, is taken as political during a campaign.' He indicated that he felt it was his duty as Crash Advocate-General to ensure their protection.

'The Crash have been a city-wide treasure for as long as anyone can remember,' Latham said. 'Obviously something is going on, but I can't believe that any thinking person, having grown up with The Crash, would want to just get rid of them at the first sign of something unusual. We owe it to them, we owe it to ourselves, to find out what exactly is happening.'

When asked if he suspected malicious interference or foul play surrounding Maggerty's death, Latham declined to rule them out. 'All I will say,' he said, 'is that the turn of events is suspicious, to say the least.'

Latham did not give a timetable for the release of The Crash from custody, but said that the round-up of the animals was scheduled for this morning at dawn.

96. The Living River.

The herd streamed up and down hills, through fences, across roads, roaming, searching, always moving until they felt ready to collapse from exhaustion. At last, she stopped them in a remote gully. It offered no food or water, but it kept them out of sight for a time. Time enough, she hoped, for the members of the herd to sleep, to heal, and mourn. Many animals were injured, either from the stampede out of the woods or from bleeding wounds from the same kind of explosion that had hit her horn, shredding its front end and causing a throb of pain that still pulsed through her skull.

She walked a brisk circle around the limping, struggling herdmembers as they made their way to the center of the gully. She signaled for them to rest, to gather themselves and their energy for whatever it was that lay ahead, a prospect that she herself equally feared. The gully wasn't really big enough to hold them all, but none seemed to mind the close company just now, leaning on one another for comfort and support even in the already sweltering heat of early morning. Two newly orphaned calves lay whimpering in a circle of older females, all pressed together offering protection.

But protection from what? What had actually happened?

Her instincts seemed to be of no use anymore. She had killed the thin creature that had followed them for reasons she could not quite grasp. She had led them away to the woods, to a place where many of them lost their lives and many others were injured and maybe dying. Now she had led them here, to a valley of stone with no water and no food and no future. Why did they still follow her when she had failed so badly? Was she capable of leading them out of this, or would the next steps lead just as inevitably to more death, 403 to more destruction? Yet still they stopped and slept at her indication. Still they looked to her for direction, even through the places she had led them, even to this place here, this stopping point on the road to who knew where.

All right then. She led them because a leader was needed, and at no time was a leader needed more than now. She would continue to lead them until they ceased to follow her. That was her duty to the herd. That was what they expected of her. She no longer wanted to lead, but the choice was not hers. If they still wanted her, as it seemed they did, then there was nothing she could do. Why? If the answer was not forthcoming, then perhaps one did not exist. They demanded her leadership. She would give it. That was all.

Dawn was breaking. The animals were finally quietening down to sleep. She was on her last circuit around them before collapsing into rest herself when she heard the sound. A jostling of rocks from just over the edge of the gully. And again. More coming from all sides, and then a twisting cloud of scent blew its way down among them. Thin creatures. Lots of them. So quickly, so stealthily.

Were they safe nowhere, then? Was there no end to this?

(—*Remember, everyone, slowly slowly slowly. We don't want a stampede on our hands. Everyone ready up on the north ridge? Over.*

—*Ready up here. Over.*

—*Then wait for my signal. Over.*)

Gathering what energy she had left, she raised yet another alarm call. There was audible groaning as the herdmembers twisted themselves out of sleep, then a second series of groans as the scent of the thin creatures filled their nostrils. She noticed three of the group fail to rise from their slumber. Three more lost, then. At least they'd had a chance to rest.

404   She paced back and forth in front of the members of the herd

until all who could get up had arisen, all eyes on her. She turned towards the far end of the gully and with what seemed like only the latest in a long series of grunts, she ran forward as the first line of thin creatures crested the little valley.

Too exhausted even to be properly frightened, the herd made its way to the end of the gully and over its lip, a massive living river of gray. The sounds of the thin creatures behind them disappeared quickly as they plunged forward, but she heard a new sound on either side. Glancing around, she saw the loud, rumbling squares that the thin creatures often rode in pull up on each flank of the advancing herd, leaving nowhere to run except forward.

The ache from her horn pounded her head with each step. Her legs seemed heavy and airy at the same time. There was simply no way that weaker and younger members of the herd were ever going to be able to keep this up. She looked behind her and could already see the herd stretching itself thin. She had no idea what propelled them onward, but onward they went, only slowly, ever more slowly. Some animals were beginning to be left behind.

If the herd must not divide, then the herd must take a stand.

She stopped, almost abruptly, surprising the animals closest behind her, who nevertheless seemed barely able to keep upright when they too stopped running. The rest of the remaining herd caught up with them, the members looking dazed and haggard, more than one falling to the ground out of pure fatigue. This was it then. This was the beleaguered group that would have to defend itself. So be it. If this was the end of the herd, then the herd would end together. She circled the group as best she could, nudging younger and weaker animals to the center, leaving what remained of the bigger animals on the periphery.

The boxes with the thin creatures seemed to be keeping their distance for now. She brought all the herdmembers as close together as she could, then she called to them with a long, low groan. Of sorrow. Of apology. Of defiance. Of the duty that she felt for them. Of her place and position as leader. Their eyes met hers, and they seemed to understand. Slowly, she walked towards the assembled herd and took her place at the outer edge, to wait and see what the thin creatures would do, to wait and see what fate had planned for them in this sad, strangely unhurried, final moment.

Part VI.

Election Day.

97. One Up, One Down.

The newspaper headline read, DOWN TO THE WIRE ON ELEC-
TION DAY. Was it Election Day already? The last thing Peter
had heard was that that Rumour guy, Mark something, was
running unopposed. Why was it 'down to the wire'? He
stopped to look at the newsrack a little closer. *Thomas Banyon*
was running? When did that happen? Had he really been away
from the world that long? He picked up the paper and quickly
folded it into his basket. Food at the house had finally run
out, and he was having to risk a trip to the little grocer around
the corner to get something to eat. A few bananas, lots more
soup (it was cheap), and not much else. Nothing frozen,
because the house had no electricity. The gas still worked for
cooking, but there was no telling when that would be shut
off as well. And though he was keeping his spending to a
minimum, a newspaper was an allowable expense. Thomas
Banyon? For *Mayor*? That would more or less be the end of
everything, wouldn't it?

Peter paid the tiny, ancient man perched behind the counter
and left. It was barely dawn, the sun merely a possibility
beyond distant hills as the sky grew from black to blue. He
put his groceries in the back compartment of his motorcycle
and pulled off towards the house, hoping to get there before
the sun reached the sky. The streets were deserted, not even
a sign yet of the early-morning commute. That's right, Election Day was a holiday in Hennington so everyone could
vote. Peter rolled past a gray sedan parked across the street and
turned into the driveway of the house where Luther waited.

He hid the cycle in the ever-taller grass in the backyard,   409 reached through the broken screen on the back door, and let himself inside. It was still dark enough for the kitchen to be dim. He piled the soup into a cupboard, left the bananas on the table, and made his way back downstairs to Luther. Still there. Still the slight hum. Still the faint thrill of expectation. Peter closed his eyes and said a prayer, an act that had by now become second nature.

A sound through the stillness of the house. Footsteps.

He turned. A figure was descending the darkened staircase. Peter backed hurriedly into the room. Jarvis would have announced himself. This was someone else. He moved to the other side of the bed, closer to Luther. He looked around. There was nothing to protect himself with, nothing even to hurl at an intruder, and there was no point in hiding, whoever it was would see Luther anyway and Luther needed to be protected at all costs. The footsteps stopped. Peter prayed, Protect me, protect Luther, help me know what to do. The footsteps resumed their quiet tapping down the wooden staircase. He took a deep breath. Whatever happened, the only way out of this situation was through it.

The dawning sun finally poked its way through the high windows in the basement bedroom. Peter could see a pair of legs making their way slowly down the stairs. The pair of legs grew into a body and then into a hand. A hand holding a gun. Peter cleared his mind. Courage and faith and steadiness in the face of fear, that was what was called for now, that was his test. He opened his mouth and was surprised at the authority in his voice.

—Whoever you are, this suspense serves no purpose. I'm unarmed. Show yourself and state your intentions.

The figure with the gun paused for a moment, then completed the steps into the room. He was a middle-aged man dressed unexpectedly in slacks, a pressed short-sleeved workshirt, and tie. He sized up Peter, the gun still pointing, and cast a glance around the room, stopping at Luther.

—Please tell me that's not Luther Pickett.

His voice was almost a croak, a deadpan full of contempt and an unwillingness to be challenged.

—Who do you work for?

—I don't think you're in any position to be asking me questions, Mr Wickham.

—Are you the police or did Thomas Banyon send you?

—You kept his body here? You sick fuck. Wow. Banyon's going to crucify you.

—He isn't dead.

—You're just keeping him wrapped up in mummy bandages with no airholes for fun? This is over, Mr Wickham. It's over. I suggest you come along peacefully, because make no mistake, I *will* do whatever it takes to bring you with me.

—And I'll do whatever it takes to stop you.

The man raised the gun to Peter's face.

—That's unfortunate, because there's nothing in my orders that says I have to bring you back alive. Now, once more, come with *ow*!

The man spun around. Peter saw a hand holding something raise and then fall again on the man's face as he turned.

—Shit! Fuck!

It was a can. Of soup. Jarvis was hitting the man with a can of soup. The can came down a third time as the man tried to block the blow with his hands. The can knocked the gun to the floor.

—Peter, for God's sake, help me!

Peter leapt forward and grabbed the gun from the floor as Jarvis brought the can down a fourth time, striking the man in the temple, opening a bloody gash. Jarvis dropped the soup.

411

—We've got to tie him up. Is there any rope around here?

—No but there's a trunk in the closet we can lock him in.

—We can't do that! He'll starve.

—We'll call the police anonymously and report him later. What are you even doing here?

—I came to renew my faith.

—I'm sorry?

—Later, later, let's get him in the trunk and then we have to get out of here.

Jarvis went to the closet, found the trunk, and dragged it out. He flipped the latches, opened it, and started yanking clothes out onto the floor. Peter spoke to the man on the ground.

—Get in the trunk.

—Fuck you, I'm bleeding!

—Get in or I *will* shoot you. If you think I murdered Luther Pickett then you won't doubt my capability of that.

The man got to his hands and knees. Jarvis finished empty-ing the clothes and scooted back out of the way.

—In.

—You fucker! You'll pay for this.

Peter fired the gun at the floor behind the man. Jarvis jumped. The man scrambled into the trunk. Jarvis rushed forward and slammed the lid, flipping the latches to lock it.

—I wasn't aiming for him.

—I didn't think you were. I'd just never heard a gun fired before.

—Really?

—Where would I? I'm a minister. We have to get you and Luther out of here.

412   —Where to?

Jarvis held a finger to his lips. He pointed at the trunk.

—I have my car out front. I'll pull it to the side. Can you carry Luther?

—Of course. Thank you. Thank you so much. I—

—Later. We've got to get out of here.

Jarvis was breathing heavily. He looked at the closed trunk where the man could still be heard groaning.

—I had no idea it was so difficult to knock someone out.

—I wouldn't have thought you had it in you.

—Yeah, well, I've had a bad week. Meet you outside.

Jarvis turned and ran up the stairs. Peter went to the bed and picked Luther up. The humming was still there. He said a short prayer of thanks. It's not over, he thought. The only way out is *through*. He stepped lightly over the trunk, carrying Luther up the stairs to Jarvis' waiting car.

98. The Faces in the Distance.

Jacki sat in the car outside of Morton and Tucker's high school in the early hours of morning, the time of long shadows and school buses. Tucker, she knew, drove his own car now and would be bringing Morton to school with him. She didn't know where exactly he would park or what either of them would be wearing or even if they would both be coming to school that day. But here she was. The high school was over an hour's drive due north of the warehouse, and she had left before dawn, hoping to escape Hennington under the cover of darkness. Although part of her refused to believe that Thomas would be so fanatical in his search that he would track her this distance, she still drove unobtrusively, careful not to draw attention to herself, keeping to the speed limit for perhaps the first time in her life.

She had arrived before any other car to the school campus, parking in what she hoped was an unremarkable stretch of street with a long view of the school's car park. Time slowly passed. She watched as first the cleaning staff and then the teachers began to arrive for the new day. It was so quiet she could hear the pings as the car's engine cooled. She felt herself to be in a sort of no-man's-land of anticipation and daring. She was terrified, but also, surprisingly, thrilled. The danger was real, and yet here she was facing it, placing herself squarely in front of the forces coming after her, daring to choose an option that wasn't flight. Have I been transformed? she thought. Have I transformed *myself*? How can I know unless I've been tested? Or have I *already* been? And what have I transformed into?

She took the steering wheel with both hands, gradually tightening her grip until her fingers ached and what small muscles there were in her arms bulged at the tension. She grasped the wheel for as long as she could bear, then forced herself to release it slowly, letting the pain and the effort melt itself away. I'm strong, she thought. Maybe not strong enough, but I will be. I'll be strong enough.

The sun had pulled over the trees in the distance now, and the first direct rays of sunlight warmed the interior of the car. It was going to be another scorcher. Batches of kids were starting to arrive at the school. Jacki tried her best to take in each car, each group, each individual as they approached the front of the walkway which led to the large, concrete building. So many faces, so young. She hadn't realized that teenagers were still so close to being children while somehow being almost grown-up. They all seemed so small, so unprotected, even the tall ones with their outrageously long arms and hunched gaits, struggling to be fit enough for the world. The crowds grew. School buses pulled into a circular driveway, expelling bright groups of half-formed adults. Jacki felt a tenderness so pure and shocking for them that she began to cry. How could I have been so blind to this? How could I have missed this all this time? A hard kernel of hope formed in her chest. Maybe, just maybe it really wasn't too late for her, maybe this all could work. The past couldn't be reclaimed, but maybe the present could.

She saw them. A familiar face, practically her own, driving right by her. Tucker, behind the wheel, exchanging words with a smaller figure in the passenger's seat that she couldn't quite see. Morton, it had to be. She turned as Tucker's profile moved by, both boys oblivious to their mother sitting just a few feet away. She saw Tucker's head angle back as he laughed. She heard herself laugh in response, there in the silence of her car. The boys pulled away from her and turned into the student parking lot. She watched as the car searched for a space, found one, parked. The passenger side was facing her, and she saw Morton, sweet, tender Morton, open the door and step out. He fumbled with a book bag and stood near the front of the car to wait for his brother.

Only distantly realizing she was doing it, Jacki took the handle of her door and opened it. A warm breeze drifted past her face as she watched the two boys, her two sons, her two beautiful, beautiful sons join each other and disappear into the crowd of fellow students. She stepped to the pavement and stood up into the morning. Her heart thumped loudly, so loudly she could hear it in her ears, feel it in her throat. She was crying, but it was more like gasping. She couldn't see them anymore, but she remained, watching all the young almost-men and almost-women funnel forward into their day.

She didn't flinch when she felt the pull at her arm. It all seemed inevitable now, the man with the sunglasses, the somehow slightly-too-shiny car she now saw parked two spaces down from her, the grip on her firm and forceful, the sliding-away of the jacket to expose the gun. It all passed in a glimmering sheen. She wondered for a moment if she was strong enough. I'll just have to find out, she thought.

99. Thrust, Parry, Feint, Touch.

—What the hell are you doing in here?

—Cora, I have to talk to you—

—Get out of my office at once, Jon. At once! I'll have you thrown in jail—

She moved towards her phone. Jon grabbed her hand. She slapped his face, very hard, with the back of her free hand. He relented. She lifted the receiver and began to dial.

—Cora. Something's going to happen. I have to warn you—

—Don't you threaten me. My patience with you has long since expired. Hello? This is the Mayor. There's an intruder in my office—

—I'm not threatening you. I'm here to warn you. For your own safety.

—Then put me *through* to security, Goddamnit! It's an emergency!

—I believe someone's going to try and kill Thomas Banyon.

—I beg your pardon?

—And I think you might be in danger as well. I think we all might be.

—You're deranged. You've completely lost it.

—Cora, however I have acted, I would never put your personal safety at risk. However it is you feel about me, however you view the things I have done, you know that much is true. I knew you would throw me out. I knew your reaction to me would be violent, but something's going to happen. I came to warn you.

She looked at him closely, still holding the receiver in her hand. A voice chimed into the headset. She paused another second.

—It may be a false alarm. But stay ready.

She replaced the receiver.

—If this is a ploy, Jon, believe me, you *will* live to regret it.

—It's not a ploy.

—Fine then. Who would want to kill Thomas Banyon? I imagine lots of people, actually, but who now? And why on Election Day? And what does this have to do with me?

—We haven't much time, so I'll try to be brief. I worked on getting Thomas Banyon elected, true, but my interest was only ever in getting someone besides you elected Mayor and had nothing to do with Thomas Banyon personally.

—Be quick about getting to the point, Jon. It's a hell of a busy day for me as you may just possibly be able to imagine.

—It's also true that Thomas Banyon is a reprehensible man, but he was the only one around with the power to get elected on his own, without city help.

—Which is exactly what makes him so dangerous.

—Irrelevant. He was handy. I only wanted you to see how far I would go to free you from your obligations here. I wanted you to see me, to *really* see me, without anything tying you to this place.

—Forgetting, of course, my husband?

—You know I've never regarded Albert as a serious contender for your hand.

—Really, now, this is *such* an old argument. There's a saying around here, Jon, 'That joke isn't funny anymore'.

—I'm digressing. The point is that I no longer have any   417 interest in Thomas Banyon, and I've set in motion actions that will prevent him from being elected, actions that will bring your deputy the Mayor's office.

—So now you imagine you have that sort of power?

—I don't imagine it. I know it. I've enlisted the help of a former teacher who carries a great deal of influence among the, shall we say, religiously-oriented minds of this city. This man has been helping me in my work here, gathering support, spreading the message, so to speak. Applying pressure at strategic points. He has more than enough numbers to affect the outcome at the ballot box.

—The reports I've been hearing about the rise in a prophetic sect of the Bondulay.

—Yes. The size of which *I* wasn't even aware.

Cora was silent for a moment, holding Jon's gaze without blinking.

—You've lost control of your 'former teacher', haven't you?

—I'm afraid so.

—You. Dumb. Shit.

—I know—

—You traipse in here, into this city, into *my* city, after four decades with some crackpot idea of winning my hand. Out of spite you enlist the worst possible candidate to run for Mayor, and you dabble irresponsibly with some mysterious figure who you've now lost control of, putting not only your candidate but apparently everyone else in danger. Is that all about right?

—Yes, but—

—Why?

—'Why'?

—Yes, why? Putting aside how on earth I'm going to solve
this problem, why? How can you possibly think you could

have ever succeeded in your wildest dreams? How can there be any explanation for this but delusion? I mean, can you even grasp what you've done?

—We have something, you and I—

—We *had* a friendship, a decent one, for a short time. Then you went and challenged Albert to a *duel*, for heaven's sake, assuming somehow that my opinion in the matter counted not at all. An insult for which alone I would have cut you off. But then you disappeared and solved that embarrassing problem for all of us.

—We had something more than that. I think you know we did. I loved you. I *love* you. I've never stopped.

—Then I have news for you, Jon. *I* stopped. And that, unfortunately for you, is where the story ends.

—Cora—

—Enough of this. You think your accomplice would go as far as killing Thomas Banyon?

—Yes, I think so.

—Have you warned him?

—His life is his own to manage. My greater fear is that they won't stop there.

—Meaning what?

—Theophilus, my former teacher, seems to think he's fulfilling a prophecy from the Book of Ultimates. He's used avenues in the Rumour Underground, which despite all evidence to the contrary, seems to actually exist, though how much is formalized and how much is just people talking, God only knows. I'm not even sure how much of it is even Rumour, but Theophilus is determined to use it to drive out what the prophecy calls the 'dark wind'.

—Thomas being the 'dark wind'?

—That was my idea at first, but I think they've run with it. I think Theophilus has set his sights higher.

419

—So the whole city is in danger, more or less?

—I believe it may be.

—Today?

—It's the most likely day. Today would be when any action against Thomas would happen, and if they're not going to stop there, then today would be the beginning of it all.

—So you're giving me no warning whatsoever.

—I'm warning you in enough time for you to escape with me. That's why I'm here. To take you to safety.

—To take me to safety from a danger that you yourself have created.

—Cora—

—You poor, sad, misguided fool.

—*Cora*—

—As if I would ever leave my city when it's under attack. As if I would ever even have that impulse in my body. After a long, storied history of misunderstanding me, you've managed to do it yet again. So, now I mean it, get out, or I'll call security.

—Let me just—

—Somehow I have to save the life of a man I detest as well as possibly the entire future of the city where I've spent my life, and I have to do it all today. I don't really have time to listen to you anymore, Jon.

She reached for the phone, dialing numbers quickly.

—The Mayor again. I need you to remove a trespasser from my office immediately.

—Cora—

—You've got about thirty seconds to leave before a bunch of really large men come in here to drag you away.

—Listen—

—Shut up! Not another word! You no longer have any say in this. None. No more opinion, if you ever even had the right to one. Leave. Now. And never show your face to me again. Ever.

Cora raised her hand from across her desk and made a short, sharp dismissive motion to him.

—I no longer see you.

She reached for her phone again.

—Angie? I need you to track down Thomas Banyon for me. Yes, I know. I'm going to be on the phone with Albert, but I want you to interrupt me the second you get hold of him, all right? It's an emergency.

Jon stood and watched her as she ignored him, going about her business. The sounds of heavy footsteps would be arriving at any second. At last, with an effort he found excruciatingly difficult, he took his gaze from her for the last time and all but ran out of Cora's office.

100. The Message to the Light Wind.

My brothers and sisters. It does the heart of an old man good to see so many faces here, both familiar and new, and I know that each face here represents ten, twenty more out in the reaching arms of our great movement. Rumour and non-Rumour alike, banding together by divine right. More than good, it does my heart *proud* to see you and to know the extent of the unseen. My message to you this fateful morning, my dear disciples, this morning of the day that will live forever in the hearts and minds of the faithful, this morning of the day of satisfaction of the greatest prophecy our beloved Sacraments contains, my message to you this fine, fine morning is simple.

It's time. The time of the driving out of the dark wind has arrived. Many of you have asked me about the exact nature

421

of the light wind which will save us from the dark wind, the light wind which will reveal to us the truth, which will enter us into a new place and new time of worship. Some of you have even, with touching though misguided devotion, suggested that *I* might be the light wind. My beloved people. I am not a demagogue or a guru. I am not the Divine come to earth. I am merely a man who has heard the words of our Sacraments, just like all of you. If anything, I am a messenger, and I have waited my entire life to deliver this message to you. No, my brothers and sisters, I am not the light wind. Look around you. Look to your neighbor, in front and behind. Think to those outside the confines of this small church who have also heard the message. We are *all* the light wind. All of us who have heard the message, who have understood the prophecy, who have purged our church of scoffers and non-believers, who have *grown* our church outside of its very boundaries, who have swept through this city like wildfire. The light wind is here, and it is us.

Our mission is at hand. The hour of action has arrived. Are you ready? I ask you again, are you ready? If anyone has doubt in their heart, then you should leave this place. You should return to your homes and wait for whatever fate is meant to befall you. The moment has come. There is neither room nor time for doubters now. If you doubt what we do, what we are about to do, leave. I ask my brothers and sisters once more. Are you ready?

The dictates of our very own Book of Ultimates tell us what we must do. We must drive out the dark wind. Word has spread among you that the dark wind is represented in our city by the personage of Thomas Banyon. I put to you this morning that Thomas Banyon is only the beginning. He is only the symbol of the dark wind which we must drive out. Are we brave enough to truly seize our destiny? Are we strong enough to go the distance to reach what is prophesized as ours? Thomas Banyon, yes, but only for a start. Look into your hearts. When you greet Hennington with your opened eyes, with your pure hearts, with the fire of the Sacraments burning in your minds, you *will* know what to do. I give no specific order for, as I say, I am merely one of you, I am merely one representative among many of the light wind, but I will say this:

Let us not commit the sin of timidity.

The power is ours. Let us not be afraid to use it.

That is my message to you, and I want you to spread this message to our brothers and sisters who still await guidance on this bright morning. The day is here. The time for action is now. Waste no time. Brook no hesitation. Leave this place and begin your divine mission.

It's time to act. Go. You have my blessing.

101. In the Last Quiet Hours.

—I'm not sure I understand.

—I'm not sure I do either, but I'd bet my eyeteeth that the attack on The Crash was just the beginning.

—I thought that was somehow Thomas' doing.

—So did I, but things seem to have changed.

The alarming quiet that had taken hold of Hennington spread to the table between Max and Cora. On his way to City Hall, answering Cora's urgent summons, Max had noticed that half the city seemed to have vanished. Stores were closed, traffic was light, even more so than the Election Day holiday would have suggested. The few polling places he passed also seemed under-populated, some even deserted. Where was everyone?

Cora, meanwhile, had been unable to reach either Thomas or Albert. She had talked to the Chief of Police to tell him about Jon's warning, but he had told her that the opposite seemed to be true, that the streets were strangely quieter than usual, Election Day notwithstanding, a fact that Max had confirmed unsolicited on his arrival. And, forget Thomas, where was Albert? No answer at home or the gallery or on his mobile. Why on this morning of all mornings, when something momentous may or may not be about to happen, was she unable to locate her husband?

—The question I suppose then is whether you believe him or not. Would he lie? Is he delusional? Is it a ruse to woo you somehow, like you say?

—Delusional is definitely possible, but it's the way he put it that worries me. He didn't come here to threaten me with this action, whatever it is. He came here to *save* me. He thought I was in danger. He's a dangerous man, but for him to admit that he's lost control of this situation is a big deal. That's not his normal bravura. He seemed genuinely concerned for me, and to be honest, I don't know how to read that.

—Well, so far nothing seems to be happening.

—Yes, but doesn't it also seem like too *much* 'nothing'? The few poll guardians I've heard from have reported that hardly anyone is voting.

—It's early yet—

—Still, the pensioners always like to get out first thing.

—So what do we do?

—I don't know. Sit here and be unnerved is about all I've accomplished so far. I suppose we'll have to wait and see. Treat the day as normal, but with our eyes open for anything.

—I was just going to spend a quiet day with Talon until going to campaign headquarters tonight.

—For the victory rally.

—Still so sure, Cora?

—*Something* good has to happen. We've had a string of unpleasantnesses up to now. Speaking of one among many, The Crash are safe, yes?

—Definitely. The round-up went fine. They're in a secure paddock in the back of the zoo. It's not all good news. A lot of them are injured. Two of them have died in the paddock.

—If I ever get my hands on the shitheads who did that—

—Language, Cora. Talon's in the waiting room.

—She's here?

—Yes, no school and no baby-sitter.

—Of course, the holiday.

—Things are going to be in a ruckus soon enough, one way or the other. I wanted to keep her as close as possible.

—As if this whole day wasn't going to be hard enough anyway without vague, unfounded threats of who knows what.

—It's probably nothing.

—Probably. And at the end of the day, you'll be Mayor-Elect, and a new era will begin for Hennington.

—Let's wait and see.

—Oh, give an old woman her—

The door to her office swung open sharply. Albert charged in holding Talon by the hand. Kevin was behind them. Cora could hardly contain a relieved smile. Until she read Albert's face.

—What's wrong?

—Have you seen the Arboretum?

—No.

—It's on fire.

—What?

They went to the far window. A column of black-and-white smoke chugged into the air from the section of the Arboretum near the top of the hill.

—My God. Look, there's more smoke just starting. Is that near Mansfield?

—Something's happening. Something bad. The streets are deserted.

—I saw that, too.

—Hi, Max. I think you should take Talon to a safe place.

—A safe place?

—What's going on, Daddy?

—I don't know, baby. I'm sure it's nothing.

—I think we should leave, too, Cora.

—Why?

—I just have a terrible feeling. My mobile's gone dead.

—How could that happen?

—The communications relay is near the Arboretum.

—But it's not near where the smoke is coming from.

—I'm not convinced the two are unrelated.

—Jon Noth was here this morning.

—What? Why?

—I've been trying to get hold of you. He said he came to warn me.

—Oh, shit.

—He said something was going to happen and that I might be in danger.

A low thud shook the window. A black ball of smoke rose into the air, down the hill from both the University and the Arboretum.

—Daddy, something just blew up!

—We're going to head home right now, baby.

—I think that's the best idea, Max. Us, too, Cora. We should get out of here.

426   —I can't just abandon my post at the first sign of trouble!

—My first priority has to be Talon, Cora.

—Of course, Max. I wouldn't keep you two here, but Albert, *I'm* in charge of this city. My last act as Mayor will not be to leave it undefended against whatever this is.

—How come there are no sirens?

The adults paused at Talon's question. She was right. No sirens; no ambulances, police cars or fire engines. No sounds at all from the city, just livid smoke funneling up into the air like several stationary tornadoes. Another low thud shook the window matched by a new black ball of smoke appearing even further down the hill. They watched as a burning petrol-station sign made an arc in the air before coming down like a meteor and disappearing into the front of a small hotel.

Kevin broke the silence.

—Whatever it is, it's heading this way.

102. The Journey of Faith.

Peter sat low in the back seat of Jarvis' car looking out the back window. Luther lay stretched across his lap, jostling some as Jarvis sped through the city. Jarvis kept checking his rearview mirror at the increasing conflagration rolling down from the hill behind him. They had seen the Arboretum burning as they got into the car. The first explosion happened before they managed to reach the end of the block. Jarvis increased his speed down a road that was emptier than it should have been. A boom shook the car's windows.

—My God, there goes another one. What the hell's going on?

—I have my suspicions.

—You *know*?

427

—Suspicions only, but as much as I hope I'm not, I think I'm right.

—What's causing this?

—It's not a what, it's a who.

—Then who?

Jarvis turned the car around a sharp corner.

—And who the hell are *they*?

A line of people blocked the far end of the roadway. Jarvis hit the brakes, stopping a good distance from them. They walked forward – it almost looked like marching – carrying fuel cans. Jarvis and Peter watched as they poured some liquid over a parked car, then stepped back and set it aflame. The car became engulfed. Neither Jarvis nor Peter spoke as the fire reached the car's fuel tank, causing an explosion that somersaulted the car forward in the air. The line of people regrouped and began walking forward again.

—My God, it's almost—

—Orderly.

—I think we should get out of here, Jarvis.

—Yes, I think so, too.

He threw the car in reverse, squealed an impressively fast three-point turn, and rocketed the car back out the other way. He turned down another side street, coming face to face with another group making its way down the block lighting fires. Storefronts, a bus stop, a realtor's office shaped like a house. The street behind the fire lighters was working its way up into an inferno. Peter leaned forward from the back seat.

—Look. Over the rooftops.

Towers of smoke appeared down to their left and right, on the horizon. Almost the entire hill up to the Arboretum was ablaze.

—People live in that area. There must be houses burning, too. What's going *on*?

—We have to get out of here.

—I don't believe what I'm seeing.

Jarvis turned the car around yet again.

—We're going to have to head south rather than east.

—If that way's even clear.

Jarvis brought the car to a sudden halt as a ragged-looking man ran in front of them. A larger group followed him, all looking behind them as they ran. A car came lurching out of a side street, its back end in flames, careening past Jarvis and Peter. They watched it travel the length of the street until the fire met its fuel tank. It catapulted up into the air, coming to rest in the front entrance of a coffee shop. Peter spoke almost as if to himself.

—The world's ending.

—Maybe sometimes it has to.

Jarvis pulled the car around the increasing number of fleeing people, trying to aim it vaguely south. The city stretched further in that direction, but it seemed to be the only way clear from the eerily marching firestarters. Small groups of people were standing on sidewalks now, gaping at the fires burning not so far away. Jarvis and Peter passed a fire station, its trucks idle, the building looking deserted.

—That doesn't make any sense. Why aren't they responding? Jarvis, look out!

Jarvis swerved to avoid a burning police car that came screaming in from the right half of an intersection. It struck the curb and bounced through the outer pumps of a petrol station, lighting the grease-covered cement ablaze.

—Oh shit oh shit oh shit—

Jarvis hit the accelerator as the petrol station erupted in a mushroom-cloud behind them. The blast briefly lifted the rear of the car off the ground. Jarvis fought to keep control before finally skidding to a stop. A swooshing sound screamed   429 through the sky over them. They watched the petrol-station's sign, transformed into a missile by the explosion, make a horseshoe in the air before coming to earth, destroying most of the two-story façade of a small hotel. Peter pointed past Jarvis' shoulder.

—Look.

Crowds of terrified people were now running towards them. Though not as many as there should have been, Jarvis thought. Behind the running crowds, Jarvis followed Peter's finger to another ominous line of marchers heading towards them. From the south. Peter asked the question that seemed so obvious, the same one running through Jarvis' own mind.

—How can they be coming from all directions?

—The city's too big. You'd need almost the entire population . . . Uh-oh.

—You don't think—

—Maybe it's just this part of the city. It still seems concentrated here in the north.

—For now.

—We really, *really* need to get out of here.

—Do you know any shortcuts?

—After living here for so many years, I hope so.

Jarvis straightened out the car and headed down yet another side street, swerving now and then to avoid the confused, yet still oddly smallish, crowds of frightened people who seemed to be at a loss as to which direction to run. Smoke thickened the air. Jarvis kept his speed as fast as he dared, once suddenly jumping up onto the sidewalk and driving across a front lawn to avoid a mass of overturned, burning cars.

—You all right back there?

—Yeah. I've never run for my life before.

—Neither have I.

—Strange, huh?

—Yeah, hold on.

The car thumped back onto pavement again. Peter gripped Luther's body, instinctively grabbing his hand as the car sped away. Because of the noise or the adrenaline or even just the sheer impossibility of what was happening, it took a moment for Peter to realize what the pressure on his palm was. He looked down.

Luther was gripping back.

103. The View From Here.

Archie watched the north end of the city burning from his penthouse office downtown. The fire was alarmingly big for being so young. He had glanced out at the smoke rising from the Arboretum not more than an hour ago. What had only been a single column of billowing gray had quickly moved down the hill into the buildings lying to the south.

No, not moved. Moved was wrong. Because what fire moved that fast *down*hill? What happened below the first fire must have been a new fire, then a new one below that, and so on and so on. In less than an hour, the sky was already hazy to the horizon with ash and cinder. Several city blocks were on fire up there, it seemed. He was too far up to hear anything, but he had seen the large fireball that could only have been a petrol station or one of the natural-gas towers. He'd watched some sort of long projectile fly up into the air, turn, and come crashing back down. Surely they couldn't have weapons like that, could they? Whoever they were. Surely that wasn't a missile?

This isn't really happening, Archie thought. My eyes are fooling me. I'm projecting this. This is a, what do you call it, allegory. An allegory. None too subtle either.

431

He turned from the window and walked slowly back to his desk chair. His bones snapped and creaked even in the simple act of taking five steps. The age that he had ignored for going on nine decades suddenly seemed to have realized its laggardness and come upon him all at once. It was the sadness that did it, he was sure. Despair was one thing, despair had a component of energy, despair grappled and fought, despair needed you alive to feel its pain, but sadness, sadness was something else altogether. Sadness was a slow vampire. Sadness reached in and uncorked you like a full tub. Sadness was the parasite that killed its host.

He'd had despair for a while, but it had proved fruitless. Then somewhere along the line, it had turned into this terminal sadness. Maybe it was the day after day without news from Thomas, maybe the ever-dawning culpability that he felt for sending Luther away that afternoon, the last time he ever saw him; maybe when the anger, that most temporary of demons, fled in a rush on the morning when he had surrendered and enlisted Thomas' help. Whatever the reason, the despair had turned to sadness, and Archie was slowly suffocating in it. He had sold Banyon Enterprises, a decision that made sense at the time and right now didn't even really seem to matter at all. He had sent Cora away, his true love, his – well she would have to be, wouldn't she? – closest friend. He had lost Luther for good. His other son had proved unreachable, though Archie admitted he hadn't tried all that hard to reach him over the years.

No, what he hadn't lost, he had severed himself. The only thing remaining was the sadness. He leaned back into it once again in his luxurious leather chair. He began to cry but stopped for lack of energy. *It's over, isn't it? That fake fire out there on the horizon, that's what it means, right? It's over,* 432 *all of it. At the end of it all, I failed. All that work, all that time spent was for nothing, because at the end, I failed. Luther is dead. That's all this has amounted to. Luther is dead, and I'm responsible.*

Archie relaxed back in his chair to a position almost comfortable. He took a few shallow breaths. His chest hurt. He could feel the sadness reach in for the last of him, reach in and squeeze the final anguish of pain from his heart.

Oh, my son, what have I done?

He couldn't quite tell when death came upon him, which was a shame because it would have been a relief from the unbearable ache of his body. But his heart finally stopped, his breath left him for the last time, and he did die, deep in the vast silence of the office he would have to have left soon anyway. The fire continued outside. The day's destinies were beginning to be met all over the city.

A low hum could be heard by anyone walking by Archie's office, if anyone did, a hum that seemed to be coming from the chair where Archie sat slumped, his arms hanging low to the floor on either side of him. A low hum, yes, but unmistakably there.

104. War It Is, Then.

A distant smell of smoke filled the air, and members of the herd were growing agitated. She had jumped to her feet at the sound of the first distant explosion. Even though it was far off, the tremble in the ground was disturbing, shaking her out of what had become her first real rest in many, many days. However strange this new place was, they at least had plenty to eat and drink through the hot, dusty morning, and the few thin creatures who hovered around the edge of the herd had done nothing to bother them as they lay down, at last, to rest, a rest that had proven cruelly brief as the first explosion thundered through the ground, waking up not just her but the rest of those members of the herd who had not slipped off into permanent slumber. They stood now again. Facing an unseen threat, again. Looking to her for leadership. Again.

She had recognized at once that the path of the flight from the gully had been chosen for them. After stopping to form their defensive circle, time passed, but nothing happened. Slowly, she realized the thin creatures had left an opening in the circle around them. As nothing continued to happen, she reluctantly led the herd through that opening. The circle of thin creatures followed behind them. As they walked, there was always one clear direction in their path, so that was the way they headed, even though she knew that was what the thin creatures wanted. Trying to force the herd's way through them would prove immediately effective, but more would die. And the thin creatures would just track them down again. If the creatures wanted a fight at the end of this run, then a fight it would be, but with the full numbers of the remaining herd.

Yet at the end of it, they had been led into a dusty field, walled around all sides except for a gate at one end. The herd prepared itself for an attack, which then never came. Slowly, they realized that bundles of dried grass were positioned around the small field, as were standing ponds full of water. The herd grew restless until she herself went over and sniffed one of the bundles. When she took a bite out of it and chewed down the sweet grass, something approaching a sigh of relief made its way through the herd, and in no time, herdmembers were everywhere, eating and drinking their fill. As the few

434

hours passed, something resembling calm slowly descended on the group. Her own eyes began to feel heavy. She lay down with the rest of the herd and somehow went to sleep, finally forgetting the pain in her damaged horn. A few days had passed that way, a bucolia that had almost, *almost*, made her let her guard down.

And now this.

The members of the herd stood silently, not one of them moving or lowing. She raised her head high into the air, picking up the scents that lingered there as deeply as she could. Definitely burning, still at a distance but growing. She squinted. Her eyes weren't sharp enough to see the specific pillars of smoke on the horizon, but she could gauge the more general darkness of a certain section of the sky. Something else, too. Thin creatures, of course, but that smell had never quite left this little field. This was different though, wasn't it? She took a long slow breath, letting the air roll slowly through her great nose. Yes, thin creatures, but different. She smelled sweaty agitation. She smelled quick, purposeful movement, growing closer with each passing second. There, just there, lying faintly against all the other smells –

She lowered her head and snorted loudly to the herd. She threw herself into a trot around the animals as they gathered themselves quickly into the defensive circle once more. The approaching smells were becoming clearer, and now there was no mistaking it. Thin creatures, lots of them, approaching and accompanied by the same, evil metallic smell that had preceded them in the attack in the woods, the smell that had brought the explosions.

Their heads turned all at once to the sound of the gate crashing open. A thin creature appeared, walking slowly to the center of the opening. The herd pulled its circle tighter. The thin creature knelt in that strange way they had. It was   435 carrying a long slender rod that it raised towards the herd. She realized then that the circle wouldn't work. A bang exploded from the mouth of the rod. A great old female on her immediate right crumpled to her knees, pitching forward onto the dust, blood pouring out of a huge hole in her throat. The thin creature did something to the rod and raised it again. Two more thin creatures emerged behind him, each carrying their own rods. Her eyes narrowed.

So the time was now after all.

Without raising her head, she bellowed the loudest call she could muster and plummeted forward. The members of the herd could hear the rage in her cry, a rage that convinced away the fear that each of them felt. She charged, they followed, no hesitation.

The first thin creature looked up from his rod as the herd bore down. It staggered back, raising the rod again. An explosion sounded. A long thin scar of pain tripped burningly up her side. She ignored it and pounded forward. By the time the thin creature raised the rod once more, she was on it, thrusting her broken but still-effective horn up through the thin creature's crossed forelegs, through the middle of its chest, and out the other side. The smell of its blood greeted her again. She tossed its body to the side in time to see the pair of thin creatures who had emerged be gored and trampled underneath the feet of the cascade of herdmembers that now poured from the opening.

She bellowed again and looked around her. The gate opened onto a small clearing bordered by another low wall. There were thin creatures everywhere, all holding larger and smaller versions of the same rods, aiming them from sites atop the wall, leaning out from behind low trees, some resting in and on top of the metal boxes they sometimes rode around in. But the herd was here, too. The herd would not divide. The herd would face this now, she knew that. If this was the end, they would not run from it. The air filled with explosions. The animals charged forward. The battle was on.

105. A Kindness.

Eugene lived in a small flat in the southeastern part of the city, and the drive to the office took him even further south. That, combined with a certain cultivated obliviousness and the ongoing distraction of driving the Bisector, had caused him to miss completely any evidence that something odd was going on in the city that morning. In fact, the first thing he noticed that indicated something might be amiss was that Jon wasn't in the office when he arrived, which was strange because Jon, even on the days when Eugene didn't drive him, seemed to materialize there anyway, always before Eugene arrived, no matter how early. The second strange thing was that Jon stormed in five minutes later, looking unhappy.

—You have to leave here, Eugene.

—What?

—Do you know where Jill is?

—What? Yes, I—

—Where is she?

—Back at my apartment, still sleeping. Why—

—You have to go get her, and you have to get out of the city.

—What are you talking about?

Jon grabbed his wrist and nearly dragged him into the back office. The curtains were opened onto a clear, northerly view. Clear, that is, except for giant legs of smoke that seemed to be stomping on the city.

—That's what I'm talking about.

—What the hell—

—Rioters, or maybe that's not even the right word. They're too systematic to be rioters.

Eugene looked at Jon.

—Did you do this?

—Of course not. In a way. I didn't mean for *this* to happen, that's for sure.

—Was it that weird old guy?

—Yes.

A slender knife of new, white smoke rose from a location decidedly nearer to the office. Another drifted lazily up from a clock tower near City Hall.

—This can't be one man. It's too big. There have to be hundreds—

A flash of light, followed a second later by a rumble of the window as the sound wave of the explosion reached them.

—Fucking hell!

—I know. That's why you have to leave.

—This is crazy. How can you tell me one guy could do all that?

—It only takes one guy to lead. If you can convince two people, they can convince two more. Two turns into four turns into eight and on and on. It snowballs.

—But this much?

—There's this heat, for one. People get frustrated. They join in riots and mobs. It's human nature. A lit match on fuel.

—But they *live* here! They must be destroying their own homes and neighborhoods.

—No one ever said it was logical. Listen, Eugene, *you have to leave.* Go pick up Jill and get out of the city. I'm not kidding. This is not a joke.

—But aren't you kind of a friend of that guy? Aren't you
438 safe?

—When it gets to this kind of critical mass, none of that means anything. You have to go. I'm telling you for your own safety.

—What about you?

—What *about* me?

—Are you coming with me?

Jon looked surprised.

—I'm not sure I understand the question.

—How can you not understand the question? If I'm not safe and you say you're not safe, then why aren't you coming, too?

Jon considered Eugene for a moment. Eugene's face had genuine worry written on it. He really was concerned that Jon get to safety. What a heartbreakingly pleasant surprise.

—I have to stay, Eugene. The Mayor's in danger. I have to make sure she's safe.

—Can't you just call her?

—I've already been to see her this morning. She threw me out.

—Well, then, who gives a damn whether she's safe or not?

—I do. One day, you'll realize, Eugene, and I hope it's not in too painful a manner, that when you love someone rightly, when that love is your destined love, then it's completely irrelevant whether they love you back or not.

—Bullshit. How can you care when someone doesn't care back?

—I'm helpless to it, Eugene. Utterly, thoroughly, completely helpless. I love Cora Trygvesdottir, and I'm incapable of stopping.

—She's Cora *Larsson* now. She's not the same person.

—Doesn't matter.

—Yes, it does! *That's* your problem, not slavery to love. You're a slave to love that's *dead*. That's what you can't accept. 439

—You don't understand—

—Yes, I do! I understand that you're going to try and save some woman who doesn't give two shits about you and you're probably going to get killed in the process. And for what? Nothing!

Another low rumble shook the window. This time they could feel it under their feet as well.

—One of the things I've always said I liked about you, Eugene, is your ability to surprise me, and yet knowing that, I still manage to be surprised when you do.

—Oh, here we go, off on another one of Jon Noth's Thoughtful Tangents—

—You're concerned about my safety.

—Of course I am.

—Why?

—What do you mean 'why'?

—I'm just your boss, Eugene. Not your friend.

—Okay, now that hurts. If you're not my friend, why all these nice things for me, huh? Why all the new clothes and the skin doctor and the ridiculous pay checks? Huh? Why all these dinners out and the liberal lunch hours? Why all the talking and the conversation and 'Self-deprecation is destructive, Eugene' and 'How could someone as handsome as you be so shy, Eugene' and 'You deserve more credit than you give yourself, Eugene'? I finally accepted that you weren't trying to get in my pants, but if that's true, then it must be friendship, right? I've seen how you treat co-workers. I saw how you treated that idiot that you made run for Mayor. *I* was different. You treated me like—

—Like a friend, yes.

—And if you're not my friend, then why race all the way down here to warn me when you could be downtown rescuing your wannabe girlfriend?

440

Jon smiled, incongruously, warmly, gently. He even laughed.

—What a strange morning this has been.

—No kidding.

—You're right, of course, Eugene. I was a fool not to see it.

—See?

—Speaking as your friend, then, I want you to leave. I want you to go pick up Jill and leave the city. That tank you drive ought to give you plenty of protection.

—What about you?

—I'll do my best to keep myself safe. I need to do what I need to do, but you have my word as a friend that I won't be foolish.

—Depends on your definition of foolish.

—Now, please, Eugene, you must go. I'm not kidding.

—Okay, fine, enough warming of the iceberg for today, I guess.

—I guess.

Eugene held out his hand. Jon took it in a firm shake.

—Good luck.

—And to you, Eugene.

—You'll find me when it's all over?

—If it's at all possible, yes, you have my word. Now, go.

They shook again. Eugene held Jon's gaze for another moment, then released his hand and left. He looked back once when he got to the door, but neither man said anything. Jon watched him go, the most unexpected of smiles still on his lips. And Eugene, with whom this story began, now leaves it for his own safety and to his own destiny.

106. Three.

—Really, Kevin, you *must* go. You have to get to safety.

—And leave you and Albert here alone? I don't think so. Besides, this is probably the safest building in the city, right?

—I can't guarantee that.

—Then you should leave as well.

—I have to stay. I'm the Mayor.

—And Albert?

—Albert's my husband.

—Ah, the Mayor's husband. Which would make me the Mayor's what?

—Kevin, it's *because* I care for you that I'm asking you to leave.

—I understand your concern, Cora, but perhaps *you've* misunderstood *mine*. When you asked me into your lives, I knew what I was accepting. A place at your sides. A place here. Where I'm not leaving, anymore than you would leave Albert or he would leave you. Now, when it counts, believe that. The three of us is not a made-up thing. It's real, but it needs your faith in it to work.

Cora's smile was anxious, worried, but a smile nonetheless.

—So be it, Kevin. So be it all.

—That's what I like to hear.

—Now then, what's taking the third prong in our triangle so long?

City Hall was mostly empty because of the holiday, but Cora sent home the few who had trickled in, keeping only the security detail that guarded the building twenty-four hours a day anyway. Albert had gone off to see if there was any word from them. Max and Talon had left the premises an hour before, heading for the home of a distant cousin who lived out past Hennington's eastern border. Fires continued popping up on a vague path towards City Hall, though the progression was not often clear. Occasional pillars of smoke erupted from points to the far left and right of the main line. From the south-facing windows they could see spots of activity scattered throughout the city. They had also begun to see people filling the streets, sometimes marching in bands lighting fires, sometimes in groups running away in whatever direction they could. Sirens had been heard at last, but too few to assuage the feeling that there just weren't enough to handle a fire that was quickly reaching apocalyptic proportions. Cora took Kevin's hand as they watched the city burn behind the huge windows of her office.

—It's going from bad to worse, isn't it?

Albert burst through the office doors. He turned and bolted them shut. He spoke to Cora and Kevin while dragging a chair to bar the doors further.

—We're in trouble.

—How bad?

—They've surrounded the building.

—Who are 'they'?

—The rioters. Whoever is responsible.

—Are they breaking in?

—They're trying.

—What about security? Can they fend them off?

Albert's face was long and stern. He took Cora's free hand and put an arm on Kevin, the three now a circle.

—They killed one of the guards.

—What?

—The rest were being overpowered.

—My God.

—We're in danger. No mistake.

—Is there a way out?   443

—I don't think so. I think the whole building is cut off.

—How can this be happening? And so quickly?

—And from where?

A pounding at the door interrupted them.

—Shit.

—This wing goes up an extra floor above the rest of the building. If we can get up to the top, we can get out the side windows and go across the roof. The multi-story car park is on the other side. Is that where you parked, Albert?

—Yes.

—We might have to plow our way out, which is horrible but better than walking.

There was another loud thud at the door. They could hear shouting voices, too. The pounding became rhythmic as whoever it was beyond the doors began the inexorable process of beating them down. Kevin looked at them both.

—How far up is it?

—Three floors.

—Three floors, then across the roof and down through three floors of car park?

—Yes, I know it sounds risky—

—We'll never make it.

—We will if we leave right now.

—No, listen. You two go. I'll stay here and try and delay the mob.

—What?! No! Kevin—

—If they think I'm the only one here, they may not chase after you. If not, I can at least give you a little more time. Now, go, both of you, go!

—What about staying by our side? Kevin—

—I love you both. I do, and maybe this is the reason I'm here. Whatever happens remember that. If I'm meant to come out of this, I will. If we're meant to be together again, we will be. Now, go!

—No, you have to come—

—You must—

A splintering of wood cracked from the door. The frame bulged.

—If they see you, there's no point to this. Go!

He pushed them back towards the rear exit of Cora's office. He kissed Cora hard on the lips and did the same to Albert.

—It's the only way. You have to go.

—Kevin—

—You know I'm right. Trust me in this as in anything. Go.

They each hung onto him, fighting the decision until it seemed inevitable.

—We love you, you know.

—I know.

Albert brought his arm around Cora, and they turned and ran up the back stairs. They were two flights up when the mob burst in and were fortunate enough not to see Kevin die, yet they each sensed in their own way what happened, and if grief and fear can co-exist in the frenzied moments of flight, then they were each at least grateful not to be carrying that double burden alone.

107. Father and Son.

Alone in the elevator as it rocketed up towards his father's office, Thomas Banyon realized that he hadn't been inside this building for more than five years. Such was the way life went, he thought. He didn't know that Archie had sold Banyon Enterprises to Jon Noth, but he had long since ceased

445

looking at the corporate offices with anything like a pro-prietorial eye. Luther had been the heir-apparent for so long that now, even after his death – which was a certainty after what Thomas had found out this morning – he had very little doubt that Archie would find someone else to run it. Someone besides Thomas, that is. Come to that, the old man would probably find a way to lengthen his life and run it himself.

Thomas patted the pockets of his sports jacket unsuccess-fully looking for a cigarillo. No matter, there were some in the car. His calm state of mind belied the events happening outside only because he had some wonderful other matters to occupy him. He had seen the smoke rising from the Arbor-etum when he left Hennington Hills that morning but had registered only the thought, Must be a fire, before pushing it aside for the more pressing matters at hand. First, a rare trip to Banyon Enterprises to tell Archie that Peter Wickham, along with Luther's body, had been spotted by a now former employee of Paul Wadstone's security detail who had been forced to fight his way out of a locked trunk to report the sighting, and then Thomas also wanted to break it nicely to the old man that he preferred that Archie kept away from tonight's planned victory party when Thomas won the Mayor's race. Sure it might be nice to have family there, but how much family was Archie really? Besides, he'd been so glum lately that he would just bring the rest of the crowd down anyway, especially after having Luther's death con-firmed.

The second and far more important matter of the morning was the imminent return of one Jacki Strell to the entertain-ment roster. Thomas looked at his watch as the elevator doors opened into Archie's penthouse office. She had most likely arrived back at Hennington Hills safe and sound by now. All the more reason to keep this meeting with Archie as brief as

446

possible. It would be good to see Jacki again. So many questions to ask, so many things to say. Thomas' cock stirred in his pants, twisting a sprig of pubic hair painfully. He readjusted himself in the deserted reception area. Yes, it would be nice to fuck her, wouldn't it? He let the thought run for a moment, absently caressing his crotch. Maybe things could work out between the two of them, maybe he could make her see things clearly after all. She obviously wasn't happy or she wouldn't have run away. Maybe he could –

He suddenly noticed how quiet the penthouse office was. It was a holiday, sure, but shouldn't Jules have been here? Or someone, anyone? He had never known Archie to do *anything* without an assistant around to take care of the particulars. Come to think of it, that's exactly what Thomas was doing in the search for Peter Wickham. Thomas smiled sourly in the vast, empty hall. Never mind. Thomas would be Mayor soon and would no longer even be his father's lackey.

—Archie?

His call disappeared in the dusty silence.

—Archie?

He began to feel annoyed. If that old man wasn't here, after they had *specifically* arranged this meeting –

—Archie, are you here?

Thomas walked to the massive doors of Archie's office and pushed one of them open. He saw Archie asleep in his chair at the far end of the long room.

—Hey, old man, wake up! The morning's a-wasting. I've got news.

Archie didn't move. His arms were draped carelessly over the sides of his chair. His chin was on his chest, and his head leaned sharply to one side. Thomas stopped a few feet away from Archie's desk. He added up the evidence without even realizing it.

—Fuck.

He stepped around the desk and shoved two fingers onto Archie's neck. Nothing. He slapped Archie's face half-heartedly, not expecting it to do anything, and it didn't. He put his hands on his hips and looked down at the body of his father. He felt himself grow very, very angry, very, very quickly.

—You fucking old shit. Now? *Now* is when you decide to go?

The room remained quiet except for a low hum of what must have been the air conditioning. It's not working very well, thought Thomas. It's hot as hell in here.

—Couldn't stand to see your own blood son get the head-lines, could you? Could you?

Thomas knew he was being irrational, but so what? He needed a smoke. He needed to see Jacki. He needed his fuck-ing father not to be fucking dead, for fuck's sake –

Wait a minute. Wait just a minute here. No one had seen him come in. From the looks of it, no one was going to be coming in themselves today, either. Thomas scratched his chin. No particular reason why the body of Archie Banyon couldn't be found tomorrow, was there? Not until after Thomas' victory was assured and reported, not until he could officially mourn as Mayor-Elect, not until Thomas got his moment of glory first. If someone else found him, well, so be it, but if Thomas just left, just scooted out quietly without disturbing anything, then maybe there was a chance. Thomas could even 'discover' the body on his own, propelling himself right to the front of the story. Yeah. That would be good. For his image and everything. He looked down at Archie. Tomorrow was only one more day. It wouldn't matter at all, not one bit.

Thomas turned and walked briskly out of Archie's office,

not looking back. He stepped through the reception hall and into the elevator that was still waiting for him. The doors closed and he plunged down through the building towards his waiting car.

In Archie's office, there was a slight hum in the air, but it began to grow more and more faint, until after a time it hardly seemed there at all. A little while longer and there was only the silence of a dead body.

108. A Lover's Hand, A Lover's Breath.

—Jarvis?

—Yeah?

—Jarvis?

—What is it?

—I, I think—

Peter laced his fingers through Luther's own. There was definitely pressure there, definitely a feeling. Luther was still sprawled across his lap in the back seat of Jarvis' speeding car, and Peter had to bend awkwardly to put his head down on Luther's chest.

—What's going on?

—Shhh, just a second.

Peter tried to block out all the noise. It was difficult. The car jostled and squeaked, the wind rushed by the windows, the burning was so mammoth that the sounds of crackling filled the air, even in the moving car. He pressed his ear down as hard as he could against Luther. Amid all the clamor, there was silence for a moment. And then. And then.

—He's alive.

—He's what?

—He's alive. I heard his heartbeat. Oh, my God. Oh, shit, oh, my God. He's alive! He's alive!

He tore at the bandages around Luther's face, terrified and exhilarated. Impossible. Impossible. Gloriously, wonderfully impossible. He peeled off the cotton strips and wiped away the waxseed oil, uncovering Luther's face. Peter leaned forward again. His ear touched Luther's lips.

—Ha!

—What? What's going on?

—He's breathing!

Jarvis kept looking in the rearview mirror and turning round to see what was happening, all the while trying to keep the racing car steady. They weren't out of danger yet. Fires were still springing up at odd intervals all around them. Jarvis had to keep avoiding the increasing numbers of both rioters and fleeing citizens as well as a number of people in cars with the same idea. He was surprised to feel annoyed. Here was the first honest-to-goodness miracle he was witness to in his entire life as a clergyman and he wasn't able to see it because he had to keep his eyes on the road. Why were the mysteries of faith so inscrutable?

—Are you sure? Has he spoken?

—Not yet. Luther? Luther, can you hear me?

He kept pulling off bandages, freeing up Luther's arms, giving his chest room to breathe. When he reached Luther's waist, Peter realized that Luther was naked underneath the bandages. He paused but continued on. What could that possibly matter now? As he continued unwrapping him, he could feel Luther's breath grow stronger and see his muscles move as the rest of his body returned to life. The last bandages fell away from Luther's feet, and Peter embraced him, naked, pale, slippery from the waxseed oil, but alive. Alive alive alive. Peter brought his own face down again and kissed Luther on lips that tasted salty and dry but warm.

Luther opened his eyes. He made a sound as if to speak but coughed first.

—Take your time, Luther. Concentrate on waking up. Shit Almighty, I'm glad to see you!

Luther opened his mouth again. This time a word issued forth, cracking, unpracticed, but clear.

—Peter?

—Yes. It's me. It's Peter.

Luther squinted a bit, then slowly raised a hand to Peter's face.

—It's good to see you, Peter.

—Yes. Yes, Luther.

—I've been to the strangest place.

The car jolted as Jarvis narrowly missed hitting a sign.

—Where are we?

—It's a long story, Luther. I'll tell you when we're there.

—Where are we going?

—Somewhere safe.

Peter looked up and caught Jarvis' eye in the rearview mirror. Jarvis nodded and repeated what Peter said.

—Somewhere safe.

—Who's that?

—A friend.

—I'm having trouble seeing. Are my glasses around?

—I'm sorry, Luther, no. I don't have them.

—Doesn't matter.

He looked down.

—I'm naked.

—Yes.

—I don't suppose that matters either.

—No.

—I can't believe it's you, Peter.

—Who else would it be?

451

—Yes. That makes sense, doesn't it?

He reached up to touch Peter's face again.

—So many things to say.

—In time, Luther. Rest now.

—I love you. I wish I'd told you before.

Luther wiped away Peter's tears. They kissed again, and once more. Jarvis averted his eyes as the lovers embraced and caressed and reintroduced themselves, one to the other.

109. Outside City Hall.

Getting downtown proved to be more of a chore than Jon had planned, and he could feel precious time dripping away. He had sent Eugene off in the Bisector before quite realizing that this left him stranded. He didn't regret his decision, it was important that Eugene get away, but it did throw an extra wrench into the morning, one that he finally solved with a surprisingly exhilarating show of brute force. He flagged down a car that was careening away down the street, fleeing the fires coming from the north end of town. The driver, a lone middle-aged man, had almost not stopped, nearly knocking Jon over. Jon opened the driver's side door before the man had a chance to lock it, reached in, grabbed him by the lapels, and threw him briskly to the pavement.

—Sorry. Emergency.

He stepped on the gas before even closing the driver's side door. He felt a thrill through his body. He hadn't shown such physicality in years and was pleased to find himself still capable of it. For a fleeting second, he allowed himself a smile. Then he remembered what lay ahead.

The streets were filling up with streams of people either walking purposefully or running from those walking purposefully. Cars, too, skidded through intersections showing little regard for pedestrians and less, if any, for traffic signals or rules of the road. It was anarchy. Hot, loud anarchy. Horns honking, tires squealing, glass breaking, an unnerving low whoosh from the fires that burned in the middle distance. Still very few sirens, though. Theophilus' people must have somehow taken care of that. Jon found himself amazed at the scale of what Theophilus had accomplished, *was* accomplishing. Was the vein of discontent that vast and easy to tap?

—Speak of the devil.

Jon awkwardly stopped the stolen car up on a curb outside of City Hall and who should be standing in the place of glory, framed dramatically by the proscenium of the grand front doors, but Theophilus Velingtham, looking thin, tan, and smug. Crowds flitted about him, intent-looking crowds, carrying implements and what looked to be cans of fuel. They swarmed in and out of the building, surrounding it in undulating waves on all sides. A lumpen bile of anger swelled in Jon's chest. If I'm too late, he thought. If I'm too late –

—Theophilus!

He leapt from the car and up the steps.

—Theophilus! What the hell are you doing?

Theophilus turned to him with a smile, not moving, hardly seeming aware, except in the most tangential sense, of the chaos around him.

—Lagging a little bit behind the proceedings, are we, Brother Noth? Shouldn't be too much of a surprise, I suppose. You were always slow.

—Is the Mayor still inside?

—Presumably, but not, one would imagine, for very much longer.

Jon grabbed him by the shirt front.

—You son of a bitch! If you hurt her—

—You'll what?

Theophilus took hold of Jon's hands and peeled them away with surprising ease.

—I really think I've finally lost my patience with you, Jon. Forty-six years I've waited for you to fulfill the promise you displayed as the young teenager who came to me for guidance. Forty-six years. That's a long time to deprive yourself, a long time to be celibate, a long time to live only with your own thoughts. I waited through your pointless trek to university. I waited through your even more pointless love affair with that mercurial woman who stunned us all by becoming Mayor. And then I waited through nearly four decades of silence. Of no contact. Of *nothing*.

At the last word, there was finally a hint of anger.

—Theophilus—

—Oh, no, Jon, you've participated more than enough. I was overjoyed at your return. I was overjoyed to hear of your plans for Thomas Banyon. How clever of you, I thought, to bring in the dark wind yourself, so that we might then sweep through with the light wind. What a creative use of the Sacraments, I thought. Very *pragmatic*.

—I believed none of those things, you ridiculous—

—It doesn't matter whether you believe or not, you simpleton! Your faith is not required for the Sacraments to be true! All these years of carefully cultivating the germs of a movement, all these years of waiting for the catalyst that would cause those germs to bloom and expand and take this city by the storm you see before you today.

—You're mad.

Jon moved to push past him into the building. Theophilus reached out, and Jon felt a cold pain in his side. He looked down. A blade was buried to the hilt just to the right of his stomach. A slow trickle of blood quickly and quietly turned

454

into a gush that streaked down his black shirt, spilling onto his black pants. Theophilus spoke.

—A disappointingly predictable thing to say from someone who has proven to be consistently disappointingly predictable. Those who wear faith for their own purposes have a long and sordid history, my dear friend, and they almost always come to bad ends.

He flicked his wrist, pulling the blade up several inches through what felt like two of Jon's ribs. The pain was extraordinary, tempered only by an utter lack of belief that there was a knife wedged in his side.

—Theophilus—

—You see, one more thrust, and I'll reach your heart. You'd likely not survive this wound anyway, but when I reach your heart, there's no hope. So before you die, I'd like to thank you.

Jon looked into Theophilus' face.

—What?

—I said I'd like to thank you. For all this.

He motioned with his free hand to the conflagration going on around him.

—Without you, regardless of your dismal ability to follow through, none of this would have been possible. You've served your catalytic purpose quite well, and now that purpose has come to an end. Goodbye, dear friend. Maybe we'll meet again in eternity. Maybe we'll come to a better understanding there.

Jon's face contorted, uncomprehending. Theophilus flicked his wrist once more. The blade rose, reaching Jon's heart, interrupting its beat, bringing it to a final stop. Theophilus let go. Jon slumped heavily to the concrete steps, the knife still in place. His reflexes struggled for a brief moment, but they, too, soon ceased. Theophilus looked at the body for a long moment, a slight frown crossing his face. He breathed deeply, with purpose, and turned on his heels. He looked up once at City Hall towering above him. More work to do.

110. An Albert and Cora.

Cora flung a chair at the third-floor window. It struck the pane and bounced right back, not so much as chipping it.

—Goddamn safety glass!

She threw the chair again, followed by another attempt by Albert. Nothing.

—I can't believe we're going to be trapped by a fucking safety precaution!

—Is there another way out?

—I don't think so. It's all these goddamn windows as far as I can remember.

They looked through the impenetrable glass, a decades-old bar against the possibility of assassination, assassination expected to come from outside the building through either a bullet that wouldn't break the glass or from invaders who wouldn't be able to fit through the small opening that the windows allowed. The roof of the lower story lay tantalizingly close below them. A short run across it and they would reach the car park and their best chance to escape, a chance currently being thwarted by the prudence of long-dead city officials. Cora shook her head.

—Unbelievable. And the fire escape would lead us right down into that crowd of nice people.

—Is there a maintenance door or something? Surely there has to be *some* access to the roof.

456 —There is, from the parking garage on the other side.

—Then why did we come up here?

—It was our only choice, Albert! Now is not the time to argue.

—Damn! You're right, I just don't—

—Wait, listen.

—What?

—Listen.

The sounds that had been coming up the stairs behind them had ceased.

—Have they stopped?

—Maybe they don't know we're here.

—That's what Kevin was trying to do. Could we be that lucky?

—If we're unlucky enough to be stopped by safety glass, you'd think there'd have to be some justice somewhere to tip the scales back.

She took Albert's hand.

—Any ideas?

—There's no way to get out onto the lower roof?

—No. I thought we might be able to get through the windows. They'd never once been tested.

—A lousy time to pass inspection. What about the roof of this wing?

—We'd end up with a twenty-five foot jump.

—Well, if the option is that or waiting to see what the mob's got planned—

—Maybe they've stopped. It sounds like they've stopped.

—I think that'd be too much—

—What's that smell?

—Oh, no.

—It's smoke.

The air changed for a split second, almost as if it had come to life with a low and invisible crackling. There was a whoosh   457

and an impossibly large fireball engulfed the stairwell they
had used, blocking them from moving further up or down.

—No!

—Get to the fire escape!

They ran to the windows on the opposite side of the wing.
Albert struggled with the latch before the two of them finally
got it open. They looked out onto—

—Nothing.

—They've torn the fire escape down.

—How could they do that? *Why?*

The crowd frenzied itself four stories below them like a
school of beached fish fighting to breathe. A tangled pile of
metal bars and piping lay in a heap on the ground just below
where the fire escape should have been scaling its way up the
building.

—Should we scream for help?

—Do you honestly think we'd get it?

—Possible death is always a better choice than certain
death.

She turned. The room behind them was filling with smoke.
The fire from the stairwell was beginning to finger its way in
over the doorframe.

—We don't have much time, Albert.

—Help! Up here! Help!

—Help us! We're trapped!

They continued shouting for a moment or two, before Cora
began coughing from the smoke.

—I don't think they can hear us.

—Or they're ignoring us. No one has so much as looked
up.

—Let's try the safety windows again.

But the room behind them was now black with smoke, fire
458 pouring from the stairwell with blistering intensity. They were

forced to lean far out of the window to gasp at any sort of breathable air. Albert took Cora's hand and held it tightly. Each pulled the other into a close embrace. Cora spoke.

—This is it, isn't it?

—Unexpectedly, yes, it seems so.

—How strange.

—Quite.

—I'm so sorry for Kevin.

—He did what he could.

—I'm sorry that you're here with me, Albert.

—You'd rather be here alone? You think I'd let you face this without me?

—The thought of your death is so much more horrible to me than my own.

—The same is true of me, my darling, so how much better that we face it together.

—Oh, Albert. We've had a miracle, you know? You and me.

—Yes. I don't regret a moment. Don't cry, my love.

They remained wrapped in their embrace, even when the smoke caused first Albert and then Cora to lose consciousness, even when they slumped together beneath the one open window. When the fire erupted through the floor below them and turned their flesh to ash, they were still entwined. Later, after the mêlée had ended – because all mêlées, regardless of size, eventually end – and their charred remains were found, identification was not a problem, because who else could it have been, who else would remain so inextricably bound even at the very passageway to death, who else would be brave enough to face it together?

Who else but Albert and Cora?

111. The Field of Battle.

Purpose, now. Purpose was all.

To the task at hand, to the attack of the thin creatures and their metal rods, to the assistance of those members of the herd who needed it, to the protection of the young even amid the explosions and cries of battle. The herd would not divide. The herd would defend itself to the end. As an individual, she was gone. There was only the herd, one muscle with many fingers, fending off its attackers with single-minded intent.

She hooked the rear leg of a thin creature as it tried to run from her, tossing it up into the air and treading over its upper flanks when it fell back to the ground. Another one pointed a long metal rod directly towards her face. She shoved it to the side as the explosion tore from it, and drove her horn through the neck of the thin creature who held it. Another thin creature tumbled out of the smoke and dust stirred up by the fracas. She tossed it to the side with her horn.

The chaos was so thick, how would the end be signified? How would victory or defeat make itself known?

She bellowed and charged through the small, dirty yard again. Three members of the herd had managed to work their way under the large box that the thin creatures had ridden into the yard. Grunting, the herdmembers flipped it first to its side, then over onto its top. A thin creature trapped on the inside fired one of its metal rods, and one of the herdmembers dropped to its knees. The other two dragged the thin creature out with their horns and trampled it before it could make another explosion.

Knocking a yelling thin creature to the side, she saw that another group had broken through the wall that circled the yard. A thin creature was gored and another broken to pieces against the rubble of the opening, but she also saw a vibrant, healthy young male from the herd lying on the ground, trying to raise himself on back legs that lay useless and immobile beneath him. She bellowed again and threw herself forward against the back of a thin creature that had raised a metal rod to a young female calf. She pinned the thin creature to the ground with the breadth of her left shoulder and pushed hard, squeezing the air out of it. She raised herself to her feet and ushered the small, bleating calf to a safe distance.

When she turned, it was over, as suddenly as that.

Dust still hung in the air in great, greasy patches. Blood covered the ground in puddles and rivulets. Herdmembers and thin creatures littered the area in crumpled heaps, some struggling, most unmoving. She could hear the last of the thin creatures running off and the last of the herd finally giving up the chase. After the thunderous noise of the fight, the quiet was so thick it seemed almost present as a witness. Her horn throbbed. A line of pain ran up in a stripe along her right side. She could feel an unseen wound low on her back left leg. Her ears rang from the explosion that had gone off right beside them.

But she was alive.

And it was over.

She raised her head again, giving two short calls into the air. Animals turned to her and stepped forward, others emerging from the dust, some limping, most bleeding from some place or other. She walked forward to meet them, the young calf trailing her to one side. In a matter of moments, what remained of the herd surrounded her. In addition to the blood scent that seemed to be everywhere, she could smell expended energy, residual fear, overwhelming exhaustion, and something else.

461

She swung her gaze slowly to take them all in. It wasn't triumph she smelled. The losses to the herd were too numerous for that. They were now, she realized, down to less than a third of the herd's size just a few days ago. It would be enough. They would live. They would thrive. Because what she smelled was not individual herdmembers. After the losses and the battles, after all they had been through, she smelled the herd, unbowed, undivided.

They looked at her, awaiting her next move. They looked to her to lead them, still and again. Their faces were tired, worn, expectant, and yet in them, too, was an indication of her place as leader. She lowered her horn, acknowledging the responsibility. Raising it again into the smoky sky, she knew, come what may, she would never fail them.

For they would never let her.

112. The Messenger.

Alone amongst the ruckus, Theophilus was quiet.

He had initiated both the fire at the City Hall building and the destruction of the fire escape that led down from where he had guessed, correctly it turned out, the Mayor and her husband were hiding. Things were moving along nicely. The whole crisis was coming to a head. If only he could be sure they would find Thomas Banyon before the day was out, then all would be well and perfect. The dark wind would be swept away. The light wind would take its place. A new day would dawn.

—I am but Your humble messenger, O Lord. Guide my actions to make them Your own.

He had stayed in his position at the front archway of City Hall throughout the whole series of events that began with that unfortunate business of Jon Noth through the current fire that raged through the east wing and would, before long, consume the rest of the building. City Hall faced south, blocking his view of the destruction that had begun in the Arboretum to the north, but he could see on either side that the fires and demolitions had continued apace. It wouldn't be long before the cleansing powers had worked their way through the entire city, wiping it clean.

Why, then, was he feeling momentarily stuck?

—Show me what to do, O Lord. Give me a sign of action.

He trusted that when the purges were ended, he would intuitively know the epicenter of rubble from which to begin the long, glorious rebuilding process. Yet now, at this moment, he felt a faint pang of doubt that he was in the right place.

—Is it Your will that I wait, O Lord?

Rioters were deep into the process of looting City Hall, taking what they could before flames swept through the whole structure. They fled past Theophilus in both directions, sometimes buffeting him in their push to get in and out of the building through the very doors whose entrance he was blocking. He made no move to stop them. Such unpleasantness was to be expected in an operation of this scale. The fools would probably not have homes to return to by the end of the day anyway. Let them steal. Theophilus' attentions were elsewhere. The heat from the burning wing poured down around him in waves. There was something that needed to be done here. He felt it. He *knew* that somehow this was the right place. But the right place for what?

—Lord—

A sharp push from behind knocked the wind out of him. He stumbled to one knee and looked behind him. A large man carrying a computer monitor had shoved him out of the way and was struggling past. The man glared down at him.

—What're you standing there for, moron?

Theophilus raised himself up to his full height. The other man was still a bit taller, but Theophilus didn't seem to notice.

—I beg your pardon?

—Get out of the fucking way is what I said.

—I'm sorry, brother, you don't seem to quite realize who I am.

—Up yours.

The man began to trudge down the steps.

—I think you've just made a grave mistake, brother.

The man looked back up at him.

—As far as I know, asshole, we're not related.

—You should remember my face, brother, because I will certainly be remembering yours.

The man spat at Theophilus' feet.

—Fuck you. And your face.

He turned and vanished, monitor still in hands, into the passing crowds. Theophilus smiled a bit, out of annoyance more than anything else. A pity that some of the flock would still have to be dealt with when the light wind was fully in place, but such loose ends were inevitable, weren't they? He returned to his prayer.

—Guide my actions, O Lord. Steady my hand at Your wheel. Use me as Your vessel. Show me where I am to be.

He glanced at a quick movement to his left in time to see a large block of wood just before it struck him across the forehead. He stumbled backwards from the shock of it, not quite losing his balance as the pain surged through his skull and neck. He glanced up. How did I not see him? Theophilus thought, bringing up his hands to block the second blow.

—Fucking smartass. Fucking grandiosity itself.

The computer-monitor thief swung the block of wood – it looked like the leg of a thick chair – over and over again, punctuating his sentences with blows. Theophilus reeled. He moved vaguely back towards the doors of the City Hall foyer and, bleeding, went through them. The man followed.

—Stupid fucker. Thinks he can talk to *me*.

—Stop, please, I beg you.

The man brought the block of wood across Theophilus' face, knocking out several teeth, breaking Theophilus' jaw, and causing him to bite off the tip of his tongue. Help me, O Lord. Show me Your way out of this. The man raised his arm again. Theophilus turned. The block of wood struck him squarely on the back of his neck, breaking it, severing the thick cord of nerves that rested inside. He dropped to the floor in a heap. The man struck his limp body a few more times and threw the block of wood into a corner. The foyer was beginning to fill with smoke, the number of looters diminishing. The man, whose name is lost to history, kicked Theophilus a final time, then fled out the front doors.

Theophilus never rose, not even when the flames finally found their way into the mostly stone foyer, cooking the mortar until the whole reception hall collapsed into a heavy pile of blistering stone. Conjecture speculates that Theophilus was still alive for a short time through this, paralyzed from the injury, unable to feel pain but perhaps even awake and alert – though this was more from quarters who would look back on the event and still hope to make him suffer before his death.

113. Who Are You?

—Sit back, honey.

—Where are they all going?

—Sit back in your seat, Talon. Daddy's having to do some fast driving, all right?

—Are we going to be okay?

—Absolutely.

—Daddy, look! City Hall's on fire!

—What?!

Max looked into his rearview mirror. City Hall boiled under a column of flames in the distance.

—Do you think Mayor Cora and Mr Larsson and that other guy all got out?

—I'm sure they did, honey.

He debated whether to turn around and go back, but there was just too much chaos in the air, too many rioters, too many people running. He hoped Cora, Albert, and that Kevin had in fact all gotten out in time. For now, though, his main focus was getting Talon to a safe place. They had been trying for the better part of an hour to get to the house of Louise, a many-times removed cousin of Max's, who he hadn't set eyes on in several years. Her house was, however, the only place where Talon would be safely outside of Hennington's rapidly immolating borders. If only every road he'd tried so far hadn't been blocked. He pressed down on the accelerator and zoomed around a corner. A crowd of rioters barred the way yet again.

—Are they *everywhere*? Hang on, honey.

He stopped and turned in his seat to reverse the car. An explosion roared through the air and most of an office building came crashing into the street behind them.

—Shit.

—Daddy, they're getting closer.

Max looked around. They were stuck in the middle of a block. There wasn't even an alley to squeeze down. Rows and rows of office buildings and storefronts, some already burning from the explosion; no side exits of any kind.

—Uh-oh.

—Are we stuck?

—Looks like it, honey.

—What if you drive forward? Will they get out of the way?

—I don't think so. We're going to have to run for it.

—Run?

—Don't worry, baby. You'll be right with me.

He reached back and unhooked her seat belt. He put an arm around her and lifted her between the front seats to his lap.

—I'm going to open the door and carry you, all right? Hang on to me as tight as you can.

—Are they going to hurt us?

—I think they only want to hurt *things*, honey. They just want to burn the buildings and the cars. I think we'll be okay.

—Are you sure?

—Trust me, Talon. I'm not going to let anything happen to you. I promise you that. Are you ready?

—Ready.

—Here we go.

He kicked open the driver's side door, hoisted Talon to his hip, and stepped out onto the smoky street. Ten steps away from the car, he heard shouts from the crowd that sounded like his name. *It's Max Latham! What? Is it? Get him! He's part of the dark wind! Are you sure? Get him! The what? Get him! Who? No! Yes! Get him!* The crowd charged forward. Max staggered to a stop and spun back around the way he came.

—Daddy?

—Close your eyes, honey.

—Why are they shouting your name?

—We have to get back in the car.

—Are we going to drive through them?

467

—We might have to.

—Oh, no.

—Close your eyes. Everything's going to be all right.

—Daddy, behind you!

Something struck Max on the side of the head, a glancing blow that he mostly avoided. He turned Talon away from it and ran blindly forward. He could hear someone or many someones just steps behind him now. He realized he wasn't going to have time to get in the car even if he reached the door before the crowd got to them. He turned towards the hood, jumped up a step, then up again to the roof of the car. He pressed Talon's head to his neck and turned to face them. He was frightened, yes, but he was angry, too, furious that his daughter was being made to feel afraid as well, furious at the pain welling on the side of his head. It was this face of anger and parental defiance that the crowd caught as their first glimpse of just who they were chasing. Max shouted in his loudest voice.

—WHAT ARE YOU PEOPLE DOING?

There was something to his voice – witnesses later would independently describe it over and over again as 'authority' – that caused the front guard of rioters to pause where they stood near the hood of Max's car, ready to climb after him.

—Are you blind? Can't you see that I have my daughter with me? Have you all gone crazy?

Most of the crowd had stopped now, quickly, surprisingly quietly, all looking up at the man on the roof of the car, holding a girl to his side. *It's Max Latham, or so someone said. Who's the girl? Must be his kid. Why have we stopped? What's going on?*

—Are you going to attack my daughter, too? Is that what this madness is all about? Is that what it means to you? Attacking a child? Have you all taken leave of your senses?

What's he saying? Asking if we're going to attack the little girl. Well, of course not. Are we? No, I'm pretty sure. Of course not. I know I'm not.

—Does whatever your goals are include burning down your own homes, your own businesses, your own city?

Goals? What's he talking about? The dark wind. What the hell's the dark wind? I just came out because ... Who's in charge here? Well, I don't really know why, I just did.

The crowd looked up to Max on the roof of his car, delivering what he would come to realize was the first real political speech of his life. The people were silent except for a low murmuring of questions. A man who'd made it all the way up onto Max's hood held a baseball bat, the same bat that had struck Max as he ran. The man looked down at the weapon in his hands. He looked back at the crowd behind him, the one that up until just seconds ago was ready to follow him up onto the car to commit who knew what atrocities to this man and his little girl. He suddenly dropped the bat as if it were white hot. He met Max's eyes with a confused glance.

—I'm sorry. I don't know ...

He stopped. Max watched him jump off the hood and walk slowly away, cutting through the crowd, muttering something about getting home. They looked back up to Max and found themselves waiting for what he would say next.

—Daddy?

—Are you all right, pumpkin?

—Yeah. Are they waiting for you?

He cast a long sweeping glance over the upturned faces. He took a deep breath.

—For this to stop, the momentum has to be reversed.

Someone called up from the crowd.

—How?

469

Max turned again. He saw the crumpled burning pyre of the office building in the street behind him, the smoke that billowed through the air, the volcanic explosions erupting from the ground at every distance including, he knew, City Hall behind them. But he also saw the people as they began to shake themselves from whatever had come over them. More, he heard their silence. He heard their calm. He took another breath and began to speak.

114. Lair.

Jacki sat on the edge of the bed, waiting. She was in one of the apartments hidden in the back buildings of Hennington Hills Golf Course and Resort, 'apartment' being a generous term for a bed and a small bathroom for use of those clients who liked discretion over everything and preferred not to leave the grounds to get the full benefits of club membership. Jacki herself had nursed her last clip here, the toothy Councilman Wiggins, what seemed like a lifetime plus an eternity ago. Last clip. Yes, one way or another, Councilman Wiggins was going to be the last, of that she was certain.

That she had been brought to an apartment made it clear exactly how things were going to go, at least at first. Returning to be an entertainment contained all the humiliation she would need, and Thomas would know that. He would do here in the bedroom whatever it was he had in mind, though she had some good guesses, and then who knew? Her future, not for the first time, was completely open. What would go on after this evening was blank, for now, a clean slate.

And yet, she wasn't nervous, which surprised her. Surprised *and* delighted. There was even some small part of her which
470 looked forward to the coming ordeal, confrontation, whatever

it was going to be, a part which had to have come from the new Jacki because the old one, may she rest in peace, would have been up the walls with fright. But she had kicked Forum. She had seen her sons. She had been tested and found herself resilient. No, fear was there, absolutely, but it was manageable. Let Thomas come and let things proceed as they may. Her breasts had dried up during withdrawal. She would never work for him again as an accountant. He would, after all his trouble, have no more use for her.

I am facing my death, she thought. But I'll be able to see it clearly.

The door opened. Thomas Banyon stepped into the room. He was smiling, a cigarillo dangling from his lower lip.

—If it isn't the prodigal Jacki.

—Hello, Thomas.

—'Thomas'? Whatever happened to 'Mr Banyon'? You *are* an employee here after all.

—Not any more. Even you don't believe that.

He moved slowly, edging his way towards her, easing himself into a plush armchair just opposite where she sat.

—Don't I?

—If I was just an employee, why all the trouble to track me down?

—You're of great value to this company, Jacki.

—I can't give milk, Thomas. The wells have gone dry.

—Now that *is* a disappointment.

—For us all, I assure you. Now why don't you just let me go? Why can't you just let me leave in peace?

He leaned forward and raised a hand to touch her cheek. She began to flinch but forced herself not to. Instead, she raised her own hand and pushed his away.

—So she's got a new fire, huh? I like that. It could be useful.

471

—I'm not sure I'm making myself clear here, Thomas. I'm not going to be 'useful' any more. Not for you. Not ever again.

—Big talk from someone who returned here finally with so little fuss.

—I had to face you sometime, didn't I? What would my life be like if it was spent running from you?

—What, indeed? And what do you plan on doing if I don't want to let you leave?

—You don't scare me, Thomas. You can do your worst, and you'll still never win. Never. I may be here, but I've already escaped.

She held his gaze steadily, her growing surprise at her words pleasing her all the more. His eyes were bloodshot and watery, no doubt from the noxious cloud of brown smoke he was breathing into the room. Beyond the pungent tobacco mixture, she also thought she smelled alcohol on him. Drunk and stoned. In a flash realization so breathtaking she nearly allowed it to show on her face, she wondered why on earth she had ever been afraid of him in the first place. It was difficult to keep herself from smiling. Whatever happened, she had won. How great was that?

—What's so funny, Jacks?

—Just . . . things.

—Things.

—Mm-hmm.

Thomas inhaled and blew out a few smoke rings.

—I'm going to be Mayor.

—You?

—Yes, me. It's all sewn up. I've got my victory party tonight.

—You're going to be Mayor of Hennington?

—Yeah, what's so fucking funny about that?

—Mayor of the ash heap that's currently burning to the ground around us? Have you looked out a window lately?

—A few minor squabbles, nothing more. Things'll change when I take over.

—I can see that.

—What's with all this attitude, Jacki? Do you know why I brought you back here? Do you?

—I can guess.

—No, not any of that, not any of that entertainment bullshit. I don't want that.

He paused. Jacki wondered if she was being cued.

—So what do you want here, Thomas? Why drag me back against my will if you're not going to press me into service again? If you're only here to kill me, why not just get it over with so we can both get on with our individual destinies, okay?

—Kill you? Are you out of your mind? Why in the hell would I want to kill you? I'm not that kind of monster.

—Yes, you are. You're exactly that kind of monster. And worse.

The slap came so quickly, it almost didn't hurt. She felt a throbbing red glow spread across her left cheek. Then something astonishing happened. A face that nearly resembled anguish took over Thomas' features. Could this actually be Thomas Banyon apologizing, *feeling bad* about his actions? Jacki found this thought even scarier than further physical violence.

—Oh, Jacki. Jacki, Jacki, Jacki. Why did you run? Huh? Why did you leave? Why did you leave me?

—Leave *you*?

—We could have had something. We could *still* have something between us.

—You and me?

473

—Yes. I'm willing to let the past go if you are. I didn't even realize what I wanted until you had left. It didn't even come to me fully until just now, seeing you again, here in the flesh. I want you.

—You want me.

—Yes, I want you. I have to have you. You have to be mine. You have to be at my side when I'm Mayor and forever after that.

—What?

—Listen. Forget the past. Forget all that entertainment shit. Forget it. Just stay here. Just be mine. No work, no clips, nothing. Just me. Just be here for me.

She held her hand to her inflamed cheek. His look, impossibly, was imploring and she thought, at least for this brief stretch of moments here in this back room, sincere. Time had stopped. This moment would last an eternity in its complete unreality.

—Thomas—

—Wait, wait, before you say anything. I brought you something.

He reached into an inner pocket in his jacket and pulled out a small satchel. She recognized it immediately. He spoke as he removed the paraphernalia.

—I know you've been off it for a bit, not being able to get a hit of this quality, so I brought you the best there is to be found in the city. Premium stuff. You can have all you want. For free. Forever. I can get you top-notch all the time.

He inserted the syringe into the vial of golden liquid. He pulled on the tap until it reached the 50cc line. She couldn't take her eyes off it. For these weeks, these difficult, horrible weeks, she had not so much as seen a drop of Forum. Out of sight, but not out of mind. The new Jacki watched in clinical horror as Thomas tapped the syringe and squeezed a small droplet out to clear the air bubble. The old Jacki, not dead yet it turned out, whispered in her inner ear. If she had to go, was this the road she should take? One last shot of Forum, pure, grade-A, top-notch Forum, a shot so large that her deprived system would overload? Was that her destiny? To at least die of pleasure?

Thomas moved over to the bed beside her. Her eyes never left the syringe. She actually found her mouth watering. She made a decision.

—More.

—What?

—I need a bigger hit than that.

—Really? But it's—

—When you withdraw, you need more to get your proper high.

A lie. Any more Forum in that syringe, especially if it was the high grade that Thomas promised it was, would be enough to fell a rhinoceros. So be it.

—All right, Jacki. Whatever you say.

He smiled, almost gratefully. He stabbed the needle through the opening of the vial, filling the syringe up to 100ccs. He repeated the tapping and squeezing and moved the syringe over to her.

—Wait.

She leaned, unbuckled her pants, and pulled them down until her thigh was exposed. She extended her hand.

—Here.

—Oh. Do you want to do it, or shall I?

—I will, Thomas. No offense, but I'm an expert.

—None taken.

He handed her the syringe. She lifted it up so that the overhead light caught the amber glow resting in the syringe well. She ran her free hand idly over her lips. Could it be this easy? Was this the moment? Clear your mind, Jacki. The only way out is through.

Thomas put a hand on her back and another on her leg where the Forum was going to go, caressing it lightly. He leaned forward and kissed her shoulder.

—Oh, Jacki. Jacki. I'm so glad you're back.

—Me, too, Thomas. I'm glad, too.

She brought the needle down, swiftly, professionally, into the back of Thomas' hand, emptying the plunger in the same motion. The Forum spread quickly under his skin, forming a small dome between his wrist and knuckles.

—Ow!

Thomas pulled his hand back reflexively. It took him a few seconds to realize what she had done, but that was enough. By the time he raised his other hand to strike her, the willingness to do it was already leaving him.

—Jacki . . .

She stood quickly away from the bed, pulling her pants up. The look on Thomas' face was one of distant hurt, but she could see it beginning to waver. Terrific stuff, Forum. Fast-acting. Bliss came swiftly.

—Why?

His voice was thick, his tongue tripping over the single word.

—I don't have time for explanations, Thomas. I have to go.

She went to the door and found it unlocked. A good omen. She left the room without a parting word, without even a look back. She would get a car somehow. She would get out of the city. She would get to Morton and Tucker. In under three minutes, through a mixture of adrenaline and desire, she had already left the grounds of the Hennington Hills Golf

Course and Resort for the last time, not even permitting herself to spare a thought for Thomas Banyon. The opportunity to move forward was finally here. She wasn't about to lose it through hesitation.

Thomas watched her go but seemed somehow not to feel too bothered by it. He leaned back onto the bed until he was lying down. Vague, troubling thoughts hovered around the edges of his mind but only briefly before vanishing altogether. Warm molten gold filled his veins. He could never remember feeling quite this good before. He closed his eyes, and as the Forum reached his brain and his liver in a dosage so pure a quarter of it would have killed a newcomer like Thomas, he died. Euphorically, happily, perhaps unfairly so, but dead nonetheless.

And somewhere out in the still-smoldering city, Jacki was on her way to her sons.

115. To The Faithful Departing.

—I think we might finally be clear of it.

Jarvis could still see Hennington burning behind him, but the streets surrounding the moving car were empty. The drive out of the southeastern corner of the city had been touch and go, at one point almost over when a lit fire bottle hit the windshield; but it bounced free without causing any damage. They had made it. Peter spoke from the back seat.

—It's a miracle.

—Why not? A day full of them, it seems.

Jarvis looked in the rearview mirror again to reassure himself once more that Luther was actually alive. There he was, pale, shaky, naked still, but definitely, incontrovertibly there. A non-stop prayer had run through Jarvis' head for nearly the entire day. It had first asked for protection and safety,

477

but somewhere along the way, it had turned into one of thanks. Thanks for the miracle of Luther's return, thanks for their safe passage out of Hennington, but thanks most of all for being allowed to witness it all. Jarvis realized the extent of the luck and divine favor he was experiencing. He was seeing with his own two eyes a tangible, irrefutable result of faith. Despite the horrors of the day, despite running for his life, despite it all, Jarvis had never felt so happy, so humbly, utterly, thoroughly joyful.

He began to cry.

—You all right, Jarvis?

He nodded and pulled the car into the car park of a deserted playground.

—I think we're safe.

—For now.

—No, I have this feeling that we're okay. I think we're out of whatever's been happening.

Luther's voice rose so quietly from the back seat that Jarvis had to turn to hear him.

—What's been going on? Why is the city burning?

—No one knows. I mean, at least, Peter and I don't. Listen, may I . . .

He stopped.

—What is it?

—I know you hardly know me, but may I touch you, Luther?

—Of course.

Neither Luther nor Peter asked why. Jarvis reached his hand into the back seat and ran it lightly across Luther's face, running his fingers over Luther's bald head, touching both his ears, feeling the curve of his neck.

—A miracle.

—Yes.

—Impossible yet so. The definition of miraculous.

—Yes.

—Where have you been, Luther Pickett?

—I'm forgetting it, like you do a dream. I can only remember bits and pieces. It's hard to describe. I knew that I had to wait, and then all at once, I knew it was time to stop waiting. That's really all.

—I think that's probably more than enough. I know what my own two eyes saw, and I know what they're seeing now.

Luther took Jarvis' hand, squeezing it tightly. After a moment, Peter spoke.

—So what's next?

—We should get some clothes on Luther.

—I don't think we should go back to the city.

—I'd agree.

—There's nowhere for us to go back to, anyway. From all the smoke, I'm sure my old house is gone. Luther's too, probably.

—Same with the parish. In fact, I have a horrible feeling it was probably the first thing to go.

Luther spoke again in his low voice.

—We should move on.

—What do you mean?

—We're out of the city. We should keep going.

—To where?

—I want to go to Tishimongo Fair.

—Where's that?

—Due south in the Molyneux Valley. It's where I grew up.

—I know where that is. I could take you both there.

Peter interrupted.

—Jarvis, we can't ask you to do that. We have nothing to go back for, you've got—

—No, no, I could take you. I've got some money on me.

—So do I, but—

—We could get Luther some clothes on the way. It's only a day's drive. We could be there by tomorrow morning.

—We can't ask you to do that.

—I have to make sure the two of you are safe. Truly safe. Try to understand me. I have to. I don't know why I know, but I do. I'll see to it that you get to Tishimongo, and when you are—

He paused. Luther caught his eye.

—When we are, then what for you?

—I don't know.

Jarvis looked out at the horizon, at a sky filled with smoke.

—Is it my imagination or is the smoke thinning?

—Could be.

—Will you be needed back there?

—Part of me says yes.

—And the other part?

—The other part tells me that my time in Hennington is finished, that I have some new destiny, and that I should just stay out of its way.

—Come with us, then. We'll get back on our feet together.

Jarvis turned around and faced them once more.

—I'll take you to Tishimongo Fair, and I'll make sure that you're safe, like I promised.

—And then?

—And then. And then I think I'll drive to Mackettsville, on the coast.

—Why?

—I think I want to catch a ship.

—A ship? Where are you going?

—To see if I can find someone from my past who sailed across the ocean a long, long time ago.

—Lost love?

—Something like that.

—There's no better reason.

—It's probably impossible, it's been so long, but—

—But.

—Yes, I know.

Jarvis looked at the two men in his back seat.

—Miraculous.

He turned back to the wheel of his car, starting the engine. He said it again.

—Miraculous.

He put the car in gear, pulled out of the car park, and began the long journey south.

116. Ashes, Ashes.

After an endless night, the sun rose again over a damaged city, some pockets still smoldering, one fire in the northwest corner even still burning brightly as the morning light poured in from the east. Max Latham was already awake. He had slept for just an hour and only that because Talon refused to lie down unless he was there with her. They were in the back room of someone's house, a man named Richards or Richardson. Max didn't know for sure, but he would find out in the day ahead. Richards/on's house sat in a rare pocket of the city that had escaped the destruction, and he had offered it as a 'command center' (as he called it) for Max to use. There was much, much work to be done.

Max sat on a chair in Richards/on's living room, considering the daybreak. The mass hysteria – perhaps typically, though it seemed far too grave a thing to ever be called 'typical' – had turned out to be a tenuous, shimmering thing held

481

together by its misdirected passion, and like all passions, blunting it was only a matter of finding the correct dowser. Standing on the roof of that car, Talon in his arms, facing down a crowd of strangers who were about to kill them, Max had instinctively seen the means to end the madness. He had simply, intuitively reached for the lever and flipped it. Thankfully, luckily, amazingly, it was the right one. He could just as easily have been wrong.

Like a sound rippling out from its source in all directions, the small halted crowd at the foot of Max's car became a streetful of stalled rioters as more came running into the area and without knowing quite why, stopped what they were doing. One street became two, two became four. Waves of bewildered calm spread through the city like the fires that had preceded it. As mysteriously as it had all started, the rioting ebbed. A confused populace shook itself from a stupor, feeling oddly confused and ashamed, but mostly feeling lost. Max had performed, somehow, the miracle of zero becoming one.

And for that, they called him 'leader'.

He didn't like it. It didn't feel right. It didn't fit. But if someone needed to do it and if destiny or fate had selected him, then ultimately he felt he had no choice. At least for now. If they needed a leader then he would do it because there seemed to be no one else. For now.

So. The Richards/on 'command center' it was. Using an erratic phone service, he spent the night marshaling as best he could the fire and police departments, what remained of them anyway, to try to get some sort of order back into the city, but more to try to save those lives that were still within reach. It had been slow going, but sometime in the early hours he had managed to get in touch with Hennington's Fire Chief. The Police Chief was nowhere to be found, and Max presumed the worst. The Fire Chief then got hold of several of his own deputies and several police deputies who in turn got hold of several of their individual stations and so on until something resembling an organization coalesced into place.

Max then turned his attention to bringing the city's infrastructure back to life, following a similar pattern of locating top directors and spreading the message down through the networks that were already in place. How easily it could all function, but how uncomfortably necessary that someone at the top was needed to set it all in motion. It had been laborious, and it was still far too early yet to say anything for certain, but as dawn broke on the day after the riots, it somehow seemed that already a welcome quiet was settling over Hennington.

He sighed in his chair. There were still so many questions, still so many awful answers to undoubtedly discover in the days ahead. Cora and Albert had not yet been found, though City Hall was still a furnace, too hot to approach. Max would face that news when and if it came. And what of the perpetrators of this small apocalypse? He had a few clues from what Cora had said, but where were these people now? And who? And why? Would a real answer ever be forthcoming?

And what had happened to The Crash?

—Daddy?

He jumped in his seat.

—Sorry, baby. You startled me. Why are you up? It's early still.

—You left.

—I'm only here in the next room, honey. There's lots of work to do. Don't worry. I'm not going to leave you. You can count on that.

—I'm hungry.

—Yeah, it's been a while since we've eaten, hasn't it?   483

—I think since yesterday morning.

—Really? Then let's go see what this nice man has in his kitchen for you to eat.

He took Talon's hand. They wandered among all the different people who had crowded into Richards/on's house, most of whom seemed all too willing to take whatever direction Max handed to them. It was an uncomfortable feeling, but again, probably necessary. He and Talon found their way into the kitchen. He sat Talon at the dining table and started looking through cabinets.

—How about cereal?

—What kind?

—Um, lots of bran, it looks like.

—Anything sugar-frosted?

—There's sugar-frosted *bran*.

—Okay.

He poured two bowls, added milk from the refrigerator, and sat down to eat.

—So what happens now?

—Well, we try and put the city back together.

—How come you're in charge?

—It just happened that way.

—Destiny?

He shrugged.

—Maybe.

—Why did those people burn the city down?

—I don't know. I'm not sure *they* know. Some people start a thing, others join in. Movements and mobs are instantaneous and then just end. Who knows why?

—Everyone thinks you ended it.

—Why do you say that?

—I woke up and heard them talking.

—Well, I didn't. I'll have to make them understand that.

—What if you did?

—I didn't. I was lucky.

—But everyone else says—

—It's important that I don't start believing what everyone else says, honey. Otherwise, how could I lead them fairly? Time will pass, I'll do my best, and they'll decide then whether they still want me to lead them or not.

—But—

—No more 'buts', little pumpkin. That's the way it has to be if the future's going to work. I'm not a king. I'm just a man. Finish your cereal.

The sun peeked through the window of the kitchen. Father and daughter sat eating their breakfast quietly as light filled the room and dawn turned into full-fledged morning.

117. Out.

(—Would you look at that?

—What are they doing all the way out here?

—Coming from the fires, probably.

—I've never seen them this close.

—Me neither. Magnificent.

—Absolutely incredible.)

She reached the top of the hill and turned to look. This was a new place. The herd had never come this way before, so far outside the boundaries of the thin-creature city that still erupted smoke on the distant horizon. But there was grass here, she saw, green and fresh, and she could detect the faint scent of water somewhere in the distance. Over the next hill, maybe, or the one after that.

She turned to the tired herd behind her. The survivors. It was the smallest the herd had ever been, at least as far as her experience fell, but they would be enough. There were at least ten healthy males and seven females who were of age to bear calves, plus a handful of youngsters who would grow and expand the herd in their own lifetimes. The older animals that remained would help provide safety in the coming years while the herd was still small in number. They would be a great herd again. Maybe not in her lifetime but certainly in the next leader's. It was her responsibility to make it so.

The members of the herd looked at her, waiting for her next directive. She snorted once, paused, and then once again. The water was close. She could smell it. They would find it first and then settle in for a well-deserved rest. After a time, they would begin to explore this new area, find its boundaries, search for verdant pastures that could serve as temporary homes while the herd wandered. Soon. This would happen soon. Only a little more walking. Only a little bit more.

She snorted into the air again, turned, and led them down the hill and into a new day.

Acknowledgements

First and foremost, my biggest thanks to my agent, Michelle Kass, less agent than friend and champion, an absolute dream for an author. You wouldn't be holding this book in your hands if it weren't for her tremendous hard work. Special thanks also to Tishna Molla, who read the original manuscript and insisted Michelle do so. Equally enormous thanks to Philip Gwyn Jones and all at Flamingo, in particular Jon Butler and Nicola Barr.

Thanks to the early readers of this novel in its various forms. In Los Angeles: Rufino Cabang, Rick Felkins, Patrick Moore, John O'Neil and especially Caren MacDonald and Phil Rodak. In the State of Washington: my brother Joseph Ness and particularly my lifelong friend Vicki Burrows (neé Pelland). And in London: James Charles, Tony Cronin, Paul Kitchenham, Barry Quinn, Damian Strawbridge, and Andy Yorke. And also to my best-friend-of-long-standing Dave Valvoda in Los Angeles, who promises to finish it eventually.